TRESSA'S BERMUDA-STYLE LOVE TRIANGLE

Manny reached out and crushed me to his broad, manly chest, bending me over backward in a clinch worthy of Rhett and Scarlett. His lips hovered a mere fraction of an inch from my own, his dark, searching gaze locked on my own startled peepers. "Bon voyage, Barbie," he said, and put his lips to mine in a deep, hot, wet, probing kiss that stole my breath and muddled my senses. What senses I had.

When the kiss ended, I was limp and weak and clung to Manny to keep from falling. I heard a gasp. Out of the corner of my eye, I detected movement. My eyes came to rest on a hairy little piglike creature on a grungy green backpack. I had to force myself to look up and meet the stunned look of the man holding the bag.

Ranger Rick.

Jeesch. Hadn't even gained my sea legs and already I was caught between two handsome devils and the deep blue sea.

Anchors Aweigh

KATHLEEN BACUS

LOVE SPELL NEW YORK CITY

LOVE SPELL®

November 2008

Published by

Dorchester Publishing Co., Inc.
200 Madison Avenue
New York, NY 10016

ISBN 10: 0-505-52735-9
ISBN 13: 978-0-505-52735-6

The name "Love Spell" and its logo are trademarks of Dorchester Publishing Co., Inc.

Printed in the United States of America.

10 9 8 7 6 5 4 3 2 1

Visit us on the web at www.dorchesterpub.com.

It's with much appreciation, gratitude, and affection that I dedicate this book to all my awesome and wonderful readers and fans of Tressa Jayne Turner and the entire Grandville Gang. It's been a wild and wonderful ride and I have so very much enjoyed bringing these characters and their stories to you. I hope "Calamity and Company" continue to hold a special place in your hearts—and on your bookshelves.

Warmest regards,

Kathleen Bacus

Anchors Aweigh

CHAPTER ONE

A beautiful young blonde was so depressed she decided to end her life by throwing herself into the ocean. Just before she could throw herself from the docks, a handsome young sailor stopped her.

"You have so much to live for," said the sailor. "Look, I'm off to Europe tomorrow and I can stow you away on my ship. I'll take care of you, bring you food every day and keep you happy."

With nothing to lose and always having wanted to go to Europe, the blonde accepted. That night the sailor brought her aboard and hid her in a lifeboat. From then on every night he would bring her three sandwiches and make love to her until dawn.

Three weeks later she was discovered by the captain during a routine inspection.

"What are you doing here?" asked the captain.

"I had an arrangement with one of the sailors," the blonde replied. "He brings me food and I get a free trip to Europe. Plus, he's screwing me."

"He certainly is," replied the captain. "This is the Staten Island Ferry."

This particular blonde stood pier-side and cast a landlubber's eye on the huge, bright white cruise ship docked to receive passengers at the Port of Galveston. I found myself experiencing a similar sense of caveat emptor. You know: *Let the buyer beware.*

Okay, okay, so I wasn't actually the buyer of record here. My passage had been bought and paid for by my grandma and her new hubby of less than seventy-two hours. Still, that totally insignificant, piddling little detail didn't exempt this virgin sailor from feelings of nervousness and a nagging sense of unease that didn't bode well for her maiden voyage.

Can you say *Titanic*?

I watched the few remaining stragglers ahead of us as they prepared to board the vessel. They chatted and laughed while they waited to have their paperwork and identification cleared. I gnawed away at a newly-polished nail.

"Something wrong, girlie?" my seventy-something-year-old "new" step-granddaddy, Joe Townsend, asked. "Afraid you won't have sea legs?"

More like fear of design flaws, inferior steel, and too few lifeboats.

"Legs like yours and you're worried about mine?" I asked, and shrugged off my uncharacteristic anxiety. I gave "Grampa" Joe's scrawny chicken legs a nod. "Give me a break. And you should have warned us you were planning to put on shorts. You know—so we could don protective eyewear. The reflection from those white legs is brutal."

When Joe Townsend failed to fire back with one of his trademark, take-no-prisoners retorts, I frowned.

"Aren't you going to respond to that?" I asked. "You know, make a remark about how it's a wonder anyone can see you at all with my thunder thighs blocking the view? Maybe take this opportunity to remind me of the blonde pirate who walked around with a paper towel hat because she had a *Bounty* on her head?"

He shook his head.

"Nothing?" I asked, and blinked. "You got nothing?"

Joe shrugged.

"This is so not like you," I mused, and put a hand to his

forehead. "Are you sick? Too much connubial bliss, maybe? Or are you suffering from constipation? You know, not enough fiber in your diet," I suggested.

He slapped my hand away. "No!" he said. "But I'm your step-grandpa now. I have to set an example. Act like a mature adult. Be a role model."

That one got my attention. Role model? Him? Who was he kidding? This old guy had been known to maintain surveillance logs on his neighbors' comings and goings, pack unregistered heat (he considered the Colt Python a collector's item and, therefore, exempt from the law) and was probably on a government watch list somewhere for frequenting websites that featured domain names involving terms like *mercenary*, *covert*, *commando*, and *assassin*.

I admit I've pimped his predilections for snooping in the past, but always for the greater good. Joe helped me get the dirt on some prime-crime stories that not only saved my cowgirl cookies, but also resuscitated a code-blue newspaper reporting career a year or so back. Our crime-fighting collaboration makes the *Rush Hour* duo look like Holmes and Watson—a cantankerous codger who fantasizes about dressing in black masks and dark capes, paired with a blonde, frizzy-haired, aspiring reporter with two dead-end part-time jobs, a history of chronic misadventure and long-term self-esteem issues with a name that sums it all up: Calamity Jayne.

Uh, yup. That's me. Tressa Jayne Turner, aka Calamity Jayne, Grandville, Iowa's unintentional answer to extreme boredom.

Calamity. The totally misplaced moniker was bestowed courtesy of my new grampa's grandson (and my now step-cousin) Ranger Rick Townsend—yet another Townsend male who wreaks havoc on my psyche. Oh, and on certain unmentionable parts of my anatomy that will . . . go unmentioned.

I'd been doing my own funky version of the "Tressa

Turner Two-Step" when it came to Rick for years. I'm sure you're familiar with the dance called Lover's Limbo. The "should I or shouldn't I?" cha cha cha.

Ours had been a complex and volatile relationship dating back to a history of prepubescent warfare that had set the stage for adolescent antipathy and young adult angst. I'd constantly found myself the butt of Ranger Rick's repertoire of "boys will be boys" jokes, but the biggest joke of all was on me when my brother's obnoxious best bud turned out to be the best-looking guy in the greater Grandville area, and, I feared, the one male who could get me all hot and bothered with just a wink and a nod.

I'd been sorely tempted as of late to throw caution to the wind and throw myself at the magnificent male but something—an unnatural disaster, an ill-timed interruption, my own screwed-up second thoughts—always pulled me away from that particular precipice before I took the plunge. Maybe because deep down I knew if I allowed myself to fall, really fall into Ranger Rick's arms, I'd fall hard. And permanently. As in forever and ever and ever. And in today's world of disposable relationships and casual sex (surely an oxymoron) I wasn't certain such a fall might not kill me if things didn't work out.

"Calamity Jayne Turner: Fearless in all things except matters of the heart." Who knew?

Rick Townsend is a uniformed officer with the Iowa Division of Natural Resources (I love a man in uniform, don't you?) and he gives a new meaning to the term "kissin' cousins." Oh, and "keeping it in the family." Hubba hubba.

I shook my head to get myself back on topic and away from naughty thoughts.

"Excuse me, but did you just say you were a role model, Joe?" I asked. "Role model? What role, exactly? Neighborhood Watch commander? Green Hornet groupie?" This referred to a comic television crime-fighter in the sixties with whom Joe's deceased first wife was particularly enamored. "Geriatric GI Joe, maybe?"

I suggested these things, hoping to get a rise out of Joe, or at the very least a rise in his blood pressure. Something. Anything. Joe's born-again, turn-the-other-cheek attitude was giving me a pain in a couple of my own cheeks (the gluteus maximi, if you know what I mean) and making me leerier— and more suspicious—by the minute.

"Role model, as in your basic loving, caring grandparent, of course," Joe replied. "What else?"

Oh-kay. This was getting downright scary.

"Ain't that boat somethin'?" My gammy—that's what I call my grandmother—snapped a picture using the digital camera with which my folks gifted the newly married couple to use on their honeymoon cruise.

"I think this vessel qualifies as a ship, Hannah," Ranger Rick, boat aficionado and stickler for proper sailing terms, it appeared, corrected. "And it *is* something. Would you like me to take a picture of the happy couple as you embark on your very own honeymoon *Loveboat*?" He reached out for the camera. "Smile and say *bon voyage!*" After snapping the picture, he looked at it and said, "Perfect!"

"You sure it's not overexposed?" I asked. "You know, from the glare bouncing off Joe's legs?" I snorted. I crack me up sometimes.

"We can't all carry off the oh-so-attractive farmer's tan like you do, girlie," Joe said. "Those cowboy-boot lines are particularly fetching."

I searched for my customary snarky comeback, but was too relieved by the return of the cantankerous Joe to lob one back. Things were back to normal. Well, back to whatever passes as normal with a Townsend.

"You'll get rid of those tan lines in no time," Ranger Rick suggested, with a lift of his dark eyebrows. "By sunbathing as God intended," he explained, flashing me a smile hot enough to send tiny rivulets of sweat trickling between my size-B boobs.

"Maybe I'll do just that," I said, adding a challenging lift of my own eyebrow. "Care to join me?"

"I'm in!" My wrinkled, shrunken grandmother stuck her hand up faster than the time she volunteered me as Mort the Mystic's guinea pig for hypnosis at the state fair several years ago. And just so you know, I was the most realistic chicken on that stage. Okay, so I was a little handicapped in the breast department, but I kicked tail feathers with my strut and cluck.

"I don't plan on missin' out on anything," my gammy continued. "You never know if this will be my first and last cruise, so I'm goin' for the gusto. What about you, Joe? You gonna let it all hang out?"

I winced. The very thought of anything physically attached to Mr. or Mrs. Joseph Townsend, Esquire, naked and hanging out, made my innards revolt. And I wasn't even aboard the ship yet.

"You never know what this old salt'll be up to," Joe responded, his eyes on me. "One thing *I* know for sure. It's going to be a whale of a sail. 'Don't rock the boat, baby.'" He started to sing and I looked at Rick.

"Remind me again why I agreed to come on this shipwreck lookin' for a place to happen."

He put an arm around my shoulders. "Don't you remember? You signed on as my own personal purser." He squeezed my arm. "You jumped at the opportunity when you saw my benefits package. Remember?"

My cheeks burned even hotter. I needed a drink. Badly. One of those exotic fruity ones with the cute little umbrella. At the rate I was heating up, I'd have to stick the tiny umbrella upside down in my cleavage to catch the river of perspiration. Rick Townsend knew just how to turn up my internal thermometer, while he himself never appeared to break a sweat. So not fair.

"As I recall, I was promised one sweet signing bonus," I reminded Townsend. "When can I expect to see it?"

"How about when you come to turn down my bed and plump my pillows?" he replied.

"I see. So when hell freezes over, then."

"I have a stateroom all to myself, you know," Townsend reminded me, lowering his head and donning a hangdog look. "This romantic cruise ship. Couples everywhere. Me all alone. Don't you feel some sympathy?"

I might—if I didn't know that Rick was about as likely to be a lonely sailor as I was to strip down to the altogether and stretch out on the lounger next to my au naturel gammy and volunteer to apply her tanning oil. Eww.

I patted Townsend's tanned cheek. "Poor baby," I said, the heat of his face against my palm tempting me to forget about swans who mate for life and silver and gold wedding anniversaries and focus on the here and now. "But I hear these cruises are filled with tons of single and searching women looking for romance on the high seas. Maybe you'll get lucky and meet the perfect match: one who is comfort-able caring for the slithering residents of your reptile ranch while you're off on some hunting or fishing expedition, one who carries her very own impressive rack and lives only to please her man. Isn't that what most randy ranger types look for?"

"You know me better than that, Tressa," Townsend said. "But you're right about one thing. If what I've heard about these cruises is right, there's usually an abundance of young, willing flesh to keep a sailor company. Remember, though, my cabin door is always open to you."

"Uh, that's *stateroom* door, ye scurvy, ignorant wretch," I corrected in my best pirate lingo. "Arrrggh, it's the plank for you, matey!"

"You're not going to keep that up the entire cruise, are you?" Joe Townsend cut in.

"What? Keep what up?" I asked.

"All the seafaring speak and pirate prattle," he elaborated. I looked at him. "I don't know. Does it bother you?"

"It irritates the hell out of me."

I nodded and said, "Good to know, Gilligan. Good to know. And pardon me for getting into the spirit of things. Jeesch."

We made our way to the front of the line and showed our tickets and government-issued I.D. cards to the uniformed crew, then went through security before we were permitted aboard. Once we were officially checked in, strapping young porters took our carry-on luggage and secured our stateroom assignments.

Our accommodations were all located on the Verandah deck—arranged to permit the newly blended family an opportunity to blend, according to my gammy. With the exception of my sister, Taylor, and yours truly, everyone had upgraded to exterior staterooms or suites with ocean views or balconies. Taylor and I would share an interior stateroom. Can you say, claustrophobic?

Still, beggars couldn't be choosers, I knew, and I reminded myself of the "pity passage," compliments of the bride and groom, that got me here in the first place. And with all the enticements on board the vessel—okay, so I was primarily thinking about all-you-can-eat chocolate buffets—the odds of me spending much time in a cramped cabin without windows with a seasickness-prone sis was roughly the same as me signing up for *Survivor: Siberia*. Or *Survivor* anywhere for that matter.

The Townsend family contingent had shrunk to three, having lost two of their number to unforeseen circumstances. Originally Rick Townsend's older brother, Michael, and his wife Heather had booked passage, but at the last minute they decided on a family trip to Disney World instead. I suppose it could have had something to do with their son Nick getting kidnapped at the Grand Canyon the day before my gammy's wedding. Oh, he wasn't hurt or anything. In fact, knowing Nick Townsend as I'd come to over the last week, I imagine he milked the episode for all it was worth, trading up a week in Podunk, Iowa, with his maternal grandparents to a family vacation at Disney. The kid was a Townsend born and bred, after all.

My grandma and her new husband would honeymoon in an extravagant suite complete with private balcony. One could only hope that was where she intended to sunbathe "as God intended."

I was used to my gammy's . . . eccentricities. She'd been my roommate for some time before the wedding, and I was glad my days of digs-sharing with someone who collected fertility statues in various states of arousal, and who slept in cold cream, a hair net, woolly socks and nothing else, were behind me.

Townsend nudged my arm as he followed his folks down the narrow hall to their room. "You might regret not taking me up on my offer," he said. "Your sister got airsick on the plane coming here and carsick on the shuttle from the airport. I can't even begin to imagine what sea swells will do to her. Better keep the barf bags handy, mate." He grinned and saluted me before moving on down the hall.

I shook my head. We'd just set foot on the ship, and already he thought he was the friggin' lounge act.

"Here we are, ladies." The fit, blond cabin boy with short, cropped hair, highlighted tips, and cute knees slipped a computerized keycard into a slot. "Your luggage should already be in your stateroom ready for you to unpack," he said, opening the door. Once Taylor and I entered, he handed us cards of our own. His look lingered on Taylor, his fingertips slow to release her card.

"Are you by any chance a personal trainer?" he asked her. She shook her head.

"Aerobics instructor, maybe?"

I smirked. Oh, boy. Did this guy need help on his pickup lines or what?

Taylor smiled at him, her face still pale and wan from the shuttle transport. "No. I just like to keep in shape," she said.

"Oh, right," he replied, and I thought he looked a tad bewildered. "Right." He looked over at me and gave me one of those up and down looks.

I shrugged. "I just like to eat," I said.

"I see," he replied.

"From what I hear, this is the place for me," I commented, thinking of the stories I'd heard about cruises' breakfast buffets, dessert buffets, and all-night buffets. I had to fight to keep from drooling.

"You're right there," he said. "Well, I'll leave you to unpack." Taylor handed him a tip, and he nodded as he backed out of the room. "If there's anything you need, don't hesitate to let me know." He pointed at the nameplate on his shirt. "Just ask for Denny."

"You aren't by any chance affiliated with the restaurant, are you?" I joked. "Because their sausage and hash brown skillet with a side of cakes is to die for." I was already looking forward to indulging my Midwestern appreciation for good—and abundant—food.

He looked at Taylor. "Good luck," he said, and left.

I frowned. "Good luck? What did he mean by that?" I asked.

"I have no idea," my sister said, and dropped to the bunk farthest from the door and nearest the john. "I'll take this bed," she said.

"Okay," I agreed, noting the sweat beads popping out on her upper lip like tiny blisters. Her pallid complexion. The long, drawn-out moan. And we hadn't even raised anchor yet.

Ohmigawd. The puke pails! Where were the puke pails?

"Denny!" I opened the stateroom door and barreled out of the room. "Oh, Denny! Ooompf!" I plowed into something rock-hard, like a brick wall or one of those long, heavy punching bags like Rocky Balboa beat up on when he was trying to whoop Apollo Creed. Only this impenetrable object had a heartbeat. And respiration. And body heat that caused my own temperature to rise quicker than the fur on my gammy's cat, Hermione, when my two golden labs, Butch and Sundance, invaded her space.

I found my fingers tracing the outlines of abs that seemed chiseled in stone. I looked up and spotted pecs that strained the limits of the black T-shirt covering them. My eyes traveled to an arm so large it was bigger around than my thigh. (Hey, now. Be nice.) My heated gaze came to rest on a tattoo I'd seen before. A very distinctive tattoo. A tattoo that could belong to only one person.

The time it had taken for drool to collect in my mouth as I'd pondered all-you-can-eat breakfasts and all-night-long buffets—my saliva dried up in half that time once reality set in. I didn't need to examine the thick, corded neck, the rugged, stubbled jaw, or sensuous lips for positive identification. I didn't need to note the earring in a finely shaped lobe or study the arrogant contour of the nose to make sure. I didn't need to lock gazes with irises so dark against the whites of the pupils they appeared jet-black for positive identification.

But I did it all just the same.

My belly did a flip-flop that had nothing to do with moving water beneath my feet when hot breath seared my face.

"Ahoy, Barbie."

Okay, I admit it. I almost wet my pants here. Only one guy called me Barbie.

"Ahoy back," was all I could think of to say. I was in shock. Or maybe denial. This was the very last person in the world I'd expected to run into outside my stateroom on the Custom Cruise Ship *The Epiphany*: the bad-boy biker I'd first met at a smoky bowling alley bar and later bailed out of jail for fighting. A guy I next encountered in a makeshift cell on the Iowa State Fairgrounds. A specimen whose size made me feel like Tinkerbell in comparison. Okay, okay, more like Peter Pan.

Yet here he stood. All six-foot-three of him. Manny De-Marco/Dishman/da name du jour. My super-sized, super-sexy, super-secret and oh-so-faux fiancé.

Can you say, abandon ship!

CHAPTER TWO

"Barbie looks surprised," Manny observed, displaying his glaring gift for understatement.

I nodded, still stunned by this unexpected complication.

"Barbie looks confused."

I nodded again.

"Barbie looks hot."

My eyes widened. "Oh, no, really, I don't. I'm sweaty and frazzled—"

"Barbie's face is all red." Manny placed fingers on my forehead. "Definitely hot," he said, with a flash of white teeth and a gaze that rested on my lips.

"Oh. Hot, as in sweaty and perspiring and travel-grungy," I said.

This was so not the kind of banter one was supposed to engage in with a dark, dangerous dude on a fun-in-the-sun cruise ship. On the other hand, the crude overture, "Hey, babe, wanna come to my pad and roll around on my bed and get hot and sweaty?" had probably initiated more than a few sexual encounters, so I was in the ballpark. If the ballpark was "Suck at Small Talk with Big Giant Men" Stadium.

"Same ol' Barbie," was all Manny DeMarco said in response.

"What are you doing here?" I finally made myself ask after his scrutiny became too uncomfortable. "Do you work on this ship?" I reminded myself I'd never gotten a straight answer out of him as to just what he did for a living. "Are you security?" He'd be darn good at it. He'd saved Barbie's bodacious bod a time or two.

He shook his head and reached up to secure a strand of flyaway hair behind my ear. "Nope."

"Personal trainer?" I said, recalling Denny's earlier query. Manny shook his head. "Negative."

"Night club bouncer? Casino blackjack dealer? Lounge act?" I rattled off more possibilities.

"No, no, and no," he said.

"Then what are you?" I asked, frustrated.

He smiled. "On vacation," he said, and tapped my chin with his fist.

"Vacation?" I repeated. "Vacation? What about Aunt Mo?" I asked. "Her heart and all. She didn't—"

"Ahnt Mo's cool," Manny said.

I looked at him. "She is?"

"She's always wanted to go on a cruise."

"She has?"

"Manny figured now was the time."

"He did? I mean, y-you did?" I stammered.

Okay, there are a couple things you're probably wondering at this point, and now is as good a time as any to clarify matters. One: Manny likes to talk about himself in third person. Why? I have no idea. None. And I have no plans in the near future to ask him. Two: His dear, devoted, saintly "Ahnt Mo," who raised him from a whelp and who has a rather tricky ticker, thinks I'm engaged to Manny. It had been her dying wish to see him married, and I'd agreed to play along with a fake engagement. But then she hadn't died.

"You mean—"

"Ahnt Mo's on vacation, too," he said.

I stared at him.

"On vacation? On this ship? With you? And me?" And Townsend made four! I felt my throat tighten. "How?

When?" I forced the words past the constriction. I sounded like I'd reverted to some monosyllabic language from pre-history. Next I'd be bent over, my knuckles dragging the ground, grunting, sniffing an armpit and scratching myself in awkward places.

"Joltin' Joe gave us the heads-up," Manny said, and the pieces of my fragmented brain slowly began to come together.

"Joe? Joltin' Joe Townsend?" I put a hand out. "About yay tall? White hair, white skin, chicken legs? The same Joltin' Joe who hit you with pepper spray a year or so back? Who later conned you into giving my gammy and him lessons on how to run covert surveillance of my Uncle Frank when they suspected him of infidelity?"

The same Joe Townsend I'd suspected of being up to something earlier?

"That's the one," Manny confirmed.

"How? Why? When?" There went Cave Gal Tressa again. Heck, I might as well haul out a stone tablet and start chiseling away.

"Joe's grandson Nick canceled. Joe thought of Manny and Mo. He finagled some Fed he met in Arizona to push the paperwork through."

I just stared.

Finagled was right. The conniving little barnacle had orchestrated this little debacle with the finesse of Machiavelli. But why? For what reason? And did I really want to know?

"Barbie looks like Ken just told her he wants to see other people," Manny said.

Funny. I was sure my expression more closely resembled the one Barbie might wear if Ken announced he was gay. And in love with Dick Cheney.

"So what exactly is the situation with Aunt Mo?" I asked, recalling with some degree of anxiety the last time I'd encountered Manny's intimidating aunt. It had been a week earlier, back home in Grandville. She'd cornered me in

Hazel's Hometown Café, Pastor Browning in one booth, Ranger Rick in another, and demanded a date for the wedding be set posthaste.

What did I do, you ask? Why, I did what any street-smart, plucky, twenty-first-century cowgirl from the Heartland would do given the same situation: I got the heck out of Dodge. The next day I was on a big silver bird headed to Arizona.

But now it appeared the posse had caught up to Calamity Jayne, and there was no viable means of retreat at her disposal. It was Butch Cassidy and the Sundance Kid holed up in a tiny house with the Bolivian Army just outside the front door all over again.

"Does she still think we're—uh, you know—an item?" I asked, feeling my forehead crinkle.

"Manny caught Mo Googling shipboard weddings at sea before the flight," he said, and I felt the noose tighten.

"And her ticker?" I asked, steeling myself for his response.

"Manny calls it her Timex."

"Huh?" I said.

"Took a lickin' but keeps on tickin'."

Not exactly the glowing prognosis I'd hoped for, but considerably better than the "She could go at any minute" I'd heard last fall when I'd agreed to this one-take, one-time, walk-on role as Manny DeMarco's fiancée and ended up as a regular.

"So . . . her heart can probably stand the truth about our little invented engagement, then?" I asked hopefully.

Manny frowned. "Better give it a day or two," he said. "Let Ahnt Mo rest up from the flight out. Get her sea legs." He moved closer to me, his large body effectively blocking the narrow corridor to anyone not as thin as a Victoria's Secret model. "Catch her breath."

Manny took a long, deep breath himself. To my growing anxiety, a hot gust of air hit my face like a blast from the corn-burning furnace my Uncle Frank installed the winter before. But this blast held the subtle scent of mint. "It's been a long time. Manny's missed Barbie," he said, sliding even closer, if possible.

I blinked. This was a side of Manny I hadn't seen before. Or maybe permitted myself to acknowledge. A softer side. A seductive side. Dare I say, a romantic side? One of those boy-meets-girl moments. Gulp.

"Yeah, well, Barbie's been busy with school and work and weddings, and you've been . . ." I stopped and my eyes narrowed. "Where *have* you been?" I suddenly asked, recalling that every time I'd mentioned it was time for me to officially return his ring and for this couple to amicably go their separate ways, Manny had mysteriously disappeared.

"Taking care of business, Barbie," Manny replied. "Taking care of business."

Ha. But not the urgent business of setting Aunt Mo straight. That was for sure.

"Uh-huh. Business. Right. What was your line of work again?" I asked. "Consulting, wasn't it? So, have you consulted anyone on the best way to break the news to your aunt that the wedding is off?" I asked. "Or maybe we should just 'fess up and tell her the truth. That when we thought she was at death's door, we wanted to give her a parting gift to die for." I winced at my unfortunate choice of words. "Uh, you know what I mean."

Manny shook his head. "Can't do that, Barbie. Manny can't lie to Ahnt Moe."

This time, Barbie shook her head. "But you *already* lied to her. When you told her I was your girlfriend. That we were engaged," I pointed out. "That wasn't true."

"Manny gave Barbie a ring, didn't he? That's for real, isn't it?" Manny asked.

I nodded slowly. "Well, yes, but—"

"And the ring is an engagement ring? Right?"

"Well, yes—" And a heckuva big one at that.

"And Barbie still has Manny's ring, correct?"

"Well, sure—"

"And the idea of being Manny's girl didn't send Barbie running for cover."

"Well, no, but remember, I'm from the Midwest. We come from hardy stock," I said, feeling the need to lighten the mood. A lot.

"So, how about we just take things slow and easy?" Manny said. "Tressa," he added, my name sounding strange, foreign, and surprisingly seductive on his lips. Tressa—not Barbie. "You can do that, can't you, Tressa?" Goosebumps popped out on my arms and I shivered. I could tell from the twitching lips above me that the reaction had not gone unnoticed.

"Huh? What? Slow and easy?" I steered my runaway thoughts back on track. "Sure. Absolutely. No problemo. I can do slow and easy," I motor-mouthed. "That's my comfort pace. I'm built for endurance—not for speed."

Manny smiled. A dangerous smile. A Jolly Roger smile.

"Manny looks forward to confirming that fact," he said, and lowered his head—and lips—in my direction, his dark gaze confident and unwavering.

What Manny would have done—and how Barbie might've reacted—was left as your basic cliffhanger, because Denny with the cute shorts and nice knees made his way back down the narrow corridor in our direction. His eyes got huge when he spotted Manny.

"Ah," he said. "He must be your personal trainer. Looks like you're in good hands then."

I stared as Manny gently squeezed my arms and stepped back to give Denny room to pass.

"Yeah, Barbie here's in real good hands," Manny said, and winked. "She just doesn't know it yet."

The familiar feeling of things spinning out of control hit me with the force of a tidal wave, and I felt my lungs lock up.

"Air! I need air!" I managed to say, and headed for the elevator and the upper decks.

Once up top, I ran to the ship's railing, desperate as a plus-size about to be marooned on an island of cannibals. I sucked in fresh air by the gallon as I lifted a hand to my eyes and scanned the horizon in vain for a somber ship with black, billowing sails. I uttered a colorful curse.

Where the bloody hell was Captain Jack Sparrow when you needed him?

CHAPTER THREE

I made my way back to the Bat Cave—what I'd dubbed the windowless, porthole-less cabin I was sharing with my sister—keeping an eye out for a rather large, heavy-set woman who wore her gun-metal graying hair in a bun and moved like a battleship. I could have kicked myself for not asking Manny for the number of their stateroom; at least that way I'd have some inkling from whence to expect yonder attack.

I shook my head. Just my luck. My first ever cruise, and I had to share tight quarters with a sister who gave every indication of spending every day at sea with her head in a bucket, pretend to be engaged to a mystery man with a suspect past and equally questionable present or risk sending a nice old lady into cardiac arrest, come to terms with how I really felt about Ranger Rick Townsend, and still have time to extract a little payback from Mr. Chicken-Legs of the Sea, the sadistic shrimp who'd cleverly constructed this floating love triangle. Captain Steubing would so not approve.

Following a swift swipe of my key card and a quick check of the hall to my left and to my right, I entered the stateroom and found Taylor pretty much the way I'd left her: flopped face down on her tiny berth, a dark spot of drool darkening the tan comforter near her open mouth.

I threw my own emotionally drained self on the bed next to her and wondered what to do first: unpack, bait my hook for an ancient clownfish, take a nap, or hit one of the many food venues I'd heard so many cruise customers rave about. Two of the more appealing choices made me vulnerable to Wedding Planner Mo. And the others? They were just plain unfulfilling. Or un-filling.

I sighed—an exaggerated, over-the-top, long-suffering sigh.

"Is there a problem?" I heard from the bunk next to me.

I rose up on an elbow. "Maybe," I said.

"We haven't even lifted anchor yet," Taylor pointed out, still prone.

"I know," I replied.

"That's quick."

"You have no idea," I responded.

Taylor finally sat up. Her complexion had lost some of its deathly pallor, now looking more along the lines of acute anemia. "So, what is it this time? You and Rick aren't at each other's throats already, are you?"

I shook my head. A much scrawnier neck figured in my current neck-wringing fantasy.

"It's complicated," I said.

"When isn't it where you're concerned, Tressa?" Taylor asked.

I considered the wisdom of sharing with my little sister the reason for my sudden angst. Although we love each other, Taylor and I have always seemed at cross-purposes, as different in design as the shiny, sleek, luxury vessel we were about to cruise away on and a gritty, grimy, independent little tugboat who stubbornly goes about its own business, carrying others along for the ride.

Bet you can guess which one of us is the tugboat.

Taylor was the daughter who excelled at academics and extracurriculars and mature behavior, and I was the daughter who consistently scored high marks in screw-ups, madcap mayhem and chronic misadventure.

"I ran into an unexpected fellow passenger," I told her, sharing a fact that still freaked me out.

"Oh?"

"Manny."

My sister sat up straighter.

"Manny? Manny DeMarco?" she said. "The fellow you're fictionally affianced to?"

Affianced? I did an exaggerated eye roll at my sister's Jane Austen moment. Next thing I knew she'd be going all *hither and thither* on me.

"One and the same," I admitted.

"How in the world did he end up on the same cruise as our wedding party?" she asked, giving me a suspicious look. "Tressa. What did you do?"

I looked at her. "Me? I didn't do anything!" I said. "It was your brand-new step-grandpappy. He arranged this little reunion at sea."

"*My* step-grandpappy? He's yours, too, you know," Taylor pointed out.

"I refuse to claim him," I said. "Not after this little shipboard surprise."

"How do you know Joe is responsible?" she asked.

"Manny told me," I explained. "He said Joe arranged it after Mike Townsend and his family canceled. But it gets even better. Aunt Mo is here, too."

Taylor stared. "He brought his aunt? The one who is trying to pin you down on a wedding date?"

I nodded. "Talk about your fantasy cruises, huh?"

"Does Rick know?" she asked.

I shook my head. "I doubt it. If he'd run into Manny or Aunt Mo, we'd have heard the 'all hands on deck' call by now."

"So, what are you going to do, Tressa?"

"I suppose walking the plank is out of the question," I said, sinking back onto my bed.

"Uh, we're still in port, remember?" Taylor pointed out. "I don't think that would work. You could take a long walk off a short pier, I suppose," she suggested, with the beginnings of a wan smile.

"I'm so glad my situation has managed to do what megadoses of Dramamine couldn't," I observed, "and succeeded in pepping you up."

The sudden chirp of the ship's PA system got my attention: "Good afternoon. This is Captain Compton. On behalf of Custom Cruise International and the entire crew of *The Epiphany* we'd like to welcome you aboard. We very much hope that you will enjoy your Custom Cruise experience with us. We will be conducting our safety drill at 1730 hours. The safety drill is mandatory for all passengers with no exceptions. Expectations and procedure information can be found on your daily bulletin, as well as in the Custom Cruise leather-bound folder located in each stateroom. You will find the location of your mustering station on the inside door of your stateroom and on the lifejackets located in your cabins. Should you require further information regarding the safety drill, please contact the main desk or consult a steward. Once again, attendance by all passengers is compulsory. Seven short blasts on the ship's alarm whistle followed by one long blast will be your signal to report to your designated muster station. Custom Cruises appreciates your cooperation as we strive to provide a safe, enjoyable cruise experience. Thank you."

I rolled over and closed my eyes. Guess it was naptime.

"What are you doing?" Taylor asked. "Didn't you hear the captain? The safety drill is mandatory for all passengers."

I flipped back over to look at Taylor. "Are you forgetting who else will be participating in said safety drill?" I asked. "Fuggetaboutit."

"You can't stay in here the entire cruise," Taylor pointed out.

"Of course not. But losing myself on a ship this big with a thousand other merrymakers is bound to be easier than concealing my presence in a small group setting. For all I know, Manny and Mo are assigned the same emergency station we are. Townsend, too, for that matter. No way. I'm staying put. Besides, hunter orange makes my complexion appear sallow."

Taylor shook her head and donned her brightly colored vest, somehow managing to look trés chic despite her ghostly pale face and jack-o'-lantern colored attire.

"Have it your way," she said. "You usually do."

"What is that supposed to mean?" I asked.

"Just that sometimes I think you've marched to the beat of your own drum for so long that somehow you've let that independent streak define who you are and control what you do and don't do—often to your own detriment and that of those around you."

Mrrrowrr! Taylor was clearly feeling better. The claws were out! And sharp.

"Oh? Is that what three years' undergraduate study in psychology tells you?" I asked, a reference to Taylor's field of study before she unexpectedly dropped out last term. "Thanks for the analysis, sis, but if I need my head examined, Dr. Phil gets first crack."

"It's an assessment based on years of observation," she replied. She tossed my lifejacket on my bed. "In case you change your mind," she remarked, and she moved to the door and opened it.

"You take good notes for me, y'hear?" I hollered out the door after her.

When she was gone, I put my head on the pillow and thought about what Taylor had just said. Could she be right? Was I too independent? Too inclined to go my own way? Did I pursue my own agenda equipped with Tressa Turner tunnel vision so that I failed to take into account the fallout to those around me? Were they, as Taylor insinuated, merely blurs in my peripheral vision?

I made a face. I hated to think of myself in those terms.

Hated to think she thought of me that way—that *anybody* might.

I frowned. Hadn't Ranger Rick made the very same argument over the course of the last year? Hadn't he repeatedly chewed out my cowgirl tail for keeping him out of the loop and going off on one of my tangents? For continually going off half-cocked?

My independent streak had been the biggest obstacle in our relationship—a streak so big, I was assured, it could be seen from the space shuttle in orbit around the Earth. It was the thing Townsend and I argued over most, the same issue that kept me from hurling caution to the wind and throwing myself into his arms and bed. Frankly, just the idea that someone else could claim a legitimate say in what I did, where I did it, who I did it with and when I did it scared the freakin' bejeebers out of me.

I closed my eyes. Had I gotten so used to going my own way, doing my own thing, being my own person that the reality of making room for someone else in my life had become as frightening to me as the concept of cellulite to a supermodel? As likely to invoke terror as being marooned on a desert island overrun by creepy crawlies, with no food, no water, no chocolate, and my sole fellow castaway, Rosie O'Donnell? Uh, sorry, Rosie, but the view from here ain't pretty.

I shifted uncomfortably on the bed.

This vacation was supposed to be fun—a getaway from a life that, over the last couple of years, had spiraled out of control. I'd been looking forward to my first real vacation since my folks and I took a road trip when I was sixteen. Eight years had passed and the mere mention of that particular family outing still had the ability to send my father to the medicine cabinet for a handful of antacid tablets.

This past week's wedding vacation in Arizona hadn't worked out much better. In fact, it had morphed into a Southwestern scavenger hunt that, any way you looked at it,

was no *Mona Lisa* story. In addition to a Wild West intrigue, Ranger Rick and I two-stepped our way around
some serious sexual tension that rivaled a Danielle Steel
novel, with me juggling the pros and cons of giving up and
giving in to the feelings Rick inspired. Only some freaky
twist of fortune had prevented me from setting my feet (and
every other body part) down that passionate path of no return. I hadn't yet decided whether I was frustrated or relieved by that forestalled consummation, but to say I was
disappointed at the time is like me saying, "I like chocolate."

This little oceanic pleasure cruise was supposed to give
me an opportunity to take some time to figure out my feelings where Ranger Rick was concerned, to decide once and
for all if he was the man for me and I was the cow gal
for him. But now, with my "secret love" Manny and his
aunt Mo on the ship manifest, the wind had been sucked
out of my sails. I wasn't sure I was adept enough to navigate
through the jagged rocks and reefs ahead in my quest to understand and come to terms with my—scary word here,
folks—*feelings*.

You see, I don't do feelings well. I never have. Displays of
emotion come about as naturally to me as vows of silence
would to my gammy. Or abstinence to a call girl. Most of
this goes back to a longtime practice of "hiding my light under a bushel," or in my case, beneath a flaky blonde façade. It
was a comfortable persona from which to operate benignly
below others' radars—and one where all I felt required to as-
pire to was being average. I was your basic class comedienne.
The Comedy Club coed. The girl voted most likely to still
be living at home at the ten-year reunion, if she was living at
all. Hardy har har.

I didn't appear to take anything seriously, so it was little
surprise no one took me seriously. And it didn't matter that
much to me.

Until it suddenly did.

A sudden sharp burst from the PA system sent me shooting off the bed and onto the floor. It was followed by six more abbreviated taps. One more long loud sound of the horn ended the call to muster. I shook my head and sighed and got to my feet.

Great. Taylor had guilted me into leaving the relative safety of my stateroom and risking crossed swords with Marguerite Dishman, all two hundred-plus pounds of her. Somehow I had the feeling Calamity's cutlass wouldn't fare too well against Mo's meat cleaver.

I grudgingly grabbed my orange vest and headed for the door. I'd just opened it a crack and turned to pick up a copy of the daily bulletin when I heard someone outside my cabin door say, "That's good. Nope. Doesn't suspect a thing." The hushed male voice added, "This long-overdue honeymoon cruise idea was sheer genius. The kickoff to a whole new life together. A brand-new beginning." A dry laugh. "Little does the romantic fool know this will be a farewell cruise. And now that the life insurance policy has been taken care of, all systems are go."

I froze, stunned.

I chanced opening my door a fraction more, hoping to get a glimpse of the speaker. I put my eye to the crack and peeked out, but all I could see was the back of a big, ugly orange vest. Damn.

"Poor clueless woman," the voice softly said, after a short pause. "She'll never in a million years see it coming."

I swallowed—a loud gulp. Dear God, could I have heard what I thought I heard? Was some guy planning to murder his wife on this cruise? I quickly replayed the one-sided conversation in my head. A farewell cruise. An insurance policy. And one clueless wife. Put 'em all together and whaddya got?

A custom cruise to die for.

I chewed my lip and quickly mulled over my options. One, I could confront the guy with what I'd heard. I frowned. Some risk involved there. Two, I could simply forget what I'd heard. I shook my head. I know, you're shaking yours, too, thinking, *Yeah, right, like that was ever an option.* I know you too well. Guess that works both ways, huh?

And option number three? I could do what I did best—indulge that good ol' killed-the-cat Calamity curiosity and stick my nose into someone else's business—especially if that business had to do with murder. Add to the aforementioned nosy nature a certain affinity toward comrades in cluelessness (Hey, we have to stick together, don't we?) and my decision was made.

I ran over to the small desk and grabbed my backpack. Purchased in the gift shop of an historic hotel adjacent to the Grand Canyon, the bag featured "Harry" Javelina, an adorable peccary. (A peccary is a small, hairy, pig-like critter, and I'd grown especially attached to this one.) I retrieved my camera from the bag and hurried back to the door, which I yanked open, prepared to snap a picture of the conniving culprit, but instead I was greeted by a wall of orange strolling past my doorway, as scores of passengers obediently followed the captain's orders.

"Sheep," I snapped, forgetting I'd been prepared to join the flock before I'd been sidetracked by *Dial M for Murder.* I stretched up on my tippy-toes and looked down the hallway in the direction the cruise conspirator had been, but the crowd prevented any chance of identification. Great. Now how was I going to find out just who planned to turn a honeymoon cruise into a marital massacre?

I waited for a break in the stampede to shove my way into the corridor, hoping I might catch up with the culprit at the mustering station and somehow figure out who he was. I had one thing to go on: the potential victim was here on a honeymoon. A long-overdue honeymoon. There couldn't be all that many honeymoon couples aboard *The Epiphany.* Could there?

I thought of my own gammy and her new hubby, Joe. They were on their honeymoon.

I shook my head at the direction my thoughts were taking. Get real, T, I told myself. While my gammy was a pretty good catch—if you like to live dangerously, that is—her assets were hardly alluring enough to commit homicide for. And as far as I knew, my gammy didn't even carry much of a life insurance policy. So that left her out. As if she'd even been in contention. Joltin' Joe Townsend was many things: a pain in the posterior crime-fighter wannabe, legend in his own mind lothario, snoop extraordinaire. But a black widower? The idea was as likely as my gammy being a *Playboy* Playmate of the Month. Me, either, for that matter.

I followed the parade of orange to the assigned location, keeping my eyes open for anything suspicious. I studied each female passenger as we stood waiting for further instructions, hoping somehow to establish a psychic link with the unsuspecting newlywed whose husband had a grisly wedding gift in mind.

I smiled at a thirtyish, rather rotund woman. She wore a wedding ring.

"Hello," I said. "Your first cruise?"

She nodded and held out her hand.

"Joni. You?"

"First-timer, too," I responded. "I'm Tressa."

"This cruise seemed like such a fantastic opportunity. I've been wanting to do something like this for a long time and surprise my husband, so I decided to get serious about it and just do it," she said.

"Oh, you're married?" I asked, looking around.

"Ten years," she replied. "But I'm here with my sister Darla." She motioned to a younger and heavier girl to her right. "We figured we could encourage each other over the long haul. How about you? What made you decide to get serious about your health and future?"

I blinked, confused.

"Huh?"

"It's important to know you're not alone in your struggle,"

Darla chimed in. "That others are going through the exact same thing you are."

"Wh—?"

"That's true, Darla. So, when did you decide to get serious about *your* weight, Tressa?"

My mouth flew open.

"Excuse me?"

"Tressa! Tressa Turner! You stay right there! You and Mo need to talk!" The volume of that shout rivaled a bullhorn, and could belong to only one person. "I see that fight-or-flight look in your eyes, so don't you be gettin' any ideas! Hear?"

I rethought my initial impulse to flee the approaching storm as the bodies pressing around me effectively closed off all means of escape. Reluctantly I stood my ground.

"There you are. Mo's got you cornered now."

"Aunt Mo, fancy seeing you here!" I exclaimed, my acting job on par with Jessica Simpson as Daisy Duke.

"Don't you feed Mo that line, Tressa Turner. Manny told Mo he'd warned you already."

I blinked. "Warned me? I'd hardly categorize it as a warning—"

"Is this your aunt, Tressa?" Joni asked.

"Tressa's engaged to my nephew," Mo said, and I felt the deck shift beneath my feet.

"Oh, I see," Joni said. "You're taking this cruise together to bond as family and to motivate each other as you undertake this new, exciting, and challenging phase of your lives. That is so sweet."

Mo looked at me. "Who's she? What's she talking about?"

"This is Joni and her sister Darla," I said. "This is their first cruise, too. This is Marguerite Dishman. She's from my hometown back in Iowa."

"So, you're engaged, Tressa? How exciting!" Darla grabbed my left hand. "Where's your engagement ring?"

"Yes, where *is* your ring, Tressa?" Mo parroted. "It's a family heirloom and worth more than you make at that Dairee Freeze in a year."

"Ohmigawd, you work at a Dairee Freeze?" Darla's eyes got big. "Girlfriend, that explains a lot."

"Huh?" I seemed to be saying that frequently.

"Shh! Do you mind? We're trying to hear the emergency instructions," a really large man with bright red hair and freckles barked.

"Well, excuse us for breathing," Aunt Mo responded. "And what do you think's gonna happen? You think this ship is gonna sink? You think you're gonna have to haul your heavy carcass into that lifeboat? Mister, you been watchin' too many disaster movies. And just so you know, in the original *Poseidon Adventure*, Shelley Winters . . . ? She died, dude. She died. And she was about your size."

"Easy, Aunt Mo. Down, girl," I said. "She's not herself," I told the nervous passenger. "It's the seasickness patch," I whispered.

"We need to talk, Tressa," Mo said.

"We *are* talking," I pointed out.

"We need to plan," Mo said.

"She's right," Joni agreed. "It's really important to establish a realistic plan for each of you based on your specific needs and physical limitations."

"Limitations?" I stared at Joni.

"We gotta set a date," Mo said. "Figure out a menu."

"Menus are extremely important," Darla said. "They should be healthy and nutritious and, of course, low in carbs. I've been reading up on this."

I looked at Darla. A carb-free wedding cake? Nutritious cocktail weenies? What the—?

"What you been reading, girl? Weight Watchers' weddin' planner?" Aunt Mo asked.

"They make one?" Darla responded, eyes wide.

The dubious thread of this conversation quickly unraveled. I cast my eyes skyward and caught sight of a familiar dark-haired head, its owner moving slowly in my direction.

Holy harpoons! Ranger Rick!

Frantic, I looked for a place to hide. My eyes landed on the considerable girth of the red-headed guy who'd shushed us earlier. If I could just manage to get behind him . . .

I started to inch backwards, hunching over like Quasimodo in order to conceal my presence. I bumped up against said immovable object and made a quick pivot move. Preparing to make my apologies to a fellow I fully intended to use as a human shield, I turned. But instead of the chubby chider of earlier, I was stunned to look up into a striking face I'd seen on the covers of countless tabloids and magazines for well over a decade. An actress, singer and entertainer whose career had tanked as she'd piled on the pounds, this woman still exuded beauty and glamour despite the giant orange vest she wore. By comparison, I'm sure I looked like slightly bruised produce.

"You're Coral LaFavre," I said, marveling at the flawless, mocha-colored complexion, perfect makeup and divine 'do. Topping my five-feet-seven by at least three inches, she looked like a beautiful, benevolent, slightly older version of Queen Latifah smiling down on her awed subjects.

"You must be a fan if you recognized me in this getup," she said, dispelling the royal rush.

"But what are you doing here?" I asked, putting Coral LaFavre between yours truly and Rick Townsend's line of sight.

"I'm one of the lounge acts," she said. "They thought I'd be perfect for this particular cruise. You know. Theme-wise." She rolled her eyes. "The price was right and they offered some nice perks. My husband and I tied the knot almost a year ago, but we hadn't had the opportunity for a proper honeymoon so the offer came at a nice time."

"You're a newlywed?" I asked, remembering the honeymoon surprise awaiting some blushing on-board bride.

"Well, eight months' worth, if that qualifies. As a matter of fact, I was looking around for my husband when you bumped into me," she said.

I winced.

"Sorry about that, Miss LaFavre," I said. "Uh, if you'd give me a description of your husband, I'll keep an eye out for him," I offered. It was a long shot. I hadn't seen anything but the big orange back of the man on the phone, and he'd kept his voice low so chances were I wouldn't recognize him if he walked up and shook my hand. But it seemed as if this couple's honeymoon was overdue. And it was a place to start.

"Oh, here he is," Coral said. "I wondered where you ran off to, David. One minute you were there, and the next you were gone."

While Coral's husband was an inch taller than his wife, his weight was considerably less. With light brown hair and eyes, and teeth that screamed, "White strips worn here," he looked like a greasy game show host.

"Forgive me, *cara*. I wanted to make sure all the arrangements were made for your performance before we set sail. No last-minute glitches and all that." He finally noticed me. "Hello. Have you made a new friend, Coral?" he asked with a chilly smile.

I stuck my hand out. "Yes. Yes, she has," I responded. "Tressa. Tressa Turner. It's nice to meet you. I understand this is a sort of *long-overdue* honeymoon cruise for you both."

Coral's husband's smile faltered. He took my hand, his limp and moist, the bleh factor off the charts.

"Mixing business with pleasure, as it were," he said, barely squeezing my fingers. "David Frazier Compton. Good to meet you, too—Tressa, is it? Unusual name for an unusual woman, I daresay."

David Frazier Compton? As it were? Daresay? Who did he think he was?

"So, you're taking advantage of the cruise theme, as well. Good for you," he continued as I reclaimed my hand with relief. "Good for you."

"I'm actually here with a wedding group," I told him. "My grandmother got married at the Grand Canyon a couple of days ago, and some of the family accompanied them on a combination celebratory and vacation cruise."

David Frazier Compton looked puzzled. "Your grandmother, you say? How . . . interesting."

"What's the deal, Tressa? You can't just go wandering off when people are talking to you. That's downright rude!" Aunt Mo had powered her way over to us. "We got wedding stuff to decide."

"Ah, I see. This must be your grandmother, Tressa," Coral said.

"Grandmother? I'm no grandmother!" Mo barked. "Tressa here's gonna marry my nephew. If I can ever manage to set her down and get her to name a wedding date, that is." Aunt Mo paused and gave Coral the once-over. "Don't I know you?" she asked.

"I don't know. Do you?" Coral seemed amused.

"Aren't you that star who got real fat and lost all that weight and then gained it back again?" Aunt Mo said, and I wished for Jack Sparrow's kerchief so I could stuff it in her mouth.

"Aunt Mo!"

"I think you've got me confused with Oprah—or Kirstie Alley maybe, ma'am," Coral said. "Yes, I gained weight. Unfortunately, I never lost it."

"I'm Marguerite Dishman, but everyone calls me Mo."

"Oh, for God's sake! Do you people ever shut up?" I heard, and turned to see the copperhead who'd asked us to muzzle ourselves earlier pointing at me. "She's Tressa, he's David, she's Coral, that's Marguerite but everyone calls her

Mo, and I'm Lou," he said, clearly exasperated. "And I hope to hell we don't have a real emergency or, thanks to your little social club, none of us will know stem from stern!"

I winced. I hoped they didn't give a pop quiz over the safety drill or I'd be royally screwed.

"Now, why do you have to go and be so unfriendly, Lou?" Mo asked. "Your mama never teach you manners?"

I noticed other passengers beginning to disperse. Hoping to divert a nasty scene—or Mo's imminent melee—I held up my camera and suggested, "How about I commit this moment to photographic memory? Smile and say, 'Poop deck'!" I hit the button and the camera flashed. "One more—and let's get you in this one, Lou," I said, slowly inching backwards. I snapped another one. "Fantastic. A keeper!

"Well, everyone, it's been real!" I said, "but alas, all good things must come to an end, and I've really been looking forward to that touching travel tradition I've seen in the movies. You know the one: tossing streamers over the rail, waving farewell to all those poor slobs left behind on land. So, if you'll excuse me—Coral, David, Aunt Mo, Lou—it's been a pleasure."

I slipped away before Aunt Mo could stop me, but I caught her parting comment.

"If Sailor Moon there thinks she can give ol' Mo here the slip, she's been smoking too much seaweed."

I grimaced. It seemed Townsend had some stiff competition from Aunt Mo for amateur night on the Custom Cruise Comedy Club stage.

Pass the M&M's and the popcorn.

Buttered.

Naturally.

Arrgh!

CHAPTER FOUR

I made my way back to the cabin, threw my life vest in a chair and ran a brush through my straggly hair, pulling it back into a ponytail and securing it with a scrunchie. I shoved a pink baseball cap on my head that said *All Cowgirl—No Bull* and pulled my ponytail out through the opening at the back. I surveyed my reflection and stuck my tongue out. *Real mature, Tressa.*

I pulled my backpack on over my shoulders, grabbed a pink hoodie in case it got chilly, and headed out again. No friggin' way was I missing out on the traditional bon voyage festivities. And if I didn't get something to eat soon, I was never going to make cruising speed. Still, I first needed to speak with cruise security and let them know that there was mischief afoot—mischief aboard *The Epiphany* that could spell murder for one of their passengers.

I hurried up to the main desk. A dark-haired gal about Taylor's age was just finishing up with a man in line ahead of me.

"May I help you?" she asked, one eyebrow rising slightly when her eyes came to rest on my hat.

"I need to speak with security," I said. "It's a matter of life and death."

Her other eyebrow joined the first. "Life and death? What do you mean, exactly?"

I paused and put my thumb and finger to my chin. "I

don't know. How would you describe a scheme to do away with an unsuspecting spouse on a long-overdue honeymoon cruise?" I asked.

She picked up a phone and pushed a button. "This is Erica at the service desk. I have a passenger who has a, uh, security issue to discuss. Yes." She paused. "Your name?" she asked.

"Tressa. Tressa Turner," I responded.

She nodded. "Tressa Turner. Yes. Thank you," she said and hung up. "Someone from our security office will be with you shortly," she told me.

I cooled my heels for a few minutes, wondering what it was about me that so unerringly homed in on trouble and troublemakers.

"Tressa Turner? Samuel Davenport, chief security officer."

I looked up to find a hand stuck out, its owner smiling down at me. His teeth were brilliantly white against chocolate-colored skin, and he kind of reminded me of a young Bill Cosby. He looked capable and competent in his spanking-white uniform.

I held out my hand and he gripped my fingers firmly. Now *this* was a handshake.

"Tressa Turner, first-time cruise passenger." I shook his hand vigorously.

"Nice to meet you . . . Miss or is it Mrs. Turner?"

"It's Miss," I told him.

"How can I help you, Miss Turner? I understand you have a concern with regards to safety or security. Is that correct?"

I bobbed my head up and down. "That's right."

"Let me assure you, Miss Turner, you're quite safe sailing with Custom Cruise Lines. We have a stringent set of security procedures and policies and a top-notch security staff to see those policies and procedures are implemented. Our captain and crew are experienced, capable sailors, and *The Epiphany* is as seaworthy a vessel as you'll find, so you're in good hands. My recommendation? Sit back and leave the cruising to us," Samuel Davenport suggested.

"That's all very reassuring," I told him honestly. "But it's not really *my* safety I'm concerned about. It's another passenger's."

He looked confused. Gee. Imagine that.

"Who would that be?" he asked.

"I have no idea," I said.

Davenport looked even more confused. Another shocker.

"I'm not following," he said.

I took a step closer. "There's skullduggery afoot aboard *The Epiphany*," I said in a low voice. "An evil plot to turn a honeymoon cruise into a booty bonanza."

"Come again?" he said.

"Murder, man! Some groom is planning to do away with his bride aboard your vessel!" I said. "A honeymoon homicide!"

Samuel Davenport's eyes got big, the whites of his eyeballs standing out against his dark skin. He took my elbow. "If you'll come with me, Miss Turner, I think this is a discussion best conducted in private."

I didn't miss the look exchanged between Davenport and Erica, the passenger service cutie. It was your basic "Don't turn your back on her, she could be dangerous" look. No biggie. I've seen it before. On more than one occasion.

I followed Davenport to a small office several doors down a narrow corridor. He closed us in and took a seat behind an off-white workspace. A laptop computer sat to his left. Davenport grabbed a white legal pad. He pulled a silver pen from inside his jacket pocket and tossed it on the pad.

"Why don't you take it from the top, Miss Turner?" he suggested, and I explained about the phone conversation I'd overheard in the corridor outside my cabin.

"I'm actually an investigative reporter," I told him, pulling my bag off my shoulder and setting it on the surface between us. "I have a card," I assured him and unzipped my

Javelina bag, sifting through the contents. "It's in here some-where. You see, in the course of my employment I've had a bit of experience in the area of crime-detecting." I finally located a battered business card I'd made on the computer and handed it to him. "So, it's not as if I'm an amateur."

" 'Tressa Jayne Turner, *Grandville Gazette. Can we talk?'* " Davenport read. "Catchy."

"Thank you," I said. "I was torn between that tag line and 'Can I quote you on that?' but went with the shorter one. I think it works."

"And you're certain the conversation you just described to me was an accurate representation of the conversation you heard outside your cabin?" he asked.

I nodded. "Well, it's not verbatim," I admitted, "but from what I heard I don't see how it can mean anything other than that somebody out there is planning to kill his wife for insurance money. I tried to get a picture of the guy, but when I got back to the corridor the security drill was un-derway and the dude was swept away by a moving river of orange."

He looked up at me. "You didn't attend the safety drill? It's mandatory, you know," he said.

Jeesch. Talk about broken records.

"Oh, I went. I thought maybe I'd somehow be able to discover who I'd overheard by mingling with the masses."

"So, you played sleuth?" Davenport asked, twisting a dia-mond horseshoe ring on his finger.

"Investigative journalist," I pointed out.

"Ah. And in your capacity as investigative journalist did you discover anything prescient?"

I frowned. "Prescient?" I said, thinking I needed to add a new word to my dictionary.

"Were you able to discern anything useful at the safety drill?"

"Well, for one thing, you've got some really crabby pas-sengers on board, so beware," I said, thinking of Lou, the red-headed party pooper. "And I did make contact with one honeymooning couple at the drill." I took out my digital camera and hit the power button. "That's the bride, Coral LaFavre—she's a shipboard entertainer—and her new husband, David Frazier something or other." I handed him the camera.

"Okay. I'm looking at an elderly man wearing a Jackie Chan hat asleep on what appears to be an aircraft."

I grabbed the camera back. "Oh, sorry. That's just Joe—my gammy's new hubby. I'm making a book of memories for the happy couple as a wedding gift." I advanced the shots. "That's Coral and her husband."

He looked at the picture for a few seconds. "I'm acquainted with Coral," he said. "She's sailed with us before. And who are the other two people in the photo?"

"That's Aunt Mo. Not *my* aunt Mo, but my fiancé's Aunt Mo. Well, not *my* fiancé, really—my fake fiancé. And the other dude there is Lou, the crabby passenger I warned you about before. The guy seriously needs to chill out."

Davenport shook his head back and forth slowly, as if to get all the loose pieces to settle back into place. "You think Coral LaFavre's husband is the fellow you overheard?" he asked.

I shrugged. "I couldn't make a positive I.D. of the voice if that's what you mean, because he kind of whispered," I admitted. "But it's a place for you to start."

He handed me the camera. "How do you mean?"

"Why, get Coral in here and find out if she's got a hefty life insurance policy covering her," I said. "And go from there."

"Oh, I see. Just bring Coral LaFavre in and explain to her that a fellow passenger overheard one side of a very short phone conversation that might or might not point to a criminal conspiracy and, based on that information, we'd like to invade her privacy in order to ascertain if her new husband has a monetary motive for wanting her dead. Is that what you expect me to do, Miss Turner?" Davenport asked.

"Would that be a problem?" I asked, giving a weak smile.

"And where would we go from there?" he continued. "Haul every honeymooner—or second-honeymooner, for that matter—in here and grill them about their spouses' devotion and delve into personal financial information?"

"How many honeymooners could we be talking about?" I asked.

"I have no idea. And I don't feel particularly compelled to find out," Davenport said. "Listen, Miss Turner, I understand your concern in this matter, and I appreciate that you brought it to me, but I really don't think there's anything for you to be concerned about."

I sat back in my seat. I'd heard this song so often I could sing the friggin' refrain backwards.

"So, you're not planning to do anything with the information I just provided," I said.

"I didn't say that," Davenport replied, putting his pen down. "I'll certainly make sure my people are aware of this information and advise them to keep their eyes and ears open. Beyond that, I'm not sure we have the level of corroboration required to do more."

"And what kind of corroboration do you need, Mr. Davenport?" I asked. "A blood-stained canopy? A passenger who mysteriously disappears? A human chum line? Tell me. Just so I know it when I see it."

Davenport's chair squeaked as he eased back and gave me a look like the one I wear when I belly up to the Chinese buffet and the guy before me takes the last of the spring rolls and crab Rangoon.

I placed my camera back in my book bag and zipped it up. I stood. Samuel Davenport did the same.

"I do hope you can manage to take advantage of this Custom Cruise, Miss Turner, and use it as a springboard to a healthy, happy, balanced lifestyle," he said. "And leave the sailing—and the sleuthing—to the professionals."

I nodded and left. Same old song. Same old story. But was I, the same old Tressa, going to march to her own drum or take Davenport's advice and leave the sailing to someone else? Okay, folks. Place your bets.

The long loud sounding of the ship's horn and the movement of the deck beneath my feet announced we were getting underway. Great. My first cruise, and instead of waving farewell to strangers on land as we sailed away, I was stuck below deck trying to reason with a dubious security chief.

I took the elevator to an upper deck and hurried out to where I jockeyed for space at the already crowded railing.

"Excuse me," I said, squeezing in between two other tourists. They were both about the size of Crabby Lou from the drill. I checked down the deck for familiar faces and, observing none I recognized, relaxed. The ship's horn blasted, and as we slowly pulled away from the pier I put a hand up and did my best Queen Elizabeth wave.

"Good-bye! Farewell! Adios, landlubbers!" I called out, and the woman to my right gave me a half smile. I snapped a couple shots of the Galveston pier growing smaller, clicking a few pictures of the people lining the sides of the boat to bid adieu to those bound to land.

My stomach, tired of being ignored, decided to send a signal that it was time for chow, and it let out a long, loud rumble.

"Oh, dear, I guess we'd all better get used to hearing that sound a lot around here," the woman next to me commented. "I'm not sure I'm up for this. At the time it seemed like a good idea, but now that I'm here, I'm not so sure."

"Oh? Why? Are you afraid of water?" I asked.

"No. I'm afraid of starving," she replied.

I looked at her. "I don't think you'll have to worry about that," I said, my mind on all the culinary delights awaiting every cruise customer.

The woman turned to face me. "And just what is that supposed to mean?" she asked, her face turning red. "That I can live off the fat of my morbidly obese body for an extended period of time? That I'm in no danger of starving in this decade? Listen, I know I'm fat. That's why I'm here."

I stared at her.

"I'm afraid I don't quite understand——"

"Of course you don't, cowgirl. You're not in the same boat as I am. Yet," she added.

I was left to stare at her broad back as she stomped away.

"What on earth? What was that all about?" I asked the man on my other side.

"Insufferable insensitivity and an appalling lack of manners?" he answered, his accent decidedly British. "Americans," he said with a sniff.

"Now just a minute," I started to object when I felt an arm curl around my waist from behind.

"So this is where you've been hiding?" I heard, and turned around to find Rick Townsend encroaching big-time on my personal space. "I didn't see you at the safety drill. You didn't skip by any chance, did you, Tressa?"

"I was there——and I've got photos to prove it," I told him.

We stood there on the ship's deck, the sun sinking below the horizon, as we set sail. With Townsend's arm around me, his chest pressed against my back, the moment was incredibly romantic. When Townsend bent to nuzzle my neck I almost leaped over the rail.

My stomach chose that moment to gurgle louder than the cheap fountain at the butterfly garden back home.

"Hungry?" Townsend whispered in my ear.

"Always," I responded.

"They've got a nifty little thing called room service——or make that *stateroom* service——here," Townsend said, giving my neck his full attention. "We could order whatever you like."

I turned to look at him. "Whatever I like?" I asked. "What

if I wanted something like Beluga caviar or a five-hundred-dollar bottle of Dom Pérignon?"

"I know you better than that. You're more a burger-and-beer kind of date," Townsend observed.

"Yes, but I'm celebrating, remember? Once we get back to Grandville, I will have my home and hearth all to myself—and nary a 'Is that a hornbill in your pants or are you just excited to see me' statue anywhere to be found. Freedom," I said, raising my hands in the air in jubilation. "Sweet freedom!" I felt a bit like Mel Gibson as William Wallace—minus the oozing entrails and head on a pike, of course.

"Does this mean you can have friends stay over now?" Townsend asked, giving me an intent look. "If so, I say bring on the Dom."

"You are so bad," I said.

My stomach rumbled again.

"I think we'd better see about getting you fed," he said.

"We don't have to dress for dinner or anything, do we?" I asked. "Because I don't think I can wait that long."

"I'm sure there are bound to be a number of places we can pop in at for a quick bite to eat," Townsend said. "So, what's your pleasure?"

"Beef," I said without hesitation. I'd been without Iowa pork, beef or lamb for well over a week, and I was suffering from corn-fed-meat withdrawal. Although I didn't hold out hope the steak I'd get shipboard would be as good as the fare from back home, I was hungry enough to start gnawing a limb. "A thick, juicy steak. Baked potato with sour cream and butter, and a side of baked beans. Oh, and Texas toast."

"And where, pray tell, do you think you're going to find such menu items?" the Brit who had ripped into me like my hounds on table scraps inquired. "Or were you just being perverse?"

I frowned. "They don't have steak on this boat?" I asked. "What kind of cruise is this anyway?"

"A heart-healthy cruise, of course," the Brit replied.

"What are you talking about?" I asked Jeeves. (What can I say? The Brit looked like a giant-sized Ask Jeeves—minus the butler suit.) I turned to Townsend. "What is he talking about?"

Townsend just shrugged.

"It's a calorie-counting weight-watching cruise," Jeeves told me.

"I'm not following," I said. "When you say calorie counting . . ."

"It's the theme of the cruise. 'Lifestyle Facelift: Sculpt your Body, Mind, and Soul.'"

I felt my right eye begin to twitch. "Lifestyle Facelift?"

Jeeves nodded. "It's a week-long, intensive immersion into diet, exercise, and attitude with the goal of providing a jumpstart into health and happiness that we can continue after the cruise."

My mind focused on one very intimidating four-letter word: "Diet?"

Jeeves nodded. "Low-carb, low-fat, strictly monitored diet," he replied. "There will even be competitions and prizes given to winners in various categories," he said. "But mostly it's about finding balance in all areas of your life."

"Low-fat?"

"It's really an incredible opportunity. We'll be getting instruction from professional trainers. Trainers to the stars," he continued.

"Low-fat," I said.

"And there will be yoga and nutrition classes and cooking demonstrations."

"Low-fat!"

"What's the matter? You look ill. Is it the ship?" Jeeves asked. "Does she need to lie down?"

"She'll be okay. Eventually," I heard Townsend say, attempting to stifle the laughter in his voice.

Almost catatonic, I leaned slowly over the railing and

stretched out a beseeching hand toward the rapidly disappearing pier.

I could see it now, bouncing on the ocean current, my very own message in a bottle: *SOS! Chocolate Addicted Cowgirl Trapped on Fat Farm Cruise! Send Help! Send Coast Guard! Send Big Macs and Fries!*

I stuck my chin in my hands and sighed.

Now I knew how Jack Sparrow felt when the rum was gone.

Yo-ho-ho and a bottle of V-8.

CHAPTER FIVE

Townsend gently disentangled me from the ship's rail and led me safely away from the edge. "Your breaststroke might be strong, but I doubt you'd make it, Tressa," he said. "And it's only a week," he reminded me.

One week. One week of surviving on cottage cheese and carrot sticks. One week of green salads with no-cal dressing and bean sprout garnishes. One week without chocolate, doughnuts and cinnamon rolls, and where the only available cake was of the rice variety. I felt my steps falter. Townsend held me upright.

"I'll starve," I said. "I'll go mad. Like those characters in the cartoons that start seeing things and begin to eye other people with cannibalistic undertones."

"Big difference, Calamity," Townsend said. "We're not shipwrecked."

"But I am trapped aboard the S.S. Salad Barge," I grumbled.

Townsend laughed.

"You're finding this situation hilarious, aren't you?" I asked. My eyes narrowed. "You didn't know about this ahead of time, did you?"

"What? How could I?"

"Didn't your granddad book the cruise? I know he was in the know enough to make a couple of last-minute substitutions for your brother, Mike, and his family," I announced, then wanted to stuff anything—even a bran muffin—in my super-sized mouth.

"What do you mean, substitutions?" Townsend asked.

"See? I'm already talking gibberish due to hunger!" I said, grabbing hold of him and pulling him along with me. "Come on. There has to be something good to eat on board this floating fruit cup."

Townsend in tow, we located one of the various food venues.

"Uh, what is this?" I asked.

"Sushi bar!" someone squealed.

I grabbed Townsend and we moved to the next one.

"Oh! A breakfast bar! This looks promising!" I said— until I discovered the pancakes were whole wheat and the omelets made from egg substitute.

Next came the salad bar, fruit bar, and finally, thank God, the burger bar!

I tonged a thick burger on a whole grain bun and started building the perfect burger. Lettuce, tomato, onion, light mayo (bleah), cheese. I slapped the top of the bun on my sandwich. By this time my mouth was watering so badly I needed a baby drool bib to catch the moisture.

I caught Townsend's amused look as he filled a plate for himself. I headed for a nearby booth, biting into my burger before my butt hit the seat.

I chewed . . . and chewed . . . and chewed.

It had a familiar flavor and texture. One I didn't quite asso-ciate with red meat, but that was reminiscent of my gammy's rather memorable soy meatloaf.

"Something wrong?" Townsend asked, taking a big bite of his burger and wiping his mouth with a napkin.

I managed to swallow the heaping helping I'd crammed into my mouth.

"It's a soy burger, isn't it?" I asked, suddenly depressed.

Townsend nodded.

"And the hot dogs?"

"Turkey franks, I suspect," he said. "But cheer up, T," he added. "There's still the dessert bar."

"They have one?" I asked, hope in my heart.

He nodded. "And you're gonna love it. Fifty-seven different flavors!"

I stared at him. "Really?" I asked, my voice pathetic in its optimism.

He nodded. "Fifty-seven wonderful flavors of yogurt," he said. "With granola sprinkles!"

I shook my head. "Funny man."

Townsend grinned and took another bite of his soy burger. He suddenly stopped chewing. His expression changed.

"Ah, so the second bite isn't quite as good as the first one, huh?" I jeered.

Townsend continued to stare at a point beyond my head, his soy-stuffed mouth hanging open.

"Townsend? Are you okay?" I asked. "You're not allergic to soy are you?"

He shook his head and slowly started to chew again. "No, I just thought I saw someone. Nevermind," he said. "I'm mistaken. Forget it."

I frowned. "Who did you think you saw?" I asked, getting a so-don't-want-to-go-there feeling.

"Couldn't be her, so let's drop it."

"Couldn't be who?" I pressed. Darn my interrogatory nature.

"Marguerite Dishman," Townsend finally said.

I gulped. Crap.

"Aunt Mo?" I asked, my voice unnaturally high. I snorted. "What would she be doing here?" I kept my head down, picked his cup up and sniffed it. "You sure you haven't had too much grog, mate?"

Townsend grinned. "Maybe I haven't had enough," he suggested.

"Well, unless ye've smuggled yer ale aboard, there's little

chance of gettin' a buzz aboard this vessel," I said in my best pirate voice.

Townsend leaned across the table and gave me a leer. "Aye, wench, but ye and me could get high on a feelin', I wager," he pirated back. "If ye be willin'."

I stared into twinkling brown eyes that warmed me as a good stiff shot of the hard stuff couldn't. "And what would ye be havin' in mind, sailor boy?" I asked.

He took my hand. "A walk around the ship, stargazing . . . and gazing into each other's eyes," he suggested, surprising me by his romantic overture—and scaring the soy clean out of me.

"And what then?" I asked, my spit drying up faster than the farm pond in a drought year.

"I'd try some of my best pirate pickup lines, of course. Until I hit on one that worked."

I snorted. "Pirate pickup lines? Give me a break, Townsend. Since when do you know any pirate pickup lines?"

He smiled, putting Orlando Bloom's smile to shame. "Since I boned up," he responded, raising an eyebrow. "Especially for the occasion."

"Yeah, right. So? Pick me up, sailor," I challenged.

Townsend shut one eye, Popeye-like. "Aye, the fair wench is interested in paying a visit to me cabin to see me urchins then?" he said, with a ridiculous accent that sounded more silly than seafaring. "Or maybe ye wants to scrape the barnacles off me rudder?"

My mouth flew open. The scallywag *had* done his homework!

"What be the matter, wench? Parrot got yer tongue?"

I started to giggle. Tears streamed down my face. In addition to being outrageous, outspoken and out-and-out sexy, Ranger Rick Townsend had always, always been able to make me laugh.

"I hope that mirth doesn't mean ye not be taking me seriously . . ." Townsend stopped. "Because I be serious. Dead serious."

His grip on my hand tightened. I swallowed—a noisy one due to lack of throat lubrication.

"Come on," Townsend cajoled. "Take a chance, T," he said. "Another famous sailor named Columbus did and look how that turned out."

I chewed my lip.

Was I ready?

Were *we* ready?

Could we make it to Townsend's cabin without being caught by Aunt Mo?

Would I ever want to come out if we did?

"Rick? Rick Townsend? Is that really you?"

A female voice reached our table and I noticed Townsend's eyes had grown as big as pieces of eight again.

"Brianna?"

Brianna?

"Ohmigawd, I can't believe it! Rick Townsend! Ohmigosh! It's been like forever since I've seen you! What are you doing here? Oh my gawd, this is incredible!"

Townsend popped to his feet. In other circumstances I might have alerted him to the fact that he had a napkin sticking to the front of his pants, but in this case I decided to let it add to his overall charm.

"Brianna Larkin. It's been a long time," Townsend said, moving to approach the woman at my back. I turned in my seat to get a look at Townsend's mystery lady from the past. Now *my* eyes were big as silver dollars.

Of medium height, Brianna Larkin had long, straight, shiny blonde hair with perky highlights, big blue eyes (heavy on the mascara) and straight white teeth. Dressed in a navy sundress trimmed in white that showcased a tanned, toned bod, Townsend's "old" friend was definitely not in need of an Overeaters Odyssey at Sea.

"You look fantastic," Townsend continued, flashing his own pearly whites.

"Thanks! And look at you! You're more handsome than ever!" She gave him another hug, and when she pulled back I was gratified to find Townsend's napkin had attached itself to her dress front now. "What on earth are you doing here? Seriously, Rick. What are you doing on the 'blimp boat'?"

I frowned. "Blimp boat?" I said. "That's a little insensitive, isn't it?"

I finally got the blonde's attention. I tried not to fixate on the fact that her hair actually permitted a comb through it without getting hung up in the tangles.

"Oh, Rick, I didn't realize I was interrupting," she said, her mouth forming a tiny little O.

I smirked. I believed that about as much as I believed Townsend really enjoyed his soy burger.

"Hey, how ya doin'?" I smiled up at Brianna.

Townsend cleared his throat.

"Brianna, this is Tressa Turner," he said, pointing to me. "Tressa's grandmother and my grandfather recently got married. We're all here on a celebration cruise of sorts—well, or so we thought. Apparently, someone got confused when they booked the cruise and, as a result, it looks like we're doing the Custom Cruise Lite." He grinned at me and winked.

Fiend.

"Oh, I see. So you're related," Brianna said, giving me a speculative look.

"Only by marriage," I pointed out.

"You said you're all here," Brianna went on. "Does that mean your folks, too? And Mike?"

I raised an eyebrow. Apparently Brianna and Townsend knew each other very well indeed.

"My folks are on board, but Mike and his family bailed at the last minute to do Disney instead," Townsend said.

"Oh, I can't wait to see Don and Charlotte again," Brianna said. "It will be just like old times!"

"How do you two know each other again?" I asked, reminding the couple I was out of their mutual admiration society loop.

"Oh, Rick and I were college sweethearts," Brianna said. "Weren't we, Rick? We were inseparable."

Rick's smile faltered. "It's been a while," he said.

"So? What happened?" I asked.

"Oh, I wanted to see the world and Rick here wanted to settle down in Podunk, Iowa," Brianna explained, her hands on Townsend's arm. "I couldn't stand the thought of being tied down back then."

"What do you do, Brianna?" I asked, already anticipating the answer. "For a living, that is."

"I'm a fitness coach," she said. "I majored in health with a minor in nutrition. Played collegiate tennis until my hamstring gave out. How about you, Tressa?"

"I'm a print journalist," I told her.

"Oh, really? Where did you go to school? U of I? I know they have an awesome writers' workshop program there."

"Carson College," I responded.

"Oh." She nodded, judgment evident in the look she bestowed on me. "I see."

"Tressa is the star reporter for *The Grandville Gazette*," Townsend supplied. "But she's become as famous for making the news as reporting it," he said, smiling down at me.

"I see," Brianna said again.

Right.

"Listen, Rick, I've got a meeting to get to, but I'd love to get together later this evening and catch up," Brianna said. She took a business card from her tiny purse along with a pen and scribbled something on the card and handed it to Rick. "That's my cabin number. I should be done with the meeting by nine. Nine-thirty at the latest. Ring me up—or better yet, drop by if you're free. I can't wait to hear what you've been up to!"

I had a sudden desire to go for her throat but settled for

making a sudden grab at Townsend's napkin still clinging to Brianna's front. "Aaaah!" She gave a short scream and jumped back.

"Sorry," I said, holding up the napkin. "It didn't go with the outfit," I added.

She gave me an uncertain look and Townsend another fierce hug, and then bounced off.

I shook my head. Who did she think she was? Tigger?

Townsend took his seat again.

"And to think you were worried you might be lonely on this cruise," I said, patting his cheek. (Facial variety.) "I'm thinking you'd better hit the casino, Townsend, because it looks like Lady Luck is smiling on you."

"I thought we were going to take a stroll around the deck and see where that takes us," Townsend said.

I pushed my plate away. "Sorry, me hearty. Your pickup lines were good, but not quite good enough," I said. "Besides, you have a date with Brianna later. Remember?"

"But I don't want to spend the evening with Brianna," Townsend said, getting up and sliding into the booth beside me and pasting his body to my side. "I want to spend it with Tressa Jayne Turner, ace cub reporter."

Oh, God. He sounded serious.

"You do?" I asked.

He nodded.

Oh, holy shinola. He *was* serious! And what about me?

I was skank city, that's what I was. I was still wearing the clothes I'd had on that morning on the plane and on the shuttle. I'd worn them while I sweated up a storm waiting to get on the ship. Thanks to the hat I'd stuck on to hide my hair from hell, I'd bet pirate gold once I took it off I'd have a flattened ridge running the circumference of my head that on someone with silky, tame tresses like my little sister might be overlooked and forgiven, but on my crowning glory? Just the idea of Rick Townsend running his fingers through my minefield of a mane gave me intimacy nightmares.

"I'll need to, uh, freshen up," I said, my voice unnaturally high.

"Okay," he agreed, his eyes focused on my lips. I prayed to God I didn't have lettuce stuck between my teeth. "How long will it take?"

I quickly calculated the time required for a shower, shave, lotion, makeup, and polish change. Then I added an hour to that for hair care.

"I can be ready by eight," I said, adding an additional extra ten minutes to talk myself out of it. "Yeah, eight's good."

"Twenty-hundred it is," Townsend said. "How about we meet for a drink in the Pirate's Cove?"

"Works for me," I responded, finding myself staring at Townsend's mouth.

"And you won't chicken out. Right?"

I frowned. The guy was a mind reader. Or maybe not. I probably had *bwack, bwack* flashing on my forehead.

"You know me. I'm a woman of my word," I said, as he let me out of the booth.

"Yeah. And your word is 'unpredictable,'" Ranger Rick responded.

Nice.

"Enjoy the rest of your soy whopper there," I said. "Feel free to finish mine if you like." Then I hurried away.

What the devil had I committed to now?

I made my way back to my cabin, keeping a pair of dark glasses on as I traversed the decks and corridors, half expecting Aunt Mo to suddenly appear around each corner. I felt like I was in one of those scary video games where you maneuver your player cautiously through a series of passages, ever on the lookout for zombies ready to jump out at you and suck out your brains. (No comments about how blondes like me have nothing to fear from the undead, then. 'Kay? Let's play nice.)

It occurred to me to wonder why I hadn't noticed before how many of the passengers on the ship were . . . of a certain body type and weight. So much for this ace cub reporter's powers of observation. Of course, there was the glare from Joe Townsend's legs to consider. It had been blinding.

I made it to my cabin, gray matter intact. Taylor's life-jacket was on a chair, but Taylor was nowhere to be found. I wondered if she'd yet discovered the getaway glitch that placed us bunch of meat eaters from Iowa trapped on this smart-choice ship. Still, knowing Taylor, she was probably in healthy-balance heaven—and preparing to enjoy the enter-tainment factor of watching the rest of us junk-food con-noisseurs drafted to fight in the battle of the bulge.

I jumped in the shower and loofahed, buffed and polished, dried off and slipped on a set of hot pink matching undies. I pulled on a pair of low-cut denim Capri pants with a wide, white belt and wriggled into a pink T-shirt with a big heart on the front that featured silhouettes of a cowgirl resting her forehead against her horse's head. The slogan read: *Treat you like I treat my horse? You wish.* Vintage cowgirl attire.

I took more time with my makeup than usual, adding ex-tra mascara and eyeliner to make me more alluring. Okay, and slightly slutty.

Hair was next. My hair is always a challenge. A cross be-tween a lion's mane and an SOS scouring pad, I'd learned long ago that taming this particular beast required the skills of Siegfried and Roy. Or Merlin the magician. I decided to be bold and daring and wear it down for a change. Most days I stick it back in a ponytail or braid it. With generous amounts of gel, I manage to keep the frizz factor under control. Wearing it down is always risky. On a good hair day I can just about pull off a blonde Lindsay-Lohan-on-a-bad-hair-day look. On a bad hair day? Well, let's just say if Bozo the Clown was interviewing for a missus, on a bad hair day I'd be shoo-in.

Giving my head a final spritz of tresses tamer, I checked my reflection one last time, grabbed a white denim jacket and Harry Javelina and headed out the door.

"Tressa Jayne! Yoo-hoo!"

I turned to discover my grandma and her new groom, arm in arm, heading in my direction. My gammy was garbed in a mauve dress with a lightweight, lacy sweater jacket; Joe looked spiffy in dress slacks and a dress shirt.

"Well, shiver me timbers, if it isn't the infamous Captain Hook, Line and Stinker, and his lady love, Hellion Hannah!" I observed, remembering both Joe's distaste for my pirate prose and his foul deed concerning a couple stowaways. "To what do we owe yer finery? Ye be suppin' with Captain Steubing?"

Joe flashed me an irritated look. I raised an eyebrow. After all, he'd thrown down the gauntlet—in a six-foot-three form that was impossible to ignore—so as far as I was concerned, the game was on.

"We're invited to a honeymooner mixer!" Gram announced. "It's for people taking first or second or third honeymoons. I'm thinkin' that's a good thing. Right?" she said, seeking verification.

I nodded. "You'll have a chance to mix with other honeymooning sweetheart couples," I explained. "Arrgh! 'Tis a fine time ye'll be havin'," I added, about to include a warning about the stingy caloric count of the cuisine, then deciding to let the unsuspecting couple make that priceless discovery on their own. Joe was as much of a junk-food addict as I was, if not more so. And with the rapid-fire metabolism he was always touting, when he discovered a "plate worse than death" at dinner, I could only imagine his reaction. It was almost worth the suffering I would go through to see the mischievous mutineer in the same balanced-food-group boat.

"Too bad it doesn't include engaged couples," Joe said, giving me a pointed look. The perverted little puppet master.

"You think what I'm wearing will work okay?" Gram asked.

I smiled. "Aye," I said. "Ye'll be the purtiest wench at the mixer."

Gram frowned. "How come you're talkin' like that?" she asked.

"Ask Gilligan there," I replied.

"Gilligan?"

"Your new hubby. It's my nautical nickname for him," I explained. "Cute, huh?"

"So, what do you have on your itinerary for this evening?" my gammy's Little Buddy of a groom asked me. "Hide and seek? A date in a dark casino corner with a one-armed bandit? Solitaire in your cabin?"

"How about a game of battleship with an ancient mariner?" I suggested, giving Joe my best hoistin'-the-Jolly-Roger look.

"Funny," Joe said. "Let's leave your granddaughter to an exciting evening of in-over-her-head, Hannah," he said.

"Is that some kind of gambling?" Gram asked.

Joe gave me a sharp look. "Sure is," he said. "A big gamble. With a lot riding on the next play, I'm thinkin'."

I shook my head. "Give my regards to the other honeymooners, Captain Kidd," I said—and then realized what I'd just said. Honeymooners? As in, *honeymoons long overdue*? As in, an opportunity to possibly meet and greet a villain who was plotting a lost-at-sea scenario as a belated wedding gift, maybe?

I rubbed my chin. A mixer, huh? I knew how to mix. Circulate. I could chat up all the other grooms and see if I might recognize something about the individual I'd overheard in the hallway outside my cabin. If not, I could always drop a rather broad hint to the hims in each happy his-and-hers couple that I was on to them. Perhaps I could startle him into an admission of sorts, or at the very least make him rethink his plan—buy some time to narrow the field and, in the process, buy his wife a reprieve.

Okay. As a plan, it wasn't much, but I'd started with less

in other investigative endeavors. And no way could I bring myself to sail away unconcerned while there was a possibility a fellow passenger was about to be liquidated by her lover.

"Uh, where be this celebratin'?" I asked, and Gram handed me the ship's daily program of events.

"In the Stardust Lounge," she said.

I made a face. It sounded like a cheesy Vegas casino.

I checked out the ship's diagram. The Stardust was right next to Pirate's Cove, where I was supposed to meet Townsend. Still, if I went to the honeymooner mixer, I would require a husband. If I explained to Townsend first what I'd overheard, perhaps I could get him to help me out in my quest to save a damsel in distress. After all, hadn't Townsend badgered me to open up to him, to trust him? To include him in my life? How, then, could he refuse my request?

I smiled.

A handsome ranger. A star to sail by. A mystery to unravel. What more could an intrepid reporter want?

My stomach gurgled and then growled. Joe looked at me.

What more could a girl want? A meat-lover's pizza, a side of cheese bread, onion rings and a big bottle of grog. Hold the water.

CHAPTER SIX

I trailed my grandma and Joe to the Stardust. Joe kept turning around to give me puzzled looks, which I ignored. I imagine he didn't think it was safe to turn his back on me after the stunt he'd pulled bringing Manny and Mo onboard to vex my voyage. I imagine he was right.

It was five of eight when we reached the lounge. Approximately half a dozen couples of various ages were gathered there. Joe gave me another weird look as he and Gram moved into the dimly lit room.

I hovered in the doorway, eyeing each couple, trying to eliminate them one by one based on my brief glimpse of the desperado. Husband number one seemed way too short. Husband number two: too black. When I came to couple number three, I blinked. The two men stood together—both of considerable size and girth—and one had an arm around the other's waist. I looked away quickly, in case I got caught staring. I reckoned I could count them out, too. The rest of the couples were viable possibilities—with the exception of Mr. and Mrs. Joe Townsend, of course. I'd have recognized Joe's chicken legs anytime, anywhere.

I was about to go grab Townsend and explain my dilemma and enlist his aid when a heavy arm dropped over my shoulder.

"Manny's been looking for Barbie."

I turned and cast an eye up. And up.

"He has? I mean, you have?" I asked, sucking in a deep breath at the warmth of Manny's body and getting a snoot-ful of a divine, musky scent exuding from the man in exchange.

"Manny's disappointed."

"Oh?" I said.

"He didn't get to give Barbie a bon voyage kiss."

"Oh!" I said again.

"Manny felt real bad."

"Huh?"

All of a sudden the music was jacked up and a rollicking version of "Here Comes the Bride" began to play. The hostess congratulated the honeymooning couples and welcomed them to the social hour.

Manny looked confused. "What's Barbie up to now?" he asked, and I debated how much to tell him. We'd indulged in a little quid pro quo in the past to our mutual benefit, but I didn't see anything in this little intrigue for Manny. "I thought Barbie'd be hanging out with Rick the Dick."

I winced—for several reasons. First off, Manny's nick-name for Rick always prompted this reaction. Second? His remark reminded me that Townsend, who was cooling his heels in an adjacent hotspot and waiting for yours truly to take a turn on the deck, was blissfully ignorant of the fact that my make-believe fiancé was not only on board the ship but mere steps away, his muscled arm hugging me to him.

Shite.

"Townsend, uh, met an old friend from college," I evaded, which was true.

"Yeah? So what's Barbie doing at a 'just married' get-together?"

· I wondered whether a finely crafted fib would work best or if I should go the truth-is-stranger-than-fiction route. Whatever I did, I needed to do it soon or Townsend would think I'd chickened out in earnest.

"Would you believe I'm trying to figure out which one

of these grooms is hoping to disembark *The Epiphany* a wealthy widower?" I asked, quickly relaying much the same story I'd shared with Custom Cruise Security Chief Sam Davenport.

Manny shook his head. "What are the odds?" he said. "So, what's Barbie's plan?"

I then explained my long-shot idea to meet and mingle with the couples and work my "I know who you are and I know what you want to do" magic on the grooms—even though I had no idea who any of them were or what had, individually, brought them on this cruise. At the same time, I told Manny, I'd planned to subtly imply to the brides to watch their backs.

Manny smiled. "Barbie *subtle*?" He nodded. "Right. Right."

I frowned. "Barbie can do subtle," I maintained.

He raised a dark eyebrow. "Barbie's about as subtle as an iceberg." I winced. "Give Manny the ring," he ordered, and lost me.

"Ring?"

"Tressa's engagement ring," he said. "Give it to me."

I could feel my breath hitch in my throat before I expelled the contents of my lungs in a huge, heavy, loud breath.

Oh. My. Gawd! This was it! Finally! The long-awaited breakup! Hallelujah and pass the bubbly!

I unzipped my bag and retrieved the über-carat ring from a small side pocket and handed it to Manny. Whew. I let out another long sigh. I felt like Frodo Baggins relinquishing possession of the Precious. Relief flowed over me. For all of three seconds. That was about the time it took for Manny to grab my left hand and slip the ring on my unsuspecting third finger.

"We should fit in now. Sweethearts. Remember?" he said, and grabbed my hand and pulled me over to a group of three lucky couples.

"Ahoy! Congratulations! Best wishes!" Manny broadcast,

and snared a glass of what looked like champagne from a nearby waiter. He handed one to me and took a second. He raised his glass. "To new beginnings!" he toasted.

I stared at him. This was also a side of Manny I'd never seen. Exuberant. Social.

Out of his element.

Out of his gourd.

"Hear, hear!" That came from one-half of the same-sex couple. He gave Manny an appreciative look until his partner gave him an elbow in the ribs.

"Name's Manny. This is Tressa," Manny said. He still had my left hand and raised it to show off the ring.

"To Manny and Tressa!" a man in his late twenties or early thirties and who looked like the adorable Pillsbury Doughboy announced. "I'm Steve Kayser. This is my wife, Courtney," he added, putting an arm around a short, chubby, blonde woman. "That's Ben and Sherri Hall," he said, pointing to another larger-than-life pair of similar age. "The four of us are celebrating our anniversaries. We had a double wedding five years ago and decided, as a group, we needed to make a dramatic change in our lifestyles, starting with diet and exercise. This cruise offered us a chance to do that."

"Sherri and Ben have been our best friends since high school," Courtney Kayser explained. "We live in the same town on the same street! We figured this cruise was custom-made for us," she added with a giggle.

"Misery loves company, huh?" I said, and she giggled again. Cute, blonde and bubbly, Courtney had an energy and zest about her that her dark-haired friend, Sherri, didn't possess. Ben was friendly and slapped Steve on the back a lot, while Sherri was quiet and pensive. I guess opposites do attract.

Introductions were made all around. In addition to Steve, Courtney, Ben and Sherri, there was Vic and Naomi, who had just missed making *The Biggest Loser* last season and wanted to show the network they could lose the weight without its help; and Tariq and Monique, actors tired of just getting the fat roles. There was also Dolph and Major, who were on a voyage of self-discovery and identity following a civil union ceremony.

I shook my head. None of these couples seemed like candidates for a murder-for-profit conspiracy. Still, I'd learned not to take anything at face value.

"You look like a personal trainer, Manny," Major, the fellow who'd eyed Manny earlier, observed. "Am I right?"

Manny smiled. "Bodies by DeMarco," he said. "Maybe you've heard of it. I've been on *Oprah*."

I looked over at Manny. God, he was good. Or maybe he had lots of practice at fibbing on the fly. I still hadn't managed to figure out just what he did for a living. I'd convinced myself I was better off not knowing.

"Bodies by DeMarco! Oh, wow! Sure. I've heard of you. Awesome!" Major exclaimed. "Right, Dolph? Will you be one of the trainers working with us this week, Manny?" he asked, his eyes growing large at the possibility.

I did an exaggerated I'm-not-believing-this-B.S. eye roll. Manny smiled. "You never know," he said.

"So, what do *you* do?"

I stood mute until I realized Courtney was speaking to me. "Oh? Me? I, uh, sell insurance," I blurted. "Life insurance."

The group as a whole gasped and took one step back. Geez. A profession more hated than prying, snoopy reporters. Who knew?

"Yes, yes, I sell life insurance. I don't suppose any of you might be in the market for a great policy," I said, and witnessed another collective step back. "Oh, I know. I bet you all think you don't need life insurance and that you're going to live forever, but one never knows what could happen from one moment to the next. Especially on a cruise ship. You know, out on the high seas. Far from home. Unfamiliar surroundings. Changing jurisdictions. Anything could happen. You've seen the tabloid stories. Disappearing spouses.

Wheelchairs overboard. Stingrays jumping into boats. A person must always be on their guard. Remain alert and vigilant and at all times be aware of your surroundings."

I stopped to get my breath before continuing: "So? Anyone here have a good, hefty life insurance policy with reasonable premiums they'd like to brag about, because I guarantee I can beat your agent's price and benefits. Come on. Anybody? Anyone at all? I'm here to tell each of you that what I know could be a real lifesaver." I gave each couple a long, considering look. An awkward pause followed my sales pitch improv.

So much for subtlety.

"Easy, sweetheart, easy," Manny squeezed my hand. "All work and no play makes Barbie . . . scary," he said.

The group laughed and seemed to relax.

"Haa haa." I joined in the laughter, draining my glass of bogus bubbly, feeling like the Midwestern version of Bridget Jones. I looked up and caught Joe's speculative eyes on me from across the room.

Ohmigawd! Rick!

I slapped my drink in Manny's hand. "Sorry! Call of nature!" I said. "Back in a flush!"

I shook my head. I'd jumped from Bridget Jones to Mrs. Doubtfire in less time than it took my gammy to scurry out of sight when the minister came to call.

I hurried out of the Stardust, checking my watch as I jogged towards the Pirate's Cove. Eight-fifteen. Fashionably late. Still, early for me.

I discovered Townsend at a booth several tables back. "I am so sorry!" I said, sliding into the booth across from him. "It took longer to pull myself together than I anticipated," I explained. "The hair, you know."

His gaze slid over the top of my head, down to my *Pretty in Pink* T-shirt, and back up to my face, settling on my eyes. His own were bright and feverish, I thought. His expression was appreciative.

"You're well worth the wait," he said, his scrutiny intense.

"Thank you, kind sir," I replied, feeling an intense attack of nervous stomach. Nervous, empty stomach.

"Would you care for something to drink?" he asked.

I thought about the kaka champagne and was ready to pass when I saw his foamy drink. My mouth flew open.

"Is that what I think it is?" I asked.

"It depends on what you think it is," Townsend responded.

"Is that . . . beer?"

Rick nodded.

"Real beer?" I said.

Rick nodded again. "Well, light beer," he clarified.

I grabbed his glass and put it to my lips and started to drink. After three long swallows, I stopped and belched and wiped the foam from my mouth. "I'm surprised they allowed beer on a No Carnivores Allowed Custom Cruise," I said, belching again.

"Well, technically they don't," he said. "But I have contacts, remember?"

The pleasure of the brewski was dimmed by the discovery of the patroness. "Brianna," I said.

"Actually, I just happened to mention I could kill for a beer and, voila! Beer!"

Voila! Since when did Townsend speak French?

"I don't suppose you happened to mention it to that cute brunette serving wench with the rather large, er, treasure chest over there?" I said.

He smiled. "I prefer a sleeker schooner myself," he said, reaching out to take my hands.

I suddenly remembered Manny's ring gracing my left ring finger. I snatched my hands out of Rick's grasp, placing them in my lap. Townsend stared at me.

"Anything . . . wrong?" he asked.

"Wrong?" I said, desperately trying to pull the ring off my finger. "What could be wrong?" I was cursing the genetics that had given me fat knuckles.

"You just seem . . . rattled," he said.

"No. I'm fine. Really!" I said, yanking on the ring so hard I thought I was going to pull the digit out of its socket. "It's all—gooood."

"I brought you something," Townsend said, picking up a perfect, long-stemmed red rose and handing it to me.

I felt my heart begin to thump in my chest. "It's beautiful," I said, reaching out with my right hand to take the rose. "Just beautiful."

"Then you and the rose have something else in common—besides the occasional thorn, that is," he said with a wink. He caressed my hand with his thumb, his right hand poised to take my left one. I hesitated. "Your other hand, Tressa," Townsend urged.

Holy harpoon. What in Calypso's name was I going to do now?

I jumped to my feet.

"Call of nature!" I announced. "Back in a flush!" I jogged toward the exit, tugging on the friggin' ring. After this I would never, ever be able to watch *Mrs. Doubtfire* again.

I hoofed it back toward the Stardust, tired and winded. I met Joe on the way.

"Oh, there you are, girlie. Your fiancé was wondering what was taking you so long in the john. He was about to come looking for you. What's the deal? Not enough fiber in your diet?" he asked, turning the tables on me.

I took hold of his elbow and pulled him behind a fountain with potted shrubs.

"Okay, Blackbeard, what the devil are you up to?" I snapped. "Why on earth did you invite Manny and Mo on this little customized cruise from the bowels of hell?" I asked. "What are you trying to do? Screw me over?"

Joe freed his arm from my grasp. "How about to get you to fish or cut bait, girlie?" he said.

"What are you talking about?" I demanded.

"You, missy. I'm talking about you," Joe hissed. "You've

been pussy-footing around your feelings for my grandson for over a year now. Frankly, it's brutal to witness. It's time you decided once and for all how you really feel about Rick."

I stared at him. "And you thought bringing Manny DeMarco and his marriage-minded Aunt Mo along for the ride would help me decide? Are you senile? How is that supposed to help me?"

"By forcing you to choose," Joe said. "Once and for all. Don't think I haven't seen the way Manny looks at you."

"Wh-what do you mean?" I asked, terrified by what he was implying.

"There's something there," Joe said. "You know it. I know it. He knows it."

"But we're just . . ." I was about to say *friends* but stopped because I knew that wasn't true. Manny and I had never been what you'd call friends. In fact, I was hard-pressed to put into words just what we were to each other. For the first time it occurred to me to wonder why I hadn't tried to do so before now.

"Rick's my grandson," Joe went on. "You're Hannah's granddaughter. We want you both to be happy. But if you think my grandson is going to wait around forever for you to make up your mind . . ." He stopped and shook his head.

I felt bad then that I'd called him senile. He was just Joe. Tedious. Unpredictable. Eccentric. Obstinate. Joltin' Joe.

He laid a wrinkled hand on my shoulder. "I've been around a long time. Seen a lot. Believe me when I say it's for your own good. And Rick's."

I felt my eyes sting and mist up. "Cruel to be kind, huh, Joe?" I said.

"If you want to look at it that way, be my guest."

I shook my head. "I am your guest, remember?" I told him. "And look where it got me. On a week-long cruise with no breakfast buffet, no red meat, no booze and zilch chocolate, and just seven days to make the most important decision of my life. Not to mention attempting to prevent a murder no one but me believes is about to happen. Thanks, Joe. Thanks for the freakin' vegetable deluxe Custom Cruise package. I don't know how I'll ever be able to thank you."

He stared at me. "No meat? No dessert? What do you mean, no dessert? And what's this about murder?"

I left Joe and his queries in the shrubbery and hurried back to Manny.

"Took Tressa long enough. Bodies by Manny missed you. Everything come out okay?" he asked with a grin, his dark eyes roaming over me.

"I'm cool," I said, feeling anything but.

"Oh, what a lovely rose!" Courtney remarked. "Where did you get it? Are they giving them out somewhere? Oh, I suppose Manny gave you that. That's so romantic. Steve! Where's *my* rose?"

I looked down at the flower in my hand. Manny took my wrist and brought the crimson petals to his nostrils. He smelled the rose and then turned my arm slightly and kissed the soft inside of my wrist. "Very nice," he said.

I almost wet my hot pink hipsters.

"Fancy meeting you here," I heard, and turned to find Coral LaFavre and her husband with the three names had joined us. "Oh, that's right! You're engaged!" Coral grabbed my hand. "How divine," she said. "And this delicious fellow must be your fiancé," she said, her chocolate eyes giving Manny their full attention.

She held out her hand. "Coral LaFavre," she introduced herself. "My husband, David." Coral didn't bother to look at her husband, merely inclined her head in his direction. I couldn't blame her. Compared to Manny, David looked like an anemic albino.

"Manny DeMarco," Manny said, shaking Coral's hand and giving her the benefit of his commercial-grade smile. "Nice to meet you, Coral."

"I can see why you kept Manny here a secret, Tressa dear," Coral said. "Smart girl."

I managed a weak smile. If only she knew.

"Manny's a personal trainer," Courtney cut in. "I imagine you've heard of him. Bodies by DeMarco."

I cringed. This was more brutal than a stint on *The Flying Dutchman* captained by Davy Jones.

"I suppose you trainers will have us up at the crack of dawn exercising," Coral said, sticking her full lower lip out in a pout. "You'll probably have to come drag me out of bed. Will that be a problem, you think?" she asked with a wicked twinkle in her eye.

"Maybe your new husband could give you a good, swift kick—to help you out of bed," I suggested, unsure why I cared whether Coral got a personal wake-up call from Manny. Except that she thought he was my fiancé and was still putting the moves on him.

Coral's eyebrows rose and she smiled.

"This is my husband, Steve Kayser, and our best friends, Ben and Sherri Hall," Courtney told Coral. "We're doing the 'New You' Cruise together. I just have to tell you I love all your work, Miss LaFavre," she went on. "I want you to know I wrote in and told the network you should replace Star Jones on *The View* when she left. You'd be so perfect!"

"Why, thank you," she said, her lips twitching.

"You two better beware of Tressa here," Ben spoke up. "She's trolling for business."

"Oh?" David said. "What kind of business?"

"Insurance business," Courtney supplied. "Tressa here's been a herald of ill fortune with her chilling warnings of misfortune at sea," she explained. My earlier infomercial had gone way bad.

"Insurance?" Coral gave me a puzzled look. "I thought you were a newspaper reporter," she said.

I frowned. "Who told you that?" I asked, wondering if Security Sam had spoken with her after all.

"Your Aunt Mo," she said. "At the safety drill after you left she mentioned you were a reporter of some notoriety back home but that she hoped you'd settle down, have babies, and quit finding dead bodies once you and her nephew were married."

I winced. Good old one-track-mind Mo.

"Dead bodies?" Sherri finally spoke.

"I thought you said you sold insurance," Ben said.

"I did. I do," I added, looking for a way through the tangled strands of lies before I got stuck in my own outlandish web. "The insurance is a sideline. You know. A second job. You see, I own a stable of horses back home and it costs a pretty penny to keep them in grain and grass." I figured it would play better to take a kernel of truth and expand on that rather than going the pure balderdash route. "I hold down several jobs at various times of the year. Besides the newspaper job, I work at my uncle's Dairee Freeze, too. And I do seasonal work in retail, as well. It keeps me busy and keeps my little herd in hay."

"What was that about dead bodies?" Sherri asked again.

"In the course of my investigative reporting duties I might have stumbled across one or two—"

"Or four or five," Manny interjected.

"—deceased individuals in the last several years—"

"Year," Manny corrected.

"—but at least a couple of those unfortunate folks were killed before I officially got back into investigative journalism," I finished.

"Killed?" Sherri said. "As in—"

"Murder," Manny supplied. "Tressa's got a gift—for solving mysteries," he added with a wink. "She always gets her man."

"Obviously," Coral said, with another appreciative look at Manny. "How on earth did you make the leap from journalism to insurance broker?" she asked.

Via a very fertile imagination, of course.

"Well, you see," I said, thinking I was weaving so many lies I needed Spidey's cool wrist web shooters to do the job efficiently, "finding those unfortunate victims of crime like I did got me to thinking about how hard their demises would be on their families and loved ones, and I thought about how hard it would be emotionally and financially for them, which got me wondering how many of those who died unexpectedly had bothered to think about protecting their families from that very same sudden-death scenario, and that's how I got into the insurance game. If I do well this quarter, I get to begin handling annuities next annum," I added, thinking E. F. Hutton would roll over in his grave if I so much as touched anyone's annuity. Whatever that was.

"Tressa has lots of contacts in law enforcement, which can't hurt in the insurance biz either," Manny added. I looked at him, thinking that if this was his way of helping me, he was going overboard—and sending a very clear message that I was a force to be reckoned with.

Alas. More fiction.

"Oh dear, look at the time. It's been illuminating, but I have an appointment with a masseur at nine. A nice massage always relaxes me before bedtime," Coral explained. "Good night all!"

"About that life insurance?" I asked.

"I'll let you know if I'm interested," Coral responded. "Good night again."

"Good night as well," David added, giving me a quizzical look before following in his wife's wake.

I shook my head. Coral seemed different from earlier that day. I knew some women changed their personas when they were around good-looking men, so maybe that was it. Frankly, I'd never understood why women did that. You could only pretend to be someone you weren't for so long. Eventually you'd want to find someone who liked you for you. Wouldn't you?

I twirled the rose. Townsend!

"Damn!"

"Problem?" Manny asked.

"My bag! I left my bag in the restroom!" I announced. "Be right back!"

I excused myself and jogged back to the Cove. The booth was empty but there were two bottles of beer and two clean glasses sitting on the table. I filled a glass with beer and looked around for a second before I dunked my left hand in the cold liquid. Dunk. Dunk. Dunk. I pulled my freezing fingers out and twisted the ring. Progress. Dunk, dunk, dunk. Twist. Twist. Pull. Dunk. Dunk. Twist. Twist. Pull!

I yanked.

The ring came flying off. It sailed across the room and landed behind the bar.

"Son of a—!"

I chased after the ring, diving behind the bar and crawling around on my hands and knees as I searched.

"Sorry. Lost ring." I said to the young fellow tending bar. I stretched out a hand on the floor beneath the counter to locate the expensive stone. I snagged the ring and was just about to put my fingers around it when I heard a familiar voice above me.

"Mo's my name, and I'm looking for a blonde with hair out to here and, if Mo's not mistaken, she's wearing blue jeans and some kind of T-shirt with a horse or a cowboy hat or a pair of cowboy boots on it. You seen her in here?"

I saw the bartender glance down at me. I shook my head, and put my hands together as if in prayerful pleading.

"No!" I mouthed.

"Uh, why are you looking for this woman, ma'am?" the cruise line employee asked. "Has she caused some problem?" he asked.

"If you count dragging her feet about setting a wedding date worse than a pirate being forced to walk the plank, then yeah, she's causing a problem," I heard Mo respond.

"I . . . see," the bartender said. "Is she your daughter then?" he asked.

"Daughter? No. She's gonna be my niece. By marriage. If she ever gets down to brass tacks and decides to set the date. I'm beginning to think she's procrastinatin' on purpose," Mo said. "And that ain't gonna fly. You see, I got me a ticker that ain't clickin' on all the cylinders and I ain't got time to waste waitin' around for little Miss Marple to be ready to settle down. That's one reason I came on this ship. Come hell or high water, by the end of this cruise, Tressa Jayne Turner will be ready to tie that knot. Or Mo here will know the reason why."

All of a sudden my food-deprived stomach rebelled at the unaccustomed empty-cavern quality and let out a long, loud, zesty Tony the Tiger growl.

"That your stomach, boy? You need Pepto!" I heard Mo say.

"Yes, ma'am. Thank you, ma'am."

I waited a few minutes before I got off the floor.

"Thanks," I said, brushing off my Capri pants and shirt. "I owe you. Toby, is it?" I asked, reading his I.D. badge.

"That's right. So you owe me? We can take care of that quite easily," he said. "Your key card?" he queried, and I grabbed it from my back pocket and handed it to him.

"Now just how appreciative are you, Miss Turner?" he asked. "Twenty bucks' worth?"

I frowned. Blackmailing buccaneer. I hoped Joe was feeling generous.

"There you are! I thought you'd fallen overboard. You forgot your bag." My Javelina bag materialized on the bar in front of me, courtesy of Rick Townsend. "Imagine how thrilled I was to carry that into the men's restroom with me," he said, and dropped onto a barstool. "Ready for that moonlight stroll?" he asked.

"Hell, yes!" I announced, and Townsend gave me a strange look.

I remembered the ring in my hand, which reminded me of Manny next door, which reminded me of the merry-makers plus one possible murder-maker.

"I just need to let my grandma know where I'm going," I said.

"I'll go with you," Townsend offered.

"I won't be a minute."

"That's what you said the last time."

"You just wait here and get my key card back from Tobias there when he's done plundering," I said, giving Toby a dark look. "And don't go anywhere!"

I hurried away, determined to slap the ring into Manny's hand, instruct him to have the breakup talk with Aunt Mo immediately if not sooner and then haul my never-was-a-Girl-Scout-but-love-those-cookies attitude back to Ranger Rick Townsend and remain glued to his side until I knew exactly how I felt about him. And how he felt about me. If it took the entire bloody cruise to get there.

I faltered in mid-jog as I re-entered the Stardust.

Over in a dark corner, away from the others in the room, a lone couple appeared deep in conversation. The woman was talking, the man nodding, listening intently. Just like two old friends. My fingers tightened on the ring in my hand, the gem cutting into the flesh of my palm.

Manny DeMarco and Buttinskee Brianna.

Two bodies to die for.

I always knew fitness could be murder.

I strode over to Manny and, ignoring Brianna's gasp, grabbed one of Manny's muscular arms and slapped the ring into his palm.

"I wanna break up," I snapped. "So, deal with it!" I turned on my heel and marched off. I'd gone about ten feet when Manny caught up to me.

He took my arm.

"Barbie's breaking up, huh?" he said, and I nodded.

"Break it to Aunt Mo carefully, would you?" I asked.

Manny looked down at me for several long moments. "Guess there's only one thing for Manny to do then," he said.

"That's right," I agreed, with a challenging lift of one brow.

"So be it," Manny said, and reached out and crushed me to his broad, manly chest, bending me over backwards in a clinch worthy of Rhett and Scarlett. His lips hovered a mere fraction of an inch from my own, his dark, searching gaze locked on my own startled peepers. Then he said, "Bon voyage, Barbie," and put his lips to mine in a deep, hot, wet, probing kiss that stole my breath and muddled my senses. What senses I had.

When the kiss ended, I was limp and weak and clung to Manny to keep from falling. I heard a gasp. Out of the corner of my eye, I detected movement. My eyes came to rest on a hairy little pig-like creature on a grungy green backpack. I had to force myself to look up and meet the stunned look of the man holding the book bag.

I watched the emotions play across his face like a slide show. Shock. Uncertainty. Jealousy. Pain. Anger. Each one was like an arrow to my heart. I clumsily disentangled myself from Manny's embrace.

"I can explain!" I said, falling back on a familiar old Tressa Jayne Turner tune.

"Not necessary," Townsend responded. He put the book bag in my hands. "Your peccary pack," he snapped, "and cabin card." He handed that to Manny. "You'll need it more than I will," he added.

Then he left me standing there, a Javelina in my hands and a pain in my heart so intense it took my breath away.

I watched Brianna the Beauty run after Rick as he left the Stardust. I caught Joe Townsend's somber look.

"Satisfied?" I hissed at him. "Maybe next time you'll quit playing mind games, butt out and leave the chess moves to a master," I added, ripping my card out of Manny's hand. "Bon voyage, assholes," I spat, taking my leave.

I made my way to my cabin, bone-weary, tired and listless as I'd never been before: all the fight drained out of me. I felt the tears start to fall but could mount no countermeasure, could muster no resistance to staunch them. I was utterly defenseless.

They'd sunk my battleship.

CHAPTER SEVEN

This was the time I'd normally drown my sorrows in a bag of Doritos, a half-pound bag of M&M's, and a six-pack of beer. Absent that, I washed my face, brushed my teeth and crawled between the sheets of my teeny, tiny bed. Taylor was still out—no doubt enjoying the nightlife on the ship with the trainer crowd.

I pondered how this night might have been so very different. I shivered, recalling how Townsend had kissed my neck and held me against him earlier. I shut my eyes tight when I thought of Manny's sudden, shocking, searching kiss.

In hindsight I should have run after Townsend, relegated Brianna to the brig and sat on Ranger Rick until he gave me an opportunity to explain. I frowned. But what if the explanations hadn't worked? I wasn't exactly known for my oratorical skills.

Maybe then I would have let my lips do the talking—in a nonverbal kind of way, you understand. I felt my cheeks grow warm. Somehow I couldn't see myself as a femme fatale. I remembered how my semi-trampy Marilyn Monroe approach had tanked in the past and on more than one occasion. Marilyn Manson was probably a more effective vamp than I was. Rick Townsend probably would have laughed himself silly at my feeble attempt at seduction.

Also, there was that minor little thing called courage to

consider. I brought the sheet up over my head. Yo ho, me hearties. Yo ho! It's a coward's life for me.

I awoke to a loud burst of the ship's horn and promptly fell out of bed.

"Oh my God! We're foundering!" I yelled. Damn. I knew I should have paid attention at the safety drill. I jumped up and ran to retrieve my life vest.

"We're not sinking, Tressa. It's our wake-up call. Didn't you read your daily bulletin?"

I looked over to find Taylor up and dressed in a white T-shirt and lightweight, mid-calves workout pants.

"Wake-up call? Whoever heard of a wake-up call for people taking a cruise?" I asked.

"Ah, but this is not an ordinary cruise, is it?" Taylor said, and I saw the gleam in her eye. "It's a kick-start cruise. A lifestyle makeover."

"You're loving this, aren't you?" I growled. "Admit it."

She shrugged. "Let's just say it will make for an interesting study of human behavior."

"You were late getting in last night," I observed, and noticed the sudden flush in her cheeks. "Did you meet someone?" I asked.

Taylor shrugged again.

"I met a lot of people. I hung out with some of the personal trainers and passengers. I was surprised you weren't with . . ." She stopped. "I was surprised to see you in bed when I came in."

So she'd seen Townsend. I wondered if he'd been boating with Brianna. I made a face. That sounded like some lame syndicated show title.

"I had a headache," I said. "Brought on from lack of food."

"Rick didn't look like a happy cruiser," Taylor remarked.

I didn't meet her eyes. "It was probably the soy burger from supper."

"He found out about Manny DeMarco, didn't he?" Taylor asked.

I nodded, gathering my clothes from the drawer. "At the Stardust last night."

"I'm sure Rick was furious, but he can hardly blame you for Manny being on this cruise. And it wasn't as if he caught you in flagrante delicto or anything."

I was silent.

"He didn't. Did he?"

"That depends," I said.

"On what?" Taylor asked.

"If having someone stick their tongue down your throat qualifies as flagrante delicto."

Without looking up, I could imagine Taylor's stunned expression. Slack jaw. Open mouth. Bulging eyeballs.

"Are you saying Rick caught you kissing Manny De-Marco?" she asked.

"No!" I shouted. "No! I'm saying Rick caught Manny DeMarco kissing me!" I slammed the drawer shut, cursed when my panties got caught in the drawer and yanked the light blue undies free.

"How did that happen?" Taylor asked. "I thought your relationship with Manny DeMarco was all for show and all for Mo." I had to marvel at her ability to rhyme on the fly. "What in God's name was he doing with his tongue in your mouth?"

"Wishing me bon voyage?" I said, with a weak smile.

"Why didn't you push him away? Slap his face? Knee him in the groin?" Taylor asked.

I bit my lip. I'd asked myself those same questions. Well, all except for the groin one. No way was I going to try to unman Manny DeMarco with a well-placed thrust between the legs. Nuh-uh. No way, Skipper.

"I was at a bit of a disadvantage," I explained. "And it happened so quickly I didn't have time to react."

Taylor was quiet for a moment. "So, you didn't react?" she said. "One way or the other?"

"What do you mean?"

"Come on, Tressa. A great-looking, sexy, ripped male kisses you and you don't react at all? Give me a break. I'm not as gullible as that. Neither is Rick. And what kind of message are you sending to Manny when you let him kiss you like that?" she added.

"Let him? Let him! If you knew Manny DeMarco, you'd know that he isn't the kind to ask 'Mother, may I' before he does anything. And besides, it didn't mean anything. It was just playacting," I insisted.

Taylor gave me a long look. "For whose benefit?" she asked. "Tell me. Did he see Rick before or after he kissed you?"

I chewed my lip. Damn. That was a good question. And clearly one I should have asked myself but hadn't. Frankly, the possibility hadn't even occurred to me that Manny had seen Rick and then kissed me. But now that Taylor had suggested it . . .

Manny DeMarco had some 'splaining to do.

"What time is it, anyway?" I thought to ask.

"Six or so," Taylor said.

"Six? AM? What is the deal here? I'm on vacation! I want to sleep in!" I whined.

"Fine. Cower in this cabin for a week. Thumb your nose at this incredible opportunity to adopt a healthy lifestyle. Don't try to come to terms with your feelings for two very different men. Keep doing what you've been doing. It's working so well for you!" Taylor snapped.

"Maybe you should take some of your own advice, baby sister," I said. "For someone who dropped out of college after two and a half years and who is now employed at her uncle's ice cream brazier, that seems awfully judgmental, don't you think? And more than slightly one-sided. I'm thinking along the lines of removing your own log before you concern yourself with your brother's—or in this case sister's—splinter," I growled, fed up with Taylor's sanctimonious posturing. I'd put up with it for years. Before I'd always let it run off me like so much water off a quacker's back. But now? Now it was starting to tick me off. Royally.

"That's not fair, Tressa," Taylor responded. "One time! One time I'm undecided, one time I'm unsure, one time I'm unclear on what I really want to do with my life and what happens? I get this crap from you. You, who've had so many missteps and do-overs you could fill an Excel spreadsheet documenting them all."

I stared at her. I'd noticed a change in her in Arizona: an uncharacteristic bitchiness in her manner I'd never seen before. Initially I'd applauded it. Now I wasn't so sure this newfound "I am Taylor, hear me roar" approach suited her. At least, not when it was directed at me.

"Well, excuse me for being an imperfect human," I said, discouraged by the fact that it seemed we were always at loggerheads. "The difference between you and me, Taylor, is that I acknowledge my many shortcomings. How could I not when you and others are always ready, willing and eager to point them out?" I added.

Taylor looked at me. "But do you ever try to change? Improve?" she asked. She walked over and put a hand on my arm. "Regardless of what you think, Tressa, I care about you. And I want you to be safe and happy. I want you to turn this cruise into an affirmation rather than a conflagration. Turn a negative into a positive. Challenge yourself to change and grow. Live and learn. Face your feelings head-on and accept the consequences. Use this cruise as your own personal epiphany. A voyage of self-discovery."

I blinked. Her speech would have Oprah tearing up and reaching for her hanky. Who the heck did she think she was—Maya Angelou?

And then she really crossed the line. She said it: Three itty-bitty words that to me evoked much the same reaction as a red flag to a majorly pissed-off bull.

"I dare you."

I blinked. "What did you say?"

Taylor tossed me the ship's daily bulletin. "I dare you," she repeated. "I dare you to make a commitment to positive growth." She lifted her chin. "I dare you."

I considered the challenge. One week. One week without junk food, chocolate and real beer with real foam. One week of exercising, yoga, nutrition and motivational pep talks. One week of stock-taking, soul-searching and—insert stomach roiling here—getting in touch with my feelings.

"Bring it on," I finally said, sticking my hand out to shake. "By the end of this cruise, you'll have a whole new appreciation for your big sister," I promised. "You count on it."

A Tressa Turner Custom Cruise Lifestyle Makeover.

Taylor gave me an uneasy look. I suspected she wondered what she'd gotten herself into. I was more concerned with what I'd gotten myself into.

What was that saying again? Something about pride coming before a fall.

Stupid, stupid pride.

I showered and dressed in black stretchy shorts and a white T-shirt. You know, clothes you can sweat in and get away with it. I pulled my hair back in a lopsided ponytail. By the time I was through in the bathroom, Taylor had left. I stuck a black and white visor on my head and picked up the daily bulletin.

" 'Muster: 0600 hours,' " I read. " 'Weigh-in for Jumpstart participants. Body-fat index calculations. Diet and nutrition guidelines issued. Team assignments. Workshop sign-up. Breakfast: 0800 hours.' " Body-fat index? Good Lord. This was worse than I thought. A veritable smorgasbord of pain, deprivation and masochism. And all in the name of a new and improved you.

I looked in the mirror. Was I imagining it, or did my cheeks already look slightly concave? And were those dark smudges under my eyes? And talk about pale. I looked like an ad for the medieval medical practice of leeching. Or my sister, Taylor, on the plane ride. Or shuttle ride. Or merry-go-round.

I shook my head at my emaciated reflection. Who was the biggest loser on this cruise? No contest. Tressa Jayne Turner. Hands down.

I grabbed my bag, deciding if it killed me I was going to prove once and for all that Tressa Turner was possessed of willpower in sufficient quantity to last a week at sea on the S.S. *Richard Simmons*. As I left the cabin, I found myself relieved that I didn't have to play duck-and-run with Aunt Mo any longer. The secret was out. The breakup was a matter of record. I was footloose and fiancé-free! And I was starving!

I decided to take the stairs rather than the elevator. After all, I'd just pledged to focus on fitness. Well, for a week at least. I took the stairway to the upper decks, deciding that no matter how imitation it might be, I planned to have food on my plate that at least looked like bacon, sausage, and eggs. I'd just deal with any gag reflex that resulted.

I was about to climb another set of stairs when I heard someone on the staircase above me. I moved to the right to permit them to pass but no one descended.

"Tressa." My whispered name stopped me in mid-step.

"Yes?" I called up. "Hello! Who's there?"

No response other than Darth Vader-like heavy breathing.

"Hello?" I started to climb the stairs.

"Tressa!"

I stopped again at the hissed whisper. "Uh, is that you, Ranger Rick? If so, this is so not funny!" I said.

I took another step, starting to get a bit creeped out. Wait a minute. What was I thinking? It was daylight. I was on a cruise ship with upbeat people who were out to improve the landscape of their lives. So why was I lingering on these steps like some scared little girl?

I was just about to take the next step when an object

floated down the open stairway and landed a few steps up. It was a fifty-dollar bill. Like any financially challenged pinch-penny, I bent over to pick it up when something flew down the stairs at me. I caught a flash of white before I was shoved violently backwards. I frantically reached out to grip something—anything—but captured only air. The resulting backflip I performed would have brought gold in the Olympics. Unfortunately, my dismount left a helluva lot to be desired. My head smacked the wall with the force of a cannonball. My last thought before I lost consciousness?

This was no friggin' Good Ship *Lollipop*.

"Miss Turner? Miss Turner? Can you hear me?"

Blinding light dueled with blinding pain for the upper hand as I opened one eye, only to shut it again when the effort proved too taxing.

"Miss Turner? Are you okay? Your dad will be here straightaway. Miss Turner?"

I finally opened my eyes. I found the concerned gaze of what appeared to be a health care professional looking down on me.

"My dad?" My eyes filled with tears, and it had less to do with the killer headache I had and more to do with the daddy-daughter thing—that über-special connection. You daughters out there get it, right?

My dad is one of those people who would, if given the option, rather not be seen or heard. Sometimes I sit and stare at him and wonder how Hellion Hannah Turner could have birthed someone whose idea of a perfect evening is puttering with implements of husbandry (i.e. farm machinery), reading the newspaper and flipping from sports event to sports event on cable in front of his big-screen TV. A gentleman farmer (think *Green Acres* here), my dad has worked for the local telephone company for well over two decades.

My mom, a bookkeeper and tax accountant, is pragmatic

and sensible, but has a softer side. A movie buff and voracious reader, my mother is also a bit of a political junkie. I think she'd love it if they had punch cards for elections so she could check to see if her family members had dutifully voted. I'd be all in favor of it, too. If say, you got a free pizza pie for every three elections voted in, that is. Including the local ones, of course.

"Who are you?" I asked.

"I'm Doctor Baker, *The Epiphany*'s medical officer. I took the liberty of going through your bag and found your identification and was able to track down your father. He's on his way. How are you feeling? Are you up to telling me what happened?" he asked. The sound of a door closing gained his attention. "Oh, I bet that's your father now," he said, and left me long enough to steer my father into the room. The concern on my dad's face brought new tears to my eyes.

"How are you feeling, kiddo?" he asked. "The doctor said you took a tumble down the stairs."

"He did?" I asked, sniffling. My dad handed me his handkerchief and I dabbed at my eyes. "I did?"

"I was just getting ready to ask if she felt well enough to tell me what happened," Dr. Baker said.

I shut my eyes again, trying to think back. I winced. It hurt to think.

"Were you dizzy? Before you fell? Did you get a sense of vertigo or motion sickness before the fall?" he asked.

"I don't think so," I said.

"Did you trip?"

"No."

"Slip?"

"No."

"Well, then what happened?"

I opened my eyes. "I think maybe I was pushed," I admitted, as that startling revelation found its way into my addled brain. I watched as the doctor's pupils dilated. He gasped.

"Pushed? By who?" he asked.

I raised my shoulders in a tiny shrug. "I really don't know. I don't recall much," I said. "It's all fuzzy. And it happened so fast. I remember stairs. And whispering. Creepy whispering. And money. There was money. And the next thing I knew something slammed into me, knocking me off my feet and sending me down the stairs like an out-of-control human projectile. From there, everything faded to black."

"Why would anyone want to push you down a flight of stairs?" my father asked.

Another tiny shrug. "Beats me." I winced. Unfortunate choice of words and all that.

"I'm sure you're mistaken," the gaunt guy in white said, reaching out to take my wrist and check my pulse. "How's the head?"

I put a hand to the back of my noggin and frowned when I encountered a knot the size of a Cadbury crème egg. The big one, not the miniature.

"Still sore to be sure," Dr. Baker answered his own question without waiting for my response. "Are you nauseous now? Dizzy?" He took a thin silver penlight from his pocket and shined it in one eye and then the other. "I don't think we're dealing with a concussion here, but we can't be certain. You should remain here and take it easy for the day so we can keep an eye on you. Just in case."

Spend my vacation cruise in the sick bay with Bones Baker hovering over me? Yeah, right. When peccaries fly.

I sat up. "I'll be fine," I said. "The pain has already subsided some. It's gone from a bass drumbeat to a bongo in the last several minutes," I told the doctor. "So, I should be fine."

"I really wish you'd reconsider," Dr. Baker went on. "I could monitor you here, make sure you had supplemental nutritional opportunities that aren't available to the passengers at large," he said.

I tried in vain to read between the lines. "What kind of nutritional opportunities?" I asked, realizing how long it had been since I'd eaten, and just how gaunt and withered I must look to the good doctor.

"Pretty much whatever you like," Baker said. "One of the perks that comes with being the doctor in residence," he added.

"So, say I felt like bacon," I asked. "Would that be real bacon or synthetic?"

"The real thing," the doctor replied. "If you like."

"And if I had, say, a hankering for hashed brown potatoes and eggs sunny-side up? Would that be a pipedream?"

"Not at all."

"What about coffee—and don't hold the caffeine? What about that?"

"Not a problem."

A phone rang nearby.

"Excuse me. I need to get that. And Mr. Turner, if you could come with me and fill out some forms, that would be helpful."

My father nodded. "Be right back," he said, and followed the doctor into an adjacent room.

I pressed my fingertips to my goose egg again—stark and painful evidence of my freefall down the flight of stairs. And the wicked whisper before said tumble? I hadn't imagined that. I recalled at the time how it gave me the willies. And I hadn't imagined the violent shove, either. I lie there quietly, trying to figure out what the assault meant for me.

And, why *me*? Unfortunately, this was a recurring refrain where I was concerned.

I thought some more. The effort hurt less than it had before. The attack had been planned and targeted. That was clear. So who on board this vegetarian vessel had a beef with me?

Aunt Mo. But she wanted me married, not buried.

Townsend? He definitely wanted a piece of me, but that particular piece started with an "a" and rhymed with bass (as in a species of fish, not a musical reference).

Beyond that? Nobody. Nobody at all. Unless . . .

I slapped a hand to my mouth. My huge, gaping, ginormous cavern of a mouth.

The greedy groom! I'd forgotten all about him. The captain of deceit. The hateful herald of the old high seas honeymoon heave-ho.

Oh. My. Gawd! I'd done it! I'd thrown down my very own gauntlet. My impromptu insurance infomercial the other night at the Stardust, coupled with Manny's depiction of me as a youthful Jessica Fletcher cum Bob Woodward had struck a nerve with a cold, calculating cutthroat looking to improve his bottom line through marriage, then murder.

I'd rattled his chain.

Rocked his boat.

Taken the wind out of his slimy sails.

And, as a result, I'd placed a big, ol' target on my back.

The truly sobering rub to all this? I had no clue who aboard this calorie-counting cruise held the revolver and was fixing to take aim and pull said trigger.

I went through the previous night's activities in my addled pate. It had to be someone who'd been at the Stardust, someone in the group Manny and I had spoken to. Someone who had overheard my over-the-top, in-your-face performance of Blind Cowgirl's Bluff and taken it to heart. I ticked them off one by one.

There was Steve and Courtney, married five years, and their bosom buddies, Ben and Jerry. I mean, Ben and Sherri. Vic and Naomi, the *Biggest Loser* losers and the typecast actors, and Tariq and Monique. And then there was Dolph and Major, who were both life partners and lifestyle partners.

Other possibilities occurred to me, rolling through my addled mind like a frightening flipbook, leaving me vulnerable and exposed. Maybe the would-be killer had seen little Tressa with her ear to the crack in her cabin door. Maybe the girl at the front desk had blabbed about the quirky paranoid tourist and her crazy conspiracy theories. Maybe Security Chief Davenport had decided to put a bug in Coral LaFavre's ear after all, and that's how she really found out I was a reporter.

Maybe, maybe, maybe.

What did all this mean for me?

It meant there was no way of knowing just who had it in for this spunky sailor girl reporter who just happened to have a talent for trouble, and who had no clue beyond the fact that it involved a honeymooning couple and a life insurance policy.

So, how did I protect myself from an unknown enemy on a ship full of strangers? How did I protect a nameless victim-to-be from a faceless, faithless lover with murder on his mind? I considered the possibilities.

I could stay in the sick bay or locked in my cabin for the duration of the cruise, I supposed. But that would only draw more attention to me. More suspicion. And what if the murderer-to-be wanted to play hardball? What if he thought I'd told Taylor what I'd overheard? Or my folks? Or my grandma? Or Rick? Could they all be in danger because of my big ears and even bigger mouth?

I thought back on what Taylor had implied earlier, about how I was oblivious to those who inhabited my ordinary world. How I was insensitive to their feelings. Their needs. Taylor was wrong. I knew that now. Even the slim chance that I'd placed them in peril scared me witless. But what could I do? How could I begin to keep everyone safe?

The doctor returned, and behind him my father. "You look a bit more alert, Miss Turner," the doctor said. "Are you remembering more about your mishap now?" he asked. "You were somewhat fuzzy on details earlier."

I stared at him.

Remember?

A sudden image of Aunt Mo refusing to accept said broken engagement, stalking me up and down the decks of *The Epiphany* like the obsessed paparazzi shadowing Britney Spears appeared in my head, of Mo shoving that humongous ring on my finger, nagging me to set a date, harping on and on about Ranger Rick—it all played like a video loop on the tiny screen in my head.

Remember?

One matchmaking mama-bear type.

Remember.

A murderer who thought I knew too much. (Hah!)

Remember.

Time to sort out my feelings.

Remember.

It was sheer lunacy.

Total madness.

Extreme psychosis.

Remember!

It was pure genius!

"You seem confused, Miss Turner. Disoriented. Are you all right?"

I looked at the doctor and at my dad. I hated to deceive him in this way—hated to put my family through this worry needlessly. But what choice did I have? Sam Davenport would never believe a killer-to-be had attempted to shut me up (a killer who obviously didn't know me very well or they would have known this was futile) no more than he would believe my claims of spousal skullduggery. And that left me in a very scary and vulnerable place.

My dad came forward then. He sat on the edge of my bed and took my hand.

"Are you okay? Can you tell us about it? What happened?" he asked.

I looked at him, schooling my features to look blank,

confused. (I know what you're thinking. Not such a stretch for me. Right? Hey, cut me some slack. I'm lying to my pop's face, here. It's not a warm and fuzzy feeling.)

"I'm sorry?" I said, appearing what I hoped passed for tentative. Unsure. "Do I . . . know you?"

CHAPTER EIGHT

Okay, in hindsight I probably shouldn't have done it. To be honest, the bump to my head probably impaired my judgment more than I suspected at the time. But once the idea planted itself in my brain matter, I couldn't dislodge or disregard it. And before I knew better, I was acting on it.

Ding, ding! Tugboat Tressa, full speed ahead.

My father's face did one of those "Play it again, Sam" moves. You know, the ones where you can almost see the person replaying words in their head.

"What?" my father asked. "What do you mean, do I know you?" he said. "I'm your father!"

"You are?" I asked, blinking in rapid succession for good measure.

Dr. Baker rushed to my bedside, fumbling to get his penlight out of his pocket again. He pulled one of my eyelids back and shined the light into my pupil, blinding me and repeated the procedure in the other, his movements jerky, spastic and agitated, like those of a puppet whose puppet master had imbibed one too many fruity umbrella drinks.

"What are you saying, Miss Turner? You don't recognize your father?" He turned to my dad. "You are her father, right?"

"Only for the last twenty-four years or so," my dad snapped.

"And he doesn't look familiar to you, Miss Turner? Tressa?

Not at all?" the doctor asked, turning back to me and sticking a stethoscope to my chest.

"Maybe if I squint a little," I said.

"I've heard of this, but I never thought I'd actually see a case," Dr. Baker said, excitement tinged with concern in his voice.

"A case? A case of what?" my father asked.

"Amnesia," he replied. "Temporary amnesia."

"Amnesia?" I said, having second thoughts, thinking maybe I should rein in this farce before it was well and truly out of the gate and on its way to being a runaway.

"My daughter has amnesia?" my dad interrupted. "Amnesia?"

I winced. This was harder than I had expected, though why it should be was a mystery. I had never been able to fib to my father—well, not without serious attacks of conscience, that is.

"Temporary, I'm sure," Dr. Baker said. "Sometimes a hard blow to the head scrambles things around in there a bit, mixes things up, resulting in a short-term loss of memory. Contrary to what you've seen on daytime TV, it's relatively rare but it does happen."

"And you think it's happened to me?" I asked.

"It appears so," the doctor said.

My father frowned. "How long does something like this normally last?" he asked. "It does wear off. Right?"

The doctor nodded. "It varies from patient to patient."

And this patient? I was betting about six days ought to do it.

"What is the last thing you remember?" the doctor asked.

"Waking up here," I said.

"No. Before that. Do you remember coming aboard the ship?" he asked.

"Ship? What ship?" I responded.

"This ship. You're on the Custom Cruise ship, *The Epiphany*."

"I am?" I looked at my father. "Have I ever been on a cruise ship before?" I asked.

He shook his head.

"Sweet," I said.

"Don't you remember the wedding?" my father asked.

"I'm married?" I said.

"I'll have to do some consulting, conduct some research," the doctor was saying.

"Do you recommend we transport Tressa to a hospital for further testing?" my dad asked. "Have her seen by a specialist? A head doctor maybe?"

Nice.

"No!" I yelled, and received surprised stares in return. "Uh, I mean I'm fine, really. I want to stay here on the ship. I like it here. I do. And I'm sure the doctor is right and I'll start to remember in no time. Please, if you're my dad, if you love me, you won't make me leave this ship!" I'd read somewhere that severe agitation in suspected head trauma wasn't good, so I was hoping I could convince the two to hold off on the medical evacuation for now. "I just need time," I added. "That's all I need."

My dad patted my hand. "Okay, honey. Calm down. Take it easy. What do you think, doc?" my dad asked.

"Frankly, I think it's probably best if she stayed on board the ship—for a few days at least. I'll keep a close eye on her and if she appears to be getting worse, we'll have Coast Guard choppers transport her back to the States." As Baker said this, I sighed with relief. "In the meantime, young lady, you're going to follow my orders. No exertions. No stress. Just rest, relaxation and good nutritious meals."

"I think maybe I could eat something," I said, thinking if I didn't get some food in me soon I was going to keel over again for real.

"Good. That's a start," Doc Baker said with a relieved smile. "Now, what was it that you thought sounded good again?"

I was just about to place my order and perhaps add a side of strawberry pancakes to it when my mother, sister, brother, sister-in-law, grandmother and Joe Townsend rushed in and stood staring at me from the foot of my bed. I felt like I was in a scene from *While You Were Sleeping*.

"Tressa Jayne! My God! Are you all right?" my mother exclaimed. "Your father left a note that you'd fallen down a flight of stairs! How on earth did you manage to accomplish that?"

I felt a hand on mine. My dad's hand.

"Tressa's not herself, Jean," he said.

"What do you mean she's not herself?" my grandma piped up. "Who is she?"

"There has been an unexpected side effect from her tumble down the stairs," the doctor broke in. "Now I expect Tressa here will be just fine, but the fact is she hit her head hard enough to lose consciousness, and that resulted in quite a large lump. In doing so, some thought processes have been scrambled about here and there and she's having some difficulty putting things back together again."

I frowned. He made me sound like Humpty Freakin' Dumpty.

"What do you mean, difficulty?" my mother asked, her eyes narrowing.

"She's got amnesia," my father announced.

"She's got ham and what?" my grandma asked. "Where'd she get the ham? I haven't seen a decent hunk of meat since we came on board. If you don't count them fitness gurus struttin' their stuff all over the boat," she added.

"Ship," I corrected, before I could stop myself.

"Can this be true?" my mother asked. "Tressa, is this true? You don't remember any of us? You've lost your memory?"

"I'm sorry—Jean, was it?" I asked. "That's what the doctor seems to think," I hedged. My mother was the sharpest knife in our little cutlery collection. If I could fool her, I could fool anyone.

"Shouldn't we do something?" my mother asked. "Take her somewhere? Have her head examined?"

Et tu, mother dear? *Et tu?*

"You heard the doctor, Jean," my father said. "She'll be fine. In fact, she already looks much better than she did just a few minutes ago. We'll keep an eye on her and so will the doctor here. If there's cause for concern, we'll have her off the ship and to a hospital immediately. Isn't that right, doc?"

"Absolutely," he agreed.

My grandma shoved her way to my bedside. "It's like what happened on one of my stories," she said, giving me an eagle eye. "Lily fell over this cliff and when she was rescued she thought she was still married to her ex-husband, Heath, 'cause she had no memory of her present husband, Jack. She was pregnant—it was a miracle she didn't lose the baby—and everyone thought the baby belonged to Heath . . . and Heath did, too, only Lily had slept with Jack when she thought Heath was cheating on her and she got pregnant but of course she didn't remember that and Jack didn't know anything about it—"

I put a hand to my head. It was beginning to ache again.

"Hannah, please, can't you see you're making Tressa worse?" Jean—I mean, my mother—said. Gee. Am I good or what? I think that's what you call method acting. "She obviously needs to rest."

Gram shook her head. "Leave it to Tressa," she said to the doctor. "She's known for her adventures, you see. The tales I could tell. Like the one about the shyster's stiff she found in the trunk. And the dead guy at the marina. And there was that pyro at the state fair that tried to turn her into a crispy critter."

The doctor looked at me, his expression suddenly very different from the generous healer of earlier.

"Tressa's got what they call a gift," Gram said with a proud glint in her eye.

Dr. Baker cleared his throat. "Is that right?" he said.

"I do feel tired," I interrupted before my gammy provided a complete dossier on the dead I'd discovered.

"When she gets her memory back, get her to tell you about the time we were put on ice together," Gram said. "That's a good one."

I smiled. Yeah. And while I was at it, I'd enlighten the good doctor as to how my gammy got the nickname Hellion Hannah and why I suspected my own gift was her lovely little genetic legacy to me. I wasn't the only Turner with skeletons in the closet.

"And you're sure my daughter is going to be okay?" my mother asked.

"Your daughter is going to be fine, Mrs. Turner. Just fine. As a matter of fact, she admitted to being hungry just before you arrived, so we were just going to order her a nice big breakfast—isn't that right, Tressa?" The doctor smiled down at me. "Now, weren't you thinking along the lines of some nice crisp bacon, hash browns, eggs and coffee?"

Movement at the foot of my sickbed drew my attention to Taylor. She stood there, arms folded across her chest, her head cocked to one side.

"If she lost her memory, how can she remember what she likes to eat?" Taylor asked.

Damn Taylor and her overachieving ass.

"This nice doctor insisted on a nourishing breakfast," I said, "to help me get my strength back. And, hopefully, my memory as well. Uh, by the way, who are you? A cousin? Older sister?"

Taylor frowned. "I'm her sister—her *younger* sister," she told the doctor. "And she'll have a bowl of fresh fruit, a bran muffin—no butter—a glass of orange juice and a cup of coffee."

I tried to keep from overtly gagging. At least I had my coffee, I consoled myself—for as long as it took Taylor to bark another order.

"Decaf coffee, that is," Taylor clarified, raising an eyebrow at me in silent challenge.

"Excellent choices!" Dr. Benedict Arnold Baker gushed. "Wholesome and healthful. I'll place that order right away. You're lucky to have a sister who looks out for you so capably." He hurried away.

I looked from my mother to my sister to my brother and his wife to my grandma and Joe. They looked at me like I was a specimen in a Petri dish. Or like some obscure, puzzling piece of art, and they were trying to figure out just what the heck I was supposed to be.

I put a fluttering hand to my forehead. "I feel weak," I said. "I need to rest." I looked at Taylor. "Doctor's orders, you know," I added and shut my eyes.

"Uh, he probably also cautioned that with a head injury it's best not go to sleep—or you might not wake up," Taylor said, reaching out to squeeze my big toe.

"There's one blessing in all this," Joe Townsend finally spoke up.

"What's that?" Gram asked.

"She's not talking like a pirate now," Joe said.

I rolled over on my side away from the gallery of curious spectators.

Good one, Gilligan, I thought. Good one.

Note to Tressa: Remember Joltin' Joe last.

CHAPTER NINE

My family remained with me throughout my delightful meal. I tried to act like someone who'd just lost her memory might act. You know, someone hesitant to make eye contact. Quiet. (A challenge for me in and of itself.) A little vague. A little nervous. A lot vulnerable. Since I'd never been a student of drama, I was basically winging it. Still, I'd picked up a thing or two from soap operas myself.

It was an uncomfortable breakfast—six pairs of probing eyes fixed on little ol'. . . what was my name again? Oh, yes. Tressa.

Once I'd finished every bite—remember, I was starvin', Marvin—I decided I needed some alone time, some time to figure out what in God's name I'd been thinking when I began this soap scam. I put my head back on my pillow and shut my eyes. Ever the observant physician, Dr. Baker, shooed my family members out of the room, citing my need for rest and quiet. They reluctantly agreed and, one by one, they kissed my cheek or squeezed my hand and left. My father was the last to go. Not normally a demonstrative guy— we sort of share that trait—he put a hand to my forehead and gently pushed the hair back from my face and smiled down at me.

"We'll talk later," he promised, which surprised me, too. My dad isn't the chatty type.

Once they left, I mulled over my options. I could take my

chances with a nice, long nap and, if I woke up, I could discover my memory had returned. Of course, when I did, I'd
have to watch my back for the remainder of the cruise—
meaning less time to watch the back of a wife in peril and
more time devoted to dodging Aunt Mo and questions I
wasn't ready to answer concerning the sudden "breakup"
with Manny. Still, it would take considerable skill to pull
this ruse off. And while I knew I wasn't the ditzy, dumb
blonde I'd made myself out to be for the better part of my
life, I wasn't at all certain I was ready for a prime-time role
as an amnesiac.

I supposed I could play it by ear, row with the flow, see
how it went and hope I'd know when the time was right to
drop the act. Plus, the side benefit of being able to thumb
my nose—oh so innocently—at Wedding Wrangler Mo was
nigh on to irresistible.

Drowsiness overtook me and, despite Taylor's warning
about falling asleep, I slept nonetheless.

I was dreaming. I was swimming laps, back and forth,
back and forth in the gloriously inviting waters of *The
Epiphany*'s pool, my body buoyant and alive. I got to the end
of a lap and started to shove myself up out of the water to
take a long, deep breath, but for some reason I couldn't
break the plane of the water's surface. Flailing about with
my hands, I tried to propel my head out of the water to suck
in restorative air, but it was as if there was a cover over the
entire pool. My lungs began to burn, heavy and tight in my
torso. I tried to cry out for help but found the pressure too
intense to produce more than a squeak.

It took a few more seconds before I came fully awake and
it took a few additional seconds for me to realize that, rather
than a pool cover, there was a pillow over my face. I needed
an additional ten count to realize someone was pressing
down on the pillow. Hard. Add several more seconds to the
clock before I realized this meant that someone was trying
to kill me.

Okay, okay. This was your basic bona fide blonde moment here. What can I say? I was in a weak, vulnerable state.

Pain shot through my head as the knot on my skull was pressed hard against the bed. I reached out above me in an attempt to grab something, anything, to fend off my attacker. Hair. A nose. An eyeball. I wasn't picky. Instead, when I reached out, I caught hold of fabric rather than hair or skin. I pulled. I felt my strength faltering and knew I had to do something quick before Taylor was proven right—again— and I fell into a permanent sleep.

I started to throw myself back and forth on the bed, hoping to dislodge the hands on the pillow or maybe tip the bed over. I'd kind of forgotten I was on a boat and the bed was probably bolted down. The best I could manage was to tip myself off the bed and onto the floor, bringing my bedsheets and blanket with me. Running footsteps reached me beneath my blanket tent as I fought to escape the bed linens. Too late I freed myself, and by the time I could see and breathe again, my assailant had beamed out of sickbay.

I got unsteadily to my feet, dragging the bedclothes up around me. Something floated to the floor. I bent over to pick it up. I frowned. It looked like a buff. Like the cloth kerchiefs they wear on *Survivor* to identify each tribe member. This buff was black and red, with white skulls and crossbones. This buff was one-size-fits-all. And this buff had come from the head of one very real threat. It was a buff that represented the ultimate challenge.

I stuck it on my head, tying it in the back, taking care to avoid harsh contact with the knot on my skull.

Outwit.

Outlast.

Outplay.

Outlive.

That had just become the new theme of this ultimate Custom Cruise experience.

I was just about to jot a quick thank-you note to Bones

Baker, to explain I was feeling much better and needed some fresh air and was checking myself out of the sickbay, when a noise in the outer office brought my chin up sharply. Pray, what was this—a villain returned to finish said dastardly deed?

I switched the light off and held my breath. I looked at the rumpled bed sheets and scurried over to place the pillows underneath the bedding, picking up the covers and throwing them over the pillows to make it look like someone was in the bed. I've seen this in the movies a million times and I still have to wonder how anyone can mistake pillows for a person. I looked around the room for something—anything—I could use as a weapon, just in case my opponent was returning for round two of his pillow fight.

My eyes settled on a reflex hammer and I shook my head. Too wimpy. I saw a big jar of cotton swabs, but it was plastic. Where was a cold, ruthless, stainless steel speculum when you needed one? I grabbed the plastic cotton ball container, not wanting to be empty-handed, and scurried to stand in the corner near the door.

"Knock, knock." The whispered words reached me, eliciting a shiver by bringing to mind the whispered words by the would-be murderer on his cell phone and in the stairwell. Then I frowned. What kind of premeditated murderer prefaced his dirty deed with a knock-knock joke?

"Hello? Miss Turner?"

I raised the plastic jar over my head as the door opened. A shadow fell into the room. My fingers tightened around my pathetic weapon.

A tall, dark head appeared around the door. The figure walked slowly to the bed, standing over it before a hand reached out to pull back the sheets. A fraction of a second before I brought the plastic jar down on the dark head, I recognized Sam Davenport's horseshoe ring on the hand grasping a pillow. The identification came too late to call off the hit entirely, but I managed to alter the force and path of my impromptu weapon somewhat. Instead of a full-strength blow to the head, Davenport's shoulder bore the brunt of my downward heave.

"Ooomph!" Davenport pivoted, his hands striking a macho martial arts pose that meant business.

I gulped. I was toast.

"Hold it!" I yelled, putting my hands up. "I give up!"

Security Chief Davenport froze. His eyes widened in surprise. "Miss Turner? What are you doing out of bed? What are you doing period?" he asked.

"I think it's called defending myself," I said, remembering my amnesiac role. I put some distance between me and the security chief. "Who are you?" I asked.

"You don't remember me?" he asked, and I hesitated.

"No. But I'm guessing you're not a blood relative."

He gave me a long look. "When Dr. Baker briefed me, he said you had residual memory issues. I was hoping he was mistaken," he said.

"Briefed you? Are you the captain?" I asked. "Should I, like, salute?"

He shook his head and reached a hand out in my direction, wincing as he rotated his arm a couple of times before taking my hand. "I'm in charge of security on *The Epiphany*," he said. "We met yesterday. You came to my office to report a security concern."

"I did?" I said, shaking his hand with a weak, limp grip of my own.

"You have no memory of that meeting either?" he asked, and I shook my head, thinking that bold-faced lying was becoming easier and easier all the time. Hmm. Maybe I had a future in politics.

"Everything's still a bit of a blank," I said, "but Dr. Baker assures me it's just temporary. What kind of security concern did I have?" I asked him. "Hopefully not leaky lifeboat issues or terrorism terrors," I said.

A slight smile crossed his lips. "No, nothing like that," he

said. "And it's not important, Miss Turner. I was able to assuage your anxieties, I believe," he told me.

I smiled. *Right.*

"Dr. Baker did mention that you told him you believed
someone might have pushed you down the stairs causing
your injuries," he went on. "Is that correct? Do you believe
someone pushed you?" he pressed.

I debated telling Sam Davenport the entire truth here,
spilling my guts about the fake amnesia, grabbing hold of him
and shaking him silly as I assured him that, yes! Yes! Someone
had shoved me down those stairs! And yes! Yes! Lives were in
peril aboard the *Epiphany*, but something held me back.

Maybe it was the way he'd whispered my name outside
the door. Maybe it was the way he'd crept to the side of the
bed. Maybe it was the way he'd looked at me when I'd
jumped out from behind the door and beaned him. All I
knew was that I didn't know enough to trust him. Or to
not trust him, really, but I couldn't risk sharing confidences
with no one else in earshot.

"It was really more of an impression than a recollection,"
I explained, trying to choose my words carefully. "I'd just
regained consciousness when Dr. Baker started questioning
me and the thing that stood out in my mind was the helpless
feeling of being propelled backwards by some external force
and a feeling that I wasn't alone. So that's what I told him."

Davenport hesitated. "I see. You don't recall any specifics
of your fall, just a sense that you were pushed rather than
having tripped and fallen. Right?" he asked.

"I guess," I said, putting a hand to my back of the head in
a *Poor, pitiful me* gesture. "Everything's still confused."

He nodded. "I'm sure that's true." He looked at the bed
and frowned. "You must still think someone is out to get
you or you wouldn't have staged the bed scene and hidden
in wait behind the door," he pointed out.

The guy was smart, I'd give him that. Now, how to respond?

"Falling down a flight of stairs and then waking up with a killer headache and not really recognizing anything or anybody is pretty unsettling," I pointed out. "I hope I can be forgiven for some level of paranoia," I added.

Davenport raised an eyebrow. "Of course, Miss Turner. Much can be forgiven and explained by your experience," he agreed. "But I'm glad to see you appear to be holding up well despite your ordeal. It is also part of my job to make sure you are receiving the care and support you require. You were planning to check out of our little hospital here?" he asked, nodding at the bed.

"Yes. I dozed for a while and felt much better and thought I could use some fresh air," I told him. "I was just getting ready to write a thank-you note to Dr. Baker and take my leave."

"Are you sure you shouldn't remain here for one night? Let the doctor monitor you?" he asked.

I shook my head. "I don't know for sure, but I don't think hospitals, doctors and I jell too well," I said. "I can always come back if I begin to feel worse or relapse. What I think I need right now is to get back to a regular routine and see if that helps in the memory department."

"Sounds reasonable," he said.

See? I can do reasonable.

I scratched off a hasty note to Dr. Baker, telling him I couldn't take it anymore and I was outta here, and thanking him for everything. I clipped the note to my medical chart and grabbed my book bag and left the health and medical offices. Davenport was waiting for me. After the darkness of the sickroom, the bright sunshine blinded me. I put a hand up to block the rays and fished sunglasses out of my bag.

"Interesting bag," Davenport observed. "One of a kind, I imagine. Where'd you get it?"

I was about to launch into a description of the historic Titan Hotel near the rim of the Grand Canyon where I'd found the bag, and indulge in a diatribe about the ten-year-old Townsend terror who'd ruined my original rucksack, but caught myself just in time.

"I wondered about the bag myself. My . . . father tells me I bought it at a gift shop in a hotel in Arizona. Apparently I go for function over form," I added.

"I see," Davenport remarked. "And the kerchief?" He nodded at my buff. "I believe they're using them in the team competitions. How'd you wrangle that one?" he asked.

"Someone left it for me," was all I said.

He saw me down to the main deck and left me after gaining my promise to come to him if I recalled anything relating to the incident on the stairs—or anything else that might be helpful. As if.

It was a little after two, a warm and breezy afternoon, the sky above as blue as the ocean that surrounded us. I sucked in the invigorating scent of sea breeze, and my head lost some of its fuzziness. Passengers of a certain size and shape garbed in stretchy shorts paired with wifebeater shirts, tank or sports bra tops were clustered in various groups, chatting and sipping pastel-colored drinks.

"Tressa! Tressa Turner! Over here!" I spotted Courtney Kayser waving me over. As she moved in my direction with her best bud, Sherri, in tow, I noticed she'd been with the group from the Stardust. Huddled together, they got my full attention when I noticed the buffs they sported were identical to the one my visitor had left behind in the sickbay. Coincidence? I wasn't a big believer.

"Yay! I see you're one of us!" Courtney squealed, coming up to me and pointing at the buff on my head. "Some of us got together from the Stardust the other night and decided it would be fun if we made up our own team. I'm so glad you're with us. Aren't these buffs cool? What a fun idea! We're calling ourselves the Scallywags. Cute, huh?"

Oh, crap. What to do? What to do?

"Tressa? You look weird. Doesn't she look weird, Sher? Are you all right, Tressa?"

"That seems to be the question of the day," I said.

An arm snaked its way around my waist and squeezed. "And one we're waiting with baited breath to learn the answer to," I heard.

I turned to find Ranger Rick behind me and said, "Excuse me?" I gave him a wide-eyed look.

"Who is this, Tressa?" Courtney asked, and I chewed a nervous lip.

Tressa Turner, meet your biggest hurdle.

"I'm Rick Townsend, Tressa's first cousin. By marriage," Rick supplied, and I continued to stare up at him.

"First cousin? Really?" Courtney said. "How . . . bizarre!"

"Isn't it?" Rick said. "And you're—?"

"Courtney. Courtney Kayser. I met Tressa and Manny last night at the Stardust. Didn't I see you there, too?" she asked Townsend.

He nodded. "I was in and out."

"Where is Manny, Tressa? We were hoping we could convince him to be our team trainer," Courtney said.

"Manny?" I asked, not knowing what else to say.

"Your fiancé," Courtney elaborated, and I wanted to kick her.

"I'm not sure—"

"Oh, I'm sure you can convince him to train the Scallywags. Do you like the name? We voted on it. The girls wanted Starfish but the guys nixed that. But good, right, Sherri?"

Sherri smiled and nodded at her friend. "That's right," she said.

"It sounds fine—" I said.

"Are you sure you're okay, Tressa? You don't look well at all—huh, Sherri?" Courtney asked.

"She does look a little pale," Sherri agreed.

"Well, you see what happened was—"

"What Tressa here is trying to say here—not very clearly, ladies—is that her memory is a bit fuzzy," Townsend said.

I looked up at him. "I am?" I asked.

He nodded. "You see, she took a rather bad fall down a flight of stairs early this morning and struck her head. She was out like a light for some time, and the blow seems to have wreaked havoc with the hippocampus and cerebral cortex, the areas of the brain that store memories," Townsend the resident neurologist lectured.

"They do?" I said.

"She did? Do you mean she's lost her memory?" Courtney asked. "For real? You've lost your memory, Tressa?"

"That's what they tell me," I said, not taking my eyes off Townsend for a minute. "How did you—"

"Your father told me all about it," Townsend answered, anticipating my query. "He and the rest of the family seemed to be under the impression you were resting in the health clinic. Are you sure you should be up?"

"Oh, Tressa! What an awful way to start a cruise!" Courtney said, and reached out to take my hand. "We met last night at the Stardust. I'm Courtney and this is my best friend, Sherri. You met my husband, Steve, and Sherri's husband, Ben, too. Oh, this is just terrible," she added, and surprised me by reaching out and giving me a tight bear hug. "Is there anything we can do?" she asked.

I patted her back. "Thanks, but I'll be fine," I said.

"I'm a licensed practical nurse, so if there's anything you need—anything at all—you just let me know. Oh! You'll miss out on the exercise programs and the team competitions!" she pointed out. "I'm sure you'll have to take it easy for a day or so. Rest and relaxation for you."

Cowabunga! Even more perks! I had to keep from dancing a Snoopy happy dance.

"I suppose it would be best to take it easy for a while," I admitted. "I couldn't rest all that well in the infirmary. I had some really whacked dreams. Like I was drowning. Unable to get my breath. I woke up with my pillow covering my face," I told Courtney, figuring it would get around that I placed no sinister meaning to the second attack and, hopefully, would prevent someone from coming after me again. I wasn't like my gammy's kitty cat. I only had one life to live. And I meant to hang on to it for a while.

"Head injuries can mess a person up pretty bad," Courtney agreed. "We'd better go break the news to the rest of the Scallywags. They'll be disappointed you're out of commission. Maybe you'll feel well enough to join in on some of the competitions they've got planned," she said. "They're giving away some really cool prizes."

"We'll have to see—"

"I'm sure Manny will take good care of you, Tressa," Sherri spoke up. She gave Townsend a red-faced look. "Er, and your cousin here, too," she added.

Townsend squeezed a love handle. Mine. "Even if she doesn't know it now, Tressa will soon learn she's got more than enough protectors to get her through this difficult time," he said.

"Right," Courtney agreed, pulling Sherri back to the tribe. I watched the curious glances directed my way as chatterbox Courtney broke the news about my injury and memory glitch.

Good. You spread the word, Courtney, I thought. Spread the word.

"We need to talk, Tressa," Townsend said, taking my arm. "By the way, nice buff," he said, leading me to a long row of loungers. "It suits you." He sat me in one and stretched out next to me in the other. "How's the head?" he asked, lying on one side, facing me, one tanned, toned, manly leg bent at the knee, his brown muscular arm resting on that knee. With his white Department of Natural Resources T-shirt, khaki shorts and brown Tommy Bahama sandals, he looked like the professional cover model for a cruise ad—a Kodak moment that hadn't gone unnoticed by others, as well. Believe me. While the female contingent of fellow passengers feasted their food-deprived libidos on Ranger Rick's fine looks and fantastic physique, the male population was no doubt envisioning the unsuspecting ranger slow-roasted on a spit.

I placed my head gingerly against the back of the chair. "The head's . . . improving," I said in response to his query. An awkward silence followed. And since I never saw a silence I didn't want to break, I broke it. "So? We're cousins, huh?" I asked, trying to get a feel for where Townsend was coming from—and in the process, find out just how suspicious he was of me. And suspicious he had to be.

He smiled. "Cousins for all of three days now," he said with a grin.

"I see. Do we . . . get along?" I asked, and his grin got wider.

"We're very close," he said. He crossed his fingers. "Like this," he added.

I raised an eyebrow. What was the rogue up to now?

"Really?"

"In fact, before your fiancé came on the scene, there was a time I thought—" He stopped.

"You thought . . . what?" I asked, my mouth suddenly dry.

He shrugged. "I shouldn't be bringing this up now. Not with you in such a weakened state," he said. "You've got enough to be concerned with given the sticky situation you find yourself in."

I frowned. "Sticky situation?" I echoed. "What do you mean?"

"Your fiancé, Manny DeMarco. You really don't remember him, huh?"

I shook my head. "I have no memory of having a fiancé," I said. That much was true. Manny was my *faux* beau.

"Won't that make for some—shall we say—awkward moments come time to retire to your quarters this evening?" Townsend pointed out, and I said at least half a dozen really bad words in my head. Ranger Rick *was* trying to trip me up. He knew I was sharing a cabin with Taylor. But I couldn't know that, now, could I?

"I understood from Tyler that she and I were cabin mates on this cruise," I responded.

"Tyler?"

"My sister—I guess."

Townsend nodded. "Oh, right. *Taylor.* So Taylor told you. You must've been surprised when you found out you had a fiancé on board," he suggested. "Who broke that news, by the way?" he asked, and I blinked trying to remember who knew and when they knew it. Jeesch. I sounded like I was involved in some freaking Watergate conspiracy or Arms for Hostages deal.

The truth was, my folks had no idea of my faux fiancé folly. Thank goodness. Ditto for my gammy, or everyone in Grandville would know by now. Joe I wasn't sure of, but I suspected from his foolish interference he'd somehow found out. Perhaps Manny had even told him. Beyond Manny, Mo, Taylor—who I'd 'fessed up to some time back—and my boss at the *Gazette*, Stan the Man Rodgers, I didn't know of anyone else who knew about Manny and me. Well, the let's-pretend Manny and me, that is.

"Uh, Tina mentioned Manny as well," I said.

"Tina?"

"My sister."

"*Taylor,*" he corrected again. "You two seem to be getting along for a change."

"We don't normally?" I asked, not thrilled that our sibling rivalry was apparent to those outside the family.

Townsend shook his head. "Regrettably, no," he responded. "But maybe that will change now—you being injured and all. A silver lining to your cloud."

Since when did Rick Townsend get to be so freakin' philosophical?

"Maybe," I said, noncommittal. "So, are you here with your girlfriend?" I couldn't help asking. I was either a glutton for punishment or a fool in love. Or both.

"I thought so," he said.

"You thought so? What does that mean?"

"Things got a little complicated—like they often do where she's concerned," he said with a poignant little smile. "I suspect she's commitment-phobic."

"Oh."

"But enough of me and my troubles, let's focus on you. Are you comfortable there? Do you need a pillow? Are you thirsty? How about something tall and cool to drink?" he asked. "Or am I being too bossy? You hate to be bossed around, you know," he said.

"Who doesn't?" I asked, totally taken aback by the accommodating man beside me.

He nodded. "How about that drink?"

"That would be nice."

"Lemonade maybe? With a lot of sugar?" he asked.

My eyes narrowed at the seemingly innocent query that could have been a landmine. "Who knows? Surprise me, cousin," I said, and he raised an eyebrow.

"I might do just that," he said, getting up from his lounger. "Cos," he added with a wink, bending down to give me a quick kiss on my buff. "Be right back."

I watched him walk away, tracking the easy, casual moves of his body with a hungry look. I replayed our conversation in my head but couldn't decide if Ranger Rick realized I was faking my memory loss or not. Sometimes I'd swear he was trying to trip me up. At others, he seemed genuinely concerned. Helpful. Even . . . loving. It represented a riddle. *He* represented a riddle.

I swallowed loudly. I was pretty sure that Tressa Jayne Turner couldn't resist a good riddle.

CHAPTER TEN

"Well, if it isn't the Jill of all trades, Tressa Turner! May I join you?"

I looked up to discover David Frazier Compton, the dude with three names, staring down at me. Without waiting for a response, he took the lounger Townsend had vacated. Sitting sideways on the chair, he adjusted his navy visor and pushed his sunglasses back up on the bridge of his nose. "I understand from the Scallywags over there that you sustained injuries in a fall this morning and, consequently, are having difficulties with your memory," he said. "I just had to come over and see if it was true. Is it?" he asked, wiping his sweaty face with a Scallywag tribal buff.

I stared at the buff.

"So, is it?" he asked, and I shook my head trying to get over the fact that he had access to the same buff that my attacker had left behind.

"Is it what?" I said, trying not to appear shaken.

"Is it true?"

"Is what true?"

"That you've lost your memory!"

"How would I know if it's true or not?" I responded. "All I have are other peoples' words for everything," I pointed out. "Which begs the question: Should I know you?" I asked.

He gave me a considering look. "You should. We met last night. Coral LaFavre is my wife. You met her as well."

"Coral. What kind of name is that?"

"A stage name," he said.

"Coral's an actor?" I asked.

"Among other things," DFC replied. "It is rather a bizarre stroke of fate that you're afflicted with amnesia, is it not?" he asked. "Dreadful timing and all that, I imagine," he said.

I frowned. "Is there a good time to have a case of amnesia?" I asked.

Compton leaned closer to me. "Oh, I can think of times when it could come quite in handy," he said.

I frowned. "Handy? How so?" I asked.

"Oh, say you've broken the law and you get caught. Or maybe you owe the IRS a large amount of money. You couldn't very well aid in your own defense if you lost your memory," he said, "so your case would have to be continued indefinitely. True?"

I shrugged. "Beats me," I said, thinking it odd how crime and debt figured so prominently into Compton's thought processes.

"Or maybe you have a cheating spouse—or you are a cheating spouse," he continued. "A conveniently timed case of amnesia could conceivably save a marriage."

David Frazier Compton had a weird way of looking at life—and a seriously messed-up way of promoting the perks of amnesia to a supposed victim.

"The cheating would still be there, whether or not the spouse had knowledge or recollection of it," I pointed out. "And is a marriage worth saving if one spouse cheats?" I asked, wondering if infidelity played a role in his marriage and, if so, who was doing the cheating.

"I suppose it would depend on the couple," he said. "How much they loved each other. How forgiving they could be. Could you forgive your fiancé's infidelity, Tressa?"

I swallowed. Could I? Hell, no.

"I don't remember having a fiancé," I said. "But no, I don't think I could forgive something like that," I told him.

"Coral was quite taken with your Manny the other night," David went on. He took a long swallow of his drink. "Then again, so was every other individual of the female persuasion—plus several who weren't of the female persuasion," he added, and I knew he was referring to Dolph and Major. "But of course you won't remember any of that."

I shook my head. "Did I miss something . . . significant?"

He looked at me for an uncomfortable moment before he replied, "No, no. I should think not, love." He reached over and patted my hand. "Do be a good girl and let me know when your memory returns, won't you? So I can pass on the happy news to Coral."

"Of course," I fibbed. "Of course."

"Take care, my dear," David said and left.

I put my head back on the recliner. Remembering I had no memory was exhausting. I caught a sudden movement off to my right and discovered Security Sam Davenport conducting not-so-covert surveillance from behind a potted plant. I watched as he took off in the direction of the three-name wonder with a serious case of the sweats. It appeared Davenport had taken my concerns regarding Coral to heart and was keeping a close eye on her hubby. The fact raised my spirits considerably.

"Your drink." Townsend had returned.

He handed me a cute pink drink with an adorable turquoise umbrella stuck in it. I thanked him and took a long sip, expecting the sugary sweetness of pink lemonade, and instead getting a heaping helping of total tartness. I made a *bleah* face and shivered as I managed to swallow the foul brew known as pink grapefruit juice.

"Is something wrong, Tressa?" Ranger Rick asked.

I shook my head, trying to keep from actively gagging. "No, not at all. It's good," I managed, becoming more suspicious of Townsend by the minute. "Yum yum!"

He grinned down at me. "They've asked me to help out with some of the shipboard activities, monitoring some of the teams in the workout rooms. Things like that. Are you going to be all right here?" he asked. "I could get someone to sit with you. Your grandmother. My granddad. Taylor."

"No!" I sat up. "I mean, no, I'm good. Really. It's not as if I'm helpless, you know."

"Just a little more clueless than usual. Right?" Rick said.

"Am I usually clueless?" I asked.

He looked at me for a long moment. "There are areas where you seem to be somewhat dense," he said at last.

I flinched. "Dense?"

He nodded.

"What areas are you talking about, exactly?" I asked. "Math? Foreign languages? Politics?"

"Biology. Oh, and chemistry, too," he told me with a wink.

I frowned. "Am I missing something here?" I asked.

"Of course," he said.

"Huh?"

"Your memory. Remember?"

"And apparently, according to you, I'm normally deficient in the sciences, as well."

"Maybe I should have been more specific and said that interpersonal relationships and communication are areas of concern," he amended.

"How so?" I asked. "I'm told I have a fiancé, so I must be doing something right. And you yourself told me just minutes ago that we were like *this*," I went on, crossing my fingers as he had earlier. "So I must not be a complete dud in the relationship department."

"I don't think you're a dud at all," Ranger Rick said, sitting on the edge of my chair. "In fact, I think you're dynamite," he added, taking my hand in his.

"You do?"

He nodded. "And cute," he said, leaning in my direction. "And funny." More leaning. "And sexy." Closer still, his lips mere millimeters from mine.

"You forget engaged?"

The clipped query was as effective a mood breaker as a cold glass of grapefruit juice upended over his head. Townsend straightened, his smile forced.

"Not me, Mrs. Dishman," he said. "Tressa here's the one who can't seem to remember she's engaged," he added, getting to his feet. "Looks like you're in good hands, Calamity, so I'll leave you in your Aunt Mo's custody," he said to me. "And remember. Don't overdo it," he said, wagging a finger. "Doctor's orders."

"Wait!" I yelled. "Stop! Come back!"

But he strolled off, turning more than a few heads in his direction as he swaggered away. Mo's included.

"That man's too good-lookin' for Mo's peace of mind," Mo said, settling into the seat next to me, her dyed hair pulled back into a ponytail. She wore a white shirt with light pink fringe across the front, white spandex Capri leggings, and pink and white sandals. A big, white hoop earring dangled from each lobe. "But he's right about one thing. You shore don't act like a bride who can't wait to walk down the aisle," she pointed out. "Now, I don't mean to put no pressure on you, Tressa, but the fact of the matter is I got this here heart condition to consider. You almost lost Mo here last year, you know. I was sure I was gonna go to the hereafter without seeing my Manny happily married, but the big guy up there? Well, he had other plans for Mo. Now here I am on a cruise ship of all places feeling peppier than I have in a long time—and lookin' forward to making weddin' plans and seeing my Manny and you wedded and bedded, and dandling the fruit of Manny's loins on my knee—"

An image of Manny DeMarco's muscular loins sent a rush of heat through my body and I fanned my face as I bravely took another sip of my lip-puckering drink.

"—and being here for my family," Mo said. Her Pouty Pink acrylic fingernails fished into her clunky, retro bag.

"So, when works for you?" she asked, pulling out a pocket calendar and a gel pen. She looked at the buff on my head and the tangled locks falling around my shoulders. "Mo'll have to see what Carlo at Carlo's Creations can do with that head of hair of yours. He's a miracle worker. If he can't do it, it can't be done."

She grabbed one of my hands, looked at it, dropped it, moved down to the foot of the lounger and proceeded to peruse my piggies. "Girl, you need an overhaul," she said. "Head-to-toe deluxe treatment. It comes with one of them hot stone massages and a full-body wax. Is that a problem?" she asked me.

For the waxer. I had a low tolerance for pain.

"I'm thinking we can pull this together by late summer, early fall. How does August thirtieth sound?"

Hot as hell.

"Or maybe we should wait 'til one of the first Saturdays in September. How about September eleventh?"

I looked at her. "September *eleventh*?" I said.

She winced. "Let Mo just put a big X through that date."

"Listen, Mo—"

"Mo knows. Tressa's momma needs to be involved in the process. Right? That's one reason Mo here wanted to come on this cruise. I figgered your momma and Mo here could put our heads together and do some weddin' planning. Get this show on the road. What do you think of turquoise and mauve?" she asked.

What did I think? The mints would look vomitrocious.

"Aunt Mo—"

"You could make things easy on Aunt Mo and just get married when we dock tomorrow. Did you know they have these romantic places where you can get married onshore— all legit and everything? All you need to do is show your paperwork, fill out a few forms, and go to the chapel and get yourself hitched. All legal and binding and everything. I don't know about you, but more and more Mo's thinking that's the way to go. Streamline the whole affair. No reception hall to book. No menu to plan. No dress to buy. What do you think, Tressa? Mo can get them wheels in motion in no time and have everything ready by the time the ship docks tomorrow or the next day. How about it, Tressa? Manny's waited a long time for the right woman to come along. Mo don't want to see him wait any longer."

Dear God, she was serious!

"Look, Mo, there's something you need to know," I tried again. "Things have changed—"

"Don't you be going there, girl," Mo said. "Don't you be letting that randy ranger turn your head."

"It's not about that—"

"Oh? So you do admit the man floats your boat?" she asked.

"That's not the issue—"

"So he does."

"It's not about him—"

"I know. It's about mathematics."

"Huh?"

"It's about Tressa plus Manny minus one Ranger Romeo equals wedding bells," Mo said, and I shook my head at the addled arithmetic analogy that made it irritatingly apparent Manny had not had the talk with Aunt Mo after all, the six-foot-three sissy.

I felt myself floundering. I wasn't equipped for long-term deception. I'd never had a poker face and, while I was no George "I-cannot-tell-a-lie" cherry-tree-ax-murderer Washington, I was far from a seasoned prevaricator. Skirting the truth was one thing. Being pathological about it was quite another.

"Oh, there you are, Tressa! Rick said you were taking it easy over here. I told him I'd keep you company while they were pretending to be fitness gurus. Right. Like my Craig would give up beer and Doritos willingly. In case you hadn't remembered, your brother is a pig." My sister-in-law,

Kimmie, dropped into a vacant chair on the other side of me. "Oh, hello," she said to Mo. "Have you made a new friend, Tressa? I'm Tressa's sister-in-law, Kimmie. I'm married to her brother, Craig. Isn't it just awful about Tressa's memory?" she asked. "Tressa always seems to have such abysmal luck. Imagine, the first day of your first cruise and you take a tumble down the stairs, smack your skull and knock yourself out, and when you come around you can't remember a thing. It's so . . . so . . . poignant."

Mo did a quick visual sweep of Kimmie before her eagle-eyed gaze came back to me. "What's she talking about?" she asked. "What are you talking about?" She shifted her attention back to Kimmie.

My sister-in-law bit her lip. "Oh. You don't know. Tressa has amnesia," she said. "She's lost her memory," Kimmie added, "but the doctor assures the family it's just temporary."

"Amnesia? Amnesia!" Mo looked at me. "What kind of scam you runnin' now, missy?"

"Now just a minute, ma'am," Kimmie objected.

"Mo. It's Mo, not ma'am. And I know a scam when I see it. You know how many home repair rip-off artists have knocked on my door telling me my roof is about to fall in or the siding is gonna blow off in a good stout wind? How many mechanics have tried the old squirt-oil-under-the-car scam to try and rip me off? All them calls you get to send an underprivileged kid to some show where some fundraiser pockets ninety percent of the take? I watch that mustached John Stossal on *20/20*. And I smell something fishy here."

"Well, we are on a ship," I said.

"Attitude? You're giving me attitude?" Mo asked.

I felt my eyes get big. "It was just a little seafaring levity," I explained. "You know. To ease the tension." And boy was I feeling tense.

"You're telling me you don't remember who I am?" Mo said, her eyes narrowing in on me like mine do on the last slice of chocolate cake at a church potluck. "Is that what you're telling me?"

"Is she supposed to know you?" Kimmie asked. "I mean, when she's . . . compos mentis," she clarified in a hushed tone.

Compos mentis? Suddenly Kimmie had gone all Freud on me. Next thing she'd be pointing fingers at my id. I know what you're thinking. There goes Tressa and her superego again.

"You talk about compost," Mo declared. "This whole story smells like compost!" First fish. Now manure. Ah, the attractions of a luxury cruise. "And she sure as hell should know me," Mo said. "She's engaged to my nephew."

Kimmie gasped. She stared at me, and I could see her trying to connect the dots in her head. It made me dizzy to watch.

"You're engaged?" she squealed. "When? How? Why didn't you say anything? Oh my goodness! You're Rick's aunt?" Kimmie turned to Mo and put out a hand. "I don't think we've met."

"You lost your compost mentis, too?" Mo asked. " 'Cause I ain't related to that rogue ranger. I'm Marguerite Dishman. My nephew is Manny. Manny DeMarco. Tressa and Manny got engaged last fall," she said. "I came on this cruise to plan us a wedding."

Poor Kimmie. She looked as if she'd just been told she was expecting Rosemary's baby.

"Manny DeMarco? The tattooed bad-boy biker Tressa bailed out of jail last summer? The one who looks like a bodybuilder? That Manny DeMarco?" Kimmie responded.

"Search me," I said with a shrug.

"This can't be true," Kimmie said. "Tressa is going to marry Rick."

"I am?"

"She is?"

Kimmie nodded. "Absolutely. It's her destiny," she said to Mo and turned to me. "It's *your* destiny."

"It is?" I frowned, fairly certain I hadn't yet received that particular memo.

She nodded again. "It's your karmic fate!" she said. "It's written in the stars. It's the product of intelligent design!"

"It is?" I queried.

"Yes! It's *my* design! *My* plan. My husband's best friend marries my husband's sister. It's been my dream for years. You two were meant to be, dammit! And I'm not giving up on my dream. Do you hear? I am not giving up on my dream!"

"You sure you weren't the one who addled her pate?" Mo said to Kimmie. " 'Cause you sure got it all wrong. Tressa here is gonna make *Mo's* dream come true and marry the man of *Mo's* dreams, toots," Mo snapped. "And I got seniority."

"She can't even remember your Manny," Kimmie pointed out. "So how can she marry him?"

"Oh? Well, if she really did go and lose her memory, then she don't remember Mr. Ranger Romeo either," Mo countered. "So I guess that leaves him out, too."

Kimmie's face crumbled. She looked deflated when she turned back to me. "You seriously can't remember Rick?" she said. "Not at all? You can't remember the time he snuck into your bedroom and tied all of your sports socks in knots?" she asked. "Or the time he left a rubber snake in your underwear drawer? Or dressed Butch and Sundance in Iowa State Cyclone outfits? Or when he smashed his truck through the Dairee Freeze door and probably saved your life? And how he tried to make you jealous by flirting with Taylor at the fair last summer so you'd finally come to your senses and realize how you really felt about him?"

I did a pretty good job of appearing to be unmoved by Kimmie's trip down memory lane—right up until her last revelation, that is. I could feel a wad of something heavy form in my chest and slowly expand as it made its way into both arms and lodged in my throat, and I was fairly certain the only outlet for release was to let loose with an eardrum-bursting, glass-shattering, jaw-stretching, horror-movie-queen scream.

"He did what?" I managed to hiss.

"Snakes in underwear drawers? Sounds like one sick puppy to me," Mo said.

"He saved your life, Tressa," Kimmie repeated, her eyes filling with tears as she reached to take my hand. "How can you not remember someone who loved you enough to drive his prized 4 x 4 pickup through the wall of a fast food restaurant?" She sniffled.

Loved me? *Loved* me? I shut my eyes. This was way too much for a bruised brain to consider.

"It don't matter dink if that ranger thinks he loves her," Mo said. "She's in love with my Manny. And, memory or no memory, Mo ain't letting her forget that."

"Then it appears we're at cross-purposes, Mrs. Dishman, because I don't plan on letting her forget her feelings for Rick or his feelings for her," Kimmie said.

Now this was a first. Not only was I the object of some desire between two men, but I also had two women playing tug-of-war over me.

Kinky. Yet novel.

"Mo's determined to see this wedding happen," Mo said, a hint of challenge apparent in the stubborn set of her jaw.

"And Kimmie here is equally determined her baby will have an Uncle Rick and Aunt Tressa doting over him or her." My sister-in-law lifted her chin.

"That's how it is, huh?" Mo asked.

"That's how it is," Kimmie responded.

I blinked. What had I missed now?

"Baby? What baby?" I asked. Then, "Do you have a baby?"

Kimmie shook her head. "Not yet. But I'm working on it," she snapped.

"*You're* working on it? By yourself?" I asked, wondering if Kimmie had succeeded in her yearlong campaign to convince my brother, Craig, that he was ready for fatherhood. He'd been somewhat reluctant to commit to Kimmie's family plan, and it had caused some waves in their marriage.

"Haven't you ever heard 'Sometimes the best man for the job is a woman'?" Kimmie asked. "Oh, sorry, of course you wouldn't remember, would you? Well, take my word for it. You want a job done on time and done right? Give it to a woman. We have our ways."

"Wicked ways if you ask me," Mo interrupted. "Getting your hubby's best buddy, Ranger Rick, to tie the knot with little sister here just so you can get your man to grow up and settle down and become a daddy," she pointed out. "Don't tell me you ain't got no pony in this race, missy."

"How dare you question my motives!" Kimmie said.

I slowly got to my feet.

"Where are you going, Miss Tressa?" Mo questioned. "We ain't set no date yet."

"I need to clear my head," I said. "Too much information. Or rather, not enough."

"You best be clearing your calendar instead of your head, Tressa Jayne," Mo warned, wagging a polished nail in my direction, "because we have a wedding to plan."

"Care to make a friendly wager on that, Mrs. Mo?" Kimmie countered.

Mo's eyebrows united in a marriage of their own. "They don't call me the Bingo Bandit for nothin'," she said, putting out her hand.

"So, what are we wagering?" Kimmie asked, and I hovered for a moment to find out how bad it was going to be.

"Loser has to serenade the groom at the reception," Mo suggested.

"Oh? And sing what? 'Who Let the Dogs Out'?" Kimmie asked.

One of Mo's brows jumped.

"Mo was thinkin' more along the lines of 'Celebration,'" Mo said. "Wearing a Cupid costume," she added.

"Cupid?" Kimmie's right eye twitched. "As in the diapered baby who shoots heart-tipped arrows? That Cupid?"

"Yeah. That Cupid," Mo said.

"You got yourself a bet, Mrs. Mo," Kimmie said, but not nearly as gung-ho as before. "And may the best Cupid win."

Me? I walked away thinking either wedding party was bound to be one even a drunken party crasher would regret crashing. No matter how tasty the buffet.

CHAPTER ELEVEN

I needed to think, to plan my next move in Operation: Amnesia. I needed to figure out how to chart a course through the jagged rocks and reefs of ambivalence and uncertainty that prevented Tugboat Tressa from enjoying smooth sailing on the seas of love and devotion. For this kind of heavy lifting, I needed food. Real food. Brain food. And I needed it now.

I drifted from one deck to another, rejecting each healthy food choice I came upon with an increasing sense of desperation. Or maybe that should be deprivation.

I stopped and stared at a gigantic bowl of melon balls on ice. I liked melon—especially when I got to spit watermelon seeds. Even though this fare was sans seeds, I decided to serve myself a heaping helping of the assorted melon balls and grapes, when I got one of those "I'm being watched" feelings. I looked around and thought I caught a glimpse of my folks hurrying away. I frowned. Nice that they thought enough of me to interrupt their vacation to check on the welfare of their poor, injured, amnesiac daughter.

I stabbed a ball of watermelon with a fork and popped it in my mouth, followed by another and another and another. So not filling. My stomach gurgled and I winced. Much longer without real sustenance and I wouldn't have to worry about discovering my feelings; I was gonna die of starvation well before I ever figured out who or what I wanted. Right now, the only hunk I was interested in was a hunk of triple-chocolate strawberry cheesecake. Hold the strawberries.

I thought with nostalgia of Dr. Baker's Burger King-like offer to have breakfast my way, and how Taylor had nuked that opportunity. Still, it occurred to me that somewhere on board this ship was a kitchen—or galley, or whatever they called it—with the capacity to prepare food that tasted like food with ingredients like real butter, sour cream, starch, sodium and fat. If I could somehow find my way to the kitchen.

As it turned out, I found myself wishing all my quests could be this much of a piece of cake. Yeah. I was back to thinking in terms of food again. I roamed the hallways outside cabins until I eyed a porter carrying a tray that smelled suspiciously like a Philly cheesesteak making his way down a narrow corridor along a long row of staterooms. The scent of grilled onions as he passed me from the other direction almost made my knees buckle. I had to manually shove my salivating tongue back in my mouth with my fingers to escape notice.

I looked on while he delivered said food, then stuck to him like Swiss cheese melted over grilled beef as he made his way back to the food service area of the ship. The clattering of pots and pans pinpointed the spot where—if I was lucky— I'd discover some sort of treasure of the deep-fried kind. I wasn't particularly picky about what lie beneath the deep-fried coating, either. Mushrooms, mozzarella or cheddar cheese, cauliflower, even zucchini would assuage my hunger pains.

I looked down at my shorts and top and frowned. No way would I pass for kitchen help this way. I put a hand to my buff-covered head. This I could probably get away with. Weren't kitchen workers supposed to cover their heads when preparing food? Didn't chefs wear big white hats? And what about hair nets?

I opened the door to what I thought was part of the galley and peeked in. It was a huge room, all shiny stainless steel and fluorescent lights, with a cafeteria-style line taking up one complete wall. Large tan trays with bright white placemats much like the one the room service steward had delivered waited in line for orders. Several white-coated workers were busy nearby preparing various drink orders while others put together sandwiches and salads. Each worker wore a white-linen turban-style hat. I was about to close the door when I noticed a row of hooks next to the door. On the hooks were several white coats and busboy hats.

I thought about the wisdom of what I was about to do for a full one-thousand-one, one-thousand-two, one-thousand-three count but—shocker here—hunger won out over wisdom. I reached in, grabbed a coat and hat, and shut the door quietly.

I stuck the white hat on over my buff and hurriedly shoved my arms though the sleeves of the white coat. The book bag over my shoulders beneath the coat made me look like I had one heck of a dowager's hump, but there was nothing I could do about it. If all went as planned, I'd need both my hands free for stuffing my hands and face. And pockets.

I wandered a few doors down and saw a door marked *Food Station*, opened it, and stuck my head in. A cafeteria line similar to the other one ran the length of the long, narrow room on one side, refrigerated units located above. On the other side of the room were various food stations outfitted with the items necessary for that particular meal item, each area looking almost like a mini kitchen. Bewitched, I found myself entering the room as if in a trance as assorted aromas teased my olfactory sense.

Wide-eyed, I stared at the walls of the galley, a virtual rogue's gallery of gastronomical creations, from crème brulee to baked Alaska, crab legs to caviar, all perfectly photographed so kitchen workers could see exactly how each creation should look. In my case, the effect of the victual visuals was the equivalent of water-boarding as I passed picture after picture of the palate-pleasing productions I'd expected to experience on this cruise of a lifetime.

It was then I saw it.

My tongue flopped back out of my mouth. My nostrils flared like a bloodhound's. My mouth filled with saliva. I stared as the white-jacketed chef removed the biggest, most perfect T-bone steak this side of the Missouri River I'd ever seen from a Texas-sized grill and placed it carefully on a clean white plate. He added some colorful garnish to the plate, looked up, saw me, and just like that, handed it over. I just stood there, the plate shaking in my hands, my eyes feasting on the sheer magnificence of the meat.

"Well, what are you waiting for?" the meat magician asked, passing me a slip. "Get it covered and get it on the room service tray."

"Yessir, chef sir," I said. "I'll take care of it."

And I would. Just as soon as I found a quiet corner somewhere. Utensils? I come from a state whose fair concessionaires have learned how to jam just about anything on a stick and make it taste delicious. Utensils? I don't need no stinkin' utensils!

I grabbed a stainless steel food warmer, stuck the steak beneath it, and was about to make off with my beefalicious booty when I noticed a gray-haired gentleman, garbed much as I was, standing over a deep fryer. There was something familiar about him, about the way he moved. I looked downward, and when I caught a look at the white Reeboks matched with white tube socks that reached to just under the knee, the jig was up.

"We need a jumbo order of rings and the appetizer assortment, pronto!" I barked at him. "Boy, are you busted," I added.

Joe Townsend's jump would have impressed NBA scouts. He whirled around, wire basket in hand, his face flushed from the fryer heat or, perhaps, embarrassment at being caught with his hand in the appetizer jar. Or both.

He scowled when he recognized me.

"Don't you know better than to come up like that behind someone manning a deep fryer?" he asked.

Recalling I was minus a memory at the present time, I shook my head. "Apparently not," I said. "Sorry."

His fierce frown mutated into something I wasn't sure I liked. Kind of like the look my gammy's cat, Hermione, got on a cold winter day as she sunned herself on the back of the living room sofa licking her chops and looking out the window at my labs, Butch and Sundance, jumping up and down and barking their heads off at her. *Rrrearr!*

"Apology accepted," he said, leaving me even more uneasy.

"Really?" I asked. "Because I wouldn't want to hinder you in your work. You see, nobody told me you were a chef on *The Epiphany*."

"That's because I'm not and you know it," he said.

"I do?" I asked.

He nodded. "That plate you're holding, the dilated pupils and the wide-open nostrils, not to mention the drool on your jacket there tells me you're here for the same reason I am, girlie," he said. "Survival. Of the not-so-fittest."

I blinked.

Joe must be in bad shape. He wasn't even trying to talk his way out of this.

"Now the way I see it, we can both pretend we're here for a tour of the galley or to make sure the kitchen area is up to CDC standards of cleanliness, or we can join forces and gorge ourselves as God intended folks on a cruise to do," Joe stated.

A bell sounded, and Joe turned back to the fryer, lifted a big basket of thin, crispy golden brown onion rings out of the oil and let it drain. "I've got mushrooms, cheese balls and zucchini," he said. "What about you?"

"A T-bone steak three inches thick and a plate wide," I responded.

"You in?" he asked.

I hesitated. My past collaborations with Joe had a dubious record of success. Most bordered on the absurd.

"You should get a look at the bakery down the hall," he said, delivering the sucker punch—in this case a knockout. "Pastries, cakes and confections as far as the eye can see."

I shook my head. "You're lying," I said. "I was told this is an eat-your-way-to-good-health cruise. Why would they have all those sweets around?"

"The crew has to eat, don't they?" he asked. "That's over a hundred mouths to feed who aren't counting calories. They even have brownies," he said. "Frosted and without nuts."

The plate in my hands began to shake again, the stainless steel top banging against the plate.

"Hey! You still haven't got that steak upstairs?" This bark came from the Master of Meat, the Sultan of Steak, the Chairman of the Charbroiled. "Sam Davenport's gonna chew you and me a new one if his steak is cold when it gets there," he said. "So move! The rest of the order is ready and the wine's already chilled and ready to go."

I stared at the slip he'd handed me. Davenport's name and cabin number were on it. I checked the order again. Tressa's dream dinner: Steak. Baked potato with the works. Side salad. A slice of chocolate cake. I frowned. The order also called for a grilled chicken salad, low-cal dressing and a diet drink. Apparently, Security Chief Sam was not dining alone.

"Make that order to go and you've got yourself a deal," I told Joe, setting the steak on the tray meant for Davenport and motioning to another with two covered dishes. "Dump the deep-fried goods on that tray and let's get the heck out of here," I said.

Joe's expression looked puzzled, but he quickly complied,

upending the fryer baskets onto the tray. He picked it up and we hurried out the door and into the hall.

"Reminds me of the good ol' days," Joe said, his skinny legs keeping pace with me.

"It does?" I asked.

"That marina madness you dragged me into last summer. Remember?"

I did. But I remembered it the other way around. The guy was harder to pry loose than a barnacle.

"Can't say that I do," I responded, "so I'll have to take your word for it."

"That's a first," he mumbled. "Say, where are we going?" he asked.

"We just have to deliver this tray first, and then we'll find a nice, safe place to dine in style," I told him.

"Deliver the tray? Deliver the tray! What do you mean, deliver the tray?" Joe asked. "What do you want to do something like that for?"

"I don't," I responded. "I want you to."

We stopped at the employee elevator and I hit the up button.

"Me? Why me?"

"Because I don't want to be seen," I told him.

"Seen? By who?"

"By the people we're delivering the tray to, of course," I replied.

"Why don't you want them to see you? I thought you didn't know anyone," Joe said, sharp as always.

"I know him," I said. "He's the security chief. He came to the sickbay to, uh, question me earlier."

"So?"

"So, I don't want his steak to get cold," I said, knowing that made absolutely no sense but deciding making no sense was probably to be expected from an amnesiac. Right?

The elevator dinged and the door opened. I walked in and punched Davenport's level.

"Why do you care if his steak gets cold?" Joe said, following me, doing his best bulldog impression. Once he got hold of something, he didn't let go.

"I don't know why I care!" I finally shouted. "I just do! And guess what? So do you."

He looked at me. "Me? Why should I care?"

I hit the stop button on the elevator. "Because, little man, if you don't help me deliver this tray, I'm going to tell that lovely woman you've married that you raided the *Epiphany*'s galley and didn't even think to bring her a doggie bag!" I told him. "Got it? Granddad?"

Joe looked at me. His fear was palpable.

"It's for her own good!" he yelled. "She can't eat grease!" he said. "It gives her gastritis! She toots all night!"

As if he was telling me, who'd lived with the woman for the last eight months, something I didn't know.

"Then we have an understanding?" I asked.

"What do I have to do?" he asked.

I smiled. "You are no longer a deep-fry cook," I told him. "You have been promoted. You are a room service steward. All you have to do is knock on the cabin and deliver the food. Oh, and try to see as much of the inside of the cabin as you can. You know. Be nosy. Check out the occupants. But don't be obvious about it."

"Aren't I a little on the old side to be delivering food on cruise ships?" he asked, and it struck me that this was the first time Joe had ever alluded to his age being a factor in anything. Before, he'd always maintained he had the constitution of a man twenty years his junior. Obviously, he was having serious doubts about attempting to flim-flam the head of security.

"You ever order room service?" I said.

He nodded.

"So, do you take the time to look at the delivery guy?"

He shook his head. "I generally grab the grub, say a quick thanks, and pass 'em a tip."

"There you go," I said.

"I hope you aren't planning to make me split the tip with you, because I refuse," Joe said, as I turned the elevator back on.

"You'll have earned it, laddie," I told him. "Just to be safe, we'll smash your hat down over your hair to cover the gray." I set the tray down and yanked Joe's hat down. His ears stuck out at weird angles.

The elevator opened onto Davenport's deck and we exited. I checked the cabin numbers for the right direction.

"Here's how it's gonna go down," I said, as we walked the short distance to Davenport's cabin. "I'll be standing to the side of the door so Davenport doesn't see me. I'll hold the tray like so." I raised it high, like I'd seen countless waitresses and waiters do. I'd never really mastered the technique, but figured I could hold the pose for the minute it took to deliver the goods. "You'll knock on the door. He'll open it. You'll pass him the tray and try to look into the room. Don't forget the crack in the door. And look for mirrors on the wall. You'd be amazed at what you can see reflected in a mirror," I told him.

"You've done this before," he accused.

"I have?"

He shook his head. "Just give me the damned tray," he instructed, and we switched loads.

"You know, you won't get much of a tip if you snap at the passengers like that," I pointed out. "They expect courteous service."

"And you won't find out who is in that room with the security guy if you don't pipe down," Joe said.

"Remember, just hand him the tray, take a look around, but don't be too obvious about it, and whatever you do, don't make eye contact!" I warned.

"You sure haven't forgotten how to boss people around," Joe grumbled as he straightened his jacket and hitched up his shorts.

I positioned myself to the right of the door, tray at eye level. Joe rapped on the door.

"Room service," he called out.

I smiled. So far, so good.

Just as the door started to open, I felt something cold and hard hit me in the side. I looked down and spotted the bottle of Chardonnay meant for Davenport. I frowned, and Joe jabbed me with the bottle again, harder this time. I grabbed the bottle from him with my left hand and struggled to keep the tray balanced.

The door opened.

"It took you long enough." Sam Davenport's deep voice reached me. "I was just about to make another call."

"So sorry, sir, but we got a bit behind on our orders," Joe said. "Apparently some of the passengers are already tiring of their diet regimes, and are craving the more conventional cruise fare," he said. I applauded his calm aplomb.

"I can understand that," Davenport replied, as the tray was transferred from Joltin' Joe to Security Sam. "Here, take the tray," he instructed someone in the room. Davenport fished in his pocket for a gratuity. "Here you go," he said.

"Thank you, sir. Enjoy your meals," Joe responded, and as tight as Joe was, I half expected him to unfold the bills Davenport had given him and count them right then and there. I released my breath as he pocketed the money without looking at it.

"Wait!" a voice called out. "The wine! They forgot the wine!"

It was a voice I recognized. In a place it shouldn't be.

"Oh, dear. I'm sorry," Joe apologized, checking the room service receipt. "It appears you're right. I'll see to it personally," he promised.

"Never mind," Davenport said. "We really don't have time to drink it now, anyway."

"Very good, sir." Joe was sounding more like a valet than

a room service steward. "We'll make sure your bill reflects that refund," he promised. "Good afternoon."

"But I was looking forward to a glass of wine!" The protest came from inside the room.

"Better not," Davenport said. "Good afternoon," he bade Joe, and shut the door.

I shoved the bottle of wine at Joe and lowered the tray from my aching shoulder and hurried back toward the elevator. "What was that all about?" I hissed as we waited for the elevator door to open.

"What? What was what about?"

"The wine!" I said. "Why did you pinch the wine? If he'd have gotten on the phone and called down to complain, our cover would have been blown."

"Cover? You make it sound like this is some kind of deep undercover operation," he said, and I felt the muscles of my face tighten as the blood vessels widened. A warm blush soon followed.

"You're getting all red in the face," Joe charged. "You're blushing."

"Overexertion," I explained. "Too much too soon," I added.

The elevator dinged and the door opened.

"Uh-huh," Joe said, eyeing me closer than I had that thick cut of beef earlier. "Well, forgive me for liking a glass of wine with my supper," he said.

And being too tight to pay for it himself, I suspected.

"Well? What did you see? Anything interesting?"

"That depends," Joe said.

"On what?" I asked.

"On whether you consider seeing a woman in dishabille interesting," he responded.

I looked at him. "Well, that depends," I said.

"On what?" Joe asked.

"On what dishabille means."

Joe shook his head. "Haven't you ever read a book?" he asked.

My eyes narrowed. "Apparently not the kind you have."

"It means that someone is partially unclothed," he said. "Undressed."

"Unclothed? As without clothing—i.e., naked?" I asked.

He shrugged. "If a towel counts as naked."

"A towel?"

He nodded. "A big one."

"So, Coral LaFavre was in Security Sam Davenport's cabin in 'dishabille,'" I murmured. "What do you know?"

"What's that? What did you say?" Joe asked.

"I said, I'm starving," I replied, thinking I had already said too much.

"So, where are we going to dine on this forbidden feast?" Joe asked. "Your cabin?"

I shook my head. "Not a good idea. I understand my sister is prone to motion sickness, and the smell alone would probably send her over the edge. Not exactly my idea of a congenial dining experience." Besides, I wasn't up for the ensuing tiff with Taylor should she walk into our little deep-fry fest. "And your stateroom is out due to other gastronomical issues," I said. "That leaves only one place I can be assured of eating this meal in peace and without being judged," I told Joe. "One place where a lovely thing called doctor-patient confidentiality trumps well-meaning familial interference and know-it-all-itis. A place I've stayed at before and give high marks for cleanliness and so-so marks for hospitality."

Joe nodded.

"Sickbay," we said.

CHAPTER TWELVE

It was dark when I awoke. Symphonic snoring from the cot next to me pulled me out of a dream state that had me sipping frozen margaritas on a soft blanket across a white sand beach with Captain Sparrow and Will Turner and nary an Elizabeth Swann in sight. Of course, in my dream my bikini-clad body had more in common with Knightley's twig of a frame than my more robust, farm-girl bone structure, but get real. Who puts themselves in a bikini in front of two aesthetically appealing pirates and—dream or no dream—gives herself a muffin top? Not this dream lover, that's for sure.

In my blissful dream world, Jack had just handed me his frequently malfunctioning compass, formed, rather cleverly for a dream, I thought, in the shape of a heart.

"Open it," he'd instructed, his dark eyes sporting more mascara than a working girl behind on her rent, locked on mine with an intensity that sent chills down my bare arms.

"Why?" I asked, finding my gaze drawn to his.

"You know why," Orlando Bloom aka William Turner whispered, his breath hot on the back of my neck.

"I do?"

"Open it," Orlando/William urged.

"What will I see?" I asked both men. "What will I see?"

"Why, the thing you want most, love," Johnny/Jack replied. "The thing you want most in the world."

I'd been about to lift the top of the heart-shaped compass, my eyes glued to the needle as it pointed out my heart's desire, when a loud sucking sound so not in simpatico with hot sands and hotter men pierced my dreamlike state more effectively than an urgent bladder issue that carries over into your dream state and you find yourself looking for a loo in lala land.

"Ever heard of Breathe Right?" I asked the codger in the next bed as I sat up in the darkened room and swung my feet over the side. "If you haven't yet, I'm sure your lady wife will bring them to your attention as soon as we hit port," I said, pulling my buff off my head and putting a hand to what I was sure could best be described as a shock-and-awe do. "I thought someone was after me with a buzz saw when I woke up," I told him, putting my fingers gingerly to my keepsake goose egg, and pleased to find it was now the size of one of those twenty-five cent bubblegum balls out of the machine at the video rental store—the one that never failed to drop a rancid white gumball every time I put my quarter in.

I flipped the bedside lamp on.

"Yeah, well, you pretty much keep up a running dialogue, complete with sound effects," Joe said. "I felt like I'd been caught in a time warp and was back listening to radio theater," he said.

I frowned. "I talk in my sleep?"

"Talk? No. Chatter like a mad hatter? Yes."

"What did I say, exactly?" I asked.

"It was kind of hard to tell," he said. "Between all the giggling and cooing," he added. "What were you dreaming about, anyway?"

"A pelvic exam," I snapped, still bearing a pretty big grudge because I'd been left in lover's limbo by nasal interruptus.

"It's good to see you haven't lost your sense of humor along with your memory," Joe said, and his reminder came just as I was about to make some smartass crack about how his timing had always sucked and provide examples of the same.

"It's good to know I've had a sense of humor all along," I replied. I looked at my watch. "Criminy. It's after eight!" I said. "I bet the family is frantic. Why did you let me drink that wine?" I said, pulling on my shoes.

"Let you? I don't remember you asking for permission. I no sooner had that bottle open than you had your cup handy."

Cup? I cringed. Clarity was returning.

"Tell me we didn't use urine specimen cups to drink wine out of," I begged.

"Okay," Joe said.

I frowned. "Okay, what?"

"Okay, I won't tell you we drank out of urine specimen cups," he agreed. "But it's not as if they were used. As a matter of fact, those cups are probably the most sterile thing we could have drank out of. Granted, the threads at the top of the cup posed a challenge to avoid dribbling initially, but after the first glass it was a breeze."

I winced. Okay. That was it. I was swearing off wine. No more wine.

"They've probably put out a security alert on the both of us," I told Joe. "And what are we going to say—'Oh, we just decided to impersonate food-service workers and raid the kitchen for appetizers, chicken wings and wine and drank too much and fell asleep in the infirmary'?"

"We're going to say we met up by accident, decided to have a bite to eat, stopped by the medical clinic, the doc thought you should rest, you did and I sat with you like a loving grandfather should," Joe said. "That's what we say."

I looked at him. "You're good," I told him.

He winked at me. "I learned from a master."

I nodded.

We policed up and down the area, gathered our things, and checked out of the clinic. A young girl at the desk gave us a bewildered look as we left. I couldn't blame her. We gave a whole new meaning to the term "odd couple."

I bade farewell to Joe in the hallway outside my cabin, letting myself in. Taylor was out again. Two nights in a row. A record for my sister. Miss Wang Chung Tonight she wasn't.

I dropped my bag on the desk when a gold and silver gift-wrapped box caught my eye. A card was stuck in the ribbon. It read: *Tressa.* I turned the envelope over and opened the flap and withdrew a small card. On the front was a horse's head.

Figured you could use these right about now, the card read, a single *M* the only signature.

I set the card down and picked up the package. I put it to my ear. No ticking. I shook my head. I'd seen way too many bad spy movies. Hands visibly shaking, I unwrapped the package slowly, my heart rate picking up speed as I tore the paper off. I tossed the paper aside and stared at the box of assorted—and pricey—Godiva chocolates. A gift. From Manny DeMarco. The first—and only—gift Manny had given me. Well, if you didn't count the demolition derby car he'd given me for the powder puff derby at the state fair.

But this gift? This gift was different. This gift was telling. This gift meant something. Holy Poseidon adventures! I was being courted by Manny DeMarco. In earnest! Talk about your complications. I needed to think.

I stripped and lathered up in the sarcophagus-like shower. I figured my legs were still good to go from the previous day's attentions. Besides, the chances of me seeing any action when I wasn't supposed to know Mr. Right from Mr. Rogers were slim to none. Unless . . .

I shoved all thoughts of chocolates and bad-boy bikers out of my head. As I stood beneath the hot steamy water, rinsing my body, I found my thoughts drifting to my earlier dream. Dreams had meaning. Subconsciously, they had significance. In my case, I suspected my dream had more relevance than I cared to admit.

Johnny/Jack and William/Orlando. Two sexy, desirable, gorgeous men. And both of them were hot for my body. (Okay, my head on Keira's body. Mere details.) And in my dream, there was a choice to be made.

I bit my lip. Could it be true? Was it possible? Was I really in lust with two men?

I turned the shower setting to cold and let the frigid water beat down. Lover's limbo, indeed, I thought as I let the sting-ing drops of moisture punish me. Try coward's quandary, I thought, shutting off the shower only when my backside felt like a block of ice.

I wrapped up in a towel and sat on the edge of my bed, staring at the box of chocolates.

"Open it and you'll see the thing you want most in life."

Fairy tales and hokum. And too much red wine. And I was not going near that chocolate!

Once I'd dried off, dressed in blue jeans, a wide pink belt, a crop-top white polo and white wedges, put on a face that wouldn't scare little children and braided my hair in a tight braid, I felt somewhat better about things. I was suffering from amnesia. I couldn't be expected to make major deci-sions concerning my future.

Of more immediate concern than my freak show of a love life, however, was this honeymoon harbinger of death I'd stumbled into. Every minute that went by, somewhere out there a woman could be walking arm in arm with her beloved mate, completely unaware he was waiting for the opportune moment to place a hand in the small of her back and send her tumbling overboard into the deep, dark waters of death. I shivered, cold again.

I thought about what I'd learned that afternoon—about Sam Davenport and Coral LaFavre. I wondered where Coral's husband had been while she was having a late lunch/early dinner/honey-nooner with the security chief. I recalled the vibes between Coral and David hadn't seemed all that lovey-dovey, newly wedded blissful to me. In fact, Coral had hit on Manny right in front of David. If Davenport and Coral were having an affair, I had to wonder just how long it had been going on and why Coral had married David Frazier Compton so recently if she had genuine feelings for Sam Davenport.

I shook my head.

It was worth keeping an eye on.

Two eyes.

I was just getting ready to leave the cabin when the phone rang. I picked it up. "Hello?"

"Tressa?"

"Yeah."

"Where have you been? We've been worried sick."

"Taylor?"

"Who else?"

"Where are you? I can hardly hear you."

"We're in the Fish Bowl lounge," Taylor said. "It's a karaoke bar. You've got to get up here. Our grandmother is bound and determined to perform. I need someone to help me talk her out of it."

I made a face. Little Miss Party Pooper was back. Maybe she needed to be set up with her male counterpart on board ship, Leo the Laugh-killer. Why shouldn't our grandma cut loose with a little karaoke? She was on her honeymoon, after all.

"I don't see the big deal," I told Taylor.

"Tressa. She wants to sing Madonna's *Like a Virgin*," Taylor said.

"I'm on my way."

I grabbed my Javelina bag and room key card, took one long last look at the box of chocolates and left.

Cruise ships are like huge, floating resort communities. Almost any service or entertainment you can imagine is within walking distance. Photo galleries, shops, movies, golf lessons, casinos, spa treatments, hair salons, music and dancing, Vegas-style shows, even body art is available.

I hadn't gone far when I felt uncomfortably certain I was being followed. I glanced behind me several times but didn't notice anyone suspicious.

I was passing the Casino Royale when raised voices got my attention.

"What are you thinking, Courtney? We're not made of money. We had to cut corners to afford this cruise in the first place. We're on a budget here, remember? And we didn't budget for the level of gambling you're doing. Or the losses."

I looked up to find Steve and Courtney Kayser standing just outside the casino. Steve ran a hand through his hair. Hands clenched in tight fists at her sides, Courtney's anger with her husband was apparent.

"I'm sick of living on your budget," Courtney hissed, "with you telling me what I can and cannot buy or do or have. I'm sick of it! Do you hear? Sick, sick, sick! This cruise was supposed to be fun. You don't hear Ben harping on Sherri every time she spends a dime."

"We're not talking about Ben and Sherri. We're talking about you and me. And we're talking dollars, not dimes, here, Courtney. Lots of them. I thought you wanted to save toward a bigger house. You're always complaining about how small our home is. I'm trying to make that happen. But I need your help. It takes two, babe. Two of us committed to our future. And I've got to tell you, lately I've begun to question the level of your commitment, Courtney," Steve said.

I watched the scene with some empathy. I'd been a frequent passenger on the S.S. Past Due, the sinking ship of financial fortunes, a time or two. And I'd read somewhere that money—or rather lack of it—was the number-one cause of problems and breakdowns in marriages. Sex? It was way down the list.

Steve's words seemed to have an effect. Courtney's fingers loosened up from their earlier tenseness. She paused and seemed to be considering her next words carefully.

"You're right, Steve," I heard Courtney respond. "You're right. I'm being selfish. I'm sorry. It's just that I've had to watch what I spend most of my life and I guess I got carried away by the whole luxury-cruise experience." She took his hand. "Forgive me?" she asked.

"Always," Steve replied.

I felt the sting of tears as I watched the couple embrace. There was a lot to be said for having someone handy to help bail the water out of a leaky boat. Teamwork. That's what it amounted to. Teamwork.

I walked up to the couple. Steve's arm rested on Courtney's shoulder.

"Hello again," I said to Courtney. "Remember me?"

She smiled. "I'm not the one who lost her memory," she replied with a weak smile. "Remember?" she added with a wink.

"Courtney told us what happened," Steve said. "Tough break."

"You have no idea," I said, "but thanks."

"You look much better than you did this afternoon, Tressa," Courtney observed. "How are you feeling? Any progress in the memory department?"

"No news there yet, I'm afraid," I told her, "but I'm actually feeling not bad. I took a catnap this evening, so that probably didn't hurt." While the wine probably didn't help.

"Where are you off to?" Courtney asked.

"Karaoke at the Fish Bowl." I nodded my head in the direction I was headed. "I guess some of my family is hanging out there. You're welcome to come along—if karaoke is your thing, that is," I said, figuring the invitation was one way of getting Courtney away from the casino and the temptation of the slots and blackjack tables.

Steve smiled his appreciation. "What do you say, Court? We haven't done karaoke in a long time."

She smiled, but it never reached her eyes. She patted his arm. "You go on, Steve. I just want to run to the cabin and freshen up first," she said, dabbing at the corner of her eye with a finger. "I'll meet you there," she promised.

"Okay," Steve said. "If you're sure," he added.

Courtney walked off and Steve sighed. He looked at me. "Marriage is hard work when both partners are rowing in the same direction," he said. "When they're paddling against each other?" He shook his head. "Sometimes you can be dead in the water."

I grimaced. It was a depressingly graphic picture of marriage.

"Sorry," I said, unable to think of anything else to offer. What did I know of marriage, anyway? Or rowing? I was Tugboat Tressa. I was powered by obstinacy and motored by bull-headedness. Oars optional.

"When you tie the knot, Tressa, be sure. Be sure you're ready and be sure he's ready. And most of all, be sure he's the one," Steve said. "Marriage is difficult enough when you are sure. It's a calculated risk when you aren't."

I nodded, not missing the fact that he'd used insurance-industry lingo in his last observation for my benefit.

We made our way to the Fish Bowl. I didn't have to look long to locate my gammy. Dressed in a silver sequined top and black pants, she stood to the left of the stage, apparently next up to perform. Taylor appeared to be trying to talk our gammy out of her chance in the limelight. At a large table close to the stage sat my brother, Craig, Kimmie, and Joe Townsend. My stride faltered when I caught sight of the dark-headed ranger-type sitting across from Craig.

Kimmie saw me and got up to greet me. "Thank goodness you're here," she said, grabbing my arm. "You're always so good at talking your grandmother out of something. Or into something, depending on how you want to look at it," she said. "I just hope you remember how you do it," she added, "or we're screwed."

"I thought maybe the folks would be here to spend some time with the family," I said sounding like one of the Corleone clan. "And Taylor didn't mention Rick Townsend would be here," I told Kimmie.

"She didn't?" Kimmie remarked with a wide-eyed, innocent look that I wasn't buying. "Oh, and who's this?" she asked, motioning to Steve.

"This is Steve," I said. "A new friend."

"Steve Kayser. Hi." Steve put out a hand. "My wife Courtney and I met Tressa and Manny at the Stardust last night," he said.

Kimmie's expression looked like she'd bitten down on gristle. "Oh, really," she said. "Tressa was with Manny? Isn't that sweet?"

"All the newlyweds, honeymooners, second-honeymooners and engaged couples were there," Steve said.

"No doubt someone's idea of a little joke," Kimmie said.

"Joke?" Steve repeated.

"Do you like sports, Steve?" Kimmie asked. "You look like someone who likes sports." She let go of me and took Steve's arm. "Come meet my husband, Craig. He loves sports. He can talk sports day and night. And frequently does." She pulled him to the chair she'd vacated and shoved him into it. "Steve, Craig. Craig, Steve. Steve, Rick. Rick, Steve. Steve, Joe. Joe, Steve," she made the frenzied introductions. "Steve happened to make the observation that he felt the Vikings were destined never to win the big one," she said. She squeezed Steve's shoulder. "Enjoy!" Then she tugged me to the stage.

"It took you long enough," Taylor said as we approached. "Why didn't you let anyone know you'd checked yourself back into the infirmary?" she asked.

"Joe knew," I pointed out. "Hey, you," I said, reaching out to pat my gammy on the shoulder, trying not to appear too comfortable and familiar. "Big night, huh? I bet you've got some really romantic song selected to croon to your new husband," I commented. "Too bad you can't talk Joe into a duet. That would really be romantic," I observed.

"It would?" Gram asked.

I gave Taylor and Kimmie each a pointed look.

"It would! It would!" they parroted.

"It would be sooo romantic, Gramma Hannah," Kimmie added.

"Joe can't carry a tune in a bucket," Gram said. "He's got what they call a tin ear."

"Isn't there a saying like 'Love's the greatest beautifier'?" I asked. "So, maybe all you'll hear is Joe's sweet, sweet love washing over you," I suggested, "and not all those sour notes."

Meet Tressa Jayne Turner, romantic philosopher.

"And Craig has our video camera, so he can record your dynamic duet for posterity," Kimmie said.

"Posterity who?" my gammy asked.

"Kimmie means you'll have a DVD keepsake of this special honeymoon moment, Gram," Taylor explained.

"And when you get back home, you can invite your friends over for cake and coffee and entertain them with your and Joe's moving Fish Bowl performance," I interjected, motioning for Joe to join us.

Meanwhile Gram pursed her lips. "What would we sing?"

"'Memories'?" Taylor suggested. "Are you comfortable with Barbra Streisand?"

"If I don't have to look at her while she's singing," Gram said. "That nose."

"How about that Elton John song, 'Don't Go Breakin' My Heart'?" Kimmie suggested. "That's got a beat to it."

"Didn't he sing that one with a man?" Gram asked, and I began to think we were going to be stuck with Grandma sailing into "Virgin" waters.

"'Endless Love,'" I heard, and turned to find Joe had joined us and taken my gammy's hand. "That's the one, Hannah. 'Endless Love.'" I watched as moisture entered my grandmother's eyes. She smiled.

"Trust you to come up with the perfect love song," Gram said, clutching his hand to her dry, rouged cheek.

My gammy's very own knight in shining armor, I thought as I watched their poignant exchange.

"This will be fun," Gram told her husband. "Just try to stay on key. Craig's recording the performance for posterior."

I shook my head. I loved my gammy.

Kimmie and Taylor wished them luck and returned to their seats at the table. I moved to stand along the wall to the side of the stage so I could watch the performance without others watching me. It promised to be an excruciating assault on the eardrums or one hell of a tearjerker. Or both. Either way, I planned to maintain a how-low-can-you-go profile during this lovey-dovey duet.

You see, although I don't cry very often, on those occasions that I do, I really let loose. And I'm not one of those neat, petite criers. I'm a messy bawler, complete with red splotches, loud hiccups and lots of snot. Not a pretty sight.

Gram and Joe were introduced and took the stage, microphones in their left hands and their partner's hand in the other. The music started. They hadn't finished the first two lines of lyrics and Messy Tressa was already reaching into her bags of tricks for tissues to mop up the tears.

It didn't matter that Joe really couldn't carry a tune in, over, above or inside a bucket, or that my gammy was always a few words ahead of her hubby. It didn't matter that Joe muffed the lyrics and Gram started singing his part. It didn't matter that Joe wore white tube socks and Reeboks. It simply didn't matter. It was the single most romantic thing I'd ever seen in my life.

Bogie and Bacall? Mere lightweights. Scarlett and Rhett? Couldn't hold a candle. Brangelina? Not even close. This? This was magic. This was endless love.

My nose began to run like someone had turned on the phlegm faucet. My jaws ached from the effort required to keep from wailing. I soaked the wad of tissues through and reached in my bag for more. A white linen hankie appeared in front of my puffy, red eyes.

"That bad?" Ranger Rick said, and I shook my head and took the proffered snot rag.

"That good," I said, and blew a long, loud honk into the handkerchief. "It's beautiful," I said, sniffling. "Absolutely beautiful."

"True enough," Townsend replied. He leaned one broad shoulder against the wall and looked down at me. "Just beautiful."

"Who'd have suspected?" I asked, mopping more moisture as Gram and Joe finished up their sweetheart serenade to each other and the crowd went wild. "Your granddad and my gammy are a hit. But I get dibs on the world tour," I said, trying to make the shift from Messy Tressa back to Cocky Cowgirl.

"World tour? Hmm. I think we'd better see an audition first, before we send you on tour," Rick said, and I gleaned his intent just about the time he snared my hand. "And no time like the present," he added, yanking on my arm as he pulled me toward the stage.

"Wait! What are you doing? I'm not going to get up on that stage and sing!" I argued.

"Yes, you are," he said.

I shook my head. "You're nuts. Look at me. I'm so blotchy I look like I've got some rare parasitic tropical disease. Rudolph would trade his flying ability for this red nose." I pointed at the proboscis in question. "I've so much mucus in my nasal passages I feel like I've got a deviated septum. Or two. And my head feels like it's stuffed with cotton balls. Plus this crowd doesn't look like it goes for hillbilly rock," I told him.

"That's okay," he said, "because we're not singing hillbilly rock."

I stared at him. "We? What do you mean 'we'? Are you going to sing?"

In all the time I'd known Rick Townsend, never once had I known him to get up and perform in a karaoke bar. Not once. He hated karaoke. Despised it.

"What? You don't think I can sing?" Townsend asked.

I shook my head and tried to pull away. "Everybody can sing but not everybody should," I pointed out. "Besides, you don't seem like the type who enjoys karaoke," I observed.

"I've never been a fan," he admitted.

"Then why are you planning to sing?" I asked. "And why are you insisting I join in your impromptu sing-along?"

"You'll see," he said.

"I'd rather see from the audience," I told him.

"You don't want me to be totally humiliated on this, my karaoke debut, do you?" Townsend asked. "I need you, Tressa. I can't do it alone. It's a duet."

"Ask Taylor," I suggested, "because I do not want to sing. I probably won't even know the song," I said. "Or have you forgotten the files that have been temporarily deleted from my memory banks?"

"They've got a teleprompter," he said. "And you've always been pretty good at improv," he said with a wink.

"No. Really." I resisted but didn't make any progress in forestalling Townsend's march to the stage.

Now don't get me wrong. I've had my musical moments. I performed quite a memorable rendition of "Shoulda Been a Cowboy" several years back at the Bud Tent at the state fair. Add to that "I Shot the Sheriff," "Mamas Don't Let Your Babies Grow up to Be Cowboys" and "Bang, Bang, You Shot Me Down" and I had a rather respectable karaoke cowgirl repertoire. (We won't talk about the time I had a beer or two too many and brutalized "Over the Rainbow." I got booed off the stage. The beer and peanuts were flying that night, I can tell you.)

I was still arguing with Townsend when the bright lights hit me and I realized I was on stage. The musical host, King Karaoke, slapped a microphone in my hand.

"Ladies and gentlemen, put your hands together for another dynamic duo, Rick and Tressa, who will be performing a song selected especially by Rick," he urged. "Made popular by Kenny Rogers and Dolly Parton, please welcome Rick and Tressa performing 'Islands in the Stream.' Take it away, dynamic duo!"

He passed the other microphone to Townsend. I just stood there and stared at Ranger Rick. The music started to build. He put his mouth to the mike. I still stared. He started singing the opening lyrics. I stared some more. He took hold of my hand and almost shoved the mike up my nose when he stuck it in front of my mouth.

But I couldn't make a sound. Yes, folks, it is possible. All of a sudden I made like a friggin' mime, gut-kicked by the lyrics coming out of Ranger Rick Townsend's mouth. Lyrics he'd hand-picked. Lyrics he sang. Lyrics he sang . . . to me!

And what those words said. Tender words of love that spoke of heartbeats and dedications. Of making love. With no one in between. Words that implored me to sail away with him to a different world. A world where the two of us start and end as one. A world where there was no need for words, and pain was muted when hearts were joined.

The clear, strong, sure tones that came from Ranger Rick shocked me, shook me to my very core, his hold on my hand so tight my fingers began to cramp. This was a side of Rick Townsend I never in my wildest dreams (and believe me when I say I've had some wild dreams about Ranger Rick) suspected existed. And it occurred to me that maybe this was a Rick Townsend who hadn't existed until now.

But why now? I wondered as his words proclaimed that this could be the real thing.

My hand holding the microphone began to palsy. Badly. So much, in fact, I smacked myself in the mouth, nearly chipping a tooth, but somehow didn't feel a thing. Didn't feel anything but stunned shock and amazed awe. And the suffocating certainty of time running out.

Why now? Because it was now or never, that's why, I thought. Time for Tressa to put up or shut up. High noon for Calamity Jayne Turner. Speak now or forever hold her yip.

Rick's dark, intense gaze didn't move away from me throughout the entire song. His rich baritone remained powerful, potent and passionate, weakening not one iota.

As he came to the end of the song, I felt my composure slipping. I couldn't believe what I was seeing—what I was hearing. What it meant.

Talk about those in peril on the sea! I, Calamity Jayne Turner, was being courted by not one man, but *two* men!

Then it happened. He came to the lyrics that were my undoing. " 'Sail away with me,' " he said. " 'Let's rely on each other.' "

From one lover to another, he confided.

It was too much. He was too much. And in that moment I knew. As sure as Joe would make another raid on *The Epiphany*'s galley, I knew. As certain that as soon as I got back to my cabin I was going to rip into that box of chocolates and gorge myself, I knew.

And that knowledge scared me to death.

So I did what had to be done. I tossed the microphone at King Karaoke, twisted my hand out of Townsend's tight grasp, jumped from the stage to the audience below and ran like a little girl.

Messy Tressa had left the building.

CHAPTER THIRTEEN

The next morning when Reveille blew, I woke with my fingers clutched around the box of chocolates.

I'd returned to the cabin prepared to rip the paper off the box with my teeth, close my eyes, select a surprise chocolate and begin to eat my way through those pricey crèmes and caramels, but for some reason, once I actually stood there, box in hand, fingers at the ready, I couldn't make myself open the box. Maybe because I knew this was one case where chocolate wouldn't comfort me. Wouldn't make me feel better.

Instead, I'd slipped into bed and held the box to my chest all night as I lay awake and pondered what kind of *Truman Show* extravaganza was playing out around me that cast me as the object of desire to two knock-down-drop-dead-gorgeous men.

A cockeyed cowgirl courtship fantasy, that's what.

I squeezed my eyes shut as I recalled Ranger Rick's shocking stage debut. For him to put himself out there like that, to profess his feelings so publicly, so compellingly, in such an uncharacteristic way, was the very last thing I'd expected from Rick Townsend. The very last.

I was still trying to wrap my head around all the implications. For me. For him.

For us.

And while I wasn't sure Townsend bought the whole

amnesiac Tressa story, either way, he seemed to be sending me a very clear message. And that message had the L-word in it.

I began to softly hum the music to the song that, from this day forward, would be known as "our song." No matter what happened. It would forever be our song.

"Oh. You're awake." Taylor walked out of the bathroom and greeted me, her gait a bit unsteady. Her eyebrows shot up when she saw the chocolate box in my hands. "Most people prefer to cuddle a pillow or a stuffed animal," she observed.

"I'm not most people," I said. "I'm me."

"Are you sure?" she asked. "Because the Tressa I know would have been on those chocolates like there was no tomorrow, especially given the dietary restrictions onboard. Yet, that box appears to be unopened. What gives?"

I sat up. "Maybe the fall down those stairs affected more than my memory," I said. "Maybe I'm becoming a different person."

"A person who no longer craves chocolate like a drug?" Taylor asked. "That's not a change. That's a miracle."

"They do happen," I said, thinking once again about Ranger Rick's crooning. "By the way, how are you feeling?" I asked, thinking it was really suspicious Taylor hadn't had any motion sickness since that first night.

She frowned. "I'm fine. Why do you ask?" she said as she fiddled with a baggie containing pills. Vitamins, I'd bet.

I shrugged out of the covers and put the box of candy at the foot of the bed. "Someone mentioned something about seasickness and I just wondered because you look just fine."

"I am fine," she snapped.

"Good. So . . . you've found something that calms the swells in your stomach. That's good. Do you mind me asking? What's your miracle remedy for motion sickness? Just in case I happen to be similarly afflicted at some point." I asked primarily because Taylor, the health and fitness nut, had bitten my head off when I'd suggested she take motion sickness pills, preferring instead to rely on gingersnaps and natural remedies. Since I hadn't seen any ginger tablets or cookies around the cabin, I smelled a rat. Of the hypocritical variety.

"I don't have a miracle remedy," she said, her movements jerky and spastic as she attempted to stuff the bag of tablets back into her carry-on case. A tablet rolled off the edge of the desk and onto the floor.

"Really?" I said, jumping to scoop it up. "What is this?" I asked, putting the pill up to the light and recognizing it as one of the same motion sickness pills the family had tried to get Taylor to take for the plane rides. And the car trips. And the shuttle.

"A vitamin," Taylor hissed.

"This isn't the vitamin you took yesterday," I said. "You broke that one in two and took one half in the morning and the other half at bedtime. No, this is something else," I said. "Maybe something for bloating and cramps?" I added. "Or is it a secret cure for motion sickness?"

"It's none of your business, that's what it is," Taylor replied, snatching the pill from my fingers.

I put my hands up. "Sorry to offend," I said. "I was just making polite conversation."

"You don't 'just' do anything," Taylor said.

"Sooorrreee," I said again. "So, what happened at the Fish Bowl after . . . after I left?" I asked, deciding if I wanted to get any information from Taylor I'd better not risk ticking her off.

"You mean after you ran off and left the guy who'd just sung his heart out to you on that stage looking like a fool? You mean after that?" she said, zipping her bag and putting it in the closet.

I winced. "What was I supposed to do given the circumstances?" I asked, hoping she would understand I meant the memory thing. And I did. If I had reacted in any way other than I had, the jig might well have been up. And because I knew that fall down the stairs was no act of clumsiness on my part, and because I suspected it had everything to do with someone thinking I knew more than I did about who was planning a send-off for their sweetheart, I also knew I had to keep my cover intact. Shaky as it was. To have reacted to Ranger Rick's blow-me-down performance in any way other than exiting center stage would have made it clear I was remembering things. Remembering people. Remembering how Ranger Rick made me feel. And to remember before I'd discovered whom I'd overheard was to put not only me at risk, but possibly everyone close to me.

"I don't know what you should have done," Taylor said. "Maybe acknowledge the courage it took for him to do that. Express some gratitude. Make some kind of response. You left him floundering on that stage like a bloody mackerel," she told me.

I sighed. "You don't understand what I'm going through," I said.

"No. *You* don't understand," Taylor replied. "You don't understand that this may well be your last chance. Your last opportunity. The end of the road for you and Rick. I'm telling you here and now and, memory or no memory, don't forget it! The heart doesn't lie. Regardless of what your brain knows or doesn't know, your heart will always tell you the truth. If you take the time to listen to it."

I sank back down on the edge of the bed. Good gawd. My sister could be one of those motivational speakers corporations bring around to energize the working class. She could write books. Sell DVDs. Make millions motivating people.

"Just think about it, will you?" she said.

I nodded. "Was . . . everybody upset with me?" I asked.

Taylor shrugged. "Kimmie was totally ticked off, and Joe kept muttering about people who would take a risk for beef but not for love—whatever that meant. Your friend Steve left to go look for his wife, who was a no-show. He was pretty peeved. At her, not you."

"And . . . Rick?"

She hesitated. "He met up with a friend from college who is on the cruise. I imagine they caught up."

I frowned. "You imagine?"

She shrugged again.

"They left."

Oh, goody. Brianna to the rescue.

"So, what's on tap today?" I asked.

"Weigh-ins. Various competitions," she said. "For all kinds of prizes."

This got my attention. "What kinds of prizes?" I asked.

"Don't you ever read your daily bulletin?" she said, frisbeeing the pamphlet in my direction. "They're giving away tons of things. From exercise bikes to treadmills. Steppers to plasma TVs."

I snapped to attention. "Plasma TV?" I said.

Taylor nodded. "Wide-screen."

"How big?" I asked.

"I don't know. Huge. Why?"

"I don't have a wide-screen plasma TV, do I?" I asked.

She shook her head.

"I didn't think so. That's why."

"You're not thinking of competing for that TV, are you?" she asked.

"Why shouldn't I?"

"Your injury. Your head—"

"Is much better." Besides, how strenuous could the competition be? Most of the competitors were not in that great of shape. Okay, me included.

"I don't know, Tressa. You'd better check with the doctor first and see if he clears you," Taylor suggested. "Then maybe if it's something fairly low-impact, it might be okay. It's probably safer than leaving you to roam free throughout the ship," she admitted.

Nice.

She got ready to leave. At the door, Taylor stopped and looked back at me. "About Rick," she began. "You'll think about what I said?"

I nodded.

Like I could think of anything else—any*one* else but Rick Townsend.

I showered and dressed quickly, putting my swimsuit on beneath a white T-shirt trimmed in brown, the silhouette of a cowgirl in chaps, boots, and spurs on the front that read *Cowgirl Attitude*. I slid my legs into a cute denim skirt and stuck my feet into brown Skechers. I stuck my hair in a ponytail, put my face on and tied the black and red buff around the top of my head.

During my shower, I'd shifted my attention to the primary dilemma at hand: discovering who was out to maim their mate on *The Epiphany*. If I was to expose that person, I could regain my memory and set about reclaiming my life—and all that entailed. But how did I begin the process of elimination?

I grabbed a notepad and wrote down the names of all the possible suspects. I'd already established that the cruise culprit more than likely had to be at the Stardust reception that first night. I listed the names of the couples that had been present. The buff I'd ripped off the head of my attacker during the sickbay assault corroborated the fact that the villain in this oceanic odyssey was one of the Scallywags—the same group who'd gathered at the Stardust. The same group who'd heard my brilliant "I don't know who you are but I know what you want to do" red alert.

I looked at the names.

I crossed Dolph and Major off the list—for obvious reasons. Vic and Naomi had split the Stardust before my impromptu pitch so it was probably safe to eliminate them. Next were Tariq and Monique. I didn't know enough about their situation to make a judgment one way or the other. I somehow had to get close to Monique and ask some probing questions before I could eliminate them.

Then there was Steve and Courtney. I couldn't think of Steve as wanting to off his wife. He seemed to genuinely love her and want a future with her, despite the fact that she liked to spend money they didn't have. People who are thinking of killing their wives for profit within a few days don't talk about budgeting so they can afford a bigger home several years down the road. Unless, of course, they thought that would throw the suspicion off them once the spouse was dead. You know, "Here we were, saving and planning for our future together and now we have no future." That sort of thing. I'd learned firsthand that people could be tricky.

Next on tap, Ben and Sherri. (I still got the urge for ice cream whenever I said their names.) I hadn't had the chance to visit with Ben much, but Sherri had seemed nice. Quiet, but nice. I'd also need to carve out some time with Sherri to scope out possible motives and clues.

And that left Coral and David. I wrote their names down and circled them. Off to the side I added Sam Davenport's name. An affair? Coral's dishabille certainly pointed to that. If David knew of Coral's feelings for Sam, he might be afraid she would leave him—and since he acted as her agent, that would leave him high and dry and on the street. But why pick this cruise? A cruise where Samuel Davenport was head of security? So maybe that meant David Frazier Compton didn't know about Sam Davenport. That didn't mean David wouldn't benefit from her death. And their behavior toward one another hadn't spoken of deep, romantic feelings for each other. More like a business relationship.

My task was set. The first order of the day was to sit down with Monique and Sherri and have a talk about financial futures and married life. What woman didn't like to dish about her husband? And I just happened to have your basic sympathetic ear.

Item two on the agenda? Winning a wide-screen plasma TV. Sweet.

My gurgling stomach reminded me the pilfered repast shared with Joe the night before had long since made it through my digestive tract and I was in need of a nutritional replacement. I grabbed Harry Javelina, slung him over one shoulder and went in search of breakfast.

I managed to replenish my dwindling reserves with whole wheat pancakes that were more than a little hard to swallow, make-believe eggs I ate with my eyes closed, turkey bacon I tried to delude myself was the real thing, and strawberries doused with Splenda. Two cups of decaf did nothing to get wind in my sails as I prepared myself for my roles as truth seeker and prizewinner.

I made my way to the contest area. Late, as usual. I figured, with such a nifty prize, by now they had all the contestants they needed.

"Hey, Tressa! Come join us!"

I looked in the direction of the call and saw Courtney and Sherri and their spouses waving at me. Nearby sat Tariq and Monique and Dolph and Major. Everyone had a buff on. Everybody, that is, except Steve. My hand went unconsciously to the buff I wore. My legs shook as I made my way to the group of cruisers.

"Hello," I said. "What's going on?"

"You should've been here earlier to watch the menfolk compete for a plasma TV," Courtney said. "It was hysterical, wasn't it, Sherri?"

Sherri nodded her agreement. "My husband sure made a big splash," she said without much emotion.

"Literally," Steve added.

I looked at him, not sure what to think of the fact that he was the only one at the table not sporting a buff.

"Oh?"

"They're holding a 'plank race,'" Courtney explained. "They have this thing that resembles a balance beam set up across the pool and you put on a grass skirt and swimsuit top, some oversized sunglasses, walk to the other side, grab a tropical drink and a rice cake and get back to the other side without falling into the pool. Once you've made it to the other side, you have to shuck the tropical get-up and hit the buzzer."

"Plus you have to have finished drinking the drink and eating the rice cake before you can jump off the plank and disrobe," Sherri added.

"Good grief," I said. "The men really have to wear grass skirts and bra tops?"

"It was the bra that did Ben in," Steve said with a chuckle. "He apparently hasn't enough experience removing them," he said.

Ben smiled.

"How did you fare, Steve?" I asked.

"I completed the mission," he said.

"You won the TV?"

He shook his head. "The people with the four best times compete in the finals," he said.

"They run four races at the same time with four separate timers," Sherri told me.

"Too bad you took that fall or you could compete," Courtney said.

"I'm pretty well healed—except for the memory glitch, that is," I explained. "And it sounds like pretty harmless fun. Not much damage water can do," I added. "Have you ladies tried your luck?"

Courtney's head snapped up and I hoped she didn't mistake my words for a gambling reference.

"I did," Courtney said. "But Sherri didn't want to. Monique's round should be coming up. Why don't you see how much longer it will be, Monique? Sherri, you should go with Tressa and sign up. It'll be fun," she said.

"Yes, do, Sherri," I said. "Please."

She looked at me and at her husband.

"Go for it, Tare," he said.

"Why not?" she said.

Monique, Sherri and I headed to the registration table. Once Sherri and I filled our cards out, I steered the women to a vacant table.

"Why don't we just wait here?" I said. "Monique will be competing any time. It'll give us a chance to visit. So, what do you and Tariq do again?" I asked.

"We're actors," Monique said.

"That's exciting. Would I have seen anything you were in?" I asked.

Monique shook her head. "You wouldn't remember if you did, but no, probably not. We're typecast. Need a porker? Call Tariq or Monique," she said.

"You're very pretty," I said.

"I do some modeling," Monique admitted. "Plus-size, of course. That's where I make most of my money."

"Do you live in L.A.?" I asked. She nodded. "Wow, it must be hard trying to make ends meet there."

"We do okay," she said. "More than okay, actually. It's just that we're not happy with the roles we get. We're both talented. We could get some substantive roles if we weren't so heavy. That's what this cruise is about. Less really is more," she said. "Especially in the entertainment industry."

I nodded. "I can understand you wanting the meatier roles," I said, and Sherri and Monique looked at each other. "Uh, I didn't mean that the way it sounded," I apologized, "I just meant that I get that you want to beef up your acting resume."

I tried to reel in the words before they got to my tongue and past my mouth and were cast out onto waiting ears, but, once fully engaged, my motormouth is nigh impossible to reel back in. Sometimes I was such a ditz.

"Are you for real?" Monique said.

I nodded. "I'm afraid so. And it looks like I'm an open-mouth-insert-big-fat-humongous-foot kind of gal," I said, realizing as I said it that I'd done it again. "Sorry," I squeaked.

She nodded. "I played a character a lot like you in a cable series," she said. "Nice girl. Good intentions. But she always seemed to say the wrong thing or do the wrong thing even though she meant well."

"What happened to the character?" I asked.

"She got killed off at the end of season one," Monique said.

I managed a weak smile. "So . . . how long have you been married, Monique?" I asked. Her gaze slid away. "Monique?"

"This is . . . awkward," she said, biting her lip.

"What is?" I asked.

Monique looked at Sherri.

"Tariq and I are not exactly married," she said.

"Engaged?" I asked.

She shook her head.

"We actually won the cruise," she admitted. "We were entered when we paid for a membership to a local fitness club. If you were newly married or planning to be married, you were entered into this contest to win this cruise. We never in a million years thought we would win. When we did and saw what the cruise offered, we couldn't pass it up. So, you see, we kind of won it under false pretenses," she said.

"You're not married?"

She shook her head.

"Not engaged?"

"Nope."

"Planning to become engaged?"

"Not in a million years. At least not to Tariq."

I looked at Sherri. She seemed as lost as I was.

"I'm not getting the big picture here," I said, and Monique winced.

"Tariq and I? We're brother and sister," Monique said.

I sat back in my chair. "Brother and sister?" I repeated. "You and Tariq are brother and sister?"

She nodded. "There was a special membership price for

couples," she said, "so we pretended we were married. Like I said, we never for a minute thought we'd win the cruise, but once we did we thought somehow it was meant to be."

There was a lot of that meant-to-be stuff going around.

"You aren't gonna out us, are you?" she asked Sherri and me.

I shook my head. "Not a chance," I said. "Sherri?"

"Mum's the word," she agreed.

"Thanks. Thanks a lot," Monique said.

Her race was called over the loudspeaker and she rose. "So, no objections if I compete for the TV?" she asked and smiled.

"Go for it," I said. "But I reserve the right to hate you if your time is better than mine," I told her.

Monique's eyes twinkled. "Fair enough," she said.

"Good luck!" Sherri called as Monique left.

So. Tariq and Monique were siblings. That meant I was down to three possible couples. Coral and David. Courtney and Steve. And Ben and Sherri. I mean, Sherri and Ben.

"So, Sherri, tell me a little bit about you and Ben," I said, thinking I might be able to narrow the field even more. "Where do you live? What do you both do for a living? How long have you been married? What brought you on this cruise?"

Sherri seemed overwhelmed by my battery of questions.

Hey, give me a break here. I'm a reporter, remember? I ask questions. That's what I do.

"We live in western Kansas in a little town called Farley. You wouldn't have heard of it. Farley's the kind of town where you celebrate a losing sports season just because you had enough people go out. Farley's the kind of community where someone buys a winning lottery ticket and loses it. Farley's the kind of community that holds a Fourth of July celebration and nobody comes."

I grimaced. In others words, Armpit, USA.

"You don't sound as if you like it much there," I said.

"I don't. I want to move back to Wichita but Ben is . . . resistant. We've been married almost five years," she said. "We both worked at a grocery store back home. Ben worked in the meat department. I was a checker working my way through community college. We started dating. Fell in love. Got married. We did everything together. Including, unfortunately, gaining weight."

Something about the way Sherri spoke struck me as strange. Maybe it was the short, clipped sentences. Maybe it was because she spoke in past tense. Maybe it was the monotone delivery. Whatever it was, it disturbed me.

"Sherri? Is everything okay?" I asked. "For being on a fun-filled cruise, you seem really sad," I observed.

She didn't respond.

"Are things okay with you and Ben?" I asked.

She smiled.

"That depends on the day," she said. "And sometimes, the hour," she added. "It's just been different lately," she said.

"How so?"

"I don't know. I'm probably imagining things. I know I don't look like it, but I have a pretty active imagination," she said. "Because most of the time things are okay. And since we've been on this cruise, Ben has been incredible. Really incredible, so I have hope. But there are times when . . ."

"Yes?"

She seemed to search for the right words.

"There are times when Ben almost seems like a stranger," she admitted.

I reached over and patted her hand. "Haven't you heard? Men are from Mars, women are from Venus," I told her. "Most of the time I'm convinced they're an alien species introduced here to drive the rightful inhabitants of this planet whacko," I told Sherri.

She smiled.

"I understand why you say that. News has it you've got a little shipboard intrigue going on," she said, and I gasped.

"You know?" I said.

She nodded.

"Everyone does. Why? Was it a secret?"

"Uh, I was under the impression only a very few people knew," I told her. "How'd it get out?" I asked.

"Get out? You and Manny told us you were engaged that night at the Stardust. But, of course, you'd have forgotten that. Then Steve told us about that guy named Rick singing to you last night. How romantic it must be to have two men competing for your hand," she said. "It's like something you read in a book or see in a movie."

Duh. I did a mental head-slap of myself. She was talking about Tressa's Bermuda Love Triangle, not Tressa's Shipboard Sleuth Fest. Man, talk about your scarifying double features.

"And with you not remembering either one of them, it makes for a powerful story," Sherri continued.

As many works of fiction were.

"It's a bit surreal," I admitted.

"I'm sure," she said. "I'd be freaking out if two hotties were after me. How do you remain so calm?"

"Wine," I mumbled.

The loudspeaker blared. It appeared our time to compete for the plasma had arrived.

"Where is the TV we win?" I asked a cute sailor as I passed the registration table. I kind of wanted to see what I was making a fool of myself over.

He handed me a postcard-sized sheet of paper. It showed a 52-inch high-def TV.

"This is it?" I turned the card over.

"You don't actually get the TV," he said. "It's a certificate for a TV. You redeem it at Electronics Central," he said. "They have outlets all over the country."

"Sweet," I said.

We were ushered to our respective starting places. Sherri was on the plank to my right. I decided to strip down to my swimsuit, figuring it would be easier to pull on a grass skirt and swimsuit top that way. I always wear a black one-piece. I've heard black slenderizes.

I looked to my left and was suddenly blinded. I almost fell in the pool, disqualifying myself in the process. I couldn't believe what I was seeing. Standing in the next lane, wearing baggy neon-green swim trunks, ear plugs, and a black and white Hawkeyes visor was Joltin' Joe Townsend. My eyes crinkled from the light reflecting off all that white skin.

"What do you think you're doing?" I asked, putting a hand to my eyes to block the glare.

"Same as you, I expect," Joe said, hitching up his trunks.

"You've got to be kidding. You're going to pull on a grass skirt and wiggle into a bra in front of all these people?" I asked.

He nodded. "And do it in the best time," he predicted.

"You're going to walk across a three-inch-wide wet bridge in a grass skirt and Reeboks?" I said. "You won't make it two yards."

"Who said I was walking?" he asked, and I looked at him.

"Whaddya mean? Of course you have to walk."

"Who said? All they said was you had to get from one end to the other without falling in."

"Yes. So?"

"So I plan to scoot across," he said.

My forehead did one of those crinkly numbers plastic surgeons make a fortune off erasing the creases from. "Scoot?"

"Scoot."

I tried to get a mental picture of how that might look. It wasn't pretty.

"You mean to scoot along the bar with it between your legs? Do you think that's a good idea?" I asked.

"Why shouldn't it be?"

"Isn't that sort of thing hard on your . . . on your . . . on the . . . prostate?" I asked.

"Don't you worry about my prostate, girl. Worry about how you're going to keep those thighs from slip-sliding away," he said.

I frowned. "That's not very nice," I observed. "You don't normally talk to me like that, do you?" I asked.

"Not at all," he said. "That's mild. I'm taking pity on you. You with your memory issues and all," he said, a glint in his eye telling me I wasn't fooling him. My bizarre request that had Joe delivering room service trays no doubt had fanned the fires of skepticism. And there was no telling what I'd divulged over that bottle of vino.

"Oh? And how would I respond?" I asked. "Would I reply in kind with something like 'Well, it's only fair you be required to wear a shirt since the light bouncing off your torso will blind the rest of the contestants and give you an unfair advantage'? Would I normally say something like that?"

"Fast learner," he snapped.

"Don't you like already have a TV?"

"Don't you?"

"I don't know. Do I?" I said, playing the game.

"You do. In fact, you already have a widescreen high-def TV," the old salt lied to my face. "So why don't you step aside and let someone else have a chance to win this prize?"

"One can never have too many TVs. Besides, there's always the chance if I did win it, I might give it away as a gift—you know, seeing as how you said I already had one and all."

"Won't matter. You aren't going to win," he said.

Okay, so there it was. The slap on the face with the glove. The challenge. I looked at my opponent. He was wiry, yes. But I had the advantage in age. And cunning? Well, that one was up for grabs.

We lined up on our marks. We would be required to grab a grass skirt and swim top from a common pile, don the grass skirt, secure it at the waist so it wouldn't end up around our ankles, put a bra top on and fasten it, and secure the over-sized sunglasses on our noses. Then, we would make our way across the planks, grab a drink in one hand and a rice cake in the other and while we made our way back across the "pirate planks" we had to eat the rice cake and drink our beverage without spilling a drop or falling off the plank. Once we reached the other side of the pool, we had to shuck the grass skirt and swimsuit bra top and hit the buzzer to stop our time.

I looked over at Joe. He cracked his knuckles. I did one of those neck-popping numbers. Let the games begin! May the best plank-walker win.

CHAPTER FOURTEEN

The starter gun sent us scrambling toward the pile of clothing. Besides Joe and Sherri, I was shocked to see red-headed party pooper, Lou, thundering toward the garment heap. I snatched a grass skirt from the pile and wrapped it around me, securing it with the drawstring. I snagged a hot pink bra top (naturally) by a strap and yanked . . . only to discover Lou had hold of the other.

"Let go!" I hissed.

"You let go!" he hissed right back.

"I can't. Hot pink's my trademark color," I said, pulling harder on the bra.

"Take the orange one!" he snapped, increasing his hold on the elastic.

"Orange! Orange makes me look sallow!" I yelled, pulling back on the bra so hard its size probably stretched from a 34C to a 36D. "Besides, it's not your size!" Mine, either, but how was he to know? I gave the item of apparel one more tug and it came loose, the elastic snapping back to bite my arm.

I stuck my arms through the loops, fasteners in front as I ran back to my plank, hooking the bra as I ran. I decided to leave it backwards, figuring it would save me time when I disrobed. I stuck a pair of big red plastic sunglasses on my nose and hurried toward my plank, stunned to find Joe Townsend had not only gotten himself garbed, but was already straddling his plank looking like something out of a cross-dressing spoof gone way bad. And he'd partnered a green grass skirt with a pink-polka-dotted purple swim top. Ugh. How gaudy.

"How'd you get dressed so fast?" I asked, stepping up on my beam.

"I didn't take time to quibble over colors like some people," he stated, beginning his awkward trek across the board.

I felt confident in my balancing act abilities. While I'd left the dance and gymnastic lessons to Taylor—I was kicked out of tumbling for harassing Dallas Boston, not only because of his name but because he was the only he in tumbling class— I'd played enough high school sports to compensate for missing out on the finer arts of dance tutelage.

I decided to use what I called the side-to-side method, being more familiar with this from my basketball guarding drills. I eased out onto the plank, curling my toes under just so to grip the plank as I made my way across, thinking I was sunk for sure if I got a toe cramp. I kept my concentration focused on the task at hand—or rather at feet—knowing I was competing against the clock rather than for a win, yet realizing if I was beaten here, I was out of contention.

"Hey, look at blondie there with the backwards boobs!" I heard, and my head snapped up. I swayed forward and almost fell in the drink. I regained my balance and frowned. That voice sounded familiar. Too familiar. The other motormouth in my family. My brother, Craig.

A long, hot-mama whistle sounded.

"That's a pretty impressive rack," another voice commented, and I felt my chest puff up with pride. That is, until the next observation.

"I always did have a thing for hot pink."

That, if I wasn't mistaken, was courtesy of my brother's cohort in adolescent comedy, Fish Bowl heartthrob, Ranger Rick. The duddly duo. They were torpedoing my chance at a high-def telly.

I blocked out the catcalls, guffaws and giggles, as well as the distracting grunts coming from the old guy next to me. We were still in a dead heat, with the first half of the race nearing its end. I had it all planned out. I'd stuff the rice cake into my mouth—one of the few benefits of having a mouth that can accommodate a Whopper—and chase it down with my drink, then haul my uni-breasted self across that plank and to the finish line.

I made it to the other side first, reaching out to take a rice cake the size of a saucer and a plastic cup full of a pink beverage with a hot pink umbrella sticking out of it. My favorite colors. A good sign. I decided to get a modest lead on my opponents, who were all nearing the end of the first leg—or, in Joe's case, already accepting the rice cake and beverage. His drink, I noticed, was orange.

I took three side steps back toward the other end.

"Don't choke to death trying to get that rice cake down," I called back to Joe. "I don't suppose you've had occasion to eat very many prior to this."

"Don't worry about me," Joe said. "I've probably put more of these away than you have."

I would have shaken my head but couldn't risk it. Instead, I continued my sidestep mode of movement. I went a few more yards when I decided it was time to consume the rice cake. I shoved it in my mouth, took a jumbo bite and started chomping, breaking off more and jamming it into my mouth.

"Wow! Look at 'Hot Pink Hooters' take a run at that rice cake," I heard. "She's got a set of jaws on her! Reminds me of a wood chipper the way she's cramming that cake in. Hope she doesn't chomp a finger off while she's at it."

I wanted to rip the speaker a new one, but my mouth was full of dry, crackly, sawdusty, rice cake. A piece of the cake protruding from the front of my mouth began to fall and I had to reach up to shove it back in. I started to sway forward and backward. Forward and backward.

"Oooh! She's gonna fall!"

I struggled to chew and swallow and regain my balance, the weight of the full glass screwing up the weight distribution. I finally got enough of a handle on the swaying to start moving again. I had no idea how close anyone except Joe was—and he was breathing down my neck.

I kicked it into gear, thinking now that I had recovered my balance, I'd simply move to the end of the plank, down my drink there, jump down, strip and enjoy the sweet taste of victory.

I sidestepped my way to the very edge of the board, gaining a modest lead over Joe who had paused to finish off his drink. I lifted my own glass and prepared to make short order of the pink lemonade. I raised the glass to my lips, took a long gulp—and my taste buds rebelled. I started to cough. My eyes watered. Ye gods! Grapefruit juice! Again! What were the friggin' odds?

Hold! I commanded the contents of my mouth that were headed for the escape hatch. Hold! I forced myself to swallow the tasty treat that rivaled a bologna-and-orange-juice combo for flavor and texture, and saw movement to my right. Joe, the straddler, was making up the distance between us in good time.

I looked at the half-full glass of grapefruit guts. (Regardless of what you hear, I really am a "glass-half-full" kind of gal.) "You've discovered dead bodies," I told myself. "You've exposed murderers and arsonists. You've faced kidnappers, evil clowns and campus kooks. You can do this!"

I put my free hand out and carefully brought it to my nose, reaching out to pinch both nostrils together tightly. I was losing valuable time, but I'd end up retching or gagging up the foul brew if I didn't pinch myself shut. I raised the glass to my lips, tipped my head back and poured it in. The juice burned the back of my throat when it hit but I kept chugalugging until I managed to drain the glass.

I slowly brought my hands away from my face. My nostrils

were stuck closed but I didn't care. I raised my hands above my head in impending victory, only to discover Gilligan had dismounted from his beam and was yanking at the drawstring of his grass skirt.

I leaped from my plank, tearing at my own skirt's waistline, untying the bow I'd made. I let my skirt drop amid cheers and some jeers. All that was left was to remove the swimsuit bra top.

Piece of cake. I wore bras all the time. And due to my clever but somewhat humiliating wardrobe reversal, guess who would be laughing now! A quick flip of the hooks and . . .

I frowned.

A quick flip of the hooks and . . .

Dang! The hooks weren't cooperating. I fumbled around and finally got one unhooked, but it was taking too much time—time enough for Joe to have dropped his own grass skirt and set to work on his Purple People-eater bra. He whipped it around, cups facing backwards, and started to work.

Whatever happened to old guys and arthritic fingers? I asked as I gave up on the hooks and eyes and began to yank the thing over my head. I had one arm out and was freeing the other when I heard a buzzer.

I looked up.

Joe was still struggling to free himself. But Party Pooper Lou? He stood by his buzzer beaming from ear to ear.

I yanked my remaining hand free and pulled the bra up over my head and tossed it back. I raced to my own buzzer and was about to pound it when another buzzer sounded. I looked over and saw Sherri smile in my direction. I grimaced, knowing my chance of cinching a place in the final round was gone, baby, gone. All that was left was to elevate myself from abject humiliation by besting Gilligan.

I saw Joe move toward his buzzer. I slammed my palm down on mine milliseconds before Joe did the same.

"Woo hoo! I win! I win!" I said, dancing a little jig. "I beat you!"

"No, you didn't," Joe said. "I beat you."

I stopped my happy dance.

"What do you mean, you beat me? I clearly hit the buzzer first," I pointed out.

"That's right, but you didn't undress first."

I stared at him. "Are you going dirty-old-man on me?" I asked, and he shook his head in disgust.

"You're still wearing the swim top," he said.

I stared some more. "What are you talking about?" I said. "I shucked that puppy already."

He put a hand toward me, reaching around to the back of my head. I felt a slight tug on my hair as he brought his hand back. I looked down to find the hot pink swim top hanging over my shoulder, a hook caught on my hair.

"Disqualified!" I heard over the loudspeaker as the gathered crowd roared.

I freed the hot pink swim accessory from my hair and flung it at Party Pooper Lou.

"You liked it so much. Be my guest," I said, making my way back to the table where I'd left my bag, silently vowing never again to touch a drop of grapefruit juice.

"Tough break, sis." My brother, Craig, handed me my bag. "But I enjoyed the show."

I grabbed my bag from him. "I might've done better had I not had to listen to sophomoric bilge-rat reprobates and their adolescent jokes," I told him. "It's sad how some people care nothing for the feelings of others." I patted his arm. "I'm so glad you're my brother because I know you wouldn't dream of doing anything like that. Would you . . . Greg?"

Craig's amused grin went bye-bye.

"Uh, it's Craig," he said. "And me? No, I would never heckle someone like that. In fact, I wanted to punch their lights out."

"What a good brother I have," I said. "One who looks

after me when I'm scared and vulnerable. Who's there to champion me when I'm down. I'm a lucky, lucky girl."

"Right," Craig said, his expression priceless. "Right."

Kimmie joined us and I smiled at her. "Well, it's been real," I said, "but as I was about to tell brother Greg here, my job is done." I was thinking what I needed most was a nice quiet corner to collect my thoughts. Since my chat with Monique and Sherri, the landscape of this lethal-lover cruise had altered significantly, with three men left vying for the role of cold-blooded killer.

"Aren't you going to hang around for the final round?" Craig asked.

"Why should I?"

"You might get a kick out of it," he said.

"I don't think I'm up for seeing any more pasty wrinkled men frolic around in grass skirts and Wonderbras," I told him.

"What about a lean mean fighting machine ranger-type?"

The query came in the form of a whisper accompanied by a hot blast of moist heat on the back of my neck.

I shivered. "What are you talking about?" I turned and saw Rick. "You don't mean . . ."

"I smoked the clock during my round," Townsend said. "Burned it."

"You? You're in the final?" I asked.

He nodded.

"You put on a grass skirt?"

He nodded.

"You wore a bikini top?"

He nodded.

"You're still in the running to win the high-def TV?" I said.

"Aye-aye," he said.

"Congratulations," I said, thinking this was so-not-fair.

"You gonna cheer me on?" he asked.

After last night? I ought to run far, far away.

"Maybe," I said.

"And you're gonna root for me?" he asked.

I frowned. "Who else would I root for?"

A not-so-subtle cough from my sister-in-law got my attention. Her eyes shifted to the right three or four times.

I followed the direction of her peepers. There he was. Six-feet-three, shirtless and ripped, Manny DeMarco stood across the deck staring right at me. My tongue got heavy and thick in my mouth. Oh. My. God. The guy was a mountain. A chiseled mountain. A sculpted rock. A hand-carved masterpiece.

"Tressa? Are you all right?" Rick asked.

Was I?

Pressure on my toes from Kimmie's foot pierced my stupor.

The loudspeaker chirped and Kimmie grabbed my arm. "That's your cue, Rick," she said. "Get out there and leave him in the dust. Just rip him up, annihilate him, humiliate him, destroy him!" she said. "Take no prisoners!"

I looked at Kimmie. She really didn't want to wear that diaper at the wedding.

"Down, girl," Craig told Kimmie, giving her a puzzled look. "It's just a friendly competition," he added.

"There's nothing remotely friendly about this competition. Nothing at all . . . Greg!" she added, giving Craig a look that made him take a step back.

"Kimmie! What's gotten into you?" he asked.

"What's gotten into me?" Kimmie's voice sounded shrill and fragmented. "What's gotten into me? Thanks to you, nothing! That's what's gotten into me. Nothing! I'm an empty vessel! Do you hear me! An empty vessel!" She let go of my arm and dashed at her eyes. "And I'm tired of waiting, Craig Turner," she said and turned and left.

"Kim? Kimmie? Kimberly!" Craig took off after her, and I stood there looking after them.

"And men think women are clueless," I commented.

"Not all the time," Rick replied.

"Shouldn't you be getting lined up?"

He nodded. "I'm going. Wish me luck?"

"Sure. Why not," I said.

"I think you can do better than that," Rick said.

"I'm not sure—" I'd started to say when he scooped me up in his arms, clutched me to his chest and covered my shocked lips with his, kissing me long, hard and well.

He let me go and I swayed like a drunken sailor. He must've caught my bemused look, because he winked.

"For luck," he said.

Luck, my pirate booty. He was looking for more than luck.

He suddenly took hold of his T-shirt and pulled it up and over his head and handed it to me. "Hang on to this for me, would you, T?" he said, giving me a smile that made me so weak in the knees, my legs buckled again. I made my way to a vacant table and sank into a chair. I mopped my hot face with Townsend's shirt and found myself closing my eyes and inhaling the seductive scent that was Ranger Rick.

"Is this seat taken?" I heard, and looked up to find Coral LaFavre at the table.

I extracted my face from the cloth. "Not at all. Have a seat," I offered, my eyes growing big when I saw the bowl of candy-coated chocolate she set on the table. For once, Lady Luck was smiling on Tressa Turner. In light of the previous afternoon's undercover operation, Coral had my vote as the candidate most likely to be the target of murderous intent for personal gain. And when that likely candidate was in the possession of a bowl of chocolate? Well, heaven was just a sin away.

She looked on as the four competitors for the TV took their places.

"Isn't that your fiancé out there?" she asked. "Oh, I forget. You don't remember. Tragic," she said, taking a long, lustful look at Manny.

"You're Coral, right? You're married to David," I said,

helping her remember she was married. "He reintroduced himself yesterday. Where is he, by the way?"

She waved a hand. "Oh, he's around," she said.

Despite the fact that the best-looking men on this—or any cruise ship anywhere—stood shirtless and flexing muscles and more, I couldn't take my eyes off the bowl of candy. My fingers crawled across the table toward the dish.

Yes, I'd been a good girl and had resisted ripping into Manny's gift of sweets the previous night, but that had had more to do with my not accepting the gift under false pretenses than a desire to abstain from the fruits of the cocoa bean. After all, I couldn't return the box to him if I opened and sampled it. And I was planning to return it to him. Of course I was. It was, after all, the right thing to do.

"And who have you been doing?" I asked, and wanted to grab my own tongue, pull it out of my mouth and twist it around my throat.

"Excuse me?" Coral asked, turning back to me.

"What have you been up to?" I re-enunciated.

She shrugged. "Relaxing. Reading. Sleeping."

Conducting a cabin check with Security Sam.

"You?" she asked.

"Me?" I said.

"What have you been doing? Besides falling down stairs, losing your memory, and waking up to discover two drop-dead alpha-male types sparring over you," Coral said, her attention wandering away again while my fingers crept closer to their hard-shelled prey.

"Same as you, actually," I said. "Relaxing. Sleeping." *Surveillance of the security chief, in cahoots with a senior citizen front man.* "Asking lots of questions."

Coral's head snapped back to me. It felt like she was watching a tennis match. "Questions? What kind of questions?"

"Oh, you know. The usual questions one asks of others when they want to know things," I responded.

"What kind of things?" she asked.

"Why, things you don't know, of course," I said, staring pointedly at the bowl of candy, no longer making any attempt to appear unaffected by the chocolate within arm's reach. She saw my interest in the milk chocolate.

"Oh. Go ahead. Help yourself," she said. "David smuggled them in for me. He thought I'd be pleased, but instead I feel like he's trying to sabotage my efforts to lose weight," she said. "So far I've resisted temptation. But now it's like who cares if I'm fat? I might as well eat what I like when I like. We all have to die of something. Right, Tressa?"

I got the feeling then she was asking me for something. Something I didn't have.

"David gave you this candy?" I said, my heart rate picking up as a horrible possibility occurred to me. "And you haven't eaten any? Any at all?" I questioned.

She shook her head. "Not one. But like I said, why bother? I was chubby as a girl and only lost the weight because I starved myself. I'm not about to go back to that kind of hell." She reached out and grabbed a handful of candies. "No way."

"What are you doing?" I asked. "Put that candy down!"

She stared at me. "What?"

"You heard me. Put that down this instant!"

Coral got an *I'm gonna need a little help here* look on her face.

"You don't need that candy!" I told her. "Resist! Resist!"

Okay, so I was getting a little agitated. But for all I knew, those cute, colorful little candies were laced with strychnine or arsenic or whatever poison tickled David Frazier's Compton fancy.

"I may not need it, but I sure as hell want it," Coral said.

I reached out and took the candy bowl. "Oh, no you don't," I said. "Now give me that. Come on. Fork it over. Now!"

"You just want it for yourself," Coral accused. "I know

that gotta-have-a-chocolate-fix look when I see it, and you got it bad, girlfriend."

"Okay. I admit it. I want to stick my mouth in that bowl and come up with a tongue that looks like Joseph's coat of many colors," I admitted. "But I won't. We can do this, Coral," I said, reaching out for her hand that clutched the candy. "We can beat this addiction together!"

She stared at me and then slowly opened her fingers. Her palm was a kaleidoscope of melded—and melted—colors. Rainbow colors. I put the bowl out to her. She dropped the deformed candies in the dish. I got up and walked to the side of the ship and dumped the candies over the side. I heaved a sigh of relief.

"I hope you know what you're doing," she said.

I nodded. "I get that a lot," I said.

By this time we'd missed the first part of the race. I decided at the very least I should have a photographic record of the historic moment that saw Rick Townsend wearing a woman's swim top. I grabbed my camera out of my bag and stood to get a better view. I captured Townsend's image with my telephoto lens.

I blinked. I couldn't believe my eyes. Townsend was clad in the same hot pink bra I'd worn. I frowned. Unbelievable. Un-freakin'-believable. Townsend and I could wear the same bra size?

Kill me. Kill me now!

Manny, tastefully attired in a light blue swim top that accentuated his dark, even tan, had just finished the rice cake and was downing his beverage in record time. Townsend, however, held the edge. He exited the plank before Manny, stripping out of his grass skirt like a pro. All he had to do was unhook the bra and he'd be the victor.

And to the victor went the high-def TV.

I found myself yelling and jumping up and down.

"Go! Go! Go!"

I frowned. Townsend seemed to be having trouble with the bra hooks. Meanwhile, Manny had reached the end of his plank and had dropped his grass skirt as well. Time seemed to stop for a second as Manny turned to look up at the audience gathered on deck. His searching gaze came to me. And stopped.

Confident and unhurried, without relinquishing my gaze, Manny's huge arm bent oh so slowly behind his back. Before you could say, "He's had lots of experience at this," the light blue swim top fell to the ground.

Manny strolled to the buzzer and smacked it. He turned and caught my stunned gaze, and winked at me. The crowd gasped.

To the victor go the spoils.

Holy hooks, eyes and winkers!

I sucked in air and looked around wildly, wondering if anyone anywhere onboard had a bag of oracle bones handy. 'Cause I predicted one heck of a squall on the horizon.

Talk about yer shaken booties and shivered timbers.

CHAPTER FIFTEEN

I gave everyone the slip. I needed some time to absorb the significance of Manny's sudden interest in me. It was flattering, certainly. What girl doesn't want to be pursued by a hot—okay, incredibly hot—guy? But just what did Manny's overt declaration mean? Could he really have feelings for me? Feelings beyond those relating to the fraudulent fiancée fantasy he'd cooked up? Feelings I'd purposely ignored up until now because I wasn't ready for the complications acknowledging Manny's feelings would bring? Now I not only had to confront the possibility that he might have deeper feelings for me, but also admit I wasn't altogether indifferent to him either. But just what were those feelings and how deep did they run? Well, that was the million-dollar question, now, wasn't it?

Stark hunger drove me to the turkey taco bar. Being a connoisseur of sorts on tacos, taco burgers, chili dogs, and beef burgers from my off-and-on employment at my Uncle Frank's Dairee Freeze restaurant, I was skeptical that the faux South of the Border fare would even remotely resemble the real thing. Nonetheless, I built my turkey taco with the skill and confidence of a pro, cramming meat, tomatoes, lettuce and cheese into the middle of the whole-grain taco shell. I drizzled a healthy amount of taco sauce on my creation and took a big bite, expecting my taste buds to rebel, but to my delighted surprise, the turkey taco was surprisingly yummy.

So yummy, in fact, I ate half a dozen of them before I realized they were actually good for me.

I was wiping taco sauce off my chin when Courtney plopped down in a seat across from me. She had a handful of scratch lottery tickets in one hand and a dime in the other. She started to scratch her way through the stack.

"A taco lover, huh?" she said, pointing at the remnants of my meal.

"I have no idea," I said. "It's turkey."

Courtney gave me a *huh?* look.

"So, I imagine you're thrilled Manny won the high-def set," she said. "I wish Steve and I could afford a fancy TV, but as you know already, we're on a budget. We even let our life insurance policy lapse to pay down our debt," she said. "And after your sales pitch that first night and all the talk about the bad stuff that can happen on a cruise, I can tell you, it sort of freaked Steve out. He's a bit superstitious," she explained, continuing to scratch her tickets.

"You don't have life insurance?" I asked, thinking this was way too easy.

She shook her head. "Only temporarily, I assure you. We figure we're both young and healthy and have relatively good jobs. Steve's a mechanic and I'm an L.P.N. We don't have children to provide for. So, it's not as much of a risk as it might be," she said, scratching another ticket. She shook her head. "You'd think I'd get tired of losing, wouldn't you? But there's this buzz you get at just the possibility that you could win. You won't tell Steve, will you?" she added. "He wouldn't approve."

I shook my head. "My lips are sealed," I said, my mind drifting to dessert and debating whether or not I had enough courage to actually try the frozen yogurt. After all, Uncle Frank, king of ice cream confections, would never know.

"I wonder. Do you have the soul of a gambler, Tressa?" Courtney asked.

I frowned. I'd never spent much time in casinos, more due to lack of funds than lack of interest. But I had the feeling others would cite my record of exploits as pointing to me being a gambler at heart. Others (notably one ranger) would observe that this risk-it-all attitude so prevalent in other areas of my life, however, did not carry over to matters of the heart.

"I don't know. I'm fuzzy on a lot of things about myself lately," I told Courtney, being über honest. "I do know I don't have an overwhelming desire to grab those lottery cards and start scratching away. But I suppose that could be because I may not be the kind of person who takes losing well. I know I didn't care much for losing that plank race earlier," I told her.

She eyeballed me. "Do you think you're the type of person who enjoys being the object of a wager?" she asked.

I drew your basic blank. "What do you mean? What kind of wager?" I asked.

"I might as well tell you. You're bound to find out somehow. There's a shipboard pool, and they're taking bets on which gorgeous hunk you'll pick."

I stared at her. A gambling pool on my personal life! The nerve. The audacity. The abject humiliation of it all.

"What are the current odds?" I asked.

Courtney's eyebrows lifted. "Split evenly," she said.

Dang. No help there.

"Care to share any inside information?" she said. "A tip?"

I shook my head. I had nothing. Nothing I was ready to disclose.

"That's okay. I already know who to put my money on, and I think it's a pretty safe bet," Courtney told me.

"Yeah? Who?" I asked.

"Rick," she said. "Hands down. You'll pick Rick."

I stared at her.

"How do you know that?" I asked.

"I'm pretty good at reading faces," she said. "But even if

I wasn't, your face gives you away every time someone says his name. You just light up. When you were talking to him on deck the other day, you couldn't keep your eyes off him. At the karaoke bar it was written all over your face. And at the plank-walking contest today, when you were jumping up and down and yelling. You were yelling for Rick. Not Manny."

I marveled at her powers of observation.

"Interesting theory," was all I said.

She smiled. "You'll pick Rick," she told me. "Just wait and see. You'll pick Rick. You won't be able to help yourself. He's doing his best to show you how he feels and he won't give up."

It occurred to me that she could very well be right.

"I like your friends, Sherri and Ben," I said, changing the subject, thinking I was moving ever closer to narrowing the field of possible perps to one. "Sherri seems really reserved," I said. "Is she always that quiet?"

Courtney stopped scratching and looked up at me. "She's always been shy. Why do you ask?"

I shrugged. "She just seems, I don't know, sad. Dissatisfied with her life. She doesn't care for your hometown, that's for sure. She made that very clear."

"Aren't we all dissatisfied with who we are and where we are at times?" Courtney said. "That's just life."

"I suppose," I agreed.

We visited for a few minutes more and I started to yawn, great big, gaping, unforgivably rude yawns. I should have known better than to eat that much turkey. Isn't there, like, some special ingredient in that particular poultry that makes you sleepy? Triptopan or something? I know I get really drowsy and have to crawl to the sofa after Thanksgiving dinner. Of course, most dinners affect me this way.

I apologized to Courtney and excused myself, citing an urgent matter I needed to attend to. One very important catnap.

When I opened the door of my cabin, a flash of pink at my feet got my attention. I bent to pick it up. It was an envelope. A hot pink envelope. My name was written on the front in big, black, block letters.

How fun. Sail mail!

I turned the envelope over, opened it up, and drew out a card. On the front were two adorable yellow lab pups. The darling duo made me homesick for my furry fellows back home. I opened the card.

I gasped. Inside was a certificate for a high-def plasma TV. A short message was scrawled on the card.

"So Barbie will get the big picture." This card also bore a single *M* as a signature.

My hand shook as I stared at it.

Big picture, indeed.

It looked like Manny DeMarco was doing his level best to broadcast his interest. I shivered. The stakes had been raised yet again. Manny sees Ranger Rick's serenade and raises him one high-def TV.

You know, a girl could get used to this contemporary courtship.

I put the card with the chocolates and drew the covers back. I slipped my shoes and skirt off and slid between the sheets of the bed. I yawned. Being the object of two suitors' affections was exhausting, and a pampered princess needed her beauty sleep.

By the time you could say, "You're gonna need a bigger boat," Princess Tressa was fast asleep.

I awoke to a dark cabin, my night-owl vision taking time to adjust. I lay there, relishing the warmth of the covers and enjoying the rare feeling of not having to be at a given place at a given time. Man, that's what I call a vacation.

I rolled over on my back and stared at the ceiling, evaluating where I was in terms of identifying the dude who wanted his better half to swim with the fishes while he reeled in a big haul. If what Courtney had said was correct and Courtney and Steve had allowed their policy to lapse, that left me with either Coral's creepy manager husband with the three names and the bleah handshake, David Frazier Compton, or Ben Hall, Sherri's sometimes-distant, sometimes-loving husband. My money was on David. I never discount the bleah factor. The guy oozed sleaze from the moment I met him.

Still, there was Steve's missing buff to consider. And from the spat I'd overheard it was clear Steve handled the money in that household—probably with good reason. And it was always possible he could have just told his wife the policy was no longer in effect when, in reality, he still held a policy on her with himself as beneficiary.

All these *what-if*s and *could-be*s made my head hurt. The truth was, I didn't want to do this. Didn't want to figure out the whodunit alone. Didn't want to do life alone any longer.

I found myself thinking about Ranger Rick: his dark brown eyes, his tanned, lean torso, his musical dedication to me. I started to hum our song.

I really wanted to trust Ranger Rick—trust him with my body and my heart. And he, too, was making an all-out effort to let me know how he felt. Maybe it was time to commit to a level of trust with Townsend I'd been squeamish about before. Be honest with Ranger Rick. Forthright. About everything. The conversation I'd overheard. My visit with Security Sam. The truth about my fall down the stairs and my subsequent memory loss. My raid on the ship's galley and Operation: Room Service that yielded Joe a handsome tip and me information on a love affair at sea.

I frowned. Better leave that last one out.

The fact of the matter was I needed someone I could trust to help me keep tabs on my cruising couples trifecta until I got the goods on the guilty party. And, regardless of our past contretemps (don't you just love that word?), the man for the job was, and always had been, Ranger Rick.

Decided, I made my way to the bathroom to splash water on my face. I was about to turn on the water when I heard the click of the keycard and the door opened. Ready to call out a greeting, I stopped when I heard the deep tones of my dad.

"You'll have to tell her, Taylor," he said. "At some point you have to tell her."

I paused. Tell who what?

"I realize that, Dad," I heard Taylor respond, "but right now is not a good time. There's the head injury and the memory thing . . ."

"She's fond of him. Maybe more. All that business earlier this spring brought them closer. You'll have to tell her."

I frowned.

What were they talking about? Who were they talking about?

"I will. Eventually. And it was only the once," she said. "We've kept away from each other since then because, frankly, neither one of us knows what—or who—they want. But if he still has feelings for Tressa, why is he kissing me?"

I clamped both hands over my mouth to keep from betraying my presence as a *What she talkin' 'bout?* exclamation almost escaped me. Kissing?

Kissing!

Kissing!!

"You're beautiful and smart and articulate, that's why," my dad said, and I shook my head. That's just what every girl wants a guy to kiss her for, right? Her . . . articulation? Ew. In that moment, I felt sorry for Taylor.

"I noticed you didn't include 'gregarious personality and delightful but quirky sense of humor' in your description," Taylor said. "Because that's not me, is it? That's Tressa. The entertaining one. The funny one. The one everybody shakes a finger at or shakes their head over, but secretly wants to be just like her."

That preposterous bit of news with all the legitimacy of a blogosphere posting caught even a seasoned, professional journalist like me off guard. Excuse me? Everyone secretly wants to be like me? Apparently Taylor had gotten into Mo's stash of seaweed and toked on one too many funny little ciggies.

"You get your serious side from your mother and me," Dad told Taylor. "Tressa is more like—"

"I know. Grandma," Taylor finished.

I heard Dad chuckle. "She sure as heck wasn't called Hellion Hannah for nothing," he said. "But that's another matter. What I'm concerned about is preserving the relationship between you two sisters. Nothing can come between sisters more than a man. You'll have to tell her before she hears from someone else."

"I will. Besides, it's not as if she has a claim on him or anything. She's kept him at arm's length for some time. Tressa seems pretty married to her footloose and fancy-free lifestyle. Who knows how she really feels in her heart of hearts."

"My point, exactly," my dad stated.

"I hear you, Dad. I hear you," Taylor said, and her hand appeared in the open door of the bathroom, and for a moment I thought she was going to come into the tiny stall, so I hurried to the shrinky-dink shower, got in and closed the curtain, and stood there for a tense few minutes praying she wasn't going to do number two while I stood concealed behind curtain number one. Togetherness only goes so far, even with sisters.

Thankfully, she grabbed her hairbrush from the sink and that was it.

I cowered behind the curtain until I heard them both leave the cabin. I stepped out, wondering just who the *who* was I'd kept at arm's length. Who the *him* was who'd kissed my little sister. Who the man was who could come between two sisters.

I remembered Kimmie telling me how Ranger Rick hadn't been above using Taylor to try and make me jealous, which wasn't like Rick Townsend at all. Still, they had spent time together last summer during the fair.

The only other men in my life over the course of the last year were Manny DeMarco, an enormous enigma of his own; Trooper Patrick Dawkins, a dishy trooper I'd met last summer and who liked me for me; Joe Townsend, who was already taken (praise the Lord and pass the Ben-Gay); my two pony-sized pups with bad hair and dog breath, and a goofy Appaloosa quarterhorse named Joker waiting for me back home.

Chances were I could eliminate Butch, Sundance, Joker, and the other joker (Joe) from consideration. That left Dishy Dawkins who, as far as I knew, had only met my sister a couple of times last summer, Manny DeMarco, who I just couldn't see having much in common with Taylor beyond a fanaticism for fitness, and Ranger Rick. My Ranger Rick.

Or not.

I mentally crumpled up my idea of spilling my guts to Ranger Rick. I'd have to switch to Plan B.

And as soon as I had one, I'd do just that.

I made my way to the ship's Internet center and decided it might be worth the considerable cost of wireless access to see what I could come up with on my prime suspects, David Frazier Compton, Steve Kayser and his best bud, Ben Hall.

I had to wait half an hour for a computer to free up. I typed in *David Frazier Compton* first and got a long list of hits, all of them related to his role as Coral LaFavre's agent. There were a number of pictures of them together. Coral looked beautiful in many of them, but in an ice-queen sort of way. I came to one entry and frowned. I clicked on it. It was an article from almost three years earlier. An article on Coral LaFavre's arrest for drunk driving. I blinked when I clicked on her mugshot. Egads. It was worse than the image I saw in the mirror every morning!

I clicked some more articles, finding that every picture of

Coral from that day on also featured her agent, David Frazier Compton. I searched for information relating to Compton but found nothing prior to his becoming Coral's representative. No other clients he repped. No other positions he'd held. Weird. It was almost as if he had done nothing before he hooked up with Coral.

Just for the heck of it, I typed in both Steve and Ben's names but discovered nothing. Ditto for Courtney and Sherri. I typed in Farley, the name of their hometown, and got several hits. Most led me to the chamber of commerce or the city hall. One headline led me to the local paper.

Lottery prize still unclaimed, it read. *Clock ticking.*

So, Sherri's little rip on Farley had been grounded in fact. Someone had purchased a winning lottery ticket worth over five million bucks at a local convenience store but so far had not turned it in to claim their prize. The article stated that the winner had until October 11th to come forward with the ticket or it would be too late.

I shook my head. I imagined the flurry of folks frantically searching pockets of jackets and coats, hauling out old purses and dumping the contents, checking in glove boxes and under car seats, junk drawers, and wastebaskets, desperate to find the winning ticket. That was why I didn't buy lottery tickets. With my luck I'd misplace the winning ticket. Of course, the fact that I had little discretionary income to spend on lottery tickets also factored into my decision not to play.

Before I logged off the computer, I couldn't resist sending a "Remember-me-I-find-dead-people" greeting to my boss, Stan the Man Rodgers, at the *Gazette,* making sure he remembered that I would be back bright and early on Monday morning ready to scope out all the news that was news in Grandville (but nowhere else) and adding another little reminder that my office chair had better not be permanently imprinted with the posterior prints of one Shelby Lynne Sawyer, aka Sasquatch to those with more courage than me.

Shelby Lynne and I had worked together on a story last fall that had more twists and turns than my hair after a night of camping out. At over six feet, the red-headed homecoming queen and wannabe reporter was hard to say "No comment" to. Shelby Lynne had her eye on my ergonomic office chair—and my job. I decided to dash off a quick "You-may-be-bigger-but-I've-got-a-nose-for-news" e-mail to Shelby Lynne.

> *Hey, Shelby.*
> *Take heart. Your mentor will be back soon! (Keep that chair warm for me, y'hear?)*
> *—Tressa*

I logged off the computer, let the attendant swipe the key card adding to Joe's bill and left. I'd gone about half a dozen steps when I stopped and slapped a hand to my forehead.

The e-mails! My e-mails! E-mails I shouldn't have sent. E-mail recipients I shouldn't remember!

"Shouldn't you be surfing the beaches and not the Web?" A tap on my shoulder spun me around. David Frazier Compton stood there, flashing a blinding white grin at me. "Trying to discover something?" he asked, and I tensed until he continued. "About yourself, I mean. Your past. To refresh your faulty memory. It's amazing what you can find out about almost anyone on the Internet," he said.

Or what you couldn't when it came to David Frazier Compton.

"I wouldn't know. I was playing solitaire," I lied.

He smiled. "A gambler at heart, eh?"

I shook my head. "Word Worm wouldn't load," I said.

I told him I was meeting people, excused myself and left, ripping myself a new one for being so careless. (Caution: self-mutilation like this is particularly painful, folks. I don't advise it.)

I dropped by the lobby area and picked up the daily

bulletin Taylor kept bugging me to read. I had a now-they-tell-me moment when I read the warning at the bottom. *Remember, the ship is moving. Please be careful, watch your step, and use the handrails.* Durr.

I checked my watch. A little after eight. I checked the activities listed for eight. Hmm. Coral's show in the Tiki Lounge had just started. I located the Tiki Lounge on the ship's diagram and started that way.

I hadn't gone too far when I got that icky feeling again, the feeling you get when you think you're being watched. You know, like when you think you're alone with a roll of chocolate chip cookie dough and you're just about to slice off a hunk and you get this feeling that someone is watching you. Just watching and waiting for you to show your true colors and to saw off a section and hightail it out of there with no one presumably the wiser. That kind of feeling. Not that I personally know about cookie dough thefts or the like. That example was fabricated for metaphorical purposes only, you understand.

I frowned. Since I was pretty sure I had a serious case of bedhead my pink ball cap couldn't quite conceal, and my clothes were probably a tad rumpled, I didn't for one moment suspect someone's scrutiny of me had anything to do with a gotta-have-a-piece-of-that state of mind. Thus, odds were someone was keeping an eye on me to catch me up in my own little version of the memory game.

Go on, punk. Make my day, I challenged. See if I betray by word or deed that I have a clue. See if I look like I even suspect anything. See if I resemble compos let alone mentis.

I frowned. I was thinking I needed therapy.

Despite my suspicion that I was being followed, I made my way to the Tiki Lounge determined to keep an eye on Coral and, hopefully, find an opportunity to discover her plans for the land excursion tomorrow.

I had hoped to maintain a low profile, enjoy the show,

have a glass of anything but grapefruit juice and keep a watchful eye. Yeah. Like that was gonna happen.

"Yoo-hoo! Tressa Jayne! Over here!" someone hissed.

I saw my grandma waving from a table right up front. Naturally. Joe was seated close to her. Coral wasn't onstage yet. A competent pianist was performing.

I joined the newlyweds, taking care to select a seat with full view of the entrance.

"Hello," I said. "How are you two?"

"It's we who should be asking you that," Joe observed. "How's the memory? Still MIA?"

"More like AWOL," I said. "But I continue to hope for the best. What have you two decided to do tomorrow when we dock at Montego Bay?" I asked, holding up the ship's brochure. "Sunbathing? Sightseeing? Golfing?"

"Snubaing," my gammy said.

I frowned. "What?"

"We're gonna snuba," she said, and I searched for any possible word substitutions that might make sense but came up dry.

"What the heck is snuba?" I asked.

"It's a combination of snorkeling and scuba diving," Joe said.

"Oh. That snuba," I said, ignoring the tremor in my right eye. "Did you clear this with your son and his wife?" I asked, thinking my folks would have a fit if they found out the newlyweds were wanting to get up close and personal with a coral reef.

My gammy shook her head.

"Haven't heard boo from them two since we set sail," she said. "I think they're spending quality time together." She pursed her lips. "That's not like my son. Mr. Romance, he ain't. Takes after your Paw Paw Will, bless his soul. Something's fishy here and it ain't got nothing to do with that crab salad they shoved at us for lunch."

"So you have no idea what my—the parents have planned for tomorrow?" I asked, cringing at the mere thought of my mother and father and shipboard sex. Eeow!

Gram shook her head.

"Probably some stick-in-the-mud, old fogey activity," she said.

"Hannah here wanted to parasail, but since she has osteoporosis and broke those bones a couple years back, they won't let her, so we had to come up with something easier on the joints," Joe said.

"Are you sure you want to try this snuba thing?" I asked. "There are tons of slippery little fish in that water, Gram. Swimming all around you. Nipping at your nose." I sounded more like freakin' Jack Frost here, but the idea of my gammy squeezing into a wet suit and stepping into the sea, given her own history of calamities, was not a Custom Cruise moment we wanted to risk taking.

I have to level with you. My reminder about the fish was deliberate—and somewhat underhanded. You see, ever since my grandma fell into the goldfish pond at the zoo and came home with not only flopping flesh but flopping fish in her bra, she'd avoided fish altogether. She forbade me to have tuna in the house. Her poor cat, Hermione, was limited to a chicken-not-of-the-sea diet. Heck, I couldn't even get her to take advantage of a buy-one-get-one-free fish filet offer at Mickey D's, and I was forced to eat both sandwiches against my will. Yes, I said forced. (Hey, didn't anyone ever tell you it's impolite to snort?) Oh, and by the way, if you see my Uncle Frank, don't tell him I prefer Mickey D's filets to his. It would devastate the poor man. 'Kay?

"Fish? What kind of fish?" Gram asked.

I shrugged. "Cute, slender little fish. And some not so little ones, too, I guess."

"How many fish?"

"Why, a virtual underwater plethora of tropical organisms, I imagine," I described.

"Huh?" Gram said.

"Lots and lots," I told her. "Oh, and do be sure you take an underwater camera and get lots of 'lovers in underwater tropical paradise' moments, would you?" I added.

Gram adjusted her brassiere as if recalling the fish fiasco. She looked at Joe.

"Let's go with Plan B," she said, and I thought surely it couldn't be as bad as Plan A.

"Plan B?" I asked.

"The camel trekking safari experience," Gram said. "Then a hike to some falls."

"Camels? Since when do you like camels?" I asked.

"Since them fish got too friendly," Gram said. I winced.

"I was looking over the shore excursion information and I saw a sweet outing and thought immediately of you two," I said.

"What? Visiting the Montego Bay senior center?" Joe asked.

"Maybe next cruise," I told him. "No, this one features an air-conditioned drive along the wonderfully scenic and lovely coast of Jamaica and up to this spectacular falls. You'll enjoy a scrumptious picnic and have a chance to get up close and personal with real live dolphins and still have time to buy lovely little souvenirs for family and friends as you take a leisurely stroll through the craft village," I said, sounding like the announcer on "Wheel of Fortune" detailing the trip contestants could win.

"Dolphins? Aren't they great big fish?" Gram asked.

I shook my head. "Actually they're not fish. They're marine mammals," I reassured her. "They're very friendly creatures," I added.

"I know what a dolphin is," Gram said. "I watched *Flipper*."

"How does that excursion sound?" I asked. "Flipper, Niagara Falls, and shopping all in one outing."

"Whaddya think, Joe?" Gram asked.

"Anywhere with you is romantic," he replied, giving my

gammy's hand a squeeze. Always the opportunist, he gave me a see-what-you're-missin'-girlie? look.

"What are your plans for tomorrow, Tressa dear?" Gram asked.

I shrugged. "With things mixed up the way they are, I don't like to plan ahead," I said, thinking more about murder plots than memory lapses. "I'll wait to see how things shake out and decide tomorrow," I told them.

"You could always snuba," Gram suggested. "We've already booked it."

As tempting as it was to suck my gut in enough to don a wetsuit and frolic with Gram's foes amid the coral reef and let the human beings sort out their own issues, I knew in good conscience I couldn't do that. As much of a long shot that I could prevent a would-be killer from acting out his fatal fantasy as it was, I still had to do whatever I could.

"Thanks for the offer, but I'm just going to play it by ear right now," I told them. "Maybe you can get a refund, or maybe your grandson might be interested, Joe."

"Rick's got a golf foursome planned with his dad, your dad and Craig," Joe informed me.

I frowned. Did I sense a shirking in the courtship competition?

The lights dimmed and the piano music ended. Coral walked out on the modest stage. In a shiny sleeveless shell teamed with a jacket of the same material and tailored black trousers, Coral LaFavre looked every inch the star—and way different from her mug shot. Her dark hair was pulled up at the sides with shiny black combs, the length of it falling onto her shoulders.

She started the show with crowd-pleasers that featured lots of energy and lots of attitude. Songs about vanity, surviving, starting over, getting even. She suddenly changed course, shifting from 'tude to substance.

"This one goes out to a new friend. Tressa. This one's for

you, babe," Coral said, before she launched into a song Babs Streisand was best known for, a song about, you guessed it: "Memories!"

Cheeky woman!

I listened as Coral sang, and as I watched her I sensed, despite her dedication, that she was not singing for me. A movement at the entrance caught my attention and I looked over to discover Security Sam Davenport standing near the entrance, his eyes never leaving Coral.

Easy now, Sam, I cautioned. One look at that face and there was no doubt of his feelings. Or, from Coral's breathless delivery, hers.

I suddenly remembered that I was sitting with the guy who'd delivered Sam Davenport's room service order, and decided no way did I want Davenport to recognize Joe, see me sitting with him and come over to demand why a passenger was posing as room service. And I really, really didn't want to hear how Joe tried to talk his way out of it.

I excused myself from the table and preempted a strike by Davenport, sorely wishing I could trust the security chief enough to confide in him. But I just couldn't put out of my mind the image of Security Sam slinking into a darkened sickbay shortly after I'd almost been smothered with a pillow.

"She's good," I said, joining Davenport near the door and tipping my head in Coral's direction. "Very good."

"That she is," Davenport replied, noncommittal.

"That husband of hers is different," I said. "Not the type I expected to see someone like Coral married to," I told him.

"Oh? And what type did you expect?" Davenport asked, his arms folded across his chest in a deceptively casual pose.

"I don't know. Someone with a little more substance and a little less . . . veneer," I said.

He didn't respond.

"So, what does a security guy like you do when the ship is in port?" I asked. "Do you have to work or can you do the sightseeing thing like a tourist?"

"Whether I remain on the ship is up in the air right now," Davenport said. "I've done most of the port activities," he said, "but it's always nice to see beautiful yet familiar scenes through the eyes of people seeing them for the first time."

Good-looking and poetic, too. No wonder Coral was in lust.

I looked back at her.

"I wonder what Coral plans to do," I said. "Maybe I'll see if I can tag along with her when we go ashore."

"I can answer that," I heard from the entrance behind me. "Coral's actually booked time at the spa," David Frazier Compton supplied. "The full treatment. So she won't be disembarking in Montego Bay."

"What about you?" Sam asked David.

"Why, I wouldn't miss a Jamaican sunrise for the world, Davenport," David remarked. "Not for the world."

The hostility between the two men was so thick a pirate's cutlass couldn't touch it.

"If Coral changes her mind and decides to go ashore, you will let her know I'd love to accompany her. Right?" I said to David.

"Of course," he replied. "But if you need an escort . . . I'd be happy to volunteer my services," he offered.

I wondered if my expression revealed I was trying to clamp down on the old gag reflex.

"Uh, I'll get back to you on that," I said, backing away—and coming up against a big, hard chest.

"Hey, babe," I heard. "Get Manny's gift?"

"About that," I said.

"Let's take a stroll around the ship, shall we, Barbie?" Manny suggested.

I let him take my hand and lead me away.

I could imagine what everyone was thinking: The odds were shifting in Manny's favor.

And what was Tressa thinking?

That Barbie was courting catastrophe.

CHAPTER SIXTEEN

I spent the rest of the evening with Manny, trying to block the image of him without a shirt from my mind. And failing miserably.

We parted ways around eleven, Manny dropping a rather nice good-night kiss on my surprised lips, pledging to stand as my escort when we dropped anchor the next morning. I dropped into bed, my high-def television certificate tucked beneath my pillow. Sweet dreams, indeed.

I was up early the next morning, but not early enough to beat Taylor out of the cabin.

I stretched, retrieved my TV certificate from my pillow, set it on the chocolate box, started to open the chocolate box, resisted the urge to open the chocolate box, and got up and around for the day.

A white top trimmed in pink, pink shorts, pink and white short socks, pink and white Skechers for walking, pink softball hat, and trademark Javelina bag made me look all put together even though my previous night's sleep had been disturbed by sword-wielding foes, hooded villains with hideous hook arms and alligators with huge, snapping jaws. Oh, and Peter Pan made a cameo appearance looking a lot like Michael Jackson. I know. Weird.

I stuffed my swimsuit in my bag just in case and decided to forego breakfast—and hunt down the real thing once on land. Getting ready to disembark, I looked around and spotted the Farley couples ahead of me in line. I shoved my way up to them, apologizing as I cut in front of others. After all, I was out to foil a capital crime here. What was a little line cutting when the stakes were so high?

I greeted the couples.

"Oh, hi, Tressa!" Courtney called out. "Isn't this a mess?"

"What's the holdup?" I asked, thinking the line was moving really slow.

"Can you believe they're weighing us?" Courtney said.

I stared at her. "What? Why?"

"It's strictly voluntary," Sherri assured me.

"They're giving prizes to those who have the least weight gain while on land," Courtney said. "Or in some cases, even lose weight. In other words, they want us to have fun but not so much fun we forget what this cruise is all about," she added.

"Well, I'm not getting on any scale," I said. "No matter what the prize is." I hesitated. "What is the prize, anyway? A stair stepper? Treadmill? A lifetime membership to a fitness center?"

"Money!" Courtney said.

"Money for clothes!" Sherri elaborated.

Money? For clothes?

"And shoes?" I asked.

"Of course," Courtney replied. "So, are you changing your mind about weighing in, Tressa?" she asked.

Was I?

I looked around.

Nobody I knew was in sight.

And I really could use some new clothes.

"Sure. Why not? Don't I strike you as a team player?" I asked.

"Of course," Sherri stated.

"Absolutely," Courtney said.

The pace picked up as scores of passengers opted not to risk public humiliation and made their way off the ship and onto dry land. And gastronomical freedom.

A little girl in line coveted my Harry Javelina bag and asked her mother if the souvenir shops would have a peccary pack. I had to break the news that unless she convinced her folks to visit the Grand Canyon, I suspected she was out of luck.

It was my turn to tip the scales. I steeled myself to accept the result. I took a step up onto the machine, deciding to shut my eyes. Nothing said I had to actually look. Ignorance could be bliss. Especially when you were talking about a woman's weight.

"That's one hundred seventy nine pounds," I heard, and my eyes flew open.

"What!" I yelled, looking at the digital reading on the scale. "One hundred seventy-nine pounds! That can't be right!" I yelled.

"You're right," the trainer recording my weight said. "It's now a hundred and eighty pounds."

"Now, just a minute—" I started to object, when I caught movement at my feet and looked down to discover somehow I'd grown an extra foot. A much larger foot.

One sneaky ranger's foot.

I turned around.

"You!" I said. "You almost gave me apoplexy," I told him, "manipulating my body mass like that."

He grinned and, as always, his smile had the ability to take my breath away—along with coherent thought.

"I couldn't resist. Besides, I couldn't pass up the chance to find out a secret more closely guarded than the nuclear codes. Tressa Jayne Turner's weight." He started to remove his foot from the scale just as I jumped down off the platform.

"Sorry, sailor," I said, "but that's one secret that goes with me to the grave. Or the occasional doctor's visit."

He shook his head. "You never let me have any fun," he scolded.

I laughed. "Right, right. I suppose golfing at a beautiful resort golf course qualifies as torture," I said.

"Not at all," he agreed. "But it could be even more enjoyable for me."

"Oh?" I said, lifting a brow.

"You could caddy for me," he suggested. "You know. Hand me the right club. Keep track of my balls."

There was that grin again, accompanied by a Groucho Marx lift of his dark brows.

"I get it. We've just docked on Ranger Rick's Fantasy Island, haven't we?" I told him. "The place where all your snow-cones'-chance-in-Jamaica fantasies can come true."

"My fantasies concerning you go a long ways beyond caddying, Calamity," Rick said. "And, if I'm not mistaken, my *odds* in seeing that fantasy come true are, oh, at least fifty-fifty, depending on the day."

My mouth flew open. The ornery ranger knew about *The Epiphany* pool—and I didn't mean the rectangular one on the main deck.

I remembered Manny's courtship token. You know. The one that measured about fifty-two inches.

"Maybe it's time to up the ante then, Ranger Rick," I said, my voice breathless, my demeanor, hopefully, seen as provocative rather than slutty as I ran my fingers up his tanned, muscled arm.

"Sounds like good advice, T," Ranger Rick said, and promptly picked me up and stepped up on the scale. Before I could scream, "Unhand this fair wench!" the traitorous trainer had reset the scale and our total weight was prominently displayed.

I shot the megaphone-mouth trainer a dark look, as it appeared he was about to herald the number.

"Don't even think about it!" I threatened, aware a simple mathematical calculation—one that Ranger Rick had probably already completed in his head—would reveal a number I'd never divulged to anyone. Most of the time, including me.

I wiggled out of the diabolically clever ranger's arms.

"If word gets out about a certain number, I will hunt you down like the cur that you are," I warned, "and the only way they will be able to identify you is by that tasteful raccoon tattoo on your behind. Have fun smacking balls with my brother and dad," I said and, tired of treading water with Townsend, I made my way to the cruise terminal.

As I stood waiting and wondering where the heck Manny was, I was joined by the Farley Foursome.

"So, what have the four of you got planned?" I asked, addressing my question to Steve.

"The girls planned today's outing," Steve said, and I could tell he wasn't exactly thrilled with what they'd come up with.

"We're river rafting," Courtney said.

"River rafting?" I repeated, alarmed at the very real danger inherent on any white-water trip yet surprised that both men looked as if they'd rather be poked in the eye with a sharp stick than participate. "That sounds exciting," I said.

"It does, doesn't it?" Steve said. "Until you find out the rafts are these squatty little two-person bamboo river rafts that are pushed along the river by means of a pole," Steve said.

I blinked. "Bamboo rafts?"

"It's romantic," Courtney insisted. "Each raft has a captain who steers you along the river while he entertains you with local folklore. You know. Like one of those gondoliers in Italy. Or is that France?"

I shrugged. It was all Greek to me. And why hadn't I known to include the low-speed, low-risk bamboo rafts in my arsenal last night when I talked Joe and Gram out of their snubaing experience?

"We'd better get going. We don't want to miss the Mountain Valley transport," Courtney said. "We take a short ride through the mountains to a village and then board our rafts. What are your plans, Tressa?"

I'd intended to eat myself into a stupor, slip into my swimsuit (if it still fit), drag my tail to a place on the beach and bake, baby, bake. But now? With Steve Kayser and Ben Hall still on my list of possible suspects, I was uneasy simply waving them off to enjoy a leisurely day of rafting on nothing more than lengths of flimsy bamboo!

"I'm not sure. Manny was supposed to meet me," I said.

Ben made a show of looking at his watch. "Hey, folks. We better hit it if we're going to catch our ride," he said, tapping his timepiece.

"Oh, you're right, Ben. Gotta go, Tressa. See you later!" Courtney said, and I watched them leave.

I looked at my own watch. Where was Manny? I needed him.

I frowned. That was a reversal for me. I'd never admitted to needing a man before. Wanting one? Yes. Lusting after one (or two)? Absolutely. But needing one? Nuh-uh. Not me. Not Tressa Jayne Turner, legend in her own mind.

I chewed a nail.

Good gawd. I *was* changing.

The old Tressa would have gone off with the two couples without a care and B.S.ed her way through any difficulties that arose. But this new Tressa found herself cooling her heels waiting for—of all things—a man. So not my SOP.

"Hey, Barbie. Sorry to be late. I had to make sure Mo got with her tour group."

Oh, crap. I guess there was still enough old Tressa left in me, because I hadn't given a thought to Aunt Mo's shore excursion experience.

"Shouldn't you be with your aunt?" I asked, and Manny shook his head.

"Mo met a nice man," he said by way of explanation.

"Oh? What are they doing?"

"Lunch. Exploring shipwrecks off Cheeseburger Reef," Manny said.

"Cheeseburger Reef?" I said, just the mention of beef making my mouth water.

He nodded. "So, what's Barbie up for?"

I looked up at him and grabbed his arm. "Does the sound of a river ride for two float your boat?" I asked, and pulled him in the direction the couples had gone earlier.

"River ride? On what?" Manny asked. "Sea spi? Jet ski? Power boat?"

"Bamboo raft," I said, dragging him along. "Trust me. You're gonna love it."

Manny shook his head and reluctantly hailed a taxi. Was ignored. I moved down from him—as if on my own—and hailed one and almost caused a traffic jam of taxis trying to grab the blonde tourist all alone. I yanked open the car door.

"Welcome to MoBay!" the taxi driver greeted me. "Where you going?"

"Mountain Valley. The bamboo river-rafting experience," I said. "But we're in a hurry," I said, climbing in.

"We?" the cabbie said, and I motioned to Manny, who was folding his long length in beside me. The cabbie's face got a puckered look. Like I do when my hipsters ride up.

"Yes, we. And step on it!"

The cabbie did just that. I'm thinking it was because he wanted Manny out of his cab ASAP because he kept giving Manny looks in the rearview mirror. And the driver was sweating. A lot.

I oohed and ahhed at the scenery as we traveled through the mountainous interior. Manny limited his responses to nods, grunts, and uh-huhs.

"You act as if you've seen all this before," I commented, and he grunted again.

I looked at him. "You *have* seen this before," I accused. "Haven't you?"

This time he shrugged.

"Manny's been here and there," he said.

"Business or pleasure?" I asked, still itching to discover Manny's vocation.

He smiled. "Both," he said.

"Do you travel a lot in your job?" I asked.

"It varies," he said.

"Does Aunt Mo know what you do?" I asked, and his hesitation and subtle shift in the seat told me I'd gotten him with that one. "Does she?" I pressed.

"Aunt Mo knows all she needs to know," Manny said. "How's the head?" he asked. He'd shifted gears so fast I got mental whiplash.

"Better," I said. "Does your 'job' require knowledge or skills of a, shall we say, criminal nature?" I asked, sending my own volley back to his side of the net.

"From time to time," he said. "Memory update?"

"The same," I said. "Where did you acquire these, uh, special skills?" *Heh heh. Right back at you, babe.*

"Around," Manny said. "Do you love Rick the Dick?"

The question hit me with the force of a line drive.

"Wh . . . wh . . . wh?"

"Do you love Rick the Dick?" Manny asked again and slid close enough that I felt the heat radiating from him.

The taxi slowed and stopped.

"We're here!" I said, escaping both the vehicle and the need to respond. "Oh, isn't this cool?"

I hurried to the area where a number of bamboo rafts approximately thirty feet in length floated alongside the shore. Each raft featured a bamboo bench-type seat just big enough for two located in the center of the raft, a red cushioned back and seat providing a comfortable sitting experience.

I scanned the length of the river that was visible, trying to find the Farley group. The greenish water, bordered on either side by tall, green trees, was calm and serene.

"I don't see them," I said. "They can't be that far ahead."

"Who?" Manny asked.

"Courtney, Steve, Ben and Sherri," I said.

"They're here?" Manny asked.

I nodded. "And we need to catch up to them," I said. "Hello there." I approached one of the "captains" dressed in a light blue shirt and long, navy blue shorts. "We really need to get rollin' on the river," I said. "You see, our friends are ahead of us and we sort of want to keep an eye on them."

The captain frowned. "Keep an eye? Not following."

"Look after them. Watch them," I said

"You want to . . . watch?" El Capitan frowned.

"Now wait—" I said.

A shadow hit the captain, covering him. "All aboard," Manny said, handing the guy some green.

"Right away, mon. This way, mon. I am Odell. So happy to be of service."

Odell helped us aboard the bamboo raft and we took a seat. He stuck a really long pole in the green river and shoved us away from shore. "I have many stories to share. Feel free to ask any questions."

"Does that pole move any faster?" I asked, and Captain Odell gave me an irritated look.

"Your lady? *Macas*," Odell told Manny, and I frowned.

"What does that mean?" I asked.

"Prickly," Manny said.

I raised an eyebrow at Odell. He did the same to me.

"What's Barbie's hurry anyway?" Manny asked.

"I told you. I want to catch up with the others," I said. "How deep is this river?" I asked Odell. "Is it over your head?"

"The Great River is ten to twelve feet deep, perhaps more in places," he said.

"How come you don't provide life vests?" I asked.

"We do have them upon request, but we have never had need of them before," Odell told me. "Each raft is captained by someone with much experience," he assured me. "And the river, it is quite narrow."

"Barbie's concerns addressed?" Manny asked. He put an arm around my shoulders. "Manny won't let anything happen to his girl," he said, and he squeezed my arm. Odell smiled and winked.

Great. Romantic raft ride. Amorous faux beau who showed every indication of wanting a little *Loveboat* action for real. A voyeur captain. What more could a girl want? For the blooming raft to turn up the knots, that's what.

"Tressa never did answer the question," I heard Manny say, and I played dumb.

"What was the question again?" I said.

"Is Tressa in love with Rick the Dick?"

I saw Odell lean in our direction, sensing a juicy bit of gossip to share with his fellow raft captains later.

"She might be," I said, "but she's not telling."

"Would Tressa know if she was in love?" Manny asked, and I thought that was a really brilliant question. Damn it.

Would I know?

How would I know?

"Love is such a subjective, individual, indefinable emotion," I said, about to launch into a really thought-provoking overview relating to what the real meaning of the word is and how it has many different facets and a kaleidoscope of textures and so many depths to plumb and levels to explore when a sudden scream from downstream got our attention.

"Help! Help! Someone!" A female voice carried back to us along the water.

Sherri!

"I think I know that voice!" I said, jumping to my feet and sending our raft bouncing. "Hurry! Work that pole, man! Work that pole!"

Odell looked at me and started yelling himself, digging the pole into the water, propelling us downriver—much too slowly for me.

"Put your arms into it!" I yelled. "Dig! Dig!"

"Sit down, please. You fall off," Odell said.

I looked at Manny—at the size of his massive arms—and grabbed hold of him and hauled him to his feet. "Take the wheel, sailor!" I said. "Or pole! Hurry!"

Manny shook his head, grabbed the pole from a protesting Odell, shook him off with a shrug of his shoulder and began navigating the bamboo raft down the river with the skill of a bamboo raft pro. In no time we had passed the other rafts and hit the bend in the river.

"There!" I screamed. "There they are! Hurry! Hurry!"

From where we were, we could see two rafts stopped in the center of the river. Two people were in the water. Two people were on the raft. Where were the captains?

"Go! Go!" I screamed.

Manny put his arms into it—and what arms! I marveled that the pole didn't break. As we drew nearer, I recognized Courtney kneeling at the side of one raft, reaching a hand out to the water, trying to grab hold of someone.

"Courtney!" I yelled. "We're coming!"

She looked up, saw us, and a hand flew to her chest.

"Hurry!" she said. "It's Ben! He's not a strong swimmer. And I can't get him on the raft."

Manny maneuvered our raft alongside Courtney's. He jumped from our raft to Courtney's, pushed her toward the center of the raft, reached down and with one big arm, plucked Ben out of the river. Ben coughed and sputtered.

"Oh, thank God!" Courtney gasped. "Thank God."

I frowned. "Uh, where's Steve?" I asked.

"Steve?" Courtney said.

"Your husband," I elaborated.

She looked around and jumped to her feet. "Oh my God, Steve! Steve!" she screamed. "He jumped in to help Ben! Steve! Steve!"

"There! He's there!" Sherri said, and pointed to a head bobbing in and out of the water, the swimmer obviously struggling to keep afloat. "There he is! Help him!"

Living near a large recreational Iowa lake has its

advantages—for all of three months out of the year. Plus, swimming was one sport I'd found where I could compete without complications, mainly because it was an individual sport.

I kicked my shoes off and dove in the river. I struck out in a long, smooth breaststroke, telling myself that there were no water snakes in the depths. None at all. (I have a serious fear of serpents. I blame Eve. Why not? She already takes the heat for PMS, monthly cramping, and the pain of child-birth.)

I reached Steve just as he appeared to be going under for the last time. Treading water, I tried to yank him up by his armpits, but his considerable weight pulled me down, too.

"Over here!" I managed to yell before my head was sub-merged. "Bring the raft!" I yelled when I bobbed back up again.

A second later Steve's weight was no longer burying me at sea—or rather river. Manny had a hold of the heavy man and me and was managing to keep both of us afloat with relative ease.

It took a minute or so for Captain Odell to move the raft alongside us. Manny grabbed hold of my waistband and hauled me up onto the side of the raft, giving me an extreme wedgie in the process. With Odell's help, I climbed on. It took both of us tugging on an arm apiece and Manny giving Steve a boost on the behind to get the exhausted Steve safely on to the raft. We lay panting and spent on the floor of the raft.

"I love you, man," I said to Manny, thinking I'd never have been able to help Steve on my own. "I love you."

"Whatever love is," Manny said.

Hoisted by my own petard.

Avast! That smarts!

CHAPTER SEVENTEEN

A bedraggled group of tourists, Steve, Courtney, Sherri, Ben, Manny and Tressa returned to *The Epiphany*. When I asked how Ben had fallen into the river in the first place and why they hadn't had captains manning their rafts, Courtney explained the men had paid the captains a nice tip so they could engage in some ridiculous competition as to who could captain their raft more competently.

"They were miffed with our choice of outings," she'd explained, "so Sherri and I gave in and let them have their way."

"So how did Ben fall in again?"

Sherri had answered that query. "He was sticking his pole in the water, it got stuck in mud or something and when he tried to pull it free, he lost his balance and went in," she explained. "Ben isn't that great of a swimmer, so Steve dove in to help haul him out."

Which begged the question:

"If Steve can swim, why did we have to save him?" I'd asked.

"I can swim," Steve said. "I'd have made it to the raft without your help," he maintained. "It was just harder pulling Ben up out of the water and keeping him afloat than I expected. I already was kind of dizzy when we left this morning."

I didn't know what to think of the incident.

"Bet this is one date Barbie won't soon forget," Manny commented to me as we parted ways back on board the *Epiphany*.

Date?

Once back in my cabin I hit the loo, the shower and the box of chocolates—not necessarily in that order. I spent considerable time in the shower, washing the Great River gunk out of my hair and body creases. My clothes were ruined. And thanks to Ranger Rick, I had zero chance to win money toward replacements.

I had just pulled on a pair of shorts and a T-shirt when there was a knock on the cabin door. I padded over to and looked out the peephole, surprised to see Coral LaFavre outside my door. I opened it.

"Hello, Coral," I said, noting she was . . . rumpled. Now, I do rumpled well. And often. But I'd never seen Coral looking anything but spit-shined. Well, except for the mug shot, that is. "What brings you to my humble bat cave?"

"May I come in?" she asked, and I opened the door and motioned her in. "I heard about the river-rafting incident. How fortunate you and Manny were there," she said.

I closed the door and took a seat on my bed. Coral choose the nearby mini sofa.

"It was definitely not in the tourist brochure," I acknowledged. "I'm just glad it had a happy ending. It would have been tragic if this cruise of a lifetime had turned out to be a death voyage," I said pointedly. "Speaking of which, how are *you* enjoying the cruise?"

She looked uncomfortable.

"It's a change," she said. "I suppose I don't have to ask you how you like it so far. Falling down the stairs, hitting your head, losing your memory, and now, jumping into a river to help save a fellow passenger."

I smiled. "I've had a busy cruise, haven't I?" I picked up the box of chocolates, selected one and handed the box to Coral. "Chocolate is my comfort food," I explained.

Coral took a chocolate and set the box down. "My comfort food is French fries with ketchup. As you can probably tell from my thighs, I've needed a lot of comfort lately."

I popped the chocolate in my mouth and put my hand out for the box. She obliged.

"You don't get comfort from your new husband?" I asked, seeing no way the sweaty-palmed fast talker could deliver the kind of attention a woman really needed. But maybe he had hidden talents. If so, they were very well hidden.

Coral took the candy box back and this time placed it on her lap. "I didn't marry David for his comfort quotient," she said.

"Why did you marry him?" I blurted.

Coral popped another chocolate in her mouth. "David was there for me during a particularly hard time," she said.

"Your drunk-driving arrest?" I asked, and she paused in the act of selecting another piece of candy.

"So you do know about that."

I nodded. "You're a star, after all."

She laughed. Not a real laugh. One of those fake ones.

"Star. Right. Well, this 'star' did something incredibly foolish and incredibly wrong. Back then, I was going through hell. My father had just died. My career was on the skids. I'd gained all this weight. I started to drink to dull the pain."

"And David was there for you? Through all that?"

"He was there," she said.

"And you were . . . grateful," I suggested. "You depended on him."

She nodded. "It was a dark time," she said.

"How did you sober up?" I asked. "David again?"

She shook her head. "I did something . . . unforgivable. It sobered me up for good," she said. I saw the pain on her lovely face.

"What did you do, Coral?" I asked, curious as to what she could have done that was serious enough to sober her up overnight.

"Something horrible," she said.

"You can tell me, Coral," I said. "I won't judge. I promise. I just want to help because I really believe you could be in serious danger here," I said.

She stared at me, her expression showing surprise.

"Danger?" she said, and looked like she was about to go on when there was a knock at the door.

"Who could that be?" I asked, jumping up and hurrying to the door. I peeked out. It was David Frazier Compton.

"It's your husband," I whispered, though why I felt it necessary to whisper I couldn't say. "How did he know you were here?" I asked, suspecting he'd followed his wife to my door.

"He knows because I told him I was going to come down and check on you and see if you were okay," she said, getting to her feet, shutting down any confidences she'd been about to share, and any opportunity I had to warn her to watch her back. I opened the door.

"Hullo, David," I greeted Coral's husband.

"Tressa! You don't look any worse for the wear," he said, stepping by me and into the tiny cabin. "Quaint," he said, and I made a face behind his back. Too late, I realized Coral saw me. "Coral, you need to be getting ready for dinner," he said. He spotted the box of chocolates. "Godiva," he commented, picking up the candy. "Well, then, I don't imagine you'll be all that hungry, will you, Coral?" he said, taking a long time to select a piece before shoving it in his mouth. I hoped it was a coconut cream. It would serve him right.

I snatched the box from him. "Actually, these are mine," I said. "Coral here's been good as gold. In fact, you'll be happy to know she didn't touch one of those M&M candies you gave her the other day. I saw to that."

He gave me a brittle smile. "How fortunate for Coral that she has found such a faithful friend. I would have thought your time was better spent with your family trying to jump-start your memory."

"Oh, I assure you, I'm working on learning new things about the people around me everyday," I said.

He blinked.

"Good to know," he said. "Coral? Shall we?" He put out a hand. I noticed she didn't take it, but walked past him to the door.

"I'm glad to see you're okay, Tressa," Coral said. "But you probably need your rest. Take care."

"You too, Coral," I said. "You take care, too."

She looked back at me and nodded. "Count on it," she said. "Coming, David?" Then she left the bat cave. David gave me a dark look and followed. I felt the love.

My gut was starting to hurt from the chocolates I'd consumed, so I decided to go in search of something more nutritious. Which wouldn't be hard at all on the "Eat, Drink, and Definitely Not Be Satisfied" *Epiphany*.

I took little time with my makeup. I considered another raid on the galley and decided I didn't have the strength it required, so I decided to load up a king-sized doggie bag with grilled chicken and veggies, assorted melons, grapes and strawberries, grab a couple bottles of water and spend the rest of the afternoon as a couch potato, watching movies and vegging out.

I was walking by the main desk when I saw Sam Davenport approach from the direction of his office. When I saw who Security Sam was with, I almost walked into the wall: the other man in my life, Manny DeMarco.

I slipped back around the corner, grabbed a *USA Today* from a nearby table and stuck it in front of my face and waited for the two men to finish talking. Five minutes later Manny walked right past me. I counted to ten and followed him. I frowned as he headed for the gangplank. Where on earth was he going? I kept pace with him—hard to do since his stride was twice the length of mine. Sure enough, he was leaving the ship again. I continued to stalk him—I mean *shadow* him—a safe distance back. He left the cruise terminal and hailed a taxi. I noticed he was having the same trouble as he had earlier signaling a taxi. He finally walked up to a taxi and jumped in the back seat.

I saw the other cabbies watching me closely, and remembered how eager they'd been to transport me the time before, when they thought I was flying solo. I was just about to approach the oldest cabbie—he kind of reminded me of Joe—thinking if I had to I could defend myself against this guy, when a hand grabbed my elbow and pulled. I swung around, prepared to use Harry Javelina to defend myself if the need arose, when I discovered it was Taylor who had a hold of me.

"Where do you think you're going?" she asked. "Wasn't today's little river-rafting adventure sufficient excitement?"

I frowned. Just who was the older sister here?

"I wanted to stretch my legs," I said. "Do a little shopping—you know, for family. To show how much I appreciate how great they've been, given my situation and all. So, if you don't mind—"

"Gifts, my bilge pump. You're following Manny De-Marco. I saw him leave the ship ahead of you."

Busted.

"Oh, really? I hadn't noticed," I maintained.

"Come on, Tressa. Level with me for once," Taylor said, and I thought about the conversation she'd had with my father.

"You might try you own advice there, sis," I said. "I know for a fact you're keeping something from me, too. I can tell," I added, giving myself some intuitive power I didn't really have.

"What are you talking about?" Taylor seemed flustered. "I'm not hiding anything."

I looked at her. "Who said hiding? I didn't say 'hiding.' That was your word."

"Oh, this is ridiculous. Let's go back to the ship."

Meanwhile, after some negotiation it appeared Manny had assuaged the cabbie's misgivings and he pulled out.

I ran to the old coot cabbie. "You go ahead, Taylor. I just want to catch up to Manny. Our river-rafting experience didn't turn out as I'd hoped and I thought maybe we could hang out."

I didn't tell her that I thought he had involved himself somehow in a murder for profit that I'd first blown the whistle on, and I wanted to know what exactly he was up to.

I jumped in the taxi. To my irritation, Taylor joined me.

"Follow that cab!" I delivered the legendary line with all the finesse of a seasoned actor. Taylor grunted.

"So, you wanted to hang out with Manny, huh? Why didn't you call out to him and tell him to wait for you instead of skulking around hiding behind that newspaper like some old-time private eye in an old-time B movie?" Taylor asked. Then she looked at me. Really looked at me. "You're sticking your nose where it doesn't belong again? Aren't you?"

Gulp. What to do without confessing the amnesia story was also so much bilge water?

"Okay, okay. So I was following Manny. I was curious. The guy has more secrets than the CIA. So what?"

"Tressa—"

"It'll be cool. We'll do some sightseeing as sisters. Hit some flea markets. Maybe spend some time wasting away in Margaritaville. Everything will be fine! Trust me!" I assured her. "Uh, make sure you don't lose that taxi!" I barked to the cabbie.

She shook her head. "You literally have no common sense, do you?" Taylor asked, and I looked over at her.

"What do you mean?"

"The cruise line warns tourists about venturing out into Montego Bay alone. They counsel us to bring ashore only those items we won't fret over should they be stolen. They educate us about drug dealers, pimps, thieves and corrupt cabbies, and you still decide to throw caution to the wind and leave the ship alone. Like I said. No common sense."

"Hey, mon. Corrupt cabbie? Who says I'm corrupt cabbie? I good cabbie. And very good driver. Get you where you want to go."

"See what you've done. You've upset him," I scolded Taylor. "No, it's fine. We're fine. You're fine!" I assured him. "If you keep that cab in sight, that is," I added.

Taylor shook her head. "You're hopeless."

We drove the several miles from the cruise terminal to the city in relative quiet. Downtown Montego Bay, or MoBay, as everyone called it, was a delightful array of colored storefronts. Yellows, pinks, mauves, oranges, purples, greens and reds, it looked like the color scheme from a children's hospital.

"This is so cool," I said. "Aren't you glad we came?"

"I was here earlier," Taylor said. "With Mom, Kimmie and Charlotte."

"Townsend's mom?" I said, surprised to find I felt a stab of some emotion I didn't care to examine at not being invited along on the outing.

Taylor nodded. "The men were golfing," she said. "I'd rather have been with them."

I raised an eyebrow. Because of Rick, maybe?

We headed down a one-way street at the far end of the Shopping Street when the taxi stopped. I looked out the front windshield. Manny was paying his cabbie.

"This will do," I told our cabbie, shoving Taylor out the door and onto the sidewalk. "Pay the man," I told her, and she shook her head and paid the fare.

"See? I told you, woman. I'm honest businessman," the cabbie said before driving away.

I pulled Taylor along, keeping a good hold on Harry Javelina in case someone coveted my cool bag. Mon.

"This is ridiculous," Taylor said.

"Oh, quitcherbitchin'," I said. "What's done is done."

"Hook you up with some ganja?" One of the less upstanding members of the MoBay community approached us.

"No, thank you," I said, sweetly. "But thanks for asking." We kept walking. "Aren't you proud of me?" I asked. "Friendly and non-confrontational. Just like the cruise line recommends. I wonder how expensive their bags are here."

"Why? Are you getting tired of that ugly warthog?" Taylor said as we entered the flea market area Manny had turned into.

"It's not a warthog. It's a peccary, and I'm very partial to Harry. But I do need something cute and colorful for summer," I pointed out.

"Oh? Peccaries are seasonal?"

"Uh, where'd he go?" I stopped. Manny had vanished. Not an easy thing for a guy that big to do. "Do you see him?"

Taylor looked around. "Nope. Guess he gave us the slip," she said. "Tough break."

"I sense your profound disappointment," I snapped, searching the crowd for a giant who should stick out like a sore thumb.

"We should go," Taylor said. "You mentioned a margarita? Well, I could use one about now."

I looked at her. "For real?" I said, and she nodded. "You and me?" She nodded again.

"Cool, mon," I said, deciding that maybe I didn't really need to know where Manny was and what he was up to all that badly.

I was just about to agree and head straight for Margaritaville when I spotted a familiar figure skulk out of a nearby stall and head away from the flea market. Squee! It was David Frazier Compton, looking guilty as sin of something. His gaze darted from side to side as headed down a side street. I grabbed Taylor's arm.

"Come with me!" I said.

"This is not the place to hail a cab," she pointed out as we made our way through a maze of narrow streets and back alleys. "And I don't think there are any bars down this way."

"So, we're off the beaten path a little," I said. "It makes things interesting."

"What are you up to now?" she asked.

Coral's husband popped into a building a ways down. I pulled Taylor to a stop. I was getting a not-so-good feeling about our situation. Less people. Less traffic. Fewer witnesses. Could spell trouble with a big T.

"Just give me a minute to look into this shop," I replied. "Then we'll go."

We came to the storefront David had disappeared into. One quick look, I told myself, and then we'd leave. I pulled Taylor around to an alley behind the building.

"This is not good," my sister said.

"Stay here," I commanded, and moved to a window to look in. It was a bar. But definitely not a tourist hotspot. So why would David come here?

"Let's go, Tressa!" Taylor said, and I nodded.

"Okay. Yeah. Fine. Let's hit it. I hear a frozen margarita calling my name, mon," I agreed.

I left the small porch to join Taylor when a dilapidated cab pulled alongside. "Taxi?" the driver asked.

"Yes, thank God!" Taylor said, but I shook my head.

"No thank you, we're good," I told the driver, a nasty-looking character with teeth that hadn't seen a toothbrush and floss in like . . . ever.

"I thought you said you were done with this little wild goose chase," Taylor said. "Face it. We lost him. So get in the taxi already!" Taylor said, and opened the back door.

"Yes. Do get in, Miss Turner." David Frazier Compton appeared from behind the corner of an adjacent building. "Please."

"No. Really. You take this taxi. We can wait for the next one," I said.

"Why don't we share?" he suggested, and I didn't care for the look in his eyes at all.

"Tressa?" Taylor questioned.

"In you go, ladies," he said, and motioned to the car, and it was then I spotted his hand in the pocket of his pants, an ominous bulge so not of the Viagra kind. "You ride up front there," he told Taylor. "Tressa and I'll take the back."

I nodded to her and we got in.

"We're headed for Margaritaville," Taylor said. "But you can have him take you where you want to go first," she added, clearly nervous.

"How accommodating," he said. "And you are sisters, right?"

I looked at him, keeping an eye on the hand in his pocket as well.

"I pay attention. I notice things. I'm in the information business much like you, Tressa," he said. "As an agent, I'm required to know who is casting for what roles, what projects are coming up, along with what PR ops are available. So I pay close attention to everything and everyone around me who can affect my world either positively or negatively. That's why I've made it a point to learn as much about you as I could, Tressa."

"I'm flattered," I said. "Do you really think I have what it takes?"

David looked puzzled. "I beg your pardon? I don't follow."

"You're thinking I might have potential as an actress, right?" I said. "You're thinking of offering me representation. Oh, I'm so happy! Down deep I always thought I could make it on the big screen. Do you think they will ever do a remake of *True Grit*, because I'd make an awesome Mattie Ross of Dardenelle County." I paused and cleared my throat. " 'Do you know a Marshall Rooster Cogburn? They say he has grit. I want a man with grit,' " I started quoting the famous movie lines. " 'If you think you can cheat me, you're mistaken. You've not heard the last of Mattie Ross. You may well hear from my lawyer, Daggett.' " I paused again. "Not bad, huh?"

"You can't be serious," David said. "I've seen better line delivery from a mime."

I resisted the urge to pummel the guy.

"I know. I know," I said. "It's probably sacrilege to even attempt such a remake. After all, there was only one Duke Wayne. Right? By the way, did you know that John Wayne's birthplace is only several counties over from my hometown? How cool is that, mon? They have a museum and everything." I finished up, my motormouth running out of steam. I opened my mouth to take another breath and ask if the agent thought Westerns would ever make a comeback when David raised a hand.

"Enough chatter. Why were you following me?"

"You? We weren't following you," Taylor put in, and I wanted to slap a muzzle on her. "We were following Manny DeMarco." She looked at me. "Weren't we?"

I nodded.

"Why were you following Mr. DeMarco?" David asked.

"You've heard of the little wager on board *The Epiphany*," I said. "You know. The one as to whether I'll end up with Manny DeMarco or Rick Townsend," I said. He nodded. "Well, I just wanted to find out everything I could about Manny. Sometimes he's a little . . . secretive, you know," I added. "Men really don't know how to communicate effectively." I shook my head sadly.

"And so?" David said.

"So, when I saw him leave the ship, I decided to follow him and see where he was going. I know. So wrong of me. I'm, like, totally ashamed. Really I am. Deeply ashamed. But there you have it."

"You expect me to believe that story," David said. "When I know you've been snooping on the Internet trying to dig up dirt on me?"

I could see the way this was going. And I was getting the feeling it was strictly one way.

"What did Coral tell you about me?" he asked, and I frowned.

"Coral? She didn't tell me anything."

"You're lying," David said. "I can see it in your face. What did she say?" He patted his bulge to make his point.

"We were talking about marriage, and she said you'd been there for her through some terrible times," I said, bending the truth a wee bit. "She said your being in her life helped her sober up. That's what she said. But that's all she said. She's a special person," I told him.

"She is that," David said, giving me a long, considering look. "And that's all she said?"

I nodded.

"You know, I'd like to believe you, but I don't," he said. "I think she shared more than that with you. Did she tell you about her drinking? About her accident? That she hit someone when she was drunk? That she blacked out and left the scene?" he asked.

I sucked in my breath.

I did something horrible.

That's what Coral had said when I'd asked how she'd sobered up. No wonder she'd quit drinking. Why wasn't there anything online about the accident when I'd Googled her then?

"Ah, as I suspected. She did mention it," David said, seeing my expression. "Coral's a fool. More so when she drank. What else did she share with her new friend? Did she also tell you that she despised me and wished me dead? Did she admit she was trying to kill me?"

"Uh, what's going on?" Taylor asked, but I could only stare at David.

"Kill you? What do you mean?" I said. "You're the one trying to kill her."

He shot a look at me.

"What the bloody hell are you talking about?" he said. "I have no intention of killing Coral. Why would I? She's my meal ticket."

"For the insurance," I said. "The policy you hold on her. The one with you as beneficiary."

"Excuse me, but what's this about murder?" Taylor asked, once again ignored.

"What policy?" David said to me. "Coral's insurance goes to her mother in the event of her death. She was adamant about that. What on earth would lead you to believe I wanted Coral dead? Actually, I'm quite fond of her, you know. In my own way, of course."

"She's your meal ticket?" I shook my head. "You're only with her because of money? You don't love her? She doesn't love you," I said, trying to sort things out by talking them out. "So why did she marry you?" I asked. "Unless." I stopped. Of course. David knew about Coral's accident yet it had never been made public. Why? Because neither of them had reported it.

I thought some more.

Blackmail! David was blackmailing Coral! It was clear now. He'd keep Coral's dirty little secret if she kept him in the manner to which he'd become accustomed.

But, if David wasn't the one planning to end his wife's life then . . . it had to be either Steve or Ben.

"Shit," I said.

"I'd say 'deep shit,' Miss Turner," David said.

"Okay. That's it! What's going on?" Taylor asked. "I don't think we're headed in the right direction," she said.

"We're taking the long way home," David said. "My new friend Cruz here has friends who know how to deal with people who can't resist sticking their noses where they really don't belong." He shook his head. "So, all this time you thought I was plotting to kill Coral. That's priceless. If only I'd known that was what you were looking into, I could have assuaged your fears quite easily. But now . . . now you really know too much. Sorry, ladies, but it looks like your Lifestyle Makeovers end here. I can't risk you getting back onboard the ship and having a little tête a tête with Coral."

He couldn't mean . . .

"Holy shit!" I reached out to punch David in the face,

reaching for the bulge in his pocket at the same time he did. "Grab the wheel, Taylor! Grab the wheel!"

I waited for the car to take a sudden veer and braced myself to plow into a building or wall but instead the car began to slow. And slow. And slow.

"Get out!" Taylor yelled. "I got the keys! Run! Run!"

I found myself locked in David's surprisingly strong grip. Had his limp-wristed overtures also been a con?

"Let go!" I yelled. "Let. Go!"

The car door behind David was unceremoniously yanked open. I took quick advantage and shoved David as hard as I could.

"I said, let go!" I yelled, and we both tumbled out into the dirt.

"Do as the lady says," I heard, and looked up to see Manny DeMarco above us, a huge foot pressing down on David's throat. David's eyes got big and buggy. He let go of me.

"I think he's got a gun," I told Manny, my breath coming in fits and starts. He shrugged.

"Who doesn't?" Manny said.

"I also believe he's blackmailing Coral," I said, getting to my feet and brushing myself off. "He sure as hell isn't much of an agent. He belittled my Mattie Ross performance. Some agent," I spat. "And this is the second set of clothes I've ruined in one day! You're gonna pay for these." I pointed to David. "You are."

"Barbie?"

I stopped. My legs were shaking so badly they almost couldn't support me, my arms and hands a palsy fest. "Yeah?"

"Get out of here."

"Huh?"

"Leave. Now!" Manny said.

"Come again?"

"You two. Vamoose. Leave. Now."

I started to object, saw the look on his face and thought better of it.

"Okay. Okay. Message received. We're gone. And you, buster?" I stepped over David as I went to leave. "You'll never work in this town again!"

I retrieved my sister, whose shaking was only slightly worse than mine, and we started walking.

"Uh, ladies? That way." Manny pointed us in the opposite direction.

We did a U-turn, finally making our way back to the bustling shopping district of MoBay, where taxis waited to take us wherever our hearts desired.

I hailed one.

"Where we going, ladies?" the cabbie said.

I looked at Taylor. "I suppose you're not up for Margaritaville now," I said, thinking I'd consider myself fortunate if I survived the tongue lashing I got from Taylor on the two-mile ride back to the cruise terminal.

"To the cruise terminal, James," I said, deciding I was going to remain onboard the *Epiphany* for the rest of the cruise. No matter what.

"Cancel that. Take us to Margaritaville," I heard Taylor say, and I looked at her.

"Taylor? Are you sure?"

"You're damn right, I am. After this shore excursion? No way am I going back to that bloody ship sober!" she said.

"Irie!" I said. "Irie!"

Jamaican translation: You've made me so happy!

Squee!

CHAPTER EIGHTEEN

We returned to the ship a full hour before departure. I helped Taylor to her cot and left her there to doze. I'd intended to ply Taylor with alcohol and then ply her with questions as to the identity of the mystery man she had a tender for, but once Taylor had a drink or two and loosened up a bit, I discovered I was actually having fun with my sister. Fun! Since this was something I'd rarely experienced with Taylor before, I found myself reluctant to spoil the moment and had avoided the subject of men altogether.

We'd get to the issue eventually, but right now I needed to talk to Coral, to tell her I knew her agent-husband was blackmailing her and tell Davenport about David's attempt to have Taylor and Tressa kidnapped—or worse. And also I had to convince Davenport that, if David wasn't out to off Coral, then that meant either Courtney or Sherri was the target.

I was headed to the security office when I spotted Courtney and Sherri in chairs near the reception area. I hurried over to them.

"Thank God you're both here. Are you okay? Has something happened? Have you figured out which one of you is married to the Black Widower? Is that why you're here?" I asked. "You should demand the FBI be brought in. Insist on round-the-clock protection. Have him thrown in the brig."

"What on earth are you talking about, Tressa?" Courtney asked. "We're here about this morning. Word got around to the cruise line of our little rafting incident, and we've got to file a report."

I frowned. "You're not here to report an attempted murder plot?" I asked.

The women stared. "Murder? Whose murder?"

Yours!" I said. Courtney and Sherri looked at each other. "Hers?"

They pointed to each other.

I shook my head. "I don't know. One of you."

They looked at each other again.

"You better sit down, Tressa," Courtney suggested, motioning to a chair. "What happened to you? You don't look good. Does she, Sherri? You're a total mess. And you've got us worried."

"You should be worried," I said, taking a seat. "Both of you. I'm sorry to have to be the one to break this to you, but Sherri . . ." I took her hand. "I think your husband may be trying to kill you," I told her.

"Huh?" Sherri looked like I did when I began the math portion of the ACT in high school.

I nodded and squeezed her hand, then released it. "However, on the off chance I could be wrong," I said, turning back to Courtney and taking her hand. "Courtney, I think *your* husband may be trying to kill you."

"Kill me? Steve?" She looked horrified. "Tressa, I think you need to go lie down and rest for a bit," Courtney said. "Don't you, Sherri? You're really not making any sense at all. That bump to your head. Now you show up here all messed up—"

"I'm fine," I snapped. "You two are the ones in peril."

"I think Courtney's right, Tressa. You need rest," Sherri said.

"You don't get it! I overheard one of your husbands!" I

smacked a hand palm-down on the table. "The first night. Before the mandatory safety drill. I overheard a husband planning to whack his wife for insurance money."

Courtney and Sherri simply sat and stared. At *me*. Then at each other. At their hands.

"Didn't you hear me? I overheard someone plotting his wife's demise for dinero!" I repeated.

"I thought you lost your memory," Courtney said. "How can you remember what happened the first night aboard ship?"

"It was a ruse!" I said. "A scam! A hoax! For self-protection. You see, I think someone became suspicious of me when I tried to tip you all off at the Stardust that first night with my insurance infomercial, and they decided I knew too much, tried to silence me by pushing me down the stairwell, failed, decided to give it another try in sickbay by smothering me with a pillow, failed once again, but left enough of a clue behind that I was able to narrow it to three or four people. Now, that appears to be down to two: your husbands, Steve and Ben."

Silence greeted my rather breathless narrative.

This time, it was Courtney who reached out to pat my hand.

"I think you're . . . confused, Tressa," she said. "You've had an . . . eventful cruise so far. First you're surprised by the unexpected appearance of a former fiancé. You're torn between two lovers, unable to make up your mind between two great guys. You take a tumble down the stairs and suffer a head injury and decide to tell everybody you lost your memory. This just isn't how normal people behave. But who can blame you? You're under a lot of stress. And people under stress imagine things. It happens all the time. Especially with head injuries. I'm a nurse. I know."

I shook my head. "I didn't make this stuff up. It happened. The conversation I overheard."

"You misunderstood it," Courtney said.

"The fall down the stairs."

"An accident. You slipped and fell," she explained.

"Almost being smothered with a pillow in sickbay," I countered.

"You dreamt it," Courtney responded. "Besides, my husband and I don't carry any life insurance. I told you that. We cut corners. Canceled our policy. And I doubt Ben and Sherri carry all that much either. What about it, Sherri?"

Her friend shrugged. "Enough to bury us, I suppose," she said, and I noticed she shivered. "I really don't know. Ben handles that stuff."

"Don't you see, Tressa?" Courtney said. "All this is just is the product of stress combined with a pretty significant head injury. You yourself have to admit you've been acting pretty strangely. Running back and forth that first night between Manny and Rick. Entering the contest to win the TV on the heels of your head injury. Jumping into the river to try and save a two hundred eighty-pound man. It all points to some skewed reasoning."

I stared at her. My God. She was actually questioning the state of my sanity. My reason. I'd been seen as eccentric before, but never psychologically disturbed.

I stood. "I know what I heard," I said. "And I know what I heard spells out an SOS for one of you. An SOS as in 'Spouse Offs Spouse.' And I'll do whatever it takes to narrow the suspects down to one. In the meantime, if I were you, I would avoid spending any alone time with my hubby. It could be hazardous to your health. Forewarned is forearmed," I added.

"I can see I've upset you—" Courtney said.

Hah. Ya think? Here I was trying to save some poor unsuspecting wife—at, I might add, considerable expense to my own cruise experience—and this was the thanks I got: A characterization just a few degrees this side of Roswell, New Mexico?

"Just remember what I said," I told them. "'Tis a foul

wind a brewin' on the *Epiphany*—and it isn't the result of trainers run amok."

I hurried over to the reception area myself. "I need to see the security chief right away," I requested.

"Is it another 'matter of life and death'?" Erica, the girl I'd spoken to the last time, referenced my previous visit.

"Wow. You're good," I said, "because it *is* a matter of life and death. Yep," I went on, wagging a finger at her. "You. You're good. Your talents are wasted on front desk duty. With your skills you should at the very least be, oh, I don't know, assisting the shipboard magician, maybe?" I said. Her attitude had given me one of my own.

"As I told your two friends, Mr. Davenport is unavailable at present," she said, giving me a get-lost look. "You're welcome to wait if you like, but I'm not sure how long it will be," she added.

I thought over my options. I could go straight to Coral with my suspicions and confront her . . .

"You wouldn't by chance be able to tell me what stateroom Coral LaFavre is in," I asked.

Erica shook her head. "I couldn't and wouldn't."

"But we're good friends, you see," I went on. "As a matter of fact, she came up to my cabin earlier and we shared a box of Godiva chocolates."

"You've been eating Godiva chocolates? On the Custom Cruise to a New You? You've been cheating and eating Godiva chocolate? They won't even let us drink soda while we're working because it sets a bad example for the passengers," she said. "And all the time you're cheating with chocolate!"

"It's my comfort food!" I defended. "Coral's is French fries and ketchup. So, what's yours?" I asked.

Erica looked to her right and left and picked up a dark drawstring pouch and shook it. "Skittles," she said.

"It's our little secret," I promised. "Now about that cabin room?"

"That's *my* little secret," she said.

Damn. Next time I'd bring the Godiva along and see how bribery worked.

I made a stop by Manny's cabin to find out what happened after Taylor and I'd left him behind on land and stuck my ear to the door to see if I could figure out if Aunt Mo was inside. When I heard the spinning *Wheel of Fortune* wheel and heard a familiar voice exclaim, "You don't need to buy no vowels! What are you? An idiot!" I hightailed it out of there.

Stonewalled, at least for the moment, I decided I'd better go back and check on my lightweight little sis. I let myself into the cabin and quietly tiptoed to her bedside. I shook my head recalling Taylor's earlier overindulgence: She would have put Jimmy Buffet to shame with her "wasting away again" routine. I had done the big sis thing, tipping back a single Red Stripe beer and letting her vent and philosophize on the sad state of things in general, lamenting my loss of memory and my talent for trouble.

As I bent over to tuck her covers around her, she grabbed my hand. "You know, I never meant for it to happen," she mumbled.

"Huh?" I said, then, "It's all right, sis. Everyone has to break loose once in a while," I said, thinking she was apologizing for getting groggy on the grog.

"It's not all right!" Taylor said. "It's not. You saw him first."

I frowned. "Who?" I said. "What are you talking about?"

"You saw him first," she mumbled. "I know that. Prior claim and all. Still, I never meant for it to happen. Honest. But I think it might be . . . at least for me . . . it just might be . . . love."

I took a step back.

Saw him first? Prior claim?

Love?

I put a hand to my suddenly heavy heart and dropped to my bed.

Ahoy, Davy Jones, we need to talk. A cowgirl from the Hawkeye state with a heartache as big as Texas really needs to know. Do tell. How did ye get the courage to cut out yer own heart?

CHAPTER EIGHTEEN

I left Taylor in bed the next morning sleeping off her excesses of the night before, my heart still hurting, my brain crammed full of information I badly needed to share and purge. Last night I'd intended to hook up with Manny and Coral, but had fallen asleep listening to my sister's drunken pillow talk and alcohol-induced snoring. But this morning found me a woman prepared to take action.

I'd initially debated my course of action. Should I save a life or ascertain if my sister was in love with a man I'd lusted after and obsessed over for more than a decade?

I'd opted to let sleeping sisters lie.

After yesterday's excursions I was content to remain hidden away on the ship, but after the situation with David, I knew I had to demand action. Tell someone. Today's port of call in Grand Cayman and the Cayman Islands might provide an opportunity for U. S. federal law enforcement to be brought in and an official investigation initiated.

I considered the situation. David Frazier Compton had denied he was trying to kill his wife. Why, if he planned to silence me anyway, wouldn't he just go ahead and admit it? In fact, he'd actually thought Coral was out to do him in— which made sense if he was blackmailing her about the accident, but made absolutely no sense when it came to the phone call I'd eavesdropped on. That had clearly been a man, and he'd been speaking about the woman in his life. And insurance policy makes three.

What were the odds that there were two murder plots afloat? Coral certainly had ample motive to do away with David. Or motives. Blackmail and a love affair made pretty compelling reasons for murder. But there was also the incident in the sickbay to consider. Sam Davenport had been Johnny-on-the-spot right after the attack. But why would he want to see me dead? He already knew what I'd overheard—already knew I'd thought it was David involved. Had he decided at that point to do away with David? For Coral? For love? Had he thought of me as a loose end who could come back to trip him up later?

Now that David had apparently been ruled out as plotting Coral's murder—who killed their only source of income, anyway?—the only other possible contenders were Ben and Steve. I sighed. I didn't have a choice. I had to level with Sam Davenport, tell him the truth about my memory just as I had with Sherri and Courtney, relate what had transpired with David Frazier Compton the night before and turn it over to him once and for all. But I wasn't going without backup. Just in case.

I thought initially about recruiting Manny. He already knew about the man on the phone. Still, after Manny's cloak and dagger routine of the evening before, and given his contact with Davenport, I wasn't comfortable keeping it in that particular family.

I thought for a second longer. Rick. I'd tell Rick. He'd be majorly bent out of shape when I told him what I'd been up to, but he was a good man to have on your side in a tight spot. Experience had taught me that.

So. I'd explain everything to Ranger Rick. He'd rant and rave and piss and moan, but he'd eventually come around. And he'd help me figure out what to do next.

I quickly showered off the smell of booze and cigarette

smoke, dressed and hurried to Townsend's stateroom. I knocked.

"Townsend, I need to talk to you," I called. "It's a matter of life and death." I was saying that a lot lately.

"Tressa?" I heard. "Just a minute."

It took another half minute for Townsend to open his door. Dressed in shorts and a T-shirt, his hair rumpled, it was clear he hadn't showered yet.

"Did I wake you?" I said, thinking that a bit odd considering Ranger Rick was one of those weird and frightening individuals known as a day person. "Have a bad night?" I asked, getting a sudden whiff of food. Food that smelled like—bacon!

"Do you have food in there?" I asked, craning my head to see more, delivering that line with as much outrage as a suspicious spouse delivers the old "Do you have a woman in there?"

"It's not a good time, Tressa," Rick said.

"Sorry. I can't wait for a better one," I said, getting the sense that Townsend was hiding something—and figuring bacon wasn't the half of it. I sniffed. "Is that a cinnamon roll I smell?" I asked, planting my foot in the door—not really all that wise considering I was wearing sandals. "Let me in," I ordered.

"Fine, but don't get the wrong idea, okay?" he said.

Now I was really concerned. I sniffed. Could we be talking eggs Benedict?

I gave him a peeved look as I stepped into the room and said, "So you lacked the resolve to resist going off the Eat Your Way to a Healthy Life plan. We can't all have the strength of character I possess. No biggie," I added, turning to discover Townsend had a co-conspirator in his illicit breakfast. Brianna, the trainer, was sitting on the tiny futon love seat feeding her face.

"I'm sorry. Am I interrupting?" I bent over and got a

whiff of hollandaise sauce. Tell me I don't have a talent for sniffing things out. "Isn't this cozy? And isn't this also like contraband?" I said, picking up a length of honest-to-goodness bacon.

"Brianna and I were just catching up," Townsend said. "You're welcome to join us."

I let the bacon fall to Townsend's plate like it was a ganja pipe. "I wouldn't dream of it," I said. "I'm actually committed to making positive changes in my diet to promote long-term good health."

"You're kidding," Townsend said.

I shook my head. "Why do you say that?"

"Because you're the girl whose idea of a nutritious breakfast is cold pizza left over from the night before. You're also the girl who keeps Cadbury crème eggs from Easter in your freezer to eat year-round," he said.

"I do not!" I said.

"Oh? How do you know? You've lost your memory. Remember?" Townsend taunted.

"I'd know if I did something like that," I said. "I'd remember."

"Right," Townsend said. "Right."

I stalked to the door and opened it. I was just about to yell "Screw you and the Starcraft speedboat you sailed in on!" and storm out of the cabin when, to my shocked surprise, those actual words did not come out. Instead, what I heard was, "Brianna? Beat it!"

She stared at me. Townsend did, too. Okay, so I was more than a little blown away, myself. This was the last thing I'd planned to do. Or say.

"What?" Brianna got slowly to her feet.

"I said beat it. Rick and I have some catching up of our own to do. And sorry, but three's a crowd, even with an ex-girlfriend."

Brianna's stunned expression was mirrored by Townsend's.

"Rick?" she said. "Do you want me to go?" she asked.

I crossed my arms and looked at Townsend. "Well?" I said. "Do you?"

His stunned expression turned to one so hot I was afraid his eyebrows would start to singe. "Beat it, Brianna," he said, his eyes never leaving mine.

It was my turn to be stunned. "Huh?"

"What?" Brianna repeated. "You want me to leave?" she asked.

Townsend shook his head. "No. But I want her to stay more." He walked Brianna to the door. "Sorry, Bree. It was good to see you," he told her, shutting the door, leaning his back against it, arms crossed, to study me.

"You never cease to amaze me," he said, shaking his head, "but I don't know why that still surprises me . . . Calamity Jayne, considering you're known for that kind of thing."

"What I know is that reputation is the product of flawed thinking—as is that catchy but misplaced moniker," I told him, feeling suddenly like I'd walked into a bull's cage, shut the door and thrown away the key. *Ay caramba!*

"So? You said we had some catching up of our own to do," Townsend said, unfolding his arms as he walked across the stateroom toward me.

"I did. We do," I agreed, panic creeping into my stammered responses. "I've got a sort of admission to make," I told him. "It can't wait."

Townsend stopped a step away. "Oh? It sounds serious."

"It is. Serious," I said, telling my eyes to look anywhere but at his lips. To gaze at anything but his gorgeous brown eyes. So they did. And to my acute embarrassment my peepers moved to the area between his legs.

Shit.

"Tressa? What are you looking at?" Townsend sounded amused.

"Nothing!" I forced my eyeballs to safer scenes and, instead, surveyed his room and the big full-sized bed that made mine look like a camping cot.

"Nice bed," I said. "I bet that it's way more comfortable than my army bunk."

"You're welcome to try it out and see," Townsend offered, and for half a second (okay, longer) I considered taking him up on his offer.

"Will you be joining me?" I teased.

"That depends," Townsend responded.

I raised an eyebrow. "On what?"

"On whether I'm invited," he said, closing the distance between us.

Okay, now here's where I might lose you all, so I have to explain what happened next and why. You know, so you'll understand.

There I was. A huge responsibility on my shoulders. Emotionally confused. Nutritionally deprived. Majorly nookie-starved. In a stateroom where you didn't stub your toe turning around. The tantalizing smells of bacon, Cinnabon cinnamon and hollandaise sauce mixing and mingling and teasing my senses. The man I personally thought should make the *People* magazine cover for sexiest man alive giving me a Long John Silver ain't got nothing on me look. Okay, I've set the scene.

And . . . action!

"It's your bed," I said, my voice shaking. "You hardly need an invitation."

He reached out and pulled me to him, his palms pressed against my lower back, his hands making soft, soothing circles, warming my skin.

"So, does this mean some things are coming back to you?" Ranger Rick asked, bringing one hand up to cup my chin. "Are you remembering?"

"I'm not quite sure. Quiz me?" I heard myself say.

Ranger Rick's gaze sharpened. The heat of his embrace ramped up, putting out only slightly less heat than Shadrach, Meshach and Abednego's fiery furnace. He gathered me close. Brushing back the hair from my face with caressing fingertips, he cradled my jaw with his hand and brought his lips to mine.

I found myself thankful I'd taken the time to brush and floss.

He kissed me softly. A nice kiss. A sweet kiss. He pulled back to look at me.

"Is that familiar?" he asked.

"Hmm," I said. "It's hard to say, given such limited exposure."

He kissed me again; this time his kiss was longer. Wetter. Hotter.

He pulled away. "How about now? Do you remember that?"

Certain key areas of my body sure did.

"I can't be positive," I said.

His next kiss was deeper, totally intense and wickedly carnal. When he ended the kiss, I could hardly stand, so it was a good thing he'd backed me over to the bed. The mattress hit the back of my knees and I dropped to the bed on my back.

"Did that ring any bells?" Townsend asked, his grin negated by the serious look in his eyes.

I looked up at him. "All of them," I said, and he eased me back onto the mattress and covered my body with his.

I vaguely remembered there was something important I needed to discuss with Ranger Rick, vaguely remembered I suspected my sister thought she was in love with him, but the feel of his tongue sliding over my neck and his teeth nipping at my earlobe all but erased any other urgency from my head. When his hand slid across my breast and cupped it, I knew I was lost in a sea of sensation that had too long been denied. I was adrift with acute awareness, an awareness of needs left unsatisfied, unfulfilled, an awareness that I was venturing into uncertain waters; but also I had the sudden clarity that here, with this man, I would find safe passage.

Every part of my body was throbbing. And I wasn't the only one. Townsend's timber was a-shiverin', too.

He kissed me again, long and hard. "Nice shirt," he said. "But I bet what's under it is even nicer." His crooked smile did a number on my vitals.

"You're talking about my sports bra. Right?" I teased, my voice breathless and husky.

He pulled at a strap. "Hot pink," he observed. "Your favorite. Mine, too. When you're in it," he added, pushing aside the opening of the white blouse I wore to nuzzle the skin at the top of my turquoise tank top. "But even more when you're out of it."

I felt Townsend's hand creep beneath my shirt and over my bare midriff. I shivered as his hand roamed upward, his thumb and finger finding and squeezing my nipple, but I was powerless to do anything but arch against him like a wanton woman in a romance novel. A woman in lust.

Or . . . love, maybe?

I felt my shirt being lifted over my head and Townsend settled over me, looking deep into my eyes as he tugged on one hot-pink bra strap.

I held my breath.

He slowly pulled the bra strap down. Cool air hit my nipple, sending a flood of feeling soaring through wondrous places.

He looked at me for a long moment.

Oh shit, oh shit, oh shit.

He bent his head and took my nipple in his mouth.

Oh. My. God.

My eyes rolled back in my head and a bolt of pure ecstasy coursed through me. This was it. This was the moment. This was the man. All bets were off. Batten down the hatches and full speed ahead. Ding. Ding. Ding. X marks the spot!

Townsend pulled my other strap down, his fingers rubbing my nipples, his tongue flicking at the tips before his lips left my breasts to come back to my mouth, his tongue swooping inside and leaving me no doubt he'd arrived at the same latitude and longitude. I moaned into his mouth, ready to demand he shuck his shirt, when the phone rang.

I tensed. He sensed it.

"You better get that," I said. "It could be important."

He grimaced. "Not more important than this," he said, and kissed me again.

"You can't just let it ring. What if there's an emergency? The ship is taking on water. The captain has had a heart attack?" *A passenger has been murdered.*

"We're in port," he pointed out. "But anything to make you happy," he said, and giving me a quick kiss he got up and answered the phone.

"Hello? Oh, hi, Taylor," Rick said.

Taylor? I instantly thought about her mumbled confession the night before.

I think—at least for me—it might just be love.

I sat up on the bed, my bra inching downward.

"As a matter of fact, she's right here. Sure. Hang on." Townsend held the receiver out to me. "It's your sister. Says she needs to talk to you."

I got up and took the phone, yanking my bra straps back up in place. "Taylor?" I answered, my tone somewhat chilly, wondering if she'd suspected I might be with Townsend, then feeling all guilty because I was with Townsend and he was presently nuzzling my neck. I shooed him away. "What is it?" I asked.

"Oh, Tressa, I'm so glad I found you. You've got to come quick. Something's happened!" Taylor said, her voice unnaturally high, her words uncharacteristically rushed.

My God! My sister with an actual, documented case of motormouth?

"What's wrong, Taylor? It's not Mom or Dad or Gammy? Or Craig or Kimmie? Is it?" I asked, my heart racing.

"No. No. It's David Frazier Compton, Coral's husband."

I frowned. "*Oo*kay. What about him?"

"He's missing. He never returned to the ship last night," Taylor said. The same blood that just seconds before had been at a high boil now cooled like pizza when the carton top is left open. My chin almost reached my bellybutton my mouth dropped open so far.

"What are you talking about? What, you mean he missed the departure?"

"Yes! That's exactly what I mean," Taylor said. "He never made it back to the *Epiphany*. Can you believe it?"

No.

And, strangely . . . yes.

"What could have happened to him?" Taylor asked.

"They do warn tourists to be careful and not go out on their own," I pointed out, but thinking no way would David have anything to fear from MoBay riff-raff. He was one of them. "I imagine he just lost track of time," I said, hoping I was correct.

"Then why doesn't he just go to the cruise terminal and have them contact the ship?" Taylor asked.

"He didn't?"

"No, he didn't."

Maybe because . . . he can't.

The thought hung there between us, and I shivered when I remembered that the last time I'd seen David he was in danger of having his windpipe crushed by a 14 wide.

"We have to tell the authorities what we know!" Taylor whispered. "Tell them what happened."

"No! We can't do that! Not yet. We need to talk. Get our stories straight," I said, and Ranger Rick's hands slid from my shoulders.

"Get your stories straight?" he mouthed, shaking his head in a "What's going on now?" motion.

I waved a hand at him.

"Listen. Stay in the cabin. I'm on my way. We'll figure out our next move. Stay there!"

I slammed the phone down, threw my shirt over my head, readjusted my clothing and grabbed Harry.

"What's going on, Tressa?" Rick said. "Who missed the ship?"

"Coral LaFavre's husband, David."

"Oh? And why are we so concerned about this David?" He looked at me in such a way I grew uncomfortable.

"Coral's become a friend," I said, wanting to tell Townsend everything but suddenly afraid that when I did someone I cared about could be in a great deal of trouble.

"What was all that about getting your stories straight?" he said.

"Oh, that. Gram and Joe want to go sailing on a catamaran but Taylor and I are trying to talk them into something safer. Like the pirate reenactment. Or going to hell."

Townsend looked at me. "And that's all?" he said. "You're sure?"

"For now," I replied. "Just for now. I'd better go. Taylor's waiting."

"You know, I had big plans for us today, too, Tressa," Townsend said, brushing the hair back out of my eyes with a tender gesture. "Will you save some time for me?"

He looked so serious that I almost stopped then and there and tossed him on the bed, leaving no doubt that that was where I wanted to be. "I'll try," I said. "I'll really try."

I headed for the door, snagging a cinnamon roll and cold bacon from the tray on the table as I left. I'd need all the strength I could get, because I just might have stumbled onto what my faux-beau/fake-fiancé Manny DeMarco really did for a living.

Manny Dishman/DeMarco/da deadliest hitman to ever sail the seven seas. My very own candy-giving, ring-bearing, life-saving assassin. What more could a woman want?

Yup, that's what you call a man to die for.

CHAPTER NINETEEN

"Okay, what's this about Coral's David?" I said, opening the stateroom door and skidding to a sudden stop when I saw Taylor and Coral sitting on the mini sofa. "Uh, hello," I said. "You, uh, haven't started without me, have you, Taylor?" I asked, wondering if my sis had already spilled the beans about our encounter with Coral's husband and Manny's walk-on role in our *The Turner Girls Go Wild in Jamaica* travel flick.

"You know the party never can begin without you being here, Tressa," Taylor said as I tossed Harry Javelina on the bed. She gave me a weird look. "Where have you been? And what is that in your hand?"

I remembered the cinnamon roll—I'd eaten the cold bacon on my sprint back to the stateroom.

"It's a bran muffin," I lied.

"With frosting?"

Eagle-eye.

"It's faux frosting," I said. "Hello, Coral. How long have you been here?" I asked.

"Long enough to get the feeling you know something about David I don't," she said.

"That long, huh?" I responded.

"Coral stopped by to tell you about David," Taylor said. "She was kind of here when I called."

Son of a barnacle.

"Are you going to tell me what's going on?" Coral asked.

I pulled the chair out from the desk and sat facing Coral and Taylor.

"Let's go in order. You first," I said.

Coral stared at me. "What do you mean?"

"Chronological order," I said. "Your story came first."

Coral's eyelids narrowed. "What story?"

"You know. The one with all the ingredients of a best-selling whodunit," I said. "The one that features the glamorous celebrity and her blackmailing agent-publicist husband. That story."

Coral put a hand to her mouth. She looked at Taylor and back at me.

"How the hell—"

"It's my gift," I said, with a shrug. "Backstory, please."

"All right, all right. Yes. David has been blackmailing me," Coral admitted.

"Over your drunk-driving accident," I said, and her eyes got big again. "When you hit someone."

"Drunk-driving?" Taylor said.

"Girl. You're good," Coral told me.

I nodded. "And David offered to keep his mouth shut about the hit and run—for a price. Right?" I said.

"Hit and run?" Taylor said.

Coral nodded. Tears filled her eyes, and I handed her a tissue box from the desk. She took one and dabbed. "You don't know the half," she said. "I didn't just hit someone." She hesitated. "I killed someone."

My own gasp was drowned out by Taylor's.

"Killed someone?" we said.

Coral blew her nose and nodded. "I know. It's horrible. Unforgivable. And I have no defense for letting this go on for so long other than the fact that I'm a craven little coward. Well, maybe not so little," she admitted.

"What happened?" Taylor asked.

"It was several years back. My career was on the skids.

My father had just died. I'd gained weight. I was miserable. David was being an ass and not getting me any new work. I was getting ready to cut him loose. I started to drink. A little at first," Coral explained. "It was a way to escape. Well, that's what I thought. Instead, it made me a prisoner. I'd had the one drunk-driving arrest. I told myself after that I'd never drink again, but I was so unhappy. And I felt better when I felt nothing at all."

"What happened that night?" I asked. "The night you hit someone?"

She shook her head. "I don't remember all that much. I'd been drinking. So what else was new? I didn't think I was all that bad off. Of course, a drunk never does, do they? I decided to go out and get another bottle of booze. I was on my way home when I hit something. I struck my head on the dashboard and passed out. David called me on my cell. It woke me up. I told him what had happened. He showed up. Told me to take his car and drive straight home, he'd take care of things. He returned to the house with my car hours later. It was then he told me I'd actually hit someone. He showed me all the blood on the grill of the car. It was ghastly. I was devastated."

"Why didn't you go to the police?" Taylor asked.

Coral dabbed furiously at her eyes. "I wanted to! I told David that. But he wouldn't hear of it. His ass was on the line, too, he said. By that time he'd already disposed of the body and he'd be charged as an accessory for tampering with evidence or something, he said. I couldn't do that to him. At the time, I was unaware of what a real asshole he was," Coral said.

"And later?" I asked. "How about then?"

She shook her head. "I won't lie to you. At that point, it was self-preservation. Or just selfishness. By then my career was back on the upswing. I'd reinvented myself. Turned my life around. Sobered up. I knew my career would never survive this kind of bombshell. Drunk driving was one thing.

Hit-and-run and vehicular manslaughter was quite another. The poor fellow was dead. Confessing now wouldn't help him. So, I kept quiet. Kept David on as my manager. Even married him to keep him quiet. I'm not proud of it. I'm no better than he is. In fact, I'm worse," she said. "I'm just ready for it to be over. Ready for it all to come out now. I can't live like this anymore."

Taylor patted Coral's shoulder.

"Who did you kill?" I asked.

"Tressa! Don't ask something like that!" Taylor scolded.

"Why not? Aren't you curious?" I asked, a niggling suspicion beginning to eat at me.

"He was a jogger," Coral said.

"My God," Taylor said. "The poor jogger."

"See? I warned you jogging could be hazardous to your health," I said to Taylor.

She shook her head.

"How exactly did you know he was a jogger?" I asked Coral, trying not to be too indelicate. "I mean, did he have on jogging clothes? Running shoes? Did he have an iPod in his ear?" *A huge dent in his head?*

"I don't know what he was wearing. I never saw him!" Coral said.

"Hello. I think we've already established that. You hit him with a car, didn't you?" I said. "I'm talking afterwards. After you hit him. What did he look like then?"

"Tressa! Eeow!" Taylor said. "That's disgusting!"

"I told you, I never saw him," Coral replied.

I looked at her. "Never? You never even took a quick peek when you got out of your car?" I asked.

"No! I told you, David didn't tell me what I'd hit until much later. He got me out of my car and led me to his and told me to drive home, he'd take care of everything. So I did."

"Then, how do you know you hit someone?" I asked.

"We already covered this. I saw the blood on the car," Coral reminded me.

I frowned. "Animals bleed," I pointed out. "How do you know it was human blood?"

She sniffled and looked up at me. "David. David told me," she said. "And later he showed me the clipping."

"Clipping?"

"The newspaper clipping. A jogger washed up on the beach a week later near where David had—disposed of the body," she said with a shudder. "It was awful. It put a name to my victim. A sense of desperate reality to that horrible, horrible night. I wanted to go to the police but somehow I let David talk me out of it again. I almost started drinking again that night."

"So, what you're telling us is you've only got David's word that you hit somebody that night," I said. "You mentioned earlier you were unhappy with David before the accident. You were planning to fire him. Right?"

Coral frowned. "What are you getting at?" she asked. "You think he made it all up? I hit something out there. I know it."

"You hit something. Something that bled. It could've been a deer, a dog, a mountain lion or whatever critters you have running across roads in your neck of the woods," I pointed out. "Did David know you planned to get rid of him as your manager at the time?"

Coral nodded. "Yes. We spoke about it a month or so before the accident. I told him if I didn't get a promising role by the end of the month, I was going to have to terminate our contract." She looked at me. "My God. You *do* think he made it all up. You think he lied about the accident, don't you?" She shook her head. "What kind of person could do something like that?"

I looked at Taylor. "The kind of man who'd rather arrange for my sister and I to be used as sex slaves or something worse than let us return to *The Epiphany* and rat him out," I told her, and explained what had happened at MoBay, leaving out Manny's timely intervention.

"Oh my God. Were you hurt?"

"Just my outfit," I said. "And my feelings. Your husband gave my Mattie Ross *True Grit* audition a big thumbs-down," I admitted.

Coral looked lost. "So, David thought once you confronted me and started to question me about that night, I might figure out there never was a pedestrian hit-and-run?" she said.

"It's the only thing that makes sense," I said. "Even if the hit-and-run death wasn't bogus, either way David was screwed if I got back to the boat. Er, ship. Being the ace cub reporter that I am, can you imagine the attention I'd grab if I claimed Coral LaFavre had committed vehicular manslaughter while driving drunk? I could sell the story for mega bucks. David would be implicated and you'd both be sent to the slammer. If the story was fake, which, after talking with you I believe to be the case, he'd lose his ability to blackmail you and, as a result, lose his cushy lifestyle," I pointed out. "Either way his gravy train would be derailed."

Coral stared. Not at me. Off into space like I do when my gammy is feeding me the latest gossip from the senior center.

I waved a hand in her face. "Coral? Are you all right? Coral?"

"Son of a bitch!" she said. "Low-down, scum-sucking bastard. Spawn of Satan. Fruit of Lucifer's loins! All this time? All this time it was a lie! I'm gonna kill that gawd-damned piece of lying trash!"

"Haven't you forgotten something?" I asked Coral. "That particular piece of poop never made it back to the poop deck last night."

"Oh. Yeah." She took a minute. "So how'd you get away from David and his minion again?" she finally asked.

I'd conveniently glossed over the part in my narrative where Manny suddenly appeared and almost pulled David through the car window.

"The Turner sisters are . . . resourceful," I told her.

"Tressa," Taylor pressed.

"What? *What?*" I asked.

"Go on." She nodded her head.

Jeesch. Bossy sister.

"Okay, okay. I have a confession to make," I told Coral. "I suppose now is as good a time as any."

"Oh?" Coral said.

"I know about you and Sam Davenport," I said.

"Oh."

"Tressa?" Taylor said.

"Oh? That's all you have to say, Coral? Oh?" I asked.

"Oh shit. Any better?"

Wow. Whoopi Goldberg in the flesh. Who knew?

"Does Davenport know about David blackmailing you?" I asked Coral.

Her sliding gaze told me affirmative.

"Did he know before the cruise?" I asked.

Again, no eye contact.

"What were you thinking?" I said. "A deadbeat husband blackmailing you. A security expert in love with you. It's almost as if you orchestrated the whole thing with the purpose of eliminating your little problem." I stopped. "You didn't. Did you?" I asked.

"Did I . . . what?" Coral asked.

"Set this whole thing up to have Davenport take your husband out," I said.

"You can't be serious," Coral said. "Is she serious?" she asked Taylor.

"Dead serious," Taylor replied. "And it's an interesting question, considering your husband missed the boat last night."

I got off my chair and sat on the cocktail table across from the singer. "Tell me, Coral, did you let Security Sam deal with your blackmail issue for you? Where's your husband, Coral?"

"I wish I knew," she said. "Because I'd tear him apart with my bare hands."

"If someone hasn't beaten you to it," I said, thinking again of Manny.

"Don't expect me to cry him a river if that's the case," Coral said.

"And all along I thought he was trying to kill you," I admitted.

Coral frowned. "Is that why you tossed my candy-coated chocolate over the side?" she asked.

I nodded. "I was desperate."

"Sounds like you need a vacation from your vacation," Coral said, getting to her feet. "I suppose I'd better go speak with Sam," she said.

"I'm coming with you," I announced, jumping up. "I need to talk to him, too." And ask him just what business he had with Manny DeMarco, and did it pertain to the now missing David Frazier Compton.

"Oh, your friends from the Stardust. They'd just finished seeing Sam when I went to meet him," Coral said.

I frowned. "You saw them this morning? Were they with their husbands?"

"One of the husbands was there, I think," she said.

"Which one?" I pressed.

"The heavy one," she said.

"Uh, not helping," I replied. "Blond or dark-haired?"

"How would I know? He had a ball cap on."

"Did they say what they were doing this morning?" I asked.

"One of the husbands, I can't remember which, was under the weather, so the other three said something about going ashore," she said. "I didn't really pay that much attention."

For the first time I started to doubt myself. I doubted my recollection of the whispered phone call. Second-guessed the attack in the sickbay. Began to wonder if it really was all in my head.

It was the buff that finally convinced me. The buff was real—concrete, physical evidence that my struggle with an unknown assailant had also been real. Real. Not made up. And considering there was no earthly reason for anyone to want to snuff me—with the exception of the murder plot I'd accidentally overheard—the attack on the stairs and in the sickbay had to be linked to that one phone conversation. That person on the phone and—I realized for the first time—the person on the other end of the conversation.

Damn.

"Tressa will catch up with you," Taylor said, and I looked at her. "We need to talk."

Coral nodded. "Okay. I'll see you shortly, I guess," she said and left.

"What's the deal?" Taylor asked as soon as the door shut. "Why didn't you tell her about Manny?"

I hesitated.

"You're protecting him," she said. "Aren't you? You do have feelings for him, don't you?"

I did. I couldn't deny it. What those feelings were and how deep they ran was a question for the jury.

"I feel a . . . connection," I admitted. "A responsibility to look out for him. He's had my back more than a few times."

"He can look out for himself," Taylor said. "We need to think about how this could affect us. What if something has happened to David? What if your match made in bedlam had something to do with it? Do you even know what the guy does for a living? Do you even care? If David's body washes up on some beach somewhere and we've kept this information to ourselves, we're screwed!"

"You're getting freaked out, Taylor. There's no way Manny DeMarco had anything to do with David disappearing. Most likely, once we got loose, he knew the jig was up and decided a nice quiet life in MoBay beat what he faced if he showed his sleazy face on this ship or in the US of A again," I said. "I know Manny. He wouldn't just kill somebody."

"How do you know?" Taylor asked. "How? Because you think you might love him? Is that how? And where does that leave Rick?"

"Why are you so concerned for Townsend all of a sudden?" I asked, but suspecting I already knew the answer.

"It's not about Rick. It's about you, Tressa," Taylor said. "About you discovering that priceless and rare treasure that only comes along once in a lifetime and having the courage to reach out and grab it before it's gone. True love is a rare and precious ultimate treasure, Tressa."

I sat down. My legs wouldn't support me. "You sound like more of an authority on true love than I am, Taylor," I told her. "Are you?"

My sister stared at me. "Am I what?"

"In love?"

Her cheeks grew pink. Her eyes wide.

"You are, aren't you?" I said.

She shook her head. "No. I don't know. Of c-course not," she stammered.

"Your tongue gets loose when you drink," I told her. "You . . . said things."

"I did?" She dropped onto her bed.

"You're in love with Rick, aren't you?" I said, wincing at the unexpectedly sharp pain I felt delivering those words. It felt as if my heart was ripped in two. Unlock the chest, Davy. Heart in hand, I'm coming.

Taylor popped back to her feet. "Rick! You think I'm in love with Rick? That's ridiculous. He's loved you since I can remember."

I flinched as if Taylor had struck me. Oh, gawd, maybe I was delusional. And it was contagious.

I got to my feet. "What are you saying, Taylor? You *don't* love Rick?"

"Of course I love him," she said.

I sat back down. "I'm confused."

Taylor joined me on the couch. "I love him like a brother!"

she said. "He's been like one to me all my life. I've never thought of him in any other way. I couldn't. It would be . . . icky."

"I'm confused," I said again. "If you don't think you're in love with Rick, then it must be . . ." I stared at her. "Manny! You're in love with Manny DeMarco?"

Taylor jumped to her feet again. "I am not!" she said. "What are you thinking?"

"I'm confused," I said for the third time.

"It's P.D.!" Taylor said, dropping back to the couch and taking my hand. "P.D.!"

"P.D.?" I repeated, stunned. Dawkins? She was in love with my trooper bud, Patrick Dawkins? The only guy I'd known who'd accepted me for me? *That* P.D. Dawkins?

"I was going to tell you. Honest. But I thought maybe it wouldn't matter. I knew you were really fond of Patrick, but I honestly thought you'd finally figure out you were meant to be with Rick and then I wouldn't feel guilty for taking Patrick away from you and we'd all live happily ever after. But you kept dragging your feet. Waffling. Wavering. Waiting, waiting, waiting. Two steps forward, three steps back. Then, when this cruise came along, I thought, yes! She'll have Rick all to herself. He'll seal the deal. Only Manny and his aunt Mo showed up and then you hit your head and there was the memory thing and I really didn't want to tell you anyway, so I just decided I'd back off and walk away from Patrick until you decided who you wanted. For however long it took. I'm sorry, Tressa. Does any of this make any sense at all?"

More than she knew. More than I knew. It seemed everyone knew how Rick felt about me. Joe. Taylor. Kimmie. Even a stranger had seen it. Why had it taken me so long to recognize what everyone else had seen all along?

I knew why.

I'd had the ultimate blonde moment and—at least where Ranger Rick was concerned—it had lasted a lifetime.

"Are you angry?" Taylor asked. "Upset? Hurt? Shocked? What?"

"I'm blonde," was all I could think to say. "Totally, undeniably blonde. But a recovering one."

She looked at me. "Does that mean you're going to be okay?" she asked.

I took her hand. "That means we're going to be okay," I told her.

I bundled up the chocolate box and grabbed the high-def TV certificate and left the stateroom and hurried down to Manny and Mo's cabin. I took a deep breath and knocked. To my relief Manny opened the door.

"Can I come in?" I asked, and he motioned me inside, closing the door behind us. Thank goodness, Aunt Mo was nowhere to be seen.

"Some of them have been eaten," I said, holding the candy box out to him, a lump in my throat the size of a coconut. Tears stung my eyes. "They were really delicious," I added.

"Barbie chose Rick the Dick," Manny said, looking at the candy box and back at me.

I was back to being Barbie.

"I'm sorry," I said, as the moisture filled to overflowing and big, fat tears spilled out onto my cheeks.

Manny reached out with a thumb and wiped the moisture from my face. "Manny's never seen Barbie cry," he said.

"Few people have," I said, snuffling up snot. "I'm a totally messy crier."

Manny smiled.

"If things had been different," I said, feeling the need to explain, "If I hadn't met Townsend first. If he hadn't been there from the beginning—"

Manny touched a finger to my lips, silencing my feeble attempts to explain. "Manny gets it," he said. "We're cool."

I started to cry even harder. I felt like I'd lost a best friend.

"Promise?" I said, blubbering.

"Totally," he said.

I dropped the box of Godivas and ran into his arms. As soon as he closed them tight around me, I realized Manny was no more capable of cold-blooded murder for hire than I was.

"About David Frazier what's-his-name," I said.

"He and Manny had a little heart to heart and he decided the climate in MoBay was healthier for him than the West Coast," he said, and I could sense the amusement in his voice. "All things considered," he added.

"So he admitted he was blackmailing Coral over a vehicular homicide that never occurred?" I asked, and I could feel Manny nod. "That's one spouse well rid of," I added.

"They aren't married," Manny said, and I finally looked up at him.

"What do you mean?" I asked.

"True confessions," Manny said. "The dude's already married—to another woman in New York. Under another name. Guy's a career con artist," he added.

"So, there's no reason for Coral to want him dead—other than the fact that she hates his guts and he's a bottom-feeding bilge rat. Right?" I said.

"Right," Manny said.

I laid my head back on his chest and listened to the strong, slow beat of his heart against my ear.

"Manny's got a confession to make, too," he said, and my breath hitched in my throat.

"Yes?" I asked, keeping my head next to his chest.

"Brianna the babe," he said, and I frowned.

"Yes?"

"Manny made a deal with her," he said.

"Deal? What kind of deal?"

"She'd keep Rick the Dick occupied so Manny could put the moves on Barbie," he confessed.

I raised my head up and took a step back.

"How underhanded! How diabolical! How . . . you!" I said. "How could you?" I asked.

Manny just smiled, his teeth indecently white. "All's fair in love and war, babe," he said.

How do you argue with that?

"So, do you want to break the news to Aunt Mo or should I?" I asked. "Or, we could do it together," I suggested.

"Manny's got it," he said. "Mo's sharp. She probably saw the way the wind was blowing way before now."

"You think so?"

He nodded.

"But just in case, you should have the ship's doctor, Bones Baker, standing by when you tell her. Okay?"

He smiled and nodded. "Roger that," he said.

I turned to leave, remembered the TV certificate in my pocket and fished it out. I reached over to put it in his hand.

"Give the TV to Aunt Mo," I said. "It might be some consolation to her," I told him.

He shook his head and closed my fingers over the prize. "Keep it," he said. "It's yours."

Like my heart.

The sentiment was there. Strong yet unspoken. And I knew I had a matter of seconds before I was bawling my eyes out again.

I nodded and walked to the door, opened it and stopped.

"What do you do for a living?" I asked, turning back to look at him one more time.

"If I told you, I'd have to kill you," he said. He smiled. Your basic killer smile.

I left the cabin in tears—and at a speed sufficient to capture the America's Cup. It was true. Breaking up was hard to do.

CHAPTER TWENTY

I sprinted back to the stateroom to finish off my crying jag and shove my face under the faucet. I stopped short when I discovered more "sail mail" had been delivered in my absence. I picked the envelope up, saw my name on the front in fancy, calligraphic handwriting, and flipped the envelope over to open it.

A one-sheet note card was inside, written in black calligraphic print as well; the print resembled the format of a formal invitation.

My mouth flopped open when I read the mysterious missive.

Ranger Rick Townsend requests the honor of your presence at Wedding Bell Isle, Grand Cayman, one PM sharp, to facilitate uniting in marriage this man and this woman, Rick Townsend and Tressa Turner, in holy matrimony. Items required:

- *Passport*
- *Cruise passenger documentation (white slip)*
- *You*

Come sail away with me to another world, Tressa.
From one lover to another,
RR

I read and reread the note ten times before it finally sank in. Once it did, I started to shake. Bad. This was what Townsend had meant when he said he had plans for us and asked me to save time for him? He'd had marriage on his mind!

I began to squeal. I jumped up and down. I danced around the stateroom like a maniac.

"He wants to marry me! He wants to marry me! Ranger Rick wants to marry me!"

Marriage!

'Til death do us part!

Forever and ever and ever.

Oh. God.

I stopped dancing.

The time had come. It was put up or shut up, hold 'em or fold 'em time. It was time for Calamity Jayne to show her cards, end her bluff, cash it in. Put up or shut up time.

Bet the farm on the Romeo Ranger.

I thought about it. What would it be like to be married to Ranger Rick, to surprise everyone with our wedding announcement? To see their faces (especially Joe's) when they found out. To know that Rick had chosen me. Wanted me. From this day forward.

I could see it all.

And I liked what I saw.

More than liked.

I embraced it.

Welcomed it.

Reveled in it.

Yeah. I thought about it.

For all of thirty seconds.

Time's up?

Big deal.

Tugboat Tressa was full steam ahead.

I checked my watch, screeched when I saw it was closing

in on eleven, and ran to the drawer to yank out clean underwear. I hoofed it to the closet and grabbed one of only two dresses I'd brought with me, a white sleeveless sundress with buttons down the front. I showered, shampooed, shaved, dried, lotioned, brushed, flossed, plucked, made up the face, braided the hair to minimize the frizz factor, and I was ready to go in under forty-five minutes. Damn, I'm good.

I stood in front of the mirror and surveyed the blushing bride. Not exactly the way I'd envisioned my wedding day. Not the place—although an island in the Caribbean was nothing to sneeze at. Not the circumstances—a brush with death, an encounter with a blackmailer and a shipboard murder mystery weren't necessarily the kind of bachelorette party games I'd dreamed of. And the dress? Definitely not the dress of my dreams. And the hair had always been subject to anyone's guess.

But the groom?

In all of my young girl wedding fantasies only one groom had waited for me at the altar. Only one man had slipped the ring on my finger. One man had pledged his love.

And that man was, at this very moment, waiting for me at Wedding Bell Isle.

Waiting for his bride.

Giddy with shock, happiness, anticipation and a feeling that this was the right man at the right time, I grabbed Harry Javelina (no way was I leaving Harry out of the moment) and hurried to find the man of my wedding-day daydreams. Oh, and the naughty dead-of-night ones, too. And no. You can't have details.

Finding my way to Wedding Bell Isle, the Mecca for couples who want to take the plunge, was easy. Everyone knew Wedding Bell Isle. It was famous. Or infamous, depending on how the quickie union played out.

Love-smitten cruisers could pick the wedding package of their choice, select the location they preferred, a quaint church, a small chapel, a famous botanical garden, a stately mansion, or an intimate ceremony on a secluded stretch of white sand.

Caribbean Weddings R Us.

How romantic.

I hurried up to the Wedding Bell Isle headquarters, keeping a lookout for one incredibly unpredictable ranger-type who just happened to be my future husband. I stumbled a little when that thought hit home.

Husband.

I was going to have a husband.

I was going to be a Mrs.

Mrs. Rick Townsend.

Tressa Townsend.

Tressa Turner-Townsend if I hyphenated.

Ye gods. What a mouthful.

I looked around for Rick. Where was the groom?

I'd decided to ask at the counter when I heard my name.

"Tressa? What on earth are you doing here?"

I spotted Courtney Kayser walking in my direction.

"I'm looking for Rick. Have you seen him?" I asked.

She frowned. "No. But we just got here a bit ago. Don't tell me. Are you and Rick getting married?" she asked. I nodded.

"I think so," I said. "At least that's what the invite said," I told her. "And you haven't seen him?"

"I'm sure he'll be along. He's probably finishing up arrangements. Come, let me buy you a rum punch over there. They're fabulous." I hesitated and she took my arm. "Come on, silly, you'll be able to see him from there." She led me to a table and went to get us each a drink.

"What are you doing here?" I asked when she returned to the table, still keeping a lookout for Ranger Rick.

"Can you believe it? Steve convinced me to renew our vows. He's off somewhere buying flowers or something. To new beginnings," she said, and raised her glass when our drinks arrived. I did the same.

"New beginnings," I said, taking a long, thirsty drink, a little out of sorts with my soon-to-be-groom. Where could he be?

"So I was right after all," Courtney said, and I took another drink, keeping an eye peeled for Townsend.

"Right about what?" I asked.

"You picking Rick. I knew it. So, how did Manny take it?" she asked. I frowned, wondering why she'd think I'd already spoken to Manny. "Was he devastated? I imagine he didn't show it. Men don't, you know. Not like we women do."

"We're cool," was all I said, my vision beginning to get fuzzy and my head loopy.

"I bet the farm on you and Rick," she said. "I'm a gambler, you know. But you already know that. It drives Steve batty. He's always lecturing me about my spending. Stop going to the casinos. Quit buying those scratch tickets. Leave off the lottery tickets. Well, the joke's on him. Drink up, Tressa. Isn't it delicious?"

It was, I decided, as I took another drink, but it sure must be potent. I was feeling goofier by the minute.

"Hey, I have an idea, Tressa. I'll be your maid of honor and you can be mine. Won't that be fun? Tressa? Tressa?"

I heard Courtney but she sounded like she was speaking to me from a long way off. I tried to focus on her but she'd become a shadowy figure without shape or definition.

"Tressa?"

"I think I'm gonna be sick," I said, feeling myself falling.

"Tressa! Tressa?"

I kissed the pavement.

Toot toot! Tugboat Tressa had just been left at the altar.

I awoke, feeling groggy, my tongue thick inside my mouth, my clothing soaked.

"She's waking up! We need to do it!"

Sunlight made my head hurt.

"Whaa?" I said, trying to open my eyes but the brightness keeping them closed.

"We need to roll her over on her stomach first. Then just keep her face in the water. That ought to do it."

I forced one eye to open. Everything was a blur.

"Help me get her over!"

"Whaa?" I sounded like a spaz.

"Welcome to Rum Point, Tressa. A rather secluded area of Rum Point, I'm afraid, that people rarely come to since that last devastating hurricane. Oh, Tressa, I'm so sorry it had to come to this," I heard through the fog in my head. "I liked you. I felt bad about writing that wedding invitation. Really, I did. But it was the only way I knew of to get you off the ship alone. I knew you'd go in a New York minute if you thought Rick was waiting to marry you. And I was right, wasn't I? Oh, Tressa. You really should've left well enough alone. You should have just enjoyed being an object of desire between two divine men. You should have minded your own business. You've really left us no choice. And now you've ruined your grandmother's honeymoon cruise. A suicide in the family tends to spoil the moment forever."

That one got my other eye open.

"Suueeside?" I managed, feeling slobber dribble out of my mouth.

"Yes. Suicide. Your suicide, Tressa, you poor, sweet, messed-up, mixed-up, delusional thing, you. And who can blame you. After all you've been through?"

"Won't bleeve sueside," I managed.

"Oh, I think they will believe, Tressa. After all, you even left a suicide note."

Suicide note? I blinked. I'd remember writing a suicide note. Wouldn't I?

"You don't remember, do you?" the shadow said. "That's priceless considering your little flim-flam. But don't worry, I'll refresh your memory. The note you left for the ship's doctor, silly. I came across it when I went back to retrieve that damned buff from the infirmary. You'd just checked yourself out. I saw the note you left for the doctor. Such a nice, courteous thing to do. I read it and thought it might come in handy. As usual, I was right. It was perfect: *'I can't take it anymore. Thank you for everything you've done, but I'm out of here. Tressa.'* "

"Siit," I said, trying to curse. That's what I got for being polite and writing friggin' thank-yous.

"Your note will be found inside your beloved Javelina pack. In fact, thanks to Harry here, that's when I first knew you were faking your memory loss. The little girl at the gangway. She asked where you got it and you told her the Grand Canyon. I knew you were faking the memory loss. So, I knew you'd have to be dealt with eventually. You just wouldn't let it go. Internet research. Your reporting background. You were like a starving bloodhound on the scent of red meat."

"Wh-why?" I finally got out.

"Oh, Tressa, you still haven't learned your lesson, have you? It's that kind of curiosity that got you here. But I suppose it doesn't matter now. You were right. It is all about money. It always has been. Just not the way you thought."

I shook my head.

"It was that stupid conversation you overheard. When I found out what cabin you were in, I knew you'd overheard our phone conversation. But you wouldn't let it go. You thought some guy was planning to kill his wife on the cruise and collect a big life insurance policy. You couldn't have been more wrong. It was the other way around. It was a wife planning to kill her husband. And not for insurance money. It was all about the lottery ticket, silly. The one sold in Farley and never claimed. A five million dollar lottery ticket—a jackpot I won and don't plan on splitting with my penny-pinching miser of a husband in a divorce settlement. But the only way to avoid that was to get rid of him and make it look like an accident, and then make it appear there was no possible motive for me to want my husband dead. No life insurance. No motive. I could move away from Farley, hold on to the winning ticket and redeem it several months down the road where nobody would be the wiser. And if they were suspicious? So what? Suspicion isn't proof. But you? You narrowed the plot down to two couples. Once you learned about the lottery winnings, you would have figured it out.

"And then there was that damned buff. The buff with my hair and my DNA all over it. I had to get that buff back, but you held on to that damned warthog backpack like it was a Gucci bag or something."

"Pecc-ry," I corrected.

"Oh, Tressa, up until you came stumbling along, my plan was foolproof," Courtney lamented.

"Sawree," I mumbled.

"I'd done my homework. All the research. I'd read stories about problems with security on cruises. How few cases were followed up on and even fewer prosecuted. How security could be lax. When I saw this cruise offered, I saw my chance. It was supposed to be over by now. But you had to spoil things by showing up on the rafting excursion. We'd planned that carefully. I slipped Steve enough of a drug to make him lethargic and dizzy. I'm an L.P.N., remember? Ben would 'accidentally' fall into the water. Poor Sherri would naturally plead for someone to save Ben. Steve being the big lug he is would jump in and die a hero trying to save his best friend. But you. You had to come along and jump in and take the hero role yourself. You just wouldn't let it go."

"The fawl?" I mumbled.

"Oh, yes, your little tumble down the stairs. I'd read about a case where a cruise passenger died from a shove down the stairs, so we tried that. Well, you survived the fall and then came up with the amnesia story—nice touch there, by the way—and that took us aback for a while. But when I found out you were faking, I started making a case for you being mentally messed up, citing your erratic and bizarre behavior, and expressing my concerns over your stability to everyone I spoke with. Including Sam Davenport. You have to admit, Tressa, your behavior is way out of the box," she said.

"I perrrfer quirky," I mumbled.

"Have it your way," Courtney said. "And that's a brief synopsis of how we've arrived at the tragic end of Tressa Turner's Jumpstart to No Life Cruise. At least Rick will have your lovely sister to console him."

Now thats what you call your low blow. And cold.

"Call?" I managed. "I heard. Man . . . wife?"

"You heard Ben checking to make sure I'd canceled the life insurance policy Steve and I held. Plus, he'd had to smooth things over with Sherri to get her to come on the cruise in the first place. Ben and I had been seeing each other for over two years—before I hit the jackpot so to speak. To make our plan work, Ben had to convince Sherri all was well in their marriage so she would make this trip. I told him if she suspected he was involved with someone else—and found out it was me later on—it could pose a real problem for us. When I bought the winning ticket, we had to cool it. So nobody would suspect. We were careful. We used untraceable cell phones to make our plans. Met in towns counties away from our homes." She shook her head. "All that time we spent. Now we'll have to go back to the drawing board. Still, accidents happen all the time. We'll think of something, won't we, Ben? But now, we need to finish our business here. Let's get on with it, shall we? No use putting unpleasant tasks off. It only makes them more difficult. Right, hon?"

Here be monsters, I thought as I began to panic in earnest.

Although my limbs felt like I was wearing heavy chain mail, I flailed around and struck out in a meager attempt to resist being rolled over on my stomach, my face submerged, my lungs filled with water. I'd seen enough of those crime shows to know I didn't want to end up a floater-and-bloater on some cold morgue slab.

My efforts were futile. I was flipped over with the ease of a pancake being turned. A heavy hand on the back of my head forced my face into the approaching tide. I held my breath for as long as I could and struggled against the weight keeping me underwater, the waves crashing over me. I was out of air.

And really out of time.

I gasped and water entered my lungs, the pain intense. Burning.

So this was how I was going out: floating up on some beach somewhere with every little guppy in the sea taking a bite out of me. Another outfit ruined.

I was close to losing consciousness. My final thoughts were of Rick.

So what if he didn't want to marry me? Who said I was ready for marriage anyway? So what if I'd made a total fool of myself in my wedding finery and my pathetic posies? None of that changed the way I felt about Ranger Rick.

And with those thoughts came the realization that, in spite of years of ambivalence, despite long-time resistance and long-term fear of heartbreak, I loved Ranger Rick— had loved him for as long as I could remember—but had never had the courage or confidence to tell him. And now, just when I had mustered up the will to do it, I'd waited too long. My time was up.

Townsend would never know how I truly felt about him. How I'd always felt about him. It looked like I was the biggest loser after all.

My lungs were in distress. My arms flopped weakly at my sides. I felt the current tug at me. All fight was now merely for stubborn show, my strength ebbing with each passing second. Who'd a-thought? Tressa Turner: guppy food. So not the way I wanted to go out.

I prepared myself to lose consciousness. To see the bright light the black-haired Melinda talked about on *Ghost Whisperer* and to run like hell toward that light like a little baby and get it over with already when the pressure forcing my face into the water suddenly disappeared and I found myself floating to the surface like a drunken bobber. As soon as my mouth broke the plane of the water, I sucked air in and spewed water out. It hurt so good.

I puked and gagged for a minute longer, then began to strike out in choppy breaststrokes in the direction of the shore. What seemed like forever later, I pulled myself up onto completely dry sand, coughing to clear my lungs, the pain in my chest easing with each purging cough. I dragged myself further up the beach, clawing at the ground like a lifeline, and then collapsed, rolling over on my back, breathing like an emphysema patient.

Something appeared above me. Not a bright light, but perhaps an angel.

"Daddy?" I said. "Daddy?"

It couldn't be. I was hallucinating. Or dead. What would my dad be doing here?

"Tressa? Honey? Are you all right?"

Tears stung my eyes. Suddenly I was six years old again with scabs on my knees, chipped front teeth, running crying to my daddy, the shivering, squealing body of a baby rabbit I'd accidentally stepped on in my arms.

"Daddy?"

"I'm here, kiddo. Dad's here," he said.

I shook my head. "Is this heaven?" I asked.

He shook his head. "No. And it sure as hell isn't Iowa either," he said. "Unfortunately."

He helped me sit up.

"What happened?" I asked. I looked over and saw Ben Hall stone-cold unconscious on the beach, a rather large rock next to him. Beside Ben, Courtney Kayser was also laid out. My mom straddled her chest, apparently maintaining enough pressure on her carotid with her knee to keep her compliant. "Mom? Mom! How? What?" I said.

"There's still a little bit of the weekend warrior in the old man," my dad said with a wink. "And your mom? She deals with the I.R.S. for a living. This little skirmish? A piece of cake."

"How did you know?"

"We followed you," my dad said.

I frowned. "You. You two were the ones who've been following me? Why?" I asked.

"That memory-loss story? I knew it was pure Tressa fiction right away," my dad said. "You forget. I was there when you told the doc that you were pushed. I could tell from your face that you meant it. I told your mom. Neither one of us was sure what was behind it—but we were determined to keep an eye on you. You sure didn't make it easy. We lost you a couple times. I had to recruit Manny and Rick at various times to help out."

I blinked. They hadn't been shacked up in their cabin, after all. They'd been the ones following me all along, looking out for their little girl. Looking out for me! My throat got tight.

"So . . . Rick knows?"

"He knew something was up with you right away, but like us he had no clue just what it was. It was only when we spoke to Manny and he told us about the conversation you overheard that we finally put it together," my dad said.

"Rick knows that I told Manny about the phone call I heard?" I said, feeling my chest tighten again. This time in stark, cold doom.

My dad nodded.

"What I can't figure out is why you went to that Wedding Bell Isle, Tressa," my mother said. "At first we thought you were just having a drink with a friend, but then you fainted and your friends scurried you off to a waiting car before we could stop them. We were fortunate we didn't lose you altogether. We lost sight of the car and it took us a while to track you down. What were you doing at that wedding service?"

"Dreaming," I said. "Dreaming of a wedding," I added, retrieving my wedding invite from Courtney's belongings. I handed my mother the card. "That's how they got me to leave the ship alone," I told her, watching her face grow solemn as she read the note.

She handed the card to my dad.

"And you went," she said. "Oh, Tressa, I'm so sorry," she said, reaching out to grab my hand and pull me down to give me a tight hug. "So, so sorry, sweetie."

"Me, too, kiddo," my dad said, coming to kneel beside us and pat my back.

"Do me a favor?" I asked my parents.

"Of course," my mother responded. "Anything."

"Don't tell Townsend," I said. "Please, please, don't tell Rick."

My mom looked at my dad and he nodded.

"Okay, kiddo," he said. "If that's what you want."

I nodded.

"So . . . what do we do now?" I said.

"Someone needs to hoof it up around the cove and get help," my dad replied.

I looked at my mom. "Rock, paper, scissors?"

She looked at me.

"I'm going. I'm going," I said.

CHAPTER TWENTY-ONE

The authorities had been notified. The FBI called in. State-
ments taken. Ben and Courtney were being held on numer-
ous charges. Sherri was in shock. Steve was incensed.

Courtney hadn't yet divulged the whereabouts of the
winning lottery ticket, but Steve planned to make a thor-
ough search for it and, if Courtney did somehow try to cash
it in, lottery officials were ordered to withhold payment until legal disputes relating to the cash award had been adjudi-
cated. I wondered if Courtney would hold on to it and let
it become worthless rather than splitting the winnings with
Steve, or if she would give it to someone else to redeem. It
would have to be someone she trusted, I decided, and I
didn't think with her recent history that would be an easy
thing to find. Still, she could decide half of five million was
better than nothing. And she might need those winnings to
bankroll her criminal defense.

I'd been checked out by Bones Baker and declared healthy
as a horse. I'd admitted my little amnesia deceit to him. He
was very understanding, considering the fact that he, as a
medical professional, had been duped.

Coral had been told the truth about David Frazier Compton and his other life and other wife and his admission that
he had, indeed, lied about the accident and Coral had struck
a critter and not a person. David had created the elaborate
hoax in order to coerce Coral into buying his continued

silence by continuing his comfortable lifestyle via a sham marriage. It seemed Coral and Sam were now free to start a life together.

All's well that ends well.

I stood on deck as we sailed away from the Cayman Islands, realizing a part of me was remaining behind on that wedding isle. The part that would have sailed away a wife. A missus. The other half of a whole.

The dreamer in me was left standing in that little white chapel on Wedding Bell Isle.

I sighed. A long, loud, what's-to-become-of-me sigh. Yeah. Pitiful.

The sunset, a spectacular blaze of peach streaked with black, was all that lovers could hope for—a breathtaking splendor I couldn't bear viewing alone. I turned to walk away and found Ranger Rick standing beside me, staring at the same striking sunset with a fierce intensity.

"Ahoy, Ranger Rick," I greeted him. "Incredible sunset, huh?"

He nodded. "It's one to remember," he said, and I shook my head.

"You're never going to let me forget that amnesia foolishness, are you?" I asked. "I admit. It wasn't one of my better ideas."

"Agreed," he said.

"So, are you looking forward to going home again?" I asked, and he took a long time answering.

"We can never go home again, Tressa," he said and turned to face me. "Not like it was. You know that as well as I do. This cruise? It was not only the beginning of something, but the ending of something else. It opened my eyes to a lot of things. Like how hard having true faith in someone else can be. How our spirit reflects who we really are despite what we may think about ourselves. How key trust is in any relationship." He paused and looked back out to sea. "You trust Manny. With the important stuff. With the stuff that counts. You trust him. You went to him. Not me. That pretty much says it all."

I opened my mouth to tell him all about the Wedding Bell Isle wedding invitation, to wave that fact in his face and exclaim, "Trust? Trust! What do you mean, I don't trust you? I was prepared to trust you with my future, my life, my heart? How can you talk about trust at a time like this?"

But the words didn't come. And I was glad I hadn't said them. Glad because I didn't want his feelings or his actions to be influenced by pity or guilt or even kindness. I didn't want his sympathy, compassion or understanding.

I wanted his love.

All of it or none of it.

How could I explain that I kept Townsend out of the loop because what he thought of me—about me—really mattered? More than any other person's opinion, his mattered. So much. How did I tell him that I was reluctant to involve him in my all too frequent imbroglios because I cared too deeply? How did I explain that if I somehow placed him in danger and, God forbid, something happened to him I would simply cease to exist? That he was my next breath. And the next. And the next. How did I explain the debilitating fear I felt of opening myself up to the possibility of happily ever after only to discover it was all a fairy tale? My fairy tale?

"You're awfully quiet," Townsend observed.

I nodded. "I guess I am," I said.

"I want you to know that it's okay, Tressa," Townsend said, taking my hand. "Despite what I've said in the past, I believe Manny has genuine feelings for you. And, I hate to admit this, but I think down deep he's a good man." He paused. "Things will be different when we get back home," he said.

"I know." Did I ever. If things went my way, it was the end of life as I knew it. It was the end of Tressa Jayne Turner being answerable only to Tressa. It was the end of

Tressa coming and going as she wanted and doing as she pleased. It was the end of shaving only up to the knees in winter.

Now all that was left to do was let Ranger Rick know how I felt.

So, tell him already, I told myself. Just open your big, fat mouth and spill it! I opened my mouth, looked up to the heavens for the right words, frowned, opened my mouth again, squinted at the sky once more . . . and just stood there.

Mime time.

Oh, irony, sweet irony, I thought as I searched in vain for words of eloquence and tenderness and devotion. Words period.

Now that the time had finally come, when all uncertainty on my part had been eliminated, all doubts vanquished, it was at this most crucial time I found myself at a total loss as to what to say or do next. After years of keeping Ranger Rick at arm's length, of doubting his level of commitment, of questioning my own readiness, here I was, ready to act, to take a leap of faith, to risk heartbreak and beyond, to reach for that elusive horizon—and I was stuck. Frozen in place. Unsure what to say. Unsure what step to take next.

This was nuts. I was the girl whose motormouth never needed a tune-up, who flew by the seat of her pants so often she had butt burn from the bumpy landings. But somehow, through it all, my lips—and yours truly—had kept moving. Kept talking. Kept on keeping on.

Until now. Now, when it mattered most, when the stakes were highest and things were at critical mass, I'd lost all avionics. Ass included.

After all the commitment-phobic feet dragging was done, after the distrust and suspicion had been laid to rest, and all doubts erased and I was ready to move forward at last, I was dead in the water. I had nothing. Nothing. What could I possibly do or say that would convince Ranger

Rick that I'd finally—and for good this time—come to my senses? What?

I thought about how this cruise had started out so promising. Back before the Bermuda Love Triangle took shape. Before a black widow and her Bluebeard sought to sever the bonds of matrimony by murder most foul. Back when I'd still had visions of dessert bars dancing in my head.

I thought about that first night, the night I'd almost signed on as Ranger Rick's cabin mate, how he'd started with those ridiculous piratical pick-up lines. He'd surprised me then. And continued to surprise and amaze me throughout this crazy courtship with his sense of humor, his steadfast faithfulness and tireless devotion to serving my best interests, often to the detriment of his own.

I bit my lip to keep from giggling as I recalled Ranger Rick's horny pirate performance.

Maybe ye wants to scrape the barnacles off me rudder.

What's the matter, wench? Parrot got your tongue?

I put a hand to my mouth.

That was it!

It might even work!

And it was way more up my alley than grabbing hold of Ranger Rick's ankle and screaming, "Don't leave me! Ever!" as he walked away, dragging me along behind him like a proverbial ball and chain.

It was decided. I'd do it.

It was time for Calamity Jayne to get her man.

"Wait right here!" I told Rick. "Don't move! I'll be right back! Promise?" I asked, and he nodded.

"Call of nature, right?" he said, a sad smile crossing his lips.

"Don't move from this spot!" I ordered, and ran to locate my props.

I was back in under ten minutes. Not bad for a girl who hates to move her arse. Breathless, I launched into my piece.

"Do you remember that first night of the cruise?" I asked

Townsend. "When you boasted about your pirate pickup lines and I challenged you to deliver?"

Rick grinned. "Apparently my execution wasn't convincing enough to win a fair wench's heart," he said.

"Oh, I wouldn't say that. I happen to know Jack Sparrow would have been very impressed," I told him.

He raised an eyebrow. "I wasn't trying for a piece of Captain Jack Sparrow's heart," he said.

"Well, if you had been, I know for a fact he couldn't have resisted your pickup lines," I said, and from the look on Rick's face, I realized I'd veered off course into uncharted waters again. "What I mean is that no one could have resisted those pickup lines."

"*You* did," he said, his smile disappearing. "You resisted them."

"I did, didn't I?" I said. "And I would again. If this very minute you penciled on the eyeliner, tied a kerchief on your head and buckled a sword to your waist and leered at me, I'd still resist the temptation to leap into your arms and find a deserted island somewhere. And do you know why?" I asked.

He nodded. "Because of Manny," he said.

I shook my head.

"No. Because of you," I said, and Townsend looked puzzled.

"Me? I'm not following. What the hell have I done?" he asked.

"Everything," I said. "That's just it. You've done everything in this relationship. You've done all the heavy lifting, all the waiting, made all the overtures. Don't you see? For you to believe in me—truly believe in the 'us' we can become—the next step has to come from me," I told him.

"I'm not following, Tressa," Ranger Rick said. "What are you exactly saying?"

I unzipped Harry Javelina and took out my props. I slid an eye patch into place over one eye, took my new souvenir buff out—the one Courtney had tried to retrieve was now evidence in the FBI's possession—and secured it to the top of my head. I slowly withdrew the kids' toy compass I'd purchased at the gift shop. I held it in my hand.

"What are you doing, Tressa?" Ranger Rick asked. "Why the getup? What's the deal with the compass?"

I looked at him. "Don't you know anything? This compass is not your ordinary run-of-the-mill compass, young sailor," I said. "This compass is magic. It always points to what I want most," I told him.

Townsend's expression shifted, his eyes wide with uncertainty.

I held the compass out in front of me in the palms of my hands. I looked down at the compass. It jiggled up and down in my suddenly shaking hands.

"Well, shiver me timbers! Whaddya know? The needle— it be pointin' straight at . . ."

I stopped and looked up into Ranger Rick's dark, dreamy eyes.

"You," I said.

I could see stunned realization in the drop of his jaw. Amazed awareness in the sudden glint of his eyes.

"Tressa?" he said.

I smiled.

"Aye, that be me name. Tressa Turner, Lady Pirate, at your service," I said, moving in, toe to toe, breast to chest. "I hear tell ye have a legendary cutlass and ye know how to use it," I growled, raising the one eyebrow that was visible beneath my kerchief. "Is there an X on the seat of your pants, me hearty? Because it appears there's wondrous booty buried beneath. What say we take ourselves off to yer cabin and ye can show Pirate Tressa how ye buries yer treasure, lad."

My face was hotter than a car roof in Iowa in mid-August—and not all due to embarrassment from my wanton pirate routine. The compass shook in my outstretched hand, the needle clicking up and down, in time to my own erratic heartbeats.

Townsend stared at my Mexican Jumping Compass and then at me.

"What say ye?" I inquired, my voice shaking as I hoped against hope I hadn't waited too long and Ranger Rick had decided to look for love in less stormy waters. "Arrrrrrrrrre ya free, lad?" I persisted.

Ranger Rick reached out and closed my fingers over the quivering compass. He took my other hand and, without a word, he led me to his cabin door.

Tense as a cat under a rocker, I felt a familiar sense of panic as I stood on the threshold of that point of no return. Townsend must have sensed fear in the air, for he got rid of any lingering thread of anxiety and uncertainty I felt by coming up with the most romantic, most touching, and by far the most effective seduction cincher of all time.

"Brace yerself, fair wench that's won this ranger's heart," he said. "Brace yerself . . . and prepare to be boarded!"

He opened the door, picked me up, and as one we crossed the threshold. Shiver me timbers, Calamity Jayne Turner has at last struck gold!

Here be real treasure.

If you enjoyed this book, be sure to look for these other great mystery romances from your favorite mystery romance authors.

Dorchester Publishing

Where mystery and romance meet.

Christie Craig
Divorced, Desperate and Dating

Sue Finley murdered people…on paper. As a mystery writer, she knew all the angles, who did what and why. The only thing she couldn't explain was…well, men. Dating was like diving into a box of chocolates: the sweetest-looking specimens were often candy-coated poison. After several bad breakups, she gave it up for good.

Then came Detective Jason Dodd.

Raised in foster homes, Jason swore never to need anyone. That was why he failed to follow up after experiencing the best kiss of his life. But when Sue Finley started getting death threats, all bets were off. The blonde spitfire was everything he'd ever wanted—and she needed him. And though this novel situation had a quirky cast of characters and an unquestionable bad guy, he was going to make sure it had a happy ending.

ISBN 13: 978-0-505-52732-5

Gemma Halliday
MAYHEM *in* HIGH HEELS

Maddie Springer is finally walking down the aisle with the man of her dreams. And she's got the perfect wedding planner to pull it all off in style. Well, perfect, that is, until the woman winds up dead — murdered in buttercream frosting. Suddenly Maddie's dream wedding melts faster than an ice sculpture at an outdoor buffet. And when her groom-to-be is made the detective in charge of the case, there goes any chance of a honeymoon. Unless, of course, Maddie can find the murderer before her big day.

With the help of her fellow fashionista friends, Maddie vows to unveil the cold-blooded killer. Is it the powerful ex-husband, the hot young boy toy, a secret lover from the past, or a billionaire bridezilla on the warpath? As the wedding day grows closer, tempers flare, old flames return, and Maddie's race to the altar turns into a race against time.

ISBN 13: 978-0-8439-6109-6

Leslie Langtry

"Mixing a deadly sense of humor and plenty of sexy sizzle, Leslie Langtry creates a brilliantly original, laughter-rich mix of contemporary romance and suspense."

—*The Chicago Tribune*

Stand By Your Hitman

A Greatest Hits romance

Missi Bombay invents things—fatal flowers, Jell-O bullets, stroke-inducing panty hose and other ways to kill a target without leaving any kind of evidence. She's a great asset to her family of assassins. The one thing she can't invent, though, is a love life. Unfortunately, her mom has decided to handle that for her. Next thing Missi knows, she's packed off to Costa Rica for a wild reality show where she's paired with Lex, the hottest contestant on TV. Too bad she also has to scope out a potential victim. But the job becomes tougher when someone starts sabotaging the show...and love-of-her-life Lex thinks she's the culprit!

ISBN 13: 978-0-8439-6037-2

KATHLEEN BACUS

CALAMITY JAYNE HEADS WEST

Tressa Jayne Turner, Grandville Iowa's own little "Calamity," is headed for the Grand Canyon State—and a wedding! It's her goofy granny gettin' hitched, and Tressa's sunny little siesta is about to have more strings attached than a dream catcher. Her cousin's keeping secrets, the roguish Ranger Rick is sending signals—more of the smokin' than smoke variety—and it seems Tressa's not the only person with an attachment to "Kookamunga," the butt-ugly fertility figurine she picked up at a roadside stand as a wedding gift. This wacky wedding's about to become an amazing race cum Da Vinci Code–intrigue. It'll be a vision quest to make Thelma and Louise's southwestern spree seem like amateur night at the OK Corral. May the best spirit guide win.

ISBN 13: 978-0-505-52733-2

ELISABETH NAUGHTON

STOLEN FURY

DANGEROUS LIAISONS

Oh, is he handsome. And charming. And sexy as all get out. Dr. Lisa Maxwell isn't the type to go home with a guy she barely knows. But, hey, this is Italy and the red-blooded Rafe Sullivan seems much more enticing than cataloging a bunch of dusty artifacts.

After being fully seduced, Lisa wakes to an empty bed and, worse yet, an empty safe. She's staked her career as an archaeologist on collecting the three Furies, a priceless set of ancient Greek reliefs. Now the one she had is gone. But Lisa won't just get mad. She'll get even.

She tracks Rafe to Florida, and finds the sparks between them blaze hotter than the Miami sun. He may still have her relic, but he'll never find all three without her. And they're not the only ones on the hunt. To beat the other treasure seekers, they'll have to partner up — because suddenly Lisa and Rafe are in a race just to stay alive.

ISBN 13: 978-0-505-52793-6

KIMBERLY RAYE

Slippery When Wet

The Flag Is Up

Jaycee Anderson is the first female to take the NASCAR Sprint Cup circuit by storm, and after finishing fourth overall last season, she has her eyes on the prize: knocking Rory Canyon out of the number three spot. She'll do anything to see the job done, too, even transform herself from a tomboy into a glamour queen if that's what it takes to get sponsorship and the edge. Rory's the kind of infuriating chauvinist who's just begging to get the pants beat off him by a woman — on the track, at least; Jaycee's fairly sure he's never had to beg anywhere else. Not with the millions of female fans who buy his shirts and caps and posters. Rory's just the type who gets Jaycee's own pistons pumping, her wheels spinning, and her engine burning oil. With their past, she's surprised they haven't already seen a smashup that ended in flames. But this track they're running has some deadly curves . . . and it's getting more slippery by the minute.

ISBN 13: 978-0-505-52773-8

KATHLEEN BACUS

In need of a break from her matchmaking mother and a score of hellish blind dates, to Debra Daniels the do-it-yourself boyfriend-in-a-box kit is a gift from Above.

Fiancé at Your Fingertips: Touted as the single woman's best defense against pitying looks and speculative stares, it comes with everything the single-and-slightly-desperate woman needs to convince friends, family and coworkers that she has indeed found Mr. Right. And "Lawyer Logan" is definitely that. Tall, handsome…and fictitious. Debra is going to have an absolute blast with her faux beau—until he shows up on her doorstep, acting as if he has every right to be there and in her arms.

Fiancé at Her Fingertips

ISBN 13: 978-0-505-52734-9

☐ **YES!**

Sign me up for the Love Spell Book Club and send my
FREE BOOKS! If I choose to stay in the club, I will pay only
$8.50* each month, a savings of $6.48!

NAME: _____

ADDRESS: _____

TELEPHONE: _____

EMAIL: _____

☐ I want to pay by credit card.

☐ **VISA**   ☐ **MasterCard.**   ☐ **DISCOVER**

ACCOUNT #: _____

EXPIRATION DATE: _____

SIGNATURE: _____

Mail this page along with $2.00 shipping and handling to:
Love Spell Book Club
PO Box 6640
Wayne, PA 19087
Or fax (must include credit card information) to:
610-995-9274

You can also sign up online at **www.dorchesterpub.com**.
*Plus $2.00 for shipping. Offer open to residents of the U.S. and Canada only. Canadian
residents please call 1-800-481-9191 for pricing information.
If under 18, a parent or guardian must sign. Terms, prices and conditions subject to
change. Subscription subject to acceptance. Dorchester Publishing reserves the right to
reject any order or cancel any subscription.